THE KILL BOX

Shattered Bone

THE KILL BOX
CHRIS STEWART

M. Evans and Company, Inc.
New York

M. Evans and Company, Inc.
216 East 49th Street
New York, New York 10017

Library of Congress Cataloging-in-Publication Data
Stewart, Chris, 1960–
    The kill box / Chris Stewart.
      p. cm.
    ISBN 0-87131-866-0 (cloth)
    I. Title.
  PS3569.T4593K55 1998
  813'.54—dc21   98-24442

Book design and type formatting by Bernard Schleifer
Manufactured in the United States of America
9 8 7 6 5 4 3 2 1

To my parents,
thank you.

ACKNOWLEDGMENTS

Special thanks to Lt Col James "Doc" Stewart, Commander 366 Aerospace Medicine Squadron, Cptn John "Sniper" Hicks, 391st Fighter Squadron, and Robert, my good friend inside the intelligence community—your assistance was invaluable. Any errors in the manuscript are not yours, but my own.

PROLOGUE

The attack chopper rose out of the night, lifting over a hill two thousand meters south of the convoy. It hovered unseen for a minute as the two pilots studied the fleeing Iraqi vehicles. The first of the Hellfire missiles was fired. The leading vehicle exploded and burst into flames. Other Hellfires were already on their way. Seconds later, the last missile impacted its target. A lone soldier scrambled out of a charred truck and staggered off into the night.

The two pilots watched him on their night-vision displays. The captain moved the control stick imperceptibly forward, nudging the deadly Apache across the desert terrain. The Iraqi soldier ran through the sand like a frightened dog. The captain pulled back on the cyclic, bringing the chopper to a stop. There was no reason to move any closer—the Apache was as deadly from this range as a .38 pistol was from two feet.

The captain studied the Iraqi as he ran, a dark-green image on his infrared screen. He could make out the flailing arms and pounding legs. He could see the pistol he held in his hand. He watched the man as he stumbled and fell, then turned and fired at the Apache three times, a burst of yellow flame emitting from the short barrel of his gun. Swinging in the sand, he began to run once again.

The pilot reached down and touched the trigger of the gun, then flipped a switch on his cyclic to take control of the weapon. The warrant officer in the front cockpit let out a cry of frustration. "Don't do it, Rayberg. Just let the poor sucker go."

The nose of the chopper lifted slightly into the air.

"Let him live, captain," the young warrant officer pleaded. "He's just another poor Arab who doesn't want to die for his country. I say we let him give up and go home to his family."

"Oh no," the captain replied. "He's the enemy and this is a legitimate kill."

The Apache sat in a stabilized hover, no more than thirty feet off of the sand. The captain flipped the helmet-mounted display down in front of his face. The tracking laser locked onto his retina, detecting even the slightest movement of his right eye. The 20mm gun that was mounted under the front nose of the chopper immediately began moving in perfect harmony with his eye, responding to the captain's commands, tracking itself to wherever he looked. It spun on its mount with unbelievable speed, sweeping from side to side as the pilot adjusted his view. The pilot picked up the target and pressed out a half-second burst. Two dozen shells were expelled from the cannon, spitting geysers of sand just aft of the target.

The fleeing man made a sudden cut to the right. The captain adjusted the gun with his eye and pressed on the trigger once again. The sand exploded in a trail leading up to the man before cutting him down in his tracks. The pilot watched the green figure spin, the force of the shell lifting him into the air and propelling him twenty feet across the sand. He fell in a heap, face down in the dirt.

The warrant officer swore in disgust. "What you just did was sickening and probably illegal. When we get back, I'm going to nail your hide to the wall!"

The captain reached down and pulled up gently on the power. The chopper began to climb into the night. He nudged the cyclic to the left, turning the aircraft back toward his battalion. The two men flew for several seconds in silence before the captain replied.

"This piece of desert is my Kill Box and he was a target. We were sent to destroy. We accomplished our mission. If you got a problem with that, go talk to the chaplain. If you think it was wrong, go talk to the JAG."

The captain flew the chopper above a rising bluff of sand and rock. He was tired and hungry and in a bad mood. He had been living in the desert for almost six months. All he wanted now was to get back to the States. And the more Iraqis he killed, the sooner that day would come.

The Apache continued to speed through the night. It was already out of Hellfire missiles. It was time to land and arm-up once again. he night was young and there were many targets yet to kill.

BOOK ONE

"An unknown number of people could die.
A million. Two million. Ten.
At this time, most agree, we are completely unprepared.
We simply could not guarantee that we could stop it."

—CDC *report to the* CIA *on the
danger of a biological attack*

"For he knew that for envy they had delivered him."

—*Matthew* 27:18

THE PENTAGON, WASHINGTON, D.C.
DAY ONE (TUESDAY)
0637 LOCAL TIME

The two men sat silently in the enormous office, an imposing mixture of over-stuffed leather, dark bookshelves, and silver-framed photos reflecting thirty years of military service. Two Micron computers sat on each side of the desk. An American flag, bright and crisp, was hanging near the rear corner of the room. On a low coffee table, along the near wall, an old, worn-out football sat on a chrome and brass tee, a reminder of the occupant's sporting days as a cadet.

General Wallet "Wally" Reynolds, the chief of staff of the air force, sat on the corner of his huge mahogany desk, the silver stars on his shoulders gleaming in the bright light. He stared out the line of tinted windows that ran along the southwest side of his office. Only one Pentagon office in ten had a window. None of them had a good view. The four-star general stared over the maze of interconnected parking lots and roadways that stretched toward I-395, the ten-lane highway that ran through the heart of the city. West, past the sea of dirty windshields, car tops, cement barriers, and black asphalt, an airliner lifted into the sky, climbing over the Potomac and away from Ronald Reagan Washington Airport.

Reynolds let out a sigh and wiped a hand across his face. Deep in thought, he ignored the other general in the room, something not many men in Washington would have ever dared do. But the two men were good friends, going all the way back to flight school, so he felt comfortable enough to consider for a while. The moments passed slowly. A teak wall clock ticked away. Turning to his superior, Reynolds finally reached out his hand.

"Could I take another look at those photos?"

General Davis Beck, the Chairman of the Joint Chiefs of Staff, reached up to pass the black-and-white photos along.

"These were taken by one of our unmanned birds flying out of Bahrain?" Reynolds asked.

The Chairman nodded. "One of the Global Hawk reconnaissance drones we shipped over there early this spring."

Reynolds studied the reconnaissance photos. They were clear and bright and startling in detail. He could see individual rocks, some no larger than pebbles, and the clumps of wiregrass sprouting through the cracks in the road. The photos had been taken very early in the day, for he noticed the shadows were all pointing to the west. He could see the ribbon of black asphalt running north and south through the desert and the trail of footprints running from the road through the sand. He turned his attention to the signal that had been left behind a high dune, an arrangement of rocks and scrap lumber not more than four or five feet across. The number 613 lay on top of the sand. He studied the signal, all the time wishing for more, some kind of hint or indication of what the sign really meant. Six-thirteen? He simply didn't know.

The air force chief of staff turned again to his friend. "And this is the third time you've found such a signal?"

The Chairman of the Joint Chiefs rose from his seat and walked to the window. Staring through the dark tinting, he watched the parking lot below. "Yes," he answered. "We saw the first signal two weeks ago, then another Saturday night. This one was detected very early this morning. The first time it was dug into the sand. The second was like this, etched out with rocks and old brush."

"And the location?"

"About seventeen miles north of Baghdad, along what the target planners have designated as Route 66, the military road that leads out to the army complex at Dhahoq es 'Ana. It's a secure road, Wally, not open to civilian traffic, but heavily traveled by security forces. So whoever left the signal knew at least two things. He knew that we would detect it with our recon flights over the complex and also that he was taking a horrible risk. His chance of being observed or detected were better than fifty-fifty. The road is well guarded and clearly under constant surveillance. To stop and form this signal may well have cost him his life."

General Reynolds looked up. "And this is all you've ever seen? Just the number? Nothing else?"

"Nope, that's it. Just the number six-thirteen. No other markings or indication of why it was there or who left it behind. It's funny. I've never seen anything quite like it before. Brent Hillard over at CIA is just about to tear out his hair. He's got his photo-analysts and Iraqi specialists working twenty hours a day. He feels its important. And in my gut, I agree.

"But so far they're dry, and they've tried every angle. Assigning the numbers letters to the alphabet, both in English and Arabic. Putting six-thirteen through half a million computerized security codes. The best they can come up with is the initials of some ancient city buried under the sand north of Baghdad. So what does that mean? We really don't know."

General Reynolds placed the photos on the side of his desk. He straightened his back and took a long breath of air. "Do you really think someone is trying to warn us? That there's a man inside Baghdad who is willing to raise the alarm?"

General Beck continued to stare out the window. "I don't know, Wally. But something is going on over there. Too many things are happening at the same time. Last week's warning from Israel. The sudden expulsion of the UN inspectors. The increased message traffic out of Baghdad and the covert activity along the Iraqi-Turkish border. Clearly, the fox is hunting. We've seen this before."

"What about the delegation to Kuwait City?" Reynolds quickly asked. "I was led to believe they might be making some progress."

"Not an inch," Beck growled. "Everyone knows they're wasting their time. The president took a huge political gamble, sending such a high-ranking delegation." Cursing, Beck thumped the top of the desk, his eyes narrowed to slits, gleaming dark with frustration. "So they leave tomorrow, and what do they have from Baghdad? More promises. More vagaries. More and more of the same.

"But I'm telling you, Wally, this thing is about to cave in. I can feel it in my gut, a growing shadow of doom. It haunts me through the day and keeps me pacing at night. It's finally going to happen and there's not a thing we can do. After years of bloating, it's about to explode. We have too many warnings and too little time."

"So, sir, you are directing me to gather a FIREBREAK team?"

Beck nodded his head. "Take the initial steps. Identify and notify the players, then give me the list. That's all I'm asking for now. Should it turn out that we need them, we'll at least be ahead. And we have to be ready Wally, even if the politicians are not. If we get caught with our pants down, we're the first ones to pay."

General Reynolds pushed himself away from the corner of his desk and walked back to his chair. "Alright then, sir. We'll get it under way. Colonel Wisner will be out there within twelve hours. I'll let you know when he's selected the team."

"Good," Beck replied. "I'll brief the president. There will be a lot of discussion, and some of the national security team won't agree, but meanwhile at least, we'll have a head start."

General Reynolds nodded. The chairman turned away from the window and headed to the private door that would bypass Reynold's front office and take him directly into the main hall. Reynolds watched him closely as he walked across the room. The chairman slowed and came to a stop at the doorway. Turning, he made a quick motion to the wall.

"You know what tomorrow is don't you?" he asked with a frown.

Reynolds hesitated, thinking, then answered, "No sir, I guess I don't."

The chairman motioned again, pointing to a calendar on the wall. "It's June, Wally. June the thirteenth. You know. Six-thirteen."

By the time the American camp in southern Iraq got the message, the sun was starting to set, a huge ball of deep orange on the desert horizon. Deep in a narrow valley along the slow and muddy Tigris River, the tiny and well-concealed camp of CIA advisors and military specialists was just coming to life. As dusk settled in, more men emerged from their tents.

The signal was sent to the camp by satellite encryption. The data-burst was short, less than a half second long. In the communications tent, the message was unscrambled and taken to the outpost commander. The major studied the note, then signaled his men. "Get the JP-4 bladders out to the chopper pads," he ordered, waving in the direction of the rubber containers of aviation fuel. "The helicopters could be here as early as tomorrow. And keep the reconnaissance teams posted on the hills to the south. I want an eye on every creature within ten miles of the camp."

MOUNTAIN HOME AIR FORCE BASE, IDAHO
DAY TWO (WEDNESDAY)
1525 LOCAL TIME

Charlie McKay was one happy guy. It was just one of those days. In two hours he would be in the air, which, by the way, was smelling very sweet, as well it should for a bright day in spring. He had just been selected for promotion and would soon pin on the gold leaves of major. To celebrate the extra seven bills a month, he'd bought a new Saab, a thousand shares of MiTech (which had immediately pushed through eight bucks a share) and donated five hundred dollars to the Salvation Army. To top off the deal, he had motored down to the mall and picked out an entire set of new underwear. Boxer shorts, his favorite kind. With tiny devils and little broken hearts. With a smile on his face he glanced in the rearview mirror. Look at that. Even his hair was looking good. He sat back in the seat. What more could he ask?

Pressing on the accelerator, he pushed his Saab up to 80. The Idaho landscape passed by very quickly, a mix of rust foothills, blue sage-brush and rock. Driving south on U.S. Interstate 84, Charlie maneuvered his car through the light traffic that led from Boise toward Mountain Home Air Force Base, forty-seven miles south of the city. The road was even and straight as it cut through the Owyhee plateau that bridged the Sawtooth and War Eagle Mountains. Charlie checked his speed and eased up on the throttle, then scanned the western horizon where the thunderstorms were starting to build, towering columns of white against the afternoon sun, their cores pushing up puffy clouds of black

and gray. The rain shafts were just beginning to develop, heavy patches of blue extending out from under the cells. Soon the lightening
would flash and the thunder would roll and the rain would come
pounding down. The desert would drink up the water like a huge,
grainy sponge, and by morning be dry once again.

Tonight, just before sunset, Charlie would lead a formation of
F-15E Strike Eagles out on what was to be the most important flying
exercise of the year. Soon after takeoff, he and his formation would join
some thirty other aircraft that were part of the same air-interdiction
operation. They would spend the next two hours and twenty minutes
flying tree-top level at 500 knots, hiding from each other in the dark
and dropping bombs on "enemy" targets. It would be a huge challenge.
But it would also be fun.

Charlie pressed a button on the side of his armrest. The driver's-
side window slid down and the air rushed in, already heavy with the
smell of rain. A gust of cottonwood fuzzballs blew across the open road,
rushing out from the core of the approaching wind. Columns of cumu-
lonimbus clouds swallowed the sun and the thin mountain air started
to cool.

Charlie studied the looming clouds. After ten years of flying he had
developed a great deal of respect for the power of just such a storm. As
the first of the lightening flashed in the distance, his good mood softened, if perhaps only slightly. Bad weather had challenged and afflicted
him before, and it looked like it would do so again.

If it didn't keep them all on the ground.

Thirty minutes later, he maneuvered into the parking lot of the
391st Fighter Squadron, the Bold Tigers. Pulling into an empty slot, he
parked his car and climbed out to check his uniform in the reflection
of his car's tinted window. After adjusting his cap to one side, he
pressed his flight suit against his chest. At six-one, Charlie was more
stocky than tall, his broad shoulders and thick arms a result of growing
up on a ranch where he had spent his summers bucking eighty-pound
bales of hay. His eyes were light blue. His skin was dark and smooth, for
he spent every second he could in the sun. He wore his sandy hair short
and it bristled on the top, especially near the cowlick at the crown of
his head. The corners of his mouth held a slight crease, for he was very
quick to smile, though his face was intense and a little bit thin.

After checking himself in the mirror, Charlie turned and strode
toward the squadron operations building, a squat brick structure with
no windows and a tiny steel door. A bright, multicolored mural of a

striped Bengal tiger hung over the doorway, its paws reaching out to each passerby. Standing near the entry was a black-and-white sign that read:

WELCOME TO THE TIGERS' DEN
HOME OF THE 391st
THE BEST FIGHTER SQUADRON IN THE WORLD

Charlie approached the front door, punched the numeric code into the cipher lock, pulled the door back and walked in. He strode to the operations desk, where the night's flying schedule was posted. He glanced at the huge plexiglass board where the sorties were scribbled in colored markers. The board was bare of red ink. No cancellations or changes. Everything was still set to go. Turning, he made his way down the narrow hall toward the mass briefing room. The flight briefing started at 1600 hours. Glancing at his watch, he checked the time: 1555. Only a few minutes to spare.

Walking past the command section, someone called out his name. He turned around but continued walking backwards, anxious to not be delayed. Lt Colonel Magill, his squadron commander, was standing outside his office door. "Need to see you," Magill said.

Charlie glanced at his watch. "Mission brief in two minutes, sir. Will it take more time than that?"

"Yep, but only a little. Get to the briefing, then stop by my office first thing when you can."

McKay nodded his head. "Okay sir, but what's it about?"

"Just stop and see me," Lt Colonel Magill replied. Charlie started to question once again, then changed his mind. Turning, he jogged down the hall.

Charlie slipped into the briefing room just as the lights were coming down. He searched for an empty seat in the semidarkness, leaning against the white cinder block wall while his eyes got used to the dim light. A gangly man was standing behind a small wood podium at the front of the room. Reaching under the stand, the man pressed a hidden button. With a solid *thunk*, the steel doors were automatically locked. The room was secure.

The briefing room was designed like a small theater, with forty seats placed on each side of a wide central aisle, facing a large, white screen. A red sign flashed the word "SECRET" from a warning box over the doorway. A computer-generated message scrolled across the projection screen:

COMBAT WEAPONS TRAINING—BLUE AIR
ATTACK PACKAGE DELTA
THIS BRIEFING IS CLASSIFIED SECRET.
TIME HACK . . . 1600:06

The seconds ticked by on the screen. Everyone checked their watches to get a good hack.

The briefing room was packed with flyers from all over base, representatives from each of the wing's five flying squadrons, each of them dressed, as was Charlie, in a dark-green flight suit and rough leather jacket. They sprawled across the reclining seats with notepads in hand. Snowman, the weather officer, was standing at the front of the room, ready to give a rundown on the weather for their late evening go.

"Everything looks good," he summarized after a series of forecast charts flashed across the screen. "Got some thunderstorms building up to the west, but as the sun sets, they should dissipate and move off to the south. Shouldn't be any trouble by the time you take off."

The room burst out in a rancorous groan. "Liar! Liar!" someone yelled from the darkness. "Burn him! Burn him! He's a witch!"

Wadded pieces of paper flew through the air, bouncing off the weatherman and the overhead projector. "Have you looked outside?" another voice called. "The thunderstorms are growing like mushrooms. Don't you have any windows down there where you work?"

Snowman stood there, unfazed. He had taken their heckling before.

"Hey," he retorted in a booming voice. "Did I say it was going to clear up? Did I say that? Yes I did! Sure, there's a little weather building right now, but I'm telling you, all of our weather models predict they will move off to the south. By the time the first flight takes off, you'll be looking at clear skies and—"

The papers came flying once again. "Sit down!" the audience cried.

Snowman smiled and waved at the men with his finger, then gathered his slides and moved back to his seat, a final piece of wadded paper flying over his head.

Charlie scanned the crowd once again, trying to pick out his friends by the back of their heads. By now, his eyes had adjusted and he could make out the pattern of familiar shapes in the dim light. Then he saw someone waving. It was Killer, Captain Alex Bennett, his back seat Weapons System Officer, or WIZZO as they were called. Killer was Charlie's best friend as well as one of the most respected aviators in the squadron. When it came to dropping bombs down the chimney, no navigator did it better than him. Killer motioned to an empty chair. Charlie slipped down the aisle and eased quietly into the seat.

The wing intelligence officer moved to the podium. "Alright," he said. "Let's start with a little target ID exercise." He tapped on the computer keyboard that controlled the overhead projector. A dark silhouette flashed on the ten-foot screen. It was only a shadow, hardly a distinguishable shape, but everyone immediately knew what it was.

"Friend or Foe?" The intel officer asked.

The audience started to boo. "Foe! Foe!" they howled.

"And what is it?"

"MiG-29!" they screamed. "Kill it! Kill it!" they cried.

The intel officer smiled.

"That's right," he said. "It is our honorable foe, the MiG-29." The officer took out a hand-held laser and pointed the tiny red beam on the screen. "As you can see, and as you all know, it's easy to distinguish the MiG-29 because of its twin vertical tails and the canted air intakes that lie just aft of the wing roots. But it could be, and has been, mis-IDed before. So take another look at it while I tell you that, according to CIA sources, and as of last week, another seventeen of these babies . . . yes, that's right, seventeen MiG-29s, one of the world's premier and most deadly fighters, are on rail and en route to Iraq. That brings their total to nearly sixty. Three full squadrons. All of them fully combat ready. And these are the new generation Mike models, which are equipped with the SLOT BACK look down, shoot down radar, as well as the laser range-finder and helmet-mounted display. Taken together, these most recent advancements make for a very, very unfriendly combination.

"So . . . for those of you heading to Saudi for the summer deployment . . . keep your eyes out for these lovely ladies, for they'll be in the skies with their radars up and running, watching you and tracking you from their base south of Baghdad."

Charlie winced at the reminder of the summer deployment. Another 120 days at Prince Sultan Air Base, in the middle of the Saudi Arabian desert. Another four months of living in tents, eating bad food, and sharing cots with scorpions and sand fleas. Another four months of droning for hours over the desert, flying in wide, search-pattern circles to enforce the southern no-fly zone over Iraq.

The intel officer continued his briefing, reviewing the detailed specifications and capabilities of the new Russian fighter that was making its way to Iraq. Most of the pilots sat listening very closely, paying special attention to the brief. Charlie leaned back and stared at the ceiling. Killer caught his eye.

"Lieutenant Colonel Magill was looking for you," he whispered in the darkness.

"Yeah, I saw him," Charlie replied

"Anything up? He seemed pretty anxious."

"Don't know. Didn't have time to talk. I'll get with him as soon as the briefing is over."

Killer hesitated, then turned back to the front of the room. They were getting to the meat of the briefing and everyone was growing intent. Major Fisher, the package commander, stepped up to the podium. He was a tall, thin man with a narrow face and a long, crooked nose, which had apparently taken its share of beatings from his sparring days back in college. As a young lieutenant, Fisher had picked up the call sign "Guppy." That lasted until the first night of the Gulf War, when Fisher had led a formation of fighters through a barrage of anti-aircraft and surface-to-air missiles over the heart of Baghdad to take out a complex of Iraqi missiles. During the sortie, he also shot down an enemy fighter, logging one of the war's few air-to-air kills. After the mission, his squadron mates decided that the call sign "Guppy" would no longer do. From that day forward they all called him "Shark."

As the Blue Air package commander, it was Shark's job to plan out the mission. He was the one who had been given the ATO, or Air Tasking Order, which defined the targets that were to be destroyed and the aircraft that would fly the mission. In this case, he had been given a powerful mix of F-15s, F-16s, B-1 bombers, and tankers. All told, 32 Blue Air aircraft were involved with the mission. About two billion dollars worth of aviation assets.

Shark reached down to organize his notes. No one spoke as he picked up the laser pointer and touched a few keys on the computer. The large center screen faded, then brightened with a map of Southwest Asia, from Turkey south to the Gulf of Aden. Shark glanced at the map, then turned to the flyers.

"Good afternoon, Gunfighters," he began, referring to the group by the wing call. "For those of you who don't know me, I'm Major Fisher. I go by Shark. I'll be your mission ground commander. Tonight's exercise is a Southwest Asia scenario. We are simulating flying out of Al Kharj, here in central Saudi Arabia." Shark turned on the red laser and used the thin beam to point to an airfield that sat approximately in the middle of the screen. "The simulated geo-political scenario is as follows:

"Over the past three weeks, there have been multiple border crossings between regular Turkish army units and Iraqi troops along the Turkish-Iraqi border. In addition, intel reports that supplies and arms have been making their way from Iranian supply centers here in Rutba to Kurdish rebels in the mountains of northern Iraq. " Again Shark used the pointer to light up the various points on the screen. "Over the past seventy hours, Hussein's elite Republican Guards have left their garrison positions around Baghdad and begun to move north.

"Early this morning, a mass of Kurdish rebels, supplied by the Iranian and Turkish underground, have staged an attack against the Iraqi stronghold city of Erbil. Satellite imagery shows a significant part of the city is burning. CNN reports there have been mass executions of Hussein loyalist party officials, and other local leaders, including an attack against one of Hussein's summer homes, where two of his daughters were staying. There are unconfirmed reports that at least one of the daughters, along with two of her children, were killed in the assault on the summer palace. Hussein has vowed retribution.

"Approximately three hours ago, intelligence reports indicated a significant flow of traffic from suspected chemical storage bunkers outside the Iraqi airfield of Falluja. Eight of Hussein's MiG-29s that are dedicated to a ground-attack role have been repositioned into hardened bunkers, presumably to be loaded with chemical weapons.

"It is our commission, derived from United Nations resolution 487, to stop the Iraqi government from the use of any weapons of mass destruction. Thus, it is our job to take out the airfield, as well as its associated support structures, hangars, command post, bunkers, weapons, and fuel-storage facilities, and of course, the suspected chemical bunkers that are hidden deep in the desert on the west side of the base.

"And it won't be as easy as you might think. For the first time since the opening days of the Gulf War, there will be opposition fighters in the air. Perhaps in significant numbers. It appears that Hussein is now willing to sacrifice his limited air assets to protect his airfield and ground forces. RC-135 reconnaissance birds in the Med have picked up radio transmission from at least twenty Iraqi combat aircraft, all marshaling in defensive positions south of Falluja.

"That, gentlemen, is a synopsis of the simulated scenario. Let me now review the real-world lineup for tonight."

He paused for a minute, then began again. "As you all know, the weapons training squadron down at Nellis Air Base in Nevada will be acting as Red Air, simulating the Iraqi aggressors. They will consist of a mix of U.S. F-15s, British Tornadoes, and navy F-18 Hornets. I don't need to remind you that, even as we speak, Red Air is sitting in a very similar briefing room, tucked away in a hangar at Nellis, planning how they intend to blow you apart.

"But the truth is, getting through the Red Air might be the easiest part of this mission, for, the simulated target at the Utah gunnery range has become one of the most heavily defended airbases in the world." A series of black and white reconnaissance photos flashed on the screen, depicting the location of the surface-to-air threats. "As you can see, multiple surface-to-air missiles sites, including the new Soviet-made SA-10s and SA-12s, have been set up on three sides of the target. In addition, four anti-aircraft batteries have been garrisoned immediately around the airfield. The target is what we would call 'rich in threats.'"

An F-16 pilot snorted under his breath. It was a huge understatement, everyone knew. Shark paused to stare at the F-16 pilots, who sat as a group on one side of the room. "That's why we love you F-16 drivers," he said. "You guys are the key to our overall success. Your only mission tonight, your only purpose in life, is to take out the enemy's radar-guided missiles. If you do it, we're happy. If you don't, we all fail. So get 'em, Vipers, we're counting on you."

Shark paused for a moment, then turned back to the screen. Pressing on, he continued to work his way through the details of the mission. All of the flyers took meticulous notes. Fifty minutes later, he was wrapping it up.

"One final thing," he concluded as he pointed his laser on Charlie. As Charlie stood up, Shark rolled the red dot around on the center of his chest. "Capt McKay and his back seater, Alex Bennett, have been working with me for the past several days to develop and perfect this whole plan. We have thought it all out. We think it will work. However, as you all know, no plan survives initial contact. If the attack is going well, it's because it's an ambush. With that in mind, Captain McKay will be acting as the airborne mission commander. He will be responsible for coordinating the attack as well as making any decisions the fluid situation may require. He will be listening up the primary strike frequency at all times. When things start to jam up, you can get ahold of him there. Any changes will be coordinated through him."

The lights in the room were slowly brought up. "Any questions?" Shark asked as the men gathered their notes. "Okay, then," he concluded, when no hands went up. "Debrief is here at 2400. Good hunting, Gunfighters. Let's go."

The aircrews rose from their seats. The KC-135s were to take off in little over an hour. The tanker crews gathered their gear and hurried out to their aircraft. Killer headed off to life support to pick up his helmet and life vest. Charlie went looking for Lt Colonel Magill.

Capt Charlie McKay tapped on the side of the doorway as he walked into his squadron commander's office. Lt Colonel Magill was standing behind his desk, a huge cherry monster that seemed to fill the room. He was leaning against a cluttered credenza while talking on the phone. Looking up, he motioned for Charlie to have a seat. Charlie settled back in a small, cloth-covered chair, facing his commander. Magill continued listening intently on the phone while staring at the floor and nodding his head.

Charlie heard footsteps behind, turned and sprang quickly to his feet him as a colonel walked into the room. Magill looked up and immediately hung up the phone.

The colonel was impeccable; dignified, confident, and sure. He was tall and slender, with dark skin, long arms, and graying salt and pepper hair. His boots had been buffed to an old fashioned shine and his flight suit was tailored to tuck in at the shoulders. His eyes were intense—a sparkling light blue that was almost unnaturally bright. The colonel stepped toward Charlie and extended his hand.

"Danny Wisner."

"Captain McKay, sir," Charlie shot back. The colonel shook Charlie's hand, then turned to Magill. "Is this the man you were talking about?" Magill nodded his head. The colonel reached behind him and pushed the door closed, then sat down on the edge of a brown leather couch and turned to face Charlie. Leaning back, he crossed one leg over the top of the other. Charlie watched him intently, then sat down stiffly in his chair.

Lt Colonel Magill came forward and sat on the edge of his desk. Folding his arms across his body, he looked down at McKay. "Colonel Wisner here is from the Pentagon," he explained. "He's working a special project for Air Staff. He reports directly to General Beck . . . "

Magill paused for a second to let Charlie think, the intentional silence emphasizing what he wanted to, but could not, say.

General Beck—Chairman of the Joint Chiefs of Staff—the most powerful man in the military. Perhaps one of the most powerful men in the world. Charlie glanced at the colonel, studying the eagles on his shoulders, which no doubt would soon be replaced by silver stars.

"Colonel Wisner has heard a little about our squadron," Magill continued. "Heard we do some good stuff. Wanted to come out and see for himself."

Charlie immediately became suspicious. The colonel was clearly a very busy man. Air Staff was killer duty for even the lowest of grunts. Working directly for General Beck surely made it much worse. No doubt the colonel could be found slaving in the bowels of the Pentagon fifteen hours a day. Yet he had flown across the country to check out their squadron? He had arrived unannounced for a quick look around?

Charlie didn't believe it. Something was going on.

He stole a quick glance in Magill's direction, but his boss avoided his eyes. Charlie shrugged his shoulders. "Sir, if you're interested in seeing our squadron in action, I invite you to check us out. Compare us to any fighter squadron in the world. We're simply the best. And we have a record to prove it."

For a moment Colonel Wisner didn't reply. He shifted in his seat, crossing one leg over the other while studying Charlie McKay.

"So, you think you're the best fighter outfit in the Air Force?"

"No sir. I do not."

"But you just said that—"

"Colonel, I said we were the best fighter squadron in the world."

The colonel stared at him. Charlie smiled again, glanced at Magill, then back to Wisner before finishing his statement with a courteous, "Sir."

"And is it true that you are the best pilot in the squadron?" Wisner asked.

Charlie was taken aback by the question, which he considered to be completely out of place. While it was true that most fighter pilots thought of themselves as the best, it was also true that they would never say so out loud. In combat there was no room to keep tally or score within the same squadron. It wasn't you against me, it was us against them. So, to have a question like that put to him so bluntly seemed inappropriate and beside the point.

For a long moment Charlie didn't respond. Finally, he answered, "Sir, I really don't know."

Colonel Wisner studied the pilot. "Well, I guess that answers my question. If you were the best you would say it. Confidence is the fighter pilot's trait. My experience has been, if you tell a fighter pilot to change a lightbulb, he will stand with the bulb in the socket, waiting for the world to revolve around him."

Charlie squirmed uncomfortably in his seat. He glanced at the colonel's chest, where he saw pilot wings. Surely the man was a fighter pilot himself, so why was he dogging one of his own?

"Sir," Charlie finally said in an irritated tone. "That may be true of some guys. But some of us like to do our talking with the jet, not standing around the office cooler or sitting at the bar."

Colonel Wisner nodded. "Fair enough," he said. "That's as it should be. Now tell me, captain, what did you do during the war?"

"F-15s, sir. C-Models. First Fighter Wing up at Langley."

"And did you have much success there?

"Some," Charlie replied.

The colonel raised his hand to his lower lip, then reached into his breast pocket and pulled out a single sheet of paper. Lifting his eyes, he recited Charlie's resume by heart.

"Distinguished graduate from flight school. Asked to stay on as a pilot instructor. One of the youngest pilots ever selected to fly the new F-15E. Top Gun winner four years in a row. Three combat kills over Baghdad. Highest number of any pilot in the Gulf. Best sortie-to-kill ratio of any pilot since Korea.

"The way I hear it, you're a regular shoot-em-up-ace kinda guy. Except for that one incident with your student back in Del Rio, your record is as good as any I've ever seen."

Charlie studied the colonel for a moment, staring into his brilliant eyes, wondering how he was supposed to respond. He was irritated and frankly just wanted to leave. He had a mission to fly. He shot another quick look to his squadron commander, hoping to get some relief. His boss caught his eye but didn't step in to help.

The colonel smiled for the first time since he'd walked into the room. Turning to Magill, he lifted himself out of his chair. "Have you got a copy of the chart?" Magill nodded his head as he walked around to the front of his desk. Opening the top drawer, he pulled out a forty-inch, multicolored flying chart and began to spread it across the top of his desk. Charlie immediately recognized it as a copy of the chart he would use for the night's mission. He and Colonel Wisner stepped toward Magill's desk.

"Okay, Captain McKay," Colonel Wisner commanded. "You're the mission commander tonight. Show me what you have in mind."

Charlie hesitated only a minute, then rotated the map toward the colonel and quickly ran through the plan, showing the different refueling, orbit, and attack routes, as well as the egress plan, bailout areas, threat locations, and air-to-air rules of engagement. The colonel nodded his head and asked occasional questions.

When Charlie was finished, Colonel Wisner took two steps back from the desk. "Okay captain, let me ask you one thing. What is the worst thing that could happen tonight? What would cause the mission to fail?"

Charlie thought for a moment before he replied. "I would have to say the weak link in this plan is the F-16s, sir. If they don't get in and take out the enemy radars that control the anti-aircraft sites, then, as the airborne commander, I would abort the whole mission. We would take too many losses to go against this target, as heavily defended as it is."

The colonel stared at the chart, then nodded. "Yes, I would have to agree. But aside from that constraint, it looks like a good plan. I look forward to watching the mission unfold."

Charlie's eyes opened just slightly in surprise. "Watching, sir?"

"Yep. I'm coming along."

Charlie grunted to himself. Coming along! A very poor choice of words. Like it was some kind of evening drive through the country.

"I'm riding on one of the tankers," Wisner explained. "It's the best way to get a good look. You know. Listen-up on the radios. Watch you do your refueling. Flight-follow you as you head into the target. It will help me get a feel for the mission. Its been a while since I've been involved with such a big package, so I thought it'd be fun to be a part of the night."

Charlie didn't respond. Let the colonel snoop if he had to. The only thing he would be was impressed. There was only one thing that had him concerned.

"Colonel," he began, trying to maintain the proper degree of respect in his voice, "you're not going to screw things up out there, are you?"

The colonel lifted an eyebrow.

"You know," Charlie continued. "Moving formations around.

Changing the targets. Screwing with the rules of engagement. Running the show or calling the shots. Doing that old 'colonel' thing where you insist on being in charge, even when you don't really know what's going on?"

A look of surprise spread across Wisner's face. If he were insulted, he didn't show it, though Charlie's chutzpah certainly caught him off guard. He wasn't used to being addressed in such a frank manner, and the fact that it came from a captain made it even more of a surprise. He almost had to suppress a quick smile. So Charlie wouldn't suck up or roll over. Good. There weren't many guys like that left around.

Wisner leaned six inches in Charlie's direction. "Is that what colonels do? Screw things up? Pretend they know what's going on?"

"Sir, I meant no disrespect. But we've both seen it before. A guy flies nothing but a desk and his son's paper kite for half a dozen years, but still considers himself one shoot-down short of ace. So I'm just asking you to understand. We've gone to a lot of work already, and it's been my experience that colonels like to do things a certain way— usually their way. But the safety and well-being of this formation has fallen on me, so I feel it appropriate to ask—"

Wisner cut him off by a lift of his hand. "You'll never even know that I'm there," he insisted. "I'll be quiet. I promise. I'm only there to observe."

"Thank you, sir," Charlie offered. "I appreciate that. I really do."

Wisner looked to Lt Colonel Magill, who glanced at the clock. "Sir, the tankers are set to take off in little less than twenty minutes. You'd better be stepping out to the jet."

Charlie glanced at Lt Colonel Magill, who gave a single nod at the door to dismiss him. Charlie turned toward Wisner. "See you in debrief, then won't we, sir?" he asked.

The colonel paused before he answered. "Probably not. But I'm sure we'll talk before I head back out to D.C."

Charlie nodded then turned and walked to the door. Pulling it open, he stepped into the hall.

The two men watched him in silence. After he was gone, Magill plopped down his wide leather chair. Wisner moved over to shut the door once again, then took a seat beside the huge desk. Magill ran his hands over his face and rubbed his eyes. He was feeling very tired, and it wasn't even late. He stared at the floor to avoid looking at Wisner, then let out a long huff of air.

"You want me to make the call?" Wisner finally asked.

"Yes, Danny, I do. In fact, I would have to insist."

Colonel Wisner reached out and picked up the phone, then dialed an on-base extension. Two minutes later, the order had been given. A message went out from the base command post to the commander of the F-16 fighter squadron on the other side of the base.

When the F-16 squadron commander read the message, he certainly didn't understand. It was one of the most puzzling things he had ever seen. But being an officer, he would follow his orders. Even those orders that didn't make any sense.

MOUNTAIN HOME AFB, IDAHO
1907 LOCAL TIME

Charlie McKay pushed through the back door of his squadron building and headed toward the fighters parked on the ramp one hundred yards to the west. His helmet and parachute harness were thrown over his shoulder, a bulky survival vest was hanging around his neck. In his left hand he carried a small, black canvas bag, which held his charts and aviator tools. He walked with an awkward stride, his abdomen and legs wrapped tightly in his anti-G suit. Capt Alex Bennett walked at his side. As the two men stepped onto the tarmac, they were met with a blast of cool air blowing down from the storm clouds that were fast approaching from the west. Charlie nodded toward the dark clouds. "So Killer, what do you think?"

Al Bennett didn't break his stride as he studied the storms. "I don't know," he answered. "Snowman might be right. They're moving south, and with the sun going down, they might lose enough energy to start dying off."

Charlie nodded his head, though he didn't agree. He knew the desert had already built enough heat to fuel the storms well into the night. They were going to have to fight their way through the weather, of that he felt sure.

The aviators strode along in silence as they approached the F-15E parking area. As they walked, a flight of two KC-135 tankers began their takeoff roll, their engines shattering the air as the heavy aircraft lumbered down the runway. Neither Charlie nor Killer looked up as they lifted into the sky. The tankers turned south and the sound of their engines quickly faded into the evening gloom.

Killer stole a quick look toward Charlie. "So, who is this Colonel Wisner guy?" he suddenly asked.

Charlie slowed his pace just a little. "You met him, too?"

"Yeah. He cornered me in the life-support room as I was gearing up. Was asking me all sorts of questions."

"Oh? Like what?"

"You know. Usual stuff. About the sortie. About the squadron. How I liked flying the jet." Killer paused and shifted the helmet to his left hand. He glanced toward his pilot, who was looking ahead.

"He also wanted to know about you, Charlie. What you were like to fly with. If you were any good."

Though Killer waited, Charlie didn't react.

"So what's the deal there Prince Charles? Why is this guy snooping around?"

"Don't really know, man. Wish that I did. But I figure I can worry about that in the morning. Right now, we have a mission to fly."

The two men stepped through the flightline security checkpoint. Reaching into their flight suits, they pulled out their line badges, clipped them onto their chest pockets, and began to walk between the rows of F-15s. The smooth aircraft glinted in the dim evening light, their noses cocked toward the runway, their canopies open. Charlie glanced down the line of gray aircraft. For ten years now he had been flying jets, and the thrill was just as intense as his first day on the flightline, walking with a tight stomach for the first sortie of his life. "What a beautiful sight," he thought to himself.

The members of the 391st Fighter Squadron were lucky enough to fly the newest version of the F-15, the Strike Eagle, or F-15E. The Strike Eagle is a tandem seat fighter. The pilot sits in the front cockpit, the Weapons Systems Officer sits in the back. The pilot does all the flying and most of the air-to-air combat, firing the missiles at the enemy bandits and, should the battle close in to a dogfight, maneuvering behind them to fire the gun. The WSO is responsible for the navigation, target selection, and bombing. It is his job to control the moving-map display, radar, and attack pods; illuminate the targets with the laser beam; operate the computer systems that release the weapons; and perhaps most importantly, keep an electronic eye out for the enemy fighters and missiles that are working so hard to shoot them down.

Together, the pilot and WSO make up a team, both of them equally important, both of them critical to getting the job done. Like the days of old back in World War II, they fly together as a crew, learning to trust one another, learning and compensating for one another's weakness, and teaching each other how to survive. Nothing comes between a pilot and a WIZZO, who almost always become very close friends.

This two-man concept, taken together with cutting-edge avionics and attack systems, made the Strike Eagle the undisputed best attack-fighter in the world. During the Gulf War, a very high percentage of the precision-guided bombs that were tossed over Iran were dropped from an F-15E. Simply put, it could fly its way in at low level, in any type of weather, night or day, nail a load of two-thousand-pound bombs down the exhaust shaft of an enemy bunker, then climb and engage in air-to-air combat, killing enemy fighters as it fought its way home. The Strike Eagle carried a double load of shot, and everyone knew it, especially the aviators who strapped on the jet.

As they walked among the fighters, Charlie glanced at a number he had penned onto the back of his hand. B-6. The parking spot for their jet. He looked up ahead to where the fighter was waiting and was a little disappointed to see it still surrounded by munitions trolleys. As the aviators approached the Strike Eagle, the crew chief trotted out to meet them, an anxious expression on his face.

"Sir, we've got a few more checks to run on the weapons, but it will only take us a few minutes," he explained in a mild New England twang.

Charlie glanced at his watch, then nodded his head. "S'okay, chief. We're a few minutes early. We'll just hang back and keep out of your way."

The chief smiled and turned back to the jet.

"Five minutes, right chief?" he called after the sergeant. "Not any longer than that? This is the biggest exercise our wing will fly this entire year. It'd be a bummer if we were late for the party."

"I guarantee it, sir. Five minutes, and you're good to go."

Charlie nodded and gave a quick thumbs up. The chief turned and trotted away. Charlie and Killer made their way toward the closest unoccupied fighter and sat their gear down under the wing. They watched as the airmen scurried around, loading the bombs on the F-15's wings. It was exhausting work, heavy and draining in precision. Despite the cool air the young men's black T-shirts were soon drenched in sweat.

Killer placed his helmet on the cement and squatted on his knees.

"You know Charles, I hate the thought of going back to the desert. Locked down in our camp, too scared to venture beyond the front gate because of the constant threat of a terrorist attack. Eating sand and getting letters from home that have been cut opened and read. Working fourteen hours a day, just to bore holes in the sky. All to remind Hussein that we're the boss.

"We barely got home from that nonsense last spring. We've been home only eight weeks, and now we're heading over again. I'm telling you, Charlie, it's starting to drag. And Linda is just about ready to shoot me."

Charlie bent stiffly down toward his WSO. "I know what you mean, Killer."

Killer poked at the rough cement with his finger. "No, Charles, and I mean no disrespect here ol' buddy, but I really don't think that you do. I'm tired of leaving my family. I've got a wife and two beautiful kids. I like to be around them. They like having me around. I miss them when I'm gone. And again, no offense, but this is my choice. Go home to my wife and a set of clean cotton sheets, or to a tent full of snoring, sweating, stinking-in-your-face pilots.

"So, I don't know. I guess the thought of going back over there," Killer nodded his head slowly out toward the east, "the thought of another four months in the sandbox—I guess it's left me thinking. I'm a dad now Charlie, and I really like my kids. When they climb on my lap, I'm as happy as I've ever been. So I don't know, but sometimes I wonder—" Killer's voice slowly trailed off.

In the moment of silence, Charlie considered his own situation. He thought of his father who had taken off when he was a kid. The old man had walked Charlie down to the bus stop one day, got on the bus, blew a kiss and wandered out of his life. Eight boyfriends and about the same number of years later, his mom had married some fellow named Lyle and settled into the good life down in east Texas, where trailers were cheap and you could fish all year long. He could picture his mother, sitting on the dock at Lake Palestine, rocking in her folding lawn chair while sipping warm beer and listening to his stepfather curse at the fish. Over the years, Charlie's relationship with his mother had grown more and more strained. He always saw her at Christmas, but that was just about all. Sometimes Lyle would call, asking to borrow some money. Sometimes his mom would call to tell him they were moving again.

Charlie thought for a moment, then turned to his best friend, whose wife he respected and whose twin daughters he adored. And it only took half a second's consideration to realize that, no, he didn't understand. He had no reason to stay. Here. There. It made no difference to him. But Al had a family. Al had a home.

Killer lifted his head and stared across the runway. "I'm just not so sure that it's fun anymore." He was speaking in nearly a whisper and Charlie realized that Killer wasn't talking to him so much as thinking out loud.

Killer looked over to Charlie. "So tell me something, will you?" he asked. "Why do I do it? Why don't I just quit? I could do that you know. I could go work with my dad and make two or three times the money. So why don't I walk and let someone else take a turn?"

Charlie leaned on the side of his helmet and rubbed the palms of his hands. "I can't say, Killer. I guess that's a question that only you can answer."

The two men sat in silence for a moment. As they did, their crew chief turned from their jet and began to make his way toward them. They lifted themselves off the tarmac and started to gather their gear. Charlie flung his parachute harness across his back and began to snap the three locking toggles while Killer did the same thing. Turning together, they made their way toward the waiting F-15.

THUNDER ONE FLIGHT
OVER THE NORTHERN UTAH DESERT
2022 LOCAL TIME

It was by any measure an awesome display. The line of thunderstorms stretched north and east for more than two hundred miles, from central Nevada through the upper quarter of Utah and past the Idaho border. Dozens of cells lifted toward the troposphere, pushed upward by the generated heat of the spring afternoon to reach altitudes above forty-five thousand feet. Vertical shafts of rain spewed from under the cells to drench the mountains and plains underneath.

Charlie scanned his eyes across the horizon while silently cursing the weather.

At least Snowman had been partially right. The storms had moved off to the south. But they had not died off. Indeed, just the opposite, they had positively exploded.

Charlie and his formation of Strike Eagles were trying to work their way south from Mountain Home Air Force Base. They had been airborne for almost thirty minutes and were already behind on their time.

Almost since takeoff, they had been trying to work their way through the line of storms that stood as a dark and seemingly impenetrable wall, separating them from the Utah Test Range where the exercise was going to take place.

Within minutes after lifting off of the runway, Charlie had requested that Air Traffic Control vector him around the line of storms. For fifteen minutes, the controller had guided the formation north and then east, thinking they could make their way around the Idaho side of the wall. But after ten minutes of flying in the opposite direction that they needed to go, Charlie could see they were wasting their time. The line of storms billowed out before him as far as he could see. After another five minutes of being vectored by ATC, he gave up, realizing the controller had no idea what he was doing. Charlie checked his fuel, then made a decision. He would turn back toward the Test Range and try to pick his own way through the storms.

Ten minutes later, Charlie found himself facing a solid wall of lightning as the thunderclouds loomed ever nearer. He tried to avoid staring at the incredible light show in order to protect what was left of his night vision. But it couldn't be helped. It was everywhere around. His radios crackled in a stream of static from the continuous lightning display. Off in the distance, directly ahead, the dark sky flashed above and below him as the electricity strobed the dry desert air. Huge anvil-shaped cells, dark and bursting at the sides, illuminating themselves from the lightning within. The lightning danced from the thunderstorm's core, flashing from cloud to cloud and cloud to ground. Charlie's canopy rattled as tiny beads of hail beat down. He glanced at his radar to measure the distance to the center of the storm. Only twenty-eight miles. He had to take action now.

He glanced over his shoulder to see the faint, blinking lights of the other three aircraft in his formation. They were lined up on his left side and spaced out in a loose trail. Like ducks on their mother, they mimicked his every move, trusting him to do the right thing.

"What do you think, Al?" Charlie asked his WIZZO. "Think we can fly over the top?"

"No way," Killer was quick to reply. "I show radar echos as high as forty-eight thousand feet. We might get around, but we're not going over. At least not with me in the jet. Now if you want to go back home and drop me off first, then . . ."

"Okay, okay," Charlie cut him off. "Bad plan. So do you think we can pick our way between the storms?"

"Don't know, boss," Killer replied. Sitting in the rear cockpit, he reached down to adjust his radar, wishing it was better at seeing through rain. He adjusted the sensitivity until the different storm cells appeared as huge, deep-green globs with traces of clear air stuck in between. He studied the radar for a moment then said, "I think if we go west, then turn back to the south, we can cut our way through the first line of storms. The problem is, we don't know what's behind the first wall. Maybe its clear weather. Maybe it's not. And if we push our way through, then find out it's just as bad on the other side, we could find ourselves completely surrounded. That would, as they say, kind of suck, don't you think? Guess the bottom line is, boss, how lucky do you feel?"

Charlie paused as he considered what Killer had said. "But the other aircraft have picked their way through," he replied.

"Yeah, Prince Charles, I know that. But they're at least thirty minutes ahead of us now. Remember, we were the last formation to take off. Then center vectored us half way to Egypt. Meanwhile the storms have had more time to build.

"But yeah, you are right. The other aircraft got through. That's a good sign for us. So I say let's give it a shot."

Killer looked forward through the empty space that separated the front and aft cockpits to see Charlie slowly shaking his head.

If there was one thing that every pilot feared, it was the power and unpredictability of severe summer storms. The winds in such thunderstorms could literally tear your aircraft apart. They could flip you and turn you and bend you in two. The hail could shatter your canopy, or worse, hammer your wings into boiled and bumpy sheets of weakened steel. And that was to say nothing of the danger of lightning.

After thinking for a moment, Charlie said, "Okay, Killer, as the navigator, you're the expert on the radar. I need to know. Can you get me through the storm and still keep us safe?"

Killer studied his scope once again, then swallowed hard. "Yeah, Charlie, I think I can do it. Get on the radio and get me a right turn. I'll pick us path through the weather. But I'm telling you now, baby, you better hold on."

Colonel Wisner sat in a small jump seat between the two pilots in the cockpit of the lead KC-135 refueling aircraft, one hundred miles to the west of Capt McKay's position. From where they had set up their orbit, the weather was bumpy, with intermittent showers, but generally clear.

For the past forty minutes, Wisner had been listening to the radios as the various formations checked in with the tankers for clearance to refuel. The F-16s had come first, followed by the F-15s and F-15Es. The B-1s, with their huge fuel tanks, loitered below, not needing additional fuel. After taking on their gas, all the fighters had immediately cleared away from the tankers and began to make their way to the south. Thunder One flight, with Charlie in the lead, had been the last formation to refuel. By the time they checked in, they were twenty minutes late.

Colonel Wisner had watched them refuel through the flat Plexiglas of the boom operator's station under the tail of the aircraft. As Charlie maneuvered his fighter behind the huge tanker, Wisner had given him a quick thumbs up, but Charlie didn't see, or a least didn't respond.

After the last of the F-15Es had cleared away from the tanker, Wisner made his way back to the cockpit and pulled a radio headset over his ears. He began to listen to several radios at one time while keeping track of the fighters on the small notepad strapped to his leg. One by one, he checked them off as the formations made their way through the storms. Off in the distance, it was easy to see the weather was getting much worse.

Charlie jammed down on his microphone switch once again. "Salt Lake Center, Thunder One," he broadcasted out in a hurried voice.

The static on his radio crackled in a nearly continuous stream of noise and the controller did not call back.

Charlie tried again. "Salt Lake Center, Thunder One, on three-eighty-five-point-eight."

After a moment of noise the radio crackled to life. "Thunder, this is Salt Lake. Go ahead."

"Thunder One is requesting an immediate right turn for weather avoidance."

For several seconds the controller didn't respond as the radio crackled and popped. Charlie squirmed in his seat as he checked the radar once again. The center of the storm was now less than ten miles away. In less than a minute they would be in the heart of the core where the wind, hail, and lightning would be at its worst. He needed a turn and he needed it now!

He simply couldn't wait any longer. Clearance or no, he needed to get away from the storm. Glancing to his left, he checked the position of his formation, then began a 90 degree turn to the right. As the lightning moved off to the side of the aircraft, Charlie got on the radio once again.

"Salt Lake, Thunder flight is now heading two-three-zero for weather avoidance. Salt Lake Center, how do you read?"

The controller's voice finally came back, obviously hurried and stressed. "Roger Thunder. Maintain that heading for now. I've got five Delta flights ahead of you trying to work their way into Salt Lake. Reduce your speed now to follow them south. An American and two Uniteds are off your left on vectors around the same cell. Advise when you're clear of the weather."

Charlie clicked the microphone and muttered a quick, "Roger, Salt Lake," then glanced at the chart on his leg.

"How far west do you think we'll have to go?" he asked Killer.

"I'm thinking about thirty miles."

Charlie glanced at the tiny illuminated clock in the corner of his instrument display. It was going to be very close. They had only nine minutes until they had to check in with the exercise controller. And because they were late, they were getting low on fuel. There just wasn't going to be time to spare.

"We'll keep this heading for another two minutes, then turn back to the south-southeast," Killer said. "I've got about a ten-mile hole between the two largest cells, but if we split the difference between them, is should work out okay."

The aircraft began to bounce and shake as the turbulence became more intense. A faint green glow of St. Elmo's Fire spread across the nose of the fighter, glowing and sparkling with a hazy, blue sheen. The radios continued to crackle and Charlie reached over to turn the volume down. Then suddenly it started to rain. Huge sheets of water poured over the aircraft, reducing the visibility to only a few feet. Charlie immediately glanced to his left to check the position of his wingmen, who had spread out behind him in a radar-trail formation. Again and again, lightning strobed the dark sky. Charlie gripped the control stick, his leather flight glove soaked with sweat. The nose of the F-15 glowed brighter as the electricity built in the air. The fighter bounced around, throwing the men about in their seats. The rain got worse as the seconds ticked by.

"Okay Killer, how much further we going?"

"Almost there, man. Another two miles and we can begin our turn back to the south. That will put us about in between the two largest storms."

Charlie focused on his instruments and lowered his head. No reason now to look outside. There was nothing to see but the rain and the dark. He concentrated on flying the aircraft and providing a smooth and predictable platform for his wingmen to follow. Every twenty seconds or so, he stole a quick glance at the clock as he counted down the time.

"Okay, Charlie. Give me a turn to one-four-zero," Killer finally said, never looking up from his radar display.

Charlie immediately began to turn while keying his microphone switch to advise Salt Lake Center they were turning southeast.

For the next four minutes the formation fought their way between the storms. Then, without any warning, the rain stopped. The night appeared to brighten and, with a huge *PANG*, the eerie glow of St. Elmo's Fire burst outward and then abruptly disappeared. The strobes of lightning began to pass behind them before fading away. Charlie looked up from his instruments. They were now in clear air. The stars were shining over his head and the half-moon glowed bright in the eastern sky. Looking down he could see the reflection of the Great Salt Lake, shimmering yellow from the bright, rising moon. Turning over his shoulder, he looked back at the wall of dark storms, then let out a huge breath of air.

"Well, that was kind of fun, wasn't it?" Killer said into his mask.

Charlie didn't react. He was too tight to laugh.

"You know what I think?" Killer went on. "I think thunderstorms are nature's way of telling us to stick it. If we could see Mother Nature, I'll bet she's rolling on the floor, holding her sides from laughing so hard."

Colonel Wisner listened on the exercise controller frequency as Charlie's formation checked in, reporting that they were clear of the storms and finally moving into position. The other aircraft were already waiting. Forty seconds later, it was time to go. Charlie called out "Boxer" on the radio, the code word for the attack to begin. The F-16s immediately pushed out, flying south toward the "enemy" targets. The F-15 air-to-air fighters circled over Charlie's head, waiting for the Red Air to come after the low-level strike forces. Charlie's Eagles and B-1s began to fall into position. As the attackers turned south, the Red

Air came up to meet them. Somewhere over his head, the first of the fighters engaged. "Fight's on!" someone barked over the common radio frequency.

Charlie and his formation were the last ones to push to the target. As the B-1s and F-16s cleared out in front of them, Charlie's F-15Es did one quick circle in the air, then pointed the noses of their aircraft toward the ground. Dropped to low level, they turned to the target and began to weave their way through the mountains. Cresting the tops of the sheer granite cliffs, the fighters would roll onto their backs and pull back toward the ground before rolling level again just a few hundred feet above the earth. Like daggers in the night, they bobbed and snaked across the terrain, leaving trails of white vapor in their wake.

Charlie searched the dark horizon, never bringing his eyes inside the cockpit. He positioned his switches and managed his system controls by punching various buttons on his control stick and throttle. HOTAS it was called—"hands-on-throttle-and-stick." This allowed the pilot to accomplish a multitude of tasks without ever removing his hands, a critical advantage in combat when even a fraction of a second might mean the difference between a kill or being killed. In addition, it allowed the pilot to control his systems while pulling 9 Gs.

Ten minutes after the exercise began, Charlie was sixty miles out from the target, flying at 200 feet and 500 knots. His wingmen were in a tactical trail, half a mile behind him and off to his right. Ahead of him, on his radar, he could see a formation of two B-1s as they crested the top of a hill. The Eagle was flying by computer command. The LANTIRN system was looking forward of the aircraft with its ultrasensitive, infrared display. Charlie watched the terrain below him on a small IR display, the trees, roads, mountains, and valleys appearing in high-contrast, green monochrome. In the bottom right corner of his Head Up Display, or HUD, a number clicked down, showing the time to the target.

Over his head, the air battle carried on as the Red Air tried to fight their way through the wall of Blue Defenders to kill the strikers that were attacking from below. There was a constant chatter on the radio, always in short grunts of code, as pilots called out bogeys, bandits, and kills to each other.

"Bogies, Bullseye two-seventy at twenty-five, hits, twenty-three thousand," a Blue Air called out, identifying an unknown aircraft radar return at ten o'clock and twenty-three thousand feet.

"Friendly!" his leader shot back.

A very short pause, then, "Bandits, BRAA, one-two-zero, twenty-one, thirty, hot." Interpretation—bad guys, bearing one-two-zero, range twenty-one miles, altitude thirty thousand feet and coming straight in their face.

The lead F-15 made the assignments. "Eagle Four, you take the two on the south."

"Roger. Tally two," the Eagle Four called back. "He's breaking—!"

"Take him! Take him!"

"Getting there!" The wingman strained in his mask, the G-forces crushing him into his seat.

Then, "Fox One times two! Eagle Four, you're dead!"

"Magic! Magic! Going evasive! Boars, we need your help!"

And so it went, the fighters mixing it up in an old fashioned furball of jets, missiles and guns and radio noise. The strikers had very little, if anything, to say as they tried to slink their way to the target.

Within ten minutes, seven Blue Air aircraft had been declared dead, shot down by the Red Air aggressors. Charlie's team had taken losses, but that was expected. All in all, it was going about like he had thought it would go.

Except for one thing. One very critical thing.

The F-16s had not called "Sterile" the codeword signifying the target area was clear. That meant they hadn't yet taken out the anti-aircraft guns and air-to-air missiles that protected the target. And until that was accomplished, there would be no attack.

And they were now only minutes away.

Charlie checked the time, glanced at his chart, then reached down to arm up his weapons. "Three minutes, ten seconds to target. Bomb release check complete?"

"Release check complete," Killer called from the back. "Radar looks good. I've got good offset and aim point. Expect first target to show in about twenty miles. Whenever you're ready, we are clear to engage."

Charlie nodded but didn't respond. He glanced at the time-to-target display and sucked in his breath.

Something wasn't right. Charlie glanced outside once again.

"Boss," Killer's voice sounded in his ears. "What's the deal with the F-16s? They should have already called the area clear."

"I know," Charlie shot back.

"Prince Charles," Killer said, "you're going to have to call an abort. If the F-16s haven't taken out the enemy radar, if the SAMS and triple

A are still active and ready, we'll get blown to bits if we fly over the target. You know the rules, Charlie. You should call an abort. You should turn the strikers around!"

Charlie didn't respond as he looked at his clock. Just under two minutes to go.

Col Wisner keyed the radio switch once again. "That is affirm, T-Bolt," he said to the F-16 flight lead. "You are ordered to abort. Withhold your HARM missiles. Leave the target area. Do not call it clear! You will comply with your previous orders."

"But, sir," the radio came back, angry and uncertain. "If we don't clear the target, the mission is over. The strikers will have to abort. And everything will be for nothing. It's a stupid thing to do, after coming this far!"

The colonel was quick to respond. "Confirm you understand, T-Bolt. Withhold your fire. Do not call the target clear. Abort now, and return to base."

The pilot in the lead F-16 swore as he tore off his mask. He didn't respond as he turned his formation around.

"Ninety seconds, Charlie. What are you going to do?" Killer's voice was nearly shrill.

Charlie didn't respond. The nightscape sped by them in a blur of moon shadows, reflected light off the desert and granite mountain peaks.

"The target isn't clear. Charlie, you should turn us around!"

For the moment, Charlie ignored his backseater and pressed on his radio switch. "T-bolts, say your position," he called out.

Nothing. The radios were silent.

"T-bolts. This is Thunder One-One. Confirm 'Sterile'. We need it now!"

Still nothing but occasional static from the storms off to the north.

Charlie tried one last thing. "Any striker on Thunder frequency. Did anyone hear the T-bolts call 'Sterile'?"

"That's a negative," a B-1 called back. "Lead, what do you want us to do?"

Charlie paused as he thought, then pressed his mike once again. "Standby—break, break—Eagles, if we press, can you still hang with us? Will you follow us up, even if the target isn't clear?"

"That's affirm, Thunder One-One," the leader of the F-15s called back. "We'll stay with you. Just let us know."

Charlie glanced at his HUD. Sixty-three seconds to go.

Killer knew what Charlie was thinking and he didn't like the plan. "The area isn't clear, Charlie," he pointed out for the third time. It was obvious what Killer wanted Charlie to do. "They haven't called 'Sterile'! If we go in, we're going to take it in the shorts. Maybe half of us will even survive."

"Look, Killer," Charlie shot back, "This exercise wasn't set up as a conventional mission. We're talking weapons of mass destruction here. And we always—always—have authority to use our best judgment, regardless of the original plan. It's possible the T-bolts called 'Sterile' and we missed it. Maybe they couldn't get through because of the radio static. Maybe their 'Sterile' call got lost in all the radio chatter. There are several possibilities, but Killer, this much is clear. The scenario is Hussein is arming and loading his fighters. He will drop those chemical weapons on the Kurds in northern Iraq."

"That's beautiful, Charlie," Killer fired back. "A fitting memorial. But listen to me, pilot. It isn't our job to get us killed. The rules of engagement are perfectly clear. If the target isn't 'Sterile,' we abort. Remember that, Charlie. It was part of the briefing."

"But I never thought—"

"Forty seconds, now pilot."

"Think of it, Al. Thousands of people will die."

"Charlie, this isn't real. It's only for practice, remember. It's only an exercise, man."

"But we train like we fight and we fight like we train. That is the whole deal. And if this were real, what would you do, Al? What would you do?"

Captain Bennett didn't reply. He paused for a moment then wiped his hands over his eyes before lowering his head to his radar display.

"Killer—tell me," Charlie pressed. "If this were the real thing, because someday it might be—I want to know, what would you want me to do?"

Killer studied the infrared image as the target came into sight. "Target environment is coming in," he called out in a tight voice. "Got an SA-10 searching us now. He's almost within range! He's trying to get a good lock!"

"Are you with me then, Killer? I want to go in!"

"Okay. Okay!" Killer screamed into his mask. "I'm with you

Charles. Now you listen to me. Give me a hard right-hand turn and get this baby down in the dirt or that SA-10 will blow us out of the sky."

Charlie was smiling as he jammed his stick hard to the right. "Way to go, Killer," he laughed. "This is going to be fun!"

"No, this is stupid," Killer called out as the jet screamed closer to the ground.

Charlie grunted against the strain of the Gs, then reached down and jammed his radio switch. "Blue Air, continue the attack," he commanded. "The area isn't clear, but I want you all in. I say again, Blue Air you're clear to engage."

Colonel Wisner smiled as he listened to Charlie's radio call. It was exactly what he had expected. The man had clearly broken the rules. It was a brave, but foolish, decision. And it was also what he was hoping Charlie would do.

AL-KUWAIT INTERNATIONAL AIRPORT, KUWAIT 1500 LOCAL TIME

Cowboy One, the presidential 747, was scheduled for a 1545 takeoff from Kuwait's international airport en route back to Washington, D.C. It would be a sixteen-hour, nonstop, lunch-for-breakfast, jetlag–inducing, killer of a flight that would take the crew and passengers through a short sunset and twilight before encountering the unsettling darkness of a midnight trans-Atlantic flight. Across an entire ocean they would fly, from the sands of Arabia to the smog of D.C., through eight time zones and for more than nine thousand miles. On board the enormous aircraft were 337,000 pounds of jet fuel and 23 tons of cargo, along with the vice president and former president, twenty-four members of their delegation, forty-nine members of the press corps, and twenty-eight members of the crew.

Sixty minutes before the presidential party arrived at the aircraft, the ground crew was still busy refueling the jet and loading half-moon–shaped baggage canisters into the luggage compartment. The pilot, an air force colonel, was just starting his preflight inspection.

At 3:27, the American party arrived in a convoy of military escorts in black Mercedes limousines. Because there was no ceremony at the airport, it took the delegation only minutes to board. At 3:36, the doors to the aircraft were shut. The passengers began to settle into their seats as the crew secured the carry-on bags and passed out refreshments. Seconds after closing the door, Cowboy One began to roll across the ramp.

As was procedure, all airport traffic was commanded to stop while Air Force One made its way to the runway. The enormous airliner lumbered along the taxiway, the two air force pilots inside the cockpit completing their predeparture checklist. By the time they approached the south end of the airport, they were ready to take off.

Following the thin, yellow taxi line, the pilot maneuvered the jet to the center of the runway and pointed the nose to the north, then held the brakes and spooled up the engines. He released the brakes and adjusted his throttles while feeling the familiar push in his seat. The aircraft quickly accelerated down the runway and lifted into the air. The wingtips bowed, bending slightly skyward, and the gear dropped against the bottom of their pistons as the 747 lost contact with the ground. The copilot reached down and lifted the gear handle, then raised the flaps from twenty to ten units. The gear thumped into place in the belly of the aircraft. The Boeing was heavy but graceful as her nose pitched up to twelve degrees. Moments later, the first wisp of cloud rushed by the tinted windscreen and the desert began to quickly fade in the haze of the dry and sandy Arabian air. At two thousand feet, the aircraft began a slight turn to the left.

Inside the presidential suite, the former president sat in a huge swivel chair. The current vice president sat as his side. Though not politically friendly, the two were now engaged in a cause. For the next three hours, they huddled in quiet conversation, discussing the failure of the United Nations sanctions against Saddam Hussein. The UN-brokered agreement of 1998 had fallen victim to his lies and deceit. What would it take to bring him into compliance this time? How much longer would he be able to hold on? What steps could they now take to destroy the most threatening weapons? What would it take to bring the man down?

After hours of discussion, they knew only one thing. The trip to Kuwait had been a complete waste of time. They were not even close to finding a solution to the situation in Iraq and the leader who had dogged them for so many years.

Turning in his seat, the former president closed his weary eyes and within minutes was breathing the heavy rhythm of sleep.

The night passed quietly. Nine hours later, Cowboy One was passing over the uneven and rocky coastline of Nova Scotia. It was early morning and the low sun cast long shadows across the green valleys of the

Canadian coast. The flight was on schedule and proceeding according to its flight path.

As the flight crossed into American airspace, Air Traffic Control, or ATC, was preparing to hand the aircraft off to New York Center, who would then coordinate for Cowboy One's approach into the extremely congested airspace that surrounded D.C.

Sitting at the controller's desk at Boston Center was a young women named Kelly Lyn. At 7:44 P.M. local, Kelly studied her display, watching the 747 track across her radar screen. The innocuous call sign gave no indication of who owned the aircraft. She didn't know where it came from. She didn't know who was on board. As she followed the aircraft across her wide radar screen, she keyed her microphone switch and called out its call sign. "Cowboy One, after crossing X-ray, descend and maintain two-niner thousand feet," she instructed.

As she waited for Cowboy One to respond, Kelly was already thinking of her next move. With the Air Force aircraft about to descend to twenty-nine thousand feet, she could move up an east-bound United, then vector a Delta flight over to Buffalo Center. With that done, she could then stack a couple of air force F-16s at thirty thousand and let them get on their way into Bangor airport. That would then allow her—

She paused in her thinking for a moment. The Cowboy Flight had not yet responded to her instructions. She keyed her radio once again.

"Cowboy One, crossing X-ray, descend and maintain flight level two-niner-zero. Contact New York Center now on one-three-two-point-four." This time she waited. Again no response. An American Airlines flight called her as it was climbing out of Boston. She glanced at her radar screen. There were three other aircraft behind it, all of them waiting for instructions.

Kelly ignored them for now. "Cowboy One, radio check. How do you read?" Nothing. She tried once again, then suddenly frowned.

With a few impatient keystrokes on her keyboard, she selected Cowboy One and asked the ATC computer to provide her with more information. The computer hummed for less than a second before illuminating the air force flight as a bright green triangle on her radar screen.

As the triangle appeared, the frown was replaced by a scowl.

The computer was asking for her job number and access code before it would give her the information she had requested. She typed very quickly, her heart beating loudly, fear beginning to rise in her chest.

She pressed the "enter" button. The details of the air force flight materialized as a series of codes and numbers next to the green aircraft symbol.

Her mouth went dry as she sucked in a breath, then jammed on her mike once again.

"Cowboy One, radio check. How do you read?" Her voice was hurried and half an octave higher. She waited and listened, but no one came back. Turning her attention to another portion of her radar screen, she called out, "American twenty-eight fifty-six, Boston Center on three-four-point-seven. Radio check. How do *you* read?"

"Boston, American has you loud and clear."

Kelly turned in her swivel chair and motioned to her watch supervisor, who immediately walked over and dropped to his knees beside her console. "What's up?" he whispered.

Kelly pointed to the aircraft symbol on her screen. "I've got a NORDO making way through my sector."

The supervisor studied the radar display. A NORDO, or No Radio Aircraft. They were infrequent, but a real pain in the neck. He studied the screen, then glanced over to Kelly and for the first time saw the fear in her eyes. Her face was white and her hands seemed to tremble as she punched up the code at her screen.

"Look at this Frank!" she whispered so the other controllers couldn't hear. "The NORDO aircraft is coded as Air Force One! And the vice president and former president Bush are on board!"

5

SHERATON WASHINGTON HOTEL
WASHINGTON, D.C.
2015 LOCAL TIME

The Secret Service team leader, code-named Bullfrog, was standing no more than thirty feet from the president. He was hidden backstage, near a fire escape door that led out onto Calvert Street. From his vantage point, he could watch as the president roused through his fund-raising speech, netting half a million dollars for twenty minutes of his time.

Bullfrog concentrated on the crowd. A pea-sized receiver was stuffed into his left ear. A tiny microphone was pinned inside his lapel. He listened to the buzz of the receiver and watched his men who were stationed throughout the huge ballroom. There were eleven Secret Service agents assigned to his detail, including four "Packers," or agents with Uzi submachine guns.

The team leader glanced around with anxious eyes. Huge groups like this always made him nervous. He hated it when the president was out in the open, especially in a crowded and unsecure room. If he had his way, he would confine the president within the walls of the White House. Only then would he feel his boss was secure.

Bullfrog half-listened as the president paused, the crowd roaring with applause. The sound of the clapping was just settling down when his radio crackled to life. Bullfrog pushed the tiny speaker further into his ear and cocked his head to one side, his eyes never leaving the president's back.

"For Daggers, for Daggers. Get Soldier down! I say again, get Soldier down!"

Instantly, Bullfrog sprang forward while reaching under his coat. Drawing his weapon, he kept it down by his thigh, the snub-nose barrel facing down, the hammer in the fire position. He ran to the edge of the curtains where he abruptly pulled himself to a stop. From the edge of the stage he surveyed the ballroom. The audience was beginning to stir, a ripple of surprise making its way through the crowd as the other secret service agents began to glide toward the front of the room.

Bullfrog lowered his head to his mike. "Dagger two, what have you got?"

His number two man, the primary observer situated at the back of the hall, surveyed the crowd with carefully trained eyes.

"Two is blank. Nothing now. But let's get him off the stage."

"Roger," Bullfrog shot back.

He was just moving forward when he heard a sound near his left ear. Turning instantly, he faced the Packer who had emerged from the back of the stage, holding the Uzi in his left hand. With a *click*, the Packer expanded the collapsible stock, then forced himself between a layer of curtains while maintaining a suspicious eye on the crowd.

Bullfrog began to move forward, walking briskly toward the podium. Two other agents moved onto the stage. As the agents moved toward the president, the audience reacted with a collective breath of alarm. The president paused, but didn't turn in Bullfrog's direction.

The president pushed himself back from the podium, a look of concern on his face. Bullfrog was the first one to reach him. He positioned himself in front of the man, placing his body between his charge and the crowd. Within seconds, the other agents stood at his side. Turning their backs on the president, they stood facing the crowd, hiding the President within of circle of men.

Bullfrog leaned over and whispered into his ear. "Sir, we need you to come with us. Please, just walk off the stage with us now."

The president glanced over to where he knew the Packer would be, looking for the glint of his gun. Bullfrog's earpiece started to squawk, asking him if Soldier was secure. The team leader muttered into his lapel, then placed a firm hand on the president's shoulder and began to nudge him toward the side door.

Bullfrog nodded his head and the men began to walk. After clearing the stage, the agents rushed the president toward the back door. Bullfrog spoke into his mike, barking a series of sharp commands.

At Bullfrog's nod, an agent slammed the stage door open and rushed into the alley, his gun pulled and at the ready position. The presidential limousine barreled down the back alley, bouncing up onto the sidewalk before squealing to a stop. The back door to the limo shot open. The team leader pushed the president toward the waiting car. The president fell in, his secret service agents behind him. The limo took off before the back door was even shut, another sedan immediately pulling into position behind it. The limo waited for only seconds at the intersection of Connecticut and Calvert before the police motorcade wailed by, then accelerated onto the road to sandwich in between the police cars. Seconds later, Bullfrog called in to the command center that Soldier was secure.

CHEVY CHASE, MARYLAND
2033 LOCAL TIME

The Speaker of the House of Representatives had just stepped out of the shower, a thick cotton bathrobe hanging from his burly shoulders. The evening sunlight spilled through his bedroom window, casting long shadows across the polished wood floor. The house had been in session until late that evening and the speaker was feeling very tired.

He heard the knock on his bedroom door and looked up at a secret service agent standing there. His wife stood in the background, a nervous look on her face.

"Mr. Speaker, I am sorry to disturb you, sir, but we have a situation with Diver. The National Command Structure has initiated a GIANT ARM recall."

The speaker opened his mouth and narrowed his eyes. His face drained of color as he glanced around the room. He stared at the wall, a faraway look on his face. His wife covered her mouth with a trembling hand but otherwise did not move.

The three individuals stood perfectly still. They all heard the sound at the same time. The bedroom windows began to vibrate very gently. The speaker listened to the whoop of the helicopter blades. Further in the distance, he heard the wail of sirens as police cars made their way down his street. He glanced to the window, unable even to think.

The agent turned toward the speaker's wife. "Ma'am," he said. "Your husband will be coming with us. Do you have something he could wear? Something that we could take with us?"

The speaker took a deep breath, then turned for his closet. "You've got to at least give me time to get dressed," he demanded.

"Mr. Speaker, we have exactly ninety seconds before you have to be on the chopper. So no, sir, you will not have time to get dressed."

The sound and vibration rolled high over their heads as the army Blackhawk pulled into a hover. Two police cruisers positioned themselves sideways in the road. The officers got out to direct traffic away. The chopper pilots surveyed the road from a height of fifty feet, then turned the tail and began to drift toward the ground. Seconds later, the chopper set down with a bounce of its tires.

The speaker glanced through the thin fabric curtains to see an army crew member throw open the helicopter's huge sliding door. He watched for a second, then felt a pull on his arm. Together, the two men ran from the room.

Fifty seconds later, the Blackhawk lifted again into the air. The speaker sat staring out the side window, his bathrobe drawn tight around his shoulders, his bare feet cold against the hard metal floor. A pair of dress slacks and a white shirt lay in a heap across his lap.

He watched as the tree-lined road slipped under his window, then turned to the colonel who was sitting at his side. The colonel opened a folder and handed him a red-covered binder. The speaker opened it and began to read. The chopper turned to the west, out away from the city. Its destination was two hundred miles away.

6

WHITE HOUSE SITUATION ROOM
WASHINGTON, D.C.
2137 LOCAL TIME

Air Force One passed abeam New York City a little over two hundred miles out over the Atlantic. The aircraft flew silent as a ghost, a mute triangle on the air traffic controller's radar screens. It proceeded on A700, a well-used and long established jet route that had been designed to feed European traffic into Dulles, Reagan, and BWI airports. Of course, the air force jet was not filed to any one of these destinations, but into Andrews AFB, home of the presidential fleet.

As the aircraft proceeded southwest, several dozen communications specialists were frantically working to contact the aircraft. They tried every available means, which were many, for Air Force One was a virtual communications center. It had radios and receivers and telephones galore. It had satellite hook-ups and high-frequency radios that could reach submarines sitting under the polar caps or aircraft flying in combat patrols over the Adriatic Sea. It could patch a phone call through to virtually any man on earth, from the leader of an east African nomadic tribe to the mayor of a tiny village in eastern Siberia.

So no one was fooled when the aircraft didn't respond. Everyone knew it wasn't simple radio failure.

The most likely scenario was the aircraft had been hijacked. Yet even that hypothesis didn't make any sense, for even if terrorists had cut off all radio communications, the crew still should have been able to activate one of the prearranged distress codes. Yet none of the onboard ATC transponders indicated any problem.

As the aircraft approached the Delaware Sound, the emergency crash net at Andrews was activated. Within seconds, huge lime-green fire trucks and foam sprayers rolled onto the flight-line and sped to both ends of the runway. A train of medical equipment—ambulances, crash-recovery vehicles, mobile trauma centers, bioenvironment hazard containment teams—everything needed to treat the injured and contain a major aircraft mishap, was also rushed to the scene. Word spread through the rescue crews like a fire in the wind. They were responding to an emergency aboard Air Force One. They were told to be prepared for the worst.

As the emergency vehicles rolled out onto the runways, the local air traffic controllers were quickly clearing the airspace around Andrews. Every aircraft, from the largest international airliners to tiny puddle-jumpers, were immediately vectored out of the area to ensure they wouldn't interfere with the emergency aircraft. Many of the airliners were diverted up to Dulles, some thirty-two miles to the east. The smaller airplanes were simply commanded to land.

As Air Force One flew to within one hundred miles of the city, the controllers expected it to descend. But the aircraft continued to cruise in level flight, undeviating in airspeed, altitude, or course. Twenty minutes later, it passed over Andrews airfield. It then began a slight veer to the left, picking up a more or less southerly direction to parallel the coastline toward the Chesapeake Bay. Passing south of the East Dismal Swamp, a huge snake-infested bog near the Pamlico Sound, the aircraft finally began to descend.

The president picked up the phone, his face hollow and tight. He listened for only a moment, then, without reacting, placed the handset back in its cradle. The crowded Situation Room, was very, very quiet. Every eye was on the president. No one spoke, no one even seemed to breath, as they studied the president's face, searching for any sign of good news.

The president's shoulders drooped as he lifted his eyes. For a moment, he sat without speaking. Then, clearing his throat, he announced to the room. "The aircraft has just passed over the South Carolina border," he said. "As the air force predicted, it has begun to descend. It is now on a constant downward glide path, losing approximately four thousand feet every minute.

"It would appear that the air force analyst called it just right. The aircraft had only a ninety-minute reserve. It has just run out of fuel. There is nothing we can do for it now."

HORRY COUNTY
TWENTY MILES EAST OF WAMPEE,
SOUTH CAROLINA
2048 LOCAL TIME

The young boy was standing at the edge of the forest when the aircraft appeared over his head like a giant, silent bird. It appeared from the shadows of the late evening light, its blue-and-white skin reflecting the dying rays of the sun. It was astonishingly quiet, no more noisy than a rustle of wind. For almost five seconds it entirely blocked out the sky as the aircraft passed over the green pasture where the boy stood, gliding not more than a hundred feet over his head. The young boy stood absolutely still, watching in amazement. He could actually hear the rush of wind passing over the wings and around the huge fuselage. The aircraft passed over him with a gentle *swoosh*, gliding peacefully toward the tall trees.

Moments later, he heard a series of brittle pops, which grew suddenly sharp and much louder. Then came the snap and crack of whole falling trees. Splinters of wood, leaves, and dust began to burst into the air, just barely over the tops of the pines. A wrenching, tearing sound ripped its way through the forest as the aircraft began to break into pieces. Slabs of steel and aluminum cut their way through the trees with the sound of brittle thunder. Huge hunks of the wing shattered and swirled through the air. The noise of the impact rolled and cracked through the forest.

In his mind, the young boy thought he could hear people scream. Frightened and trembling, he reached up and covered his ears.

HORRY COUNTY CRASH SITE
2334 LOCAL TIME

"Hold it," the colonel commanded. "Keep it right here. I want to get some photos."

The rescue helicopter pulled into a hover sixty feet over the cut in the trees where Air Force One had first impacted the forest. The colonel nodded to the military photographer who was strapped near the open door. Leaning out against the thick canvas strap, the young airman began to snap away. Night had settled over the forest. The helicopter's huge spotlights illuminated the wreckage with a bath of white light. It had been almost three hours since the aircraft went down.

As the colonel looked down at the wreckage, he estimated the jumbo jet had struck the trees at a nearly level attitude, with a fairly controlled rate of descent. He could see where the northern-most pines had experienced only a slicing of their limbs as the 747 had cut across the tallest and most flexible boughs. It wasn't until some two hundred feet beyond the initial point of impact that whole trees had begun to fall, broken into pieces by the crumbling jet.

It was at that point, where the trees lay in a tangle of splintered wood, that the real wreckage began. Shiny scraps of metal were strewn forward along the flight path for almost two thousand feet as the aircraft had been shredded apart. Looking forward, the accident investigator could see the path of the four huge engines. Because of their dense mass, their kinetic energy had propelled them forward along the flight path, cutting four separate trails through the trees. He estimated the engines were almost three thousand feet from the initial point of impact. Somewhere between them and the huge chunks of fuselage, he knew he would find the remains of the cockpit. Somewhere behind that, would be the presidential section. That was where he would begin.

The helicopter began to drift forward. The colonel stared down through the trees to the recovery effort that was ongoing below. The security forces were already on the scene, as well as the local rescue teams and county police. So far, they had found no survivors. Which was more than a little surprising. Without a post-impact fire, and with the relatively low glide-speed at impact, the colonel had hoped that some passengers would have survived.

The colonel told the pilots to set the chopper down at the end of the wreckage, where banks of portable lights had been set, illuminating the forest in an unnatural glow. The colonel climbed out of the chopper and headed through the trees toward a large, egg-shaped piece of debris. The flight deck lay in a heap on the forest floor, the cockpit battered, but more or less intact. As he approached the broken cockpit, a uniformed air force major called out.

"Sir! This way. Come quickly!" The major's name tag identified him as a flight surgeon, a member of the crash recovery team who had been flown down from D.C.

"What is it, Paul?" the colonel replied.

"Just come with me, sir. This is something you must see!"

The colonel followed the flight surgeon toward the broken cockpit. Coming around the corner of the wreckage, he was shocked to see that the two pilots were still strapped in their seats, their harnesses tight around their shoulders, their arms laying awkwardly at their sides, their heads slumped like rag dolls against their chests. The colonel could see that the pilot had an obvious broken neck. In addition, one of his legs was bent at a ninety-degree angle, cutting awkwardly off to one side. In contrast to the pilot, the copilot, the one man in the right seat, appeared to be relatively unharmed.

"Okay, Paul, what is it? I don't have a lot of time. I want to have a look at the presidential section. The White House is waiting for confirmation of their deaths." The colonel spoke as he glanced around the cockpit, taking in the rows of shattered instruments, broken switches and glass screens.

The major walked over to the copilot's seat and grabbed the man by the hair. Lifting his face, he turned it toward the colonel.

Long welts had been clawed into the copilot's face. His nose had been torn down to a mound of white cartilage. Both of his eyeballs were gone, the deep, empty sockets left gaping holes in the center of his face.

The major held the man's hair as he looked at the corpse. "These injuries didn't happen from the impact," he explained. "These injuries were self-inflicted. Look at his hands. They are covered with blood. For fifteen years I've been doing this now, and I've never seen anything like this before. And this is the fifth body found with similar wounds. Whatever happened to these men, they didn't die in the crash. All of them were dead long before that."

The colonel shuddered in fear as a terrible realization burned itself into his mind. "Get away from them, Paul." The colonel stumbled back. "Get away from them now!" He quickly turned and ran. The major sprinted behind him though not knowing why.

Reaching into his pocket, the colonel pulled out a small cell phone. He dialed the number while running through the forest, waving back a group of rescuers who were walking toward them.

He heard only one ring before the phone was picked up. He didn't wait for the person to even say hello.

"Listen to me," he spoke breathlessly into the receiver. "This is J-3. I am at the crash site and I want this area cleared out now." He waited just a moment before shouting again.

"No! No! You don't understand. We have to clear this area now! I'm declaring it hot. I want all civilians out. And tell the watch desk, we've got a firestorm on our hands. I need security and bio and everything else. Immediately. Just call them, they'll know what to do!"

The colonel didn't give the man any time to respond. He flipped the phone closed and shoved it deep into his pocket.

"Everyone!" he cried, turning to the group of local search and rescue teams. "Everyone, listen to me. Get away. Clear the area. Get away from the jet. I'm declaring this crash site a national security zone."

MOUNTAIN HOME AFB, IDAHO
2255 LOCAL TIME

The exercise was over. The jets were on their way home. The first ones to land were the refueling tankers. Minutes after his KC-135 touched down, Colonel Wisner stepped into Lt Colonel Magill's office. He was drenched in sweat and he smelled particularly foul. Magill stood up from his desk as the colonel walked in.

"He did it, didn't he?" Magill asked with a tiny smile as they sat down.

"Yep, just like you said, Paul. You know your men pretty well."

Magill leaned back in his chair. "How many aircraft did they lose?"

"It wasn't that bad, really. The range computers estimated that at most three of the bombers and maybe two of the Strike Eagles would have been shot down by enemy fire. Only five aircraft in all. And better yet, despite the SAMS and triple A, every one of the aircraft was able to deliver its weapons. The computer models predict that the entire airfield would have been completely destroyed."

"Including the hardened bunkers? And suspected chemical weapons storage sites?"

"Yep, both of them gone. So your captain will take some spears in the debrief for not adhering to the rules of engagement, but the bottom line is, despite the losses, if this had been real-world, the mission would have been a resounding success."

An urgent knock sounded at the door. Without waiting for an answer, a young airmen stuck his head into the room.

"Excuse me, Colonel Wisner, but you have a call from D.C. General Beck's office. They said to tell you it's urgent."

"Alright," Wisner replied. "I will take it in here."

"Sir, the call came in on the STU III phone. I'm afraid you'll have to came back and take the call in our vault."

Colonel Wisner frowned, then followed the airman out of the office and down a short hall. The two men passed through a steel, cipher-locked door to the secure area in the rear of the squadron building. Inside an empty briefing room, the airman pointed toward the STU III, a secure telephone that was only used for classified conversations. The colonel walked into the office. The airman pulled the door closed behind him.

Colonel Wisner picked up the phone and listened intently, his face growing pale as General Beck explained. His hands began to shake as he held the phone to his ear. He stammered just once, then closed his eyes as he thought. The conversation was brief. The colonel hung up the phone.

He stood motionless for a moment, then made his way back to Magill's office. Stalking into the room, he eyed his old friend. "I want them," he announced. "Charlie and Killer. Notify their families. We're leaving tonight."

Magill's heart skipped a beat. He had seen this before. He started to argue, then bit his tongue. The look on Wisner's face told him he better be still.

Three hours later, the colonel was sitting near the front of his jet, a small Lear that was flying at its best speed to the south. Behind him, near the aft bulkhead, Charlie McKay was asleep. Alex Bennett sat staring out the window at the darkness.

He hadn't had a chance to tell his family goodbye.

AL-HAUMAND-ELKARAR MOSQUE
DOWNTOWN BAGHDAD
0810 LOCAL TIME

The mosque was small and smooth and glaringly white, its polished marble exterior dazzling against the mid-morning sky. It was isolated behind a high wall of white brick and sand-blasted stone, a huge iron fence guarding its single entrance. Though it was a place of worship, it was not for the masses, but a sanctuary where only the privileged could go.

Inside, the mosque was nearly deserted. Only one man kneeled at the early morning prayer. The Arab leaned down and touched his head to the polished marble and muttered under his breath.

"One God, the Only God, maker of mountain and sky
Give me strength and compassion
Grant authority and mercy for all those who worship the One God
And power over those who deny
That they, like all enemies since the beginning of time,
May rest their souls on the judgments of Allah, the Only God."

The worshiper repeated the prayer several times, muttering in long cadence as he bowed his head to the floor. He prayed until he sensed the rustle of flowing fabric behind him, then the nearly imperceptible touch on his shoulder. Pushing himself up, he turned slowly around.

The cleric was dressed in a smooth white *dashiki*, which was wrapped around the front of his face and pushed back over his neck to flow down over one of his shoulders. Neither his hands nor his bare feet were visible under the flowing robe. His head was wrapped in a turban, which, against tradition, he wore in a tight wrap over his ears and around the crown of his head so that only the top half of his face was revealed. His tiny eyes were dim with age; watery, red, and diminished somehow. But though long on years, still they glared with the passion of a temper not yet fully controlled.

The younger Arab turned to follow the cleric as he walked to the front of the mosque and out a side door. Together they walked through the small garden, speaking in low voices as they talked.

"How are you feeling?" the cleric asked in a tone of great concern.

The younger man rubbed at his thigh, feeling the old wound, touching the rut in the flesh where the muscle had been stripped away, leaving a scar and a depression which in some areas went nearly down to the bone. He felt the cold steel that attached the artificial calf and wooden foot to his knee. For a moment, he flashed back to his long battle in the hospital. He almost smelled the stench of rotting flesh from the spreading gangrene. He thought of the effort to get him out of the country, to France or Italy, to where his leg could receive proper medical care, then of the American fighters who had forced his chopper to turn around, turning him back some twenty kilometers inside his own border.

The rage simmered inside him. The pain, the limp, the inability to run. He was hobbled and incomplete in a terrible way.

And he knew who to blame. Both were guilty of sin. He harbored and nursed the blame every day.

The cleric watched the younger man. Under his face-cloth, the cleric smiled, though his eyes remained dull and lifeless. The young man was ripe. He was ready. It was time.

The two walked for a moment longer, their bare feet sinking into the softness of the patch of well-watered grass. The cleric turned to the younger man and leaned toward his ear. "Listen to me, Odai," he whispered. "You are committed now. You must act. And it must be soon, or it will be too late."

Odai Hussein turned away from the cleric. "No," he started to answer. "Not yet. He might change his mind."

The old man muttered an insult. It was personal and foul and deeply offensive, yet Odai's face remained passive and unchanged.

"Your father will learn what you have done," the old man sneered. "The *Rais* will find out and you will have to explain. You must be prepared to take action! There can be no delay."

The younger man didn't respond. He stared at the grass, an awkward expression on his face. Inside his chest, his heart pounded the blood up to his ears, drumming it into his brain. His stomach rolled into a tight ball of fear. He was afraid—deeply afraid—for he knew he had crossed over the line.

7

THE WHITE HOUSE, WASHINGTON, D.C.
DAY THREE (THURSDAY)
0530 LOCAL TIME

The sun was still almost an hour from rising. Soft patches of light filtered through the bullet-proof windows from the security lights that glowed on the White House lawn. The group in the Oval Office was arranged in a rough semi-circle around a low coffee table, with the president sitting at the head. Brent Hillard, the National Security Advisor, or NSA, leaned awkwardly back in the blue leather sofa, his fingers interwoven across the back of his head, his arms acting as an improvised headrest. Michael Crosby, the director of the CIA, hunkered anxiously on the edge of another couch, his arms folded across his lap, a worried look on his face. The last of the men, the four-star Chairman of the Joint Chiefs of Staff, sat stiffly against the back of his chair.

A little less than nine hours had passed since Air Force One had crashed into the quiet Carolina forest. Since the aircraft had gone down, the White House had been a nest of upheaval, caught up in a chaos of uncertainty and fear. Lights had burned all through the long night as the staff worked to piece the story together.

President Andrew Brooks fidgeted impatiently as his men gathered their notes. He sat with his arms folded and his feet on the floor—a determined and angry look on his face. The air in the Oval Office was crackling dry and Brooks constantly sipped at a bottle of water. Leaning forward, the president pushed his fingers through his brown hair, an unconscious motion to keep it in place. He was lean and tight, with blue eyes set in a handsome, tan face—a president born for the television age. He was smooth on his feet and could schmooze like a whore—a man who was honest only when he had nothing to hide. Direct in his manner, he was aggressive, ambitious, and highly intelligent. In short, a well-studied model of the modern-day politician.

The president eyed his advisors after a quick glance at his watch. He had a press conference and he wanted some answers.

"Okay, gentlemen, what have we got?"

General Beck, a squat and powerful man with broad shoulders and thick black hair, leaned forward in his chair, a look of distress in his eyes. He was a warrior at heart and unaccustomed to fear. From the jungles of Vietnam to combat sorties over Baghdad, the general had seen firsthand every hostile situation the nation had encountered over the past twenty-eight years. But sitting in the early morning light of the Oval Office, he felt a growing sense of darkness that he couldn't deny.

The general cleared his throat as he turned to the president. "Sir," he began, "all of the early evidence indicates the aircraft simply ran out of fuel. And though it will take weeks to analyze every piece of the wreckage, over the past few hours we have been able to accomplish an initial tear-down on the engines, fuel cells, and primary mechanical components of the 747. We know for certain that none of the four engines was operating at the time of impact. We know that the fuel lines were dry. We know that the pumps in the main fuel cells had cavitated, which typically happens once they are no longer submerged in fuel.

"And while it is possible the aircraft may have experienced some kind of emergency that would explain the loss of communications and the drifting off course, it is my feeling that such a scenario is extremely unlikely."

The president studied the general without comment, waiting for him to go on. "It is my opinion, sir," General Beck continued, "based on what evidence we have already seen, that this wasn't an accident and it wasn't human error. It is my feeling, sir, that certainly the pilots, and most probably the entire crew, were dead long before the aircraft impacted the ground. They were dead before the aircraft even entered our airspace. I would guess it happened shortly after their last radio transmission, which occurred just south of the coast of Greenland."

The president leaned back in his chair, a bitter look on his face. "Alright general, so what do I say? What am I to say to the American people?"

The general looked away, shaking his head. "I wish I could tell you, sir. But the truth is, none of us know. We are looking for answers, and the answers will come. But right now, we simply don't know."

President Brooks turned to study the other two men in the room. The CIA director and National Security Advisor sat opposite each other, waiting for their turn to be grilled.

The two men were a pair of seemingly unremarkable fellows. Brent Hillard, the NSA, was forty-eight. Michael Crosby had just turned fifty-one. Hillard was huge, almost six-four and close to three hundred pounds, despite exhausting, if irregular, workouts at the White House gym. Crosby was a bald and frumpy black man with hound-dog jowls and huge ears. Neither of them played well for the camera nor circulated with much success among the sophisticates of the city. But they also happened to be two of the most intelligent and capable men in President Brooks' administration. They were shrewd, insightful, articulate, and very effective at staying above the political fray.

But more important to the president, they were also his friends. He had known both of them since their days back in college and their friendship went straight to the core. It had sustained them through times when they vehemently disagreed with each other, which of course happened all the time in their work.

Eyeing his NSA, the president said, "Okay Brent, what can you tell me? When will we have the toxicology and autopsy results?"

The NSA shifted in his seat. "Walter Reed Hospital is working on that now, sir. Blood and tissue samples were sent over to the army lab last night. But it's going to take some time before we start getting results. As you know, Mr. President, having to work at the crash site will significantly complicate the clinical investigation. Trying to match the scattered remains and the body pieces together is an extremely difficult chore. Trying to analyze the decay and determine the time and cause of death will be a painstaking and tedious job. But they have every staff member working on it, sir, and I expect to hear an initial report by later this morning.

"And as I explained to you earlier, one of our first priorities will be to identify the remains, for only by doing that can we establish if there were terrorists on board. And though I don't think it likely, we have to at least consider the possibility that someone was able to smuggle himself onto the aircraft."

"Okay," the president asked with a sense of frustration. "Then what *are* you thinking? How was the aircraft brought down?"

Dropping his shoulders, the CIA director finally began. "Mr. President, we have indications that some type of contaminant or poison may have been used. As was described to you last night, one of the pilots and several passengers suffered from violent self-inflicted wounds. While there are several possibilities to explain this, the evidence indicates some kind of hallucinogenic drug may have been involved. It could have been introduced by almost any means. In the food. In the water. A canister of aerosol placed in the vents. There are dozens of possibilities to explain how it might have been accomplished. But until we do further testing, we really won't know."

As the president listened, he sucked in a breath of dry air, filling his lungs until they pushed against the side of his ribs. He held on to the air as he glanced around the Oval Office at his desk and mementoes, the small table of gifts from his son, a coffee mug that sat near his favorite leather chair. Without knowing, he turned to the pictures of his family. A deep sense of sadness seemed to settle inside him. He was angry. He was grieved. And very confused.

And though he was searching for answers, there was this much he knew.

Someone had just assassinated two of the best men the nation had to offer—the vice president of the United States and former president. In addition, more than one hundred other people were dead. All of them Americans. Innocent civilians. It was outrageous! And he wanted revenge!

He exhaled. It was as simple as that. He wanted revenge.

And he knew. Everyone knew it was Saddam Hussein! He knew it deep in his soul. And he considered it a clear act of war.

"Gentlemen, that whore is over there laughing," the president began. Hiding in his underground palace, laughing as he watches CNN. He really believes we can't touch him, you know. I guess he thinks we won't figure it out. That we'll consider it an accident or some unknown act of God.

"For how many years has he been playing us for fools? With his buildup since the Gulf War, leading to endless inspection fiascos. And we only make things worse when we rely on the UN. Look at the '98 agreement! What more proof of incompetence do we need. But that is over. It is finished. I'm going to nail his head to the wall!"

Michael Crosby, the CIA director, stared into the president's eyes. "Sir," he said with caution, "I probably need to remind you that we don't yet have proof of who was involved in the attack. Although it's true that we have our suspicions, we really don't have any proof. And it's important here, sir, that we step back from our emotions until we have a handle on exactly what occurred. We can't go off on a rampage until we have all the facts. It wouldn't do, sir. We simply have to wait until we know."

"Let me tell you something, Michael," Brooks said in disgust. "You know, and I know, and any fool who hasn't spent the last ten years living on Mars knows that Saddam pulled the trigger on this one. He tried to assassinate President Bush once before. Don't you remember his plans back in '93? How close did he come then to getting even with him? This, Michael, was a simple act of revenge. To me that is clear. After all these years of waiting, he finally got even with Bush. So what do you want me to do! Sit here and twiddle my thumbs!"

The CIA director sat anxiously rubbing his hands. "Sir," he replied in as forceful a voice as he dared. "I'm not sure that you understand. Even if it was Saddam, we may *never* have proof. And the ugly truth is, it might not have been him. There are dozens of terrorist groups who could have carried out this attack. Hizballah. PKK. Jihad. Syria or Iran. There are so many possibilities. We have to go slow."

President Brooks lifted his hand and jabbed at the air. "Don't give me that! I don't buy any of that! I know it was him, and you know it too. He had means, he had motive. You know that is true, Michael."

"Yes, Mr. President, I understand your contention. And ninety percent of me agrees with what you have said. We know Saddam has sworn revenge. We know his standing with the militant Arabs would shoot like a rising star if he were able to complete such an attack. But still, sir, this isn't something that we can just guess on. We have to know. And we can't act. Not until we have some type of proof."

The president sat angrily against the edge of his chair. Pushing himself up, he turned and walked to the front of his desk. Leaning his fist against the highly polished wood, he stood with his back to his men before turning to look them again in the eye.

"The funeral is set for early next week, probably Wednesday morning. I will allow this time for our nation to mourn. We will focus for now on addressing our wounds." The president's voice was almost quiet now. "But listen to me, for I want to be perfectly clear. That is all the time that I'll give you, my friends. After that, I want action. I won't wait any longer. Seven days is all that you have.

"By then I want proof. I want irrefutable proof. If it was Hussein, then I want the evidence that will allow me to act. If it wasn't, that is fine. Just prove that as well. Either way, I don't care. I only want to know.

"But I guarantee you this. Whoever it was, I will stick his head on a post and display it in the center of this office. I will order the mission to go and get him myself. Murder and assassination are international crimes. If we can go after Noriega and Qaddafi, we can go after him. Now go and get me the proof that I need."

The president sat down behind his desk, a signal to the men that he considered the meeting over. Slowly, his advisors started to stir in their seats. Brent Hillard looked anxiously over to catch General Beck's eye, then quickly nodded his head. The general stood up and moved toward the president's chair.

"Mr. President," he began, "there is something else to consider. Something more that you also need to know."

The president hesitated, then nodded his head. "What is it, general?" he asked with concern.

The general glanced at Hillard, then began to explain. As he spoke, the president's face paled to a sickly gray. His eyes burned with light as he fought back the rage. And for the first time in his life, he felt the cold stab of fear as it reached down and grabbed at his heart.

8

THE PRESIDENTIAL PALACE
BAGHDAD, IRAQ
2355 LOCAL TIME

"Bloody, bloody fool! What were you thinking! Did you really believe that they wouldn't find out?"

For a long moment Odai Hussein did not respond. It was almost midnight and his brain was heavy from the Valium and wine. He sat in a stupor on the edge of a long mahogany couch, dressed only in a loose nightshirt and knitted wool socks. He smelled lightly of garlic, smoked salmon, and sweat. His hair matted with light perspiration as his father ranted and raved over his head.

"What are you speaking of, my father?" the younger Hussein finally asked. "What are you saying? What have I done?"

"Don't give me that!" President Hussein shot back. "You know what I mean! I know you, Odai. I know what's in your mind."

"My father. I felt it was safe. I felt—"

Saddam shot toward his son and shoved himself right in his face. "Shut up, you stupid fool! I've heard your excuses before. Have you nothing intelligent to say?"

Odai dropped his face to avoid his father, unable to look him in the eye. Saddam turned and cursed.

Only minutes before, Odai Hussein, the son of the Butcher, had been violently pulled from his bed after Saddam's personal guards had literally burst into his room and thrown the younger Hussein onto the floor. Grabbing him by the arms, they had jerked him to his feet. Odai fought with the guards before pushing them back. Standing, he glared at the men.

"Your father wants to see you," an army colonel declared, his voice cold as winter steel. Odai's heart nearly burst in his chest.

There were perhaps two men in the whole of Iraq who could have spoken to Odai in such a tone. As the chief of Saddam's personal guards, the colonel was one of those men, and he relished the look of fear that spread across Odai's face.

The officer took a quick step toward Odai.

So his father knew. The time had come. Midnight interviews with the president were never good news. Many men never returned from such trips. And though the president was his father, their relationship was not filled with love. Mutual need, layered with contempt and impatience, but never even a spark of affection or love. And like everyone else, Odai had developed a genuine fear of the man.

"First let me first get dressed," he demanded to the guards. He hated the thought of an encounter with his father without the benefit and security of his military rank on his shoulders.

The colonel drew a pistol and pointed it toward the door. "No," he said. "He wants you in there now." Odai shrugged and threw on a nightshirt, then hobbled between the four guards as they led the way down the hall.

He was escorted into the office, a cavernous room of tapestried walls, deep leather, silk curtains, etched windows, and polished hardwood floors. Odai positioned himself on the mahogany couch as the guards left the room with military precision. The minutes passed slowly as Odai waited for the president.

Odai Hussein was a muscular man, a somewhat smaller yet stronger version of his father. He had the same sullen eyes, broad nose, and small ears. The same hollow cheeks and short, bony hands. But unlike Saddam's bushy, black mustache, Odai preferred a well-manicured beard. At thirty-seven, he looked a little bit younger than he was.

As one of Saddam's oldest children, Odai was much like his father in demeanor and spirit, being equally unpredictable, intelligent, and crude. Like his father, he too had made an early name for himself as a thug and political assassin. He had personally overseen the execution of three of his brothers, along with their male children and most of their wives. And like his father, Odai also shared an intense hatred for Zionists and Jews. He fervently believed that Americans were Satan's children sent to this earth to destroy and laugh at his god. The feeling toward the U.S. had an iron grip on his cold heart. All he ever had to do to rekindle the hate was stare at the stub that ended his right leg, a badge he would carry for the rest of his life, for the attack helicopter had smashed his leg beyond any hope of repair.

Despite the battle injury and the handicap it had caused, soon after the war Saddam had chosen his son to rebuild his combat forces, making him the only five-star general in all of Iraq. Odai had taken command of the military with an iron-clad fist. He proved to be utterly unforgiving, a fierce and determined yet natural leader. Odai had come to thrive on the feeling of power that come from controlling men's lives, at times ordering their deaths just for the thrill of seeing fear in their eyes.

But though he was effective in ruling his army, sometimes Odai forgot that he wasn't really in charge.

And his father was just about to remind him of that.

Ten minutes passed before Saddam entered the room. The Iraqi president paced slowly toward his son, his nostrils flaring with each heavy breath. "Who told you to test the Vapor?" He demanded. "Who authorized such a foolish and mindless act?"

Odai hesitated only a second. "It was General Nedal-amal, my father. He said that you had told him—"

"Don't lie to me, you little *Kaief!*" Saddam reached out and slapped his son across the face. "Don't lie to me ever again! I know it was you. It had to be you. Do you really expect me to believe the general would act on his own? Or that somehow this wasn't your plan? Your leaders—your generals—the men you chose to serve under you, are loyal and intelligent men. Loyal to you, but also loyal to me. And they know in their hearts that I would kill them for even considering such a plan. So don't tell me that it wasn't by your order. I know you, Odai. I know how you think. And I am worried now for you, my son."

Odai touched his fingers to his lips and licked at the crimson blood with the tip of his tongue. Pulling himself upright, he looked his father straight in the eyes.

"My *Rais*, I beg you, let me speak. Listen to what I have to say. They will not know. They could not trace it to us. The aircraft was destroyed. You saw that on CNN. The bodies are nothing but mangled flesh. So how could they know? They will never trace it to Iraq."

The president rocked back on his heels. "My idiot son. How could you still be so stupid? Of course they will know. They see everything. They know when I sleep. They know when I eat. Sometimes I think that they listen when I fart. For more than a decade I have tried to foil them. And now, after all these years and billions of dollars, after working so hard, you nearly throw it away! We have come too far to let you destroy all of my plans, simply because you are an impatient man!

"Look, my son, at what is happening in Israel. The crackdown. All the arrests. The detaining of Palestinian leaders. The destruction of our warrior's homes. The sealing off of the borders. The expansion of the security zone in Lebanon. The Jews have been warned! Even as we speak, they are collecting our men, leaving us weakened and now unprepared. Is it only coincidence? Of course it is not. The Americans have traced the virus to us. They have warned the Israelis. And now what are we to do? How will we move? You have nearly destroyed our whole plan!"

"No, my *Rais*. That is not true. For every door that closes, another one opens. And that is the point I must make.

"It is the Americans we want. They are the key to the future of Islam. The Jews—we should leave them alone."

The president rubbed his hands along the side of his trousers, feeling for the smooth leather of his pistol holster, a nervous habit from his days as a rebel in the hills of northern Iraq. He turned to his son and lifted his hand once again.

"You fool, what do you mean?" he sneered. "How could you think that? What sin is running round in your head?"

Odai began to talk, speaking as fast as he dared, spilling the thoughts he had been harboring for months. "My *Rais*. If we were to attack the Israelis, what would they do? They would destroy us. We know that they would! Nuclear warheads would rain down on our cities and the cradle of Islam would be brought to her knees.

"But the Americans? They would slither away into the grass, anxious to lick their wounds and not anger us further. You know that is true, father. Despite their talk and bravado, they are weak. They lay ripe to be taken, like a fruit on a tree and it would only take once. One simple act, and they would turn their tails and run. Think of it, *Sayid*. One simple attack and they would pull out of our region. Do you think they would hold out in our corner of the world once they knew you have power to destroy?

"Think of the war. One hundred forty-eight Americans dead. And that was nearly the limit of what they would have endured. Any more than that, and they would have pulled their troops back. Their leaders are not warriors, especially this one. He is weak and craven as a child. They have no stomach for fighting. They are not like us. We lose three hundred thousand and count it a glory. They lose a few hundred, and are ready to run. They are spoiled children, with their fancy planes and fancy guns. But they are not warriors. They are not fighters. They will run.

"And that is not all, my dear *Rais*. That is not all. They have another weakness which can be exploited. A weakness, like the underbelly of a snake, where the scales are tender and the vitals can be found."

Saddam turned to face his son, his eyes burning with contempt. "And what is this weakness, Odai?" he asked with sarcasm. "What is this weakness, this mystery of feebleness that only you have found?"

Odai lifted himself from the chair and walked to stand before his father.

"Their weakness is this," he said in a whisper. "They have no fear. The arrogant Americans don't have any fear. They truly believe that they can not be hurt. Think of that, father. They don't live with any fear. When was the last time that they suffered? When was the last time they felt any pain? Generations have passed now and they have forgotten. They feel as though they are untouchable. Untouchable, as if they were gods.

"But we could touch them, father. We could hurt them. We could teach them. We could teach them to fear."

The president turned away from his son. The palace was as still as the desert that surrounded it. No wind blew through the open windows. A nighthawk cried in the distance, a sound Saddam's ancestors had heard for the past three thousand years. Odai listened to the cry as his heart beat in his chest. His father stood with his eyes to the window.

"No," Saddam finally replied in a quiet voice. "No, Odai, you are very wrong. And it will be hard to show you how disappointed I am."

Odai dropped his eyes to the floor, then lifted his head once again. "My father," he replied. "We could hit the Great Satan. Hit him but once, then demand that he take his troops and leave. The desert doesn't suit them, but it is our home—your home—the home of your fathers—and with the Americans gone, you would hold the balance of power. Then we could deal with the simple-minded Jews. And after them, Iran and everyone else. But as I have always said, the Israelis are not our primary concern. Let us forget them. They are not the key. The future lies in attacking the West."

Saddam turned away from his son and strode toward the huge window that overlooked the eastern desert. Staring into the darkness, he placed his hands behind his back as a sense of anticipation seeped deep into his soul. He was fearful—fearful for himself and fearful for Odai. His son was a foolish and manipulative man.

Saddam's instincts were screaming. He knew his son was a threat. And he would be a huge challenge to control.

Saddam turned back to Odai, his eye lids hanging low over his pupils, his spent anger having drained all the color from his face. Odai looked up to stare at his father. He took a quick step toward his leader and raised his voice. "My *Rais*," he began. "If I have not yet swayed you, then consider this one final thought.

"Three hundred thousand of your bravest soldiers lie dead and rotting out in the sand. They sacrificed their bodies for your nation. Now their blood screams out for revenge. Even now, I hear their cries from the ground, voices calling like ghosts in the wind. And only you have the power to avenge them."

As Odai spoke, his face hardened and a fire burned in his eyes. He took another step toward his father. "You owe it to them," he continued. "You owe it to them. You owe it to me. Now you have an opportunity, a sacred honor, to avenge Satan's wrong. You have been weak. And now you must be strong."

Saddam glared at his son. "No, Odai. We will do it my way. Not yours. We will do it in my time, and when I am ready. So take your ideas and shove them back into your head. And don't ever speak to me of this again."

Odai stood and stared at his father.

"Do you understand me, Odai? Or do I need to be more clear than I have already been?"

Odai thought of the family graveyard that was hidden behind the palace yard and the family blood that had been spilt by his father, then decided that the president had been clear enough. He slowly nodded his head, though his mind was still racing.

It was a terrible chance, but it was one he would take. And it was time that he stood on his own.

ALONG THE TIGRIS RIVER
NORTHERN IRAQ
0345 LOCAL TIME

Three hours later, Odai walked into the bunker. A single shaft of artificial light shone from the top of the stairway to illuminate the underground bunker with a pale, white glow. Three huge ceiling fans rotated on worn-out bearings, turning the air with a quiet *swosh* and circulating it around the room to mix the odor of sweat, silk, cumin, and incense into one indistinguishable but overpowering smell.

Odai's three men stood at rigid attention, their backs straight as iron shafts, their faces taunt, their eyes forward but looking over his head to avoid direct contact with his eyes. The general strolled past his three closest advisors in a calculated and private display of his power. Surveying each one, he passed in review, noting the expression on their faces—the tightness of their lips and the flush of their cheeks. He summed up his men as he always did, judging the feel that emanated from their souls as he peered into their eyes while forcing them to stare at the wall.

Once the inspection was over, the general turned and cleared his throat, then motioned with an abrupt gesture of his hand. The three men moved forward as one and pulled back their chairs to sit around the table. They adjusted themselves in their seats, then turned to Odai Hussein with their arms on their laps, careful to not place their hands on the table. The general waited until they had settled, then pulled back his bare wooden chair and also sat down.

Odai leaned forward in his seat. "My brothers," he began. "The glory of God has brought me to you. And now it is time that we act.

"Today I will ride up to Ubaydah. By morning, we will have our man."

9

KHALID AMR UBAYDAH PRISON
NORTHERN IRAQ
0715 LOCAL TIME

No place on earth was closer to Hell than the Khalid Amr Ubaydah prison. Situated high in the cold, winter-kill hills of Northern Iraq, Khalid Amr Ubaydah was nearly eighty kilometers from the nearest town or village. The prison jutted from the sheer walls of Mount Halgurd, just below the tree line at nine thousand feet. Stone guard towers extended skyward among the granite cliffs while thick ramparts blended with the steep canyon walls, forming a nearly seamless wall of brick and natural stone. The mountain air was cold and dry and thin enough to leave a man gasping for breath. During the winter, bitter winds howled through the ridges with gale force, driving pellets of frozen rain and sheets of snow before it. The short summer months brought chiggers, biting fleas, and hordes of venomous snakes.

The prison, older than the nation of Iraq, was twelve and a half acres of dirt floors, crumbling stone walls, rotting oak doors, and rusted steel beds. The original footings were the handiwork of Turk slaves who were born in the previous millennium. The core of the prison, the small cells, kitchen, and bastille, had been built during the weakening reign of the caliph al-Mutasim, shortly after 1000 A.D.

Arabic soldiers had designed Khalid Amr Ubaydah as a mountain fortress to help guard their empire from the threatening Mongols who were moving down from the north. During the Crusades, the fortress had been converted to a military prison. For nearly eighty years, the

Christians had used Khalid Amr Ubaydah to house and torture the godless Muslim hordes. For the next eight centuries, through various masters and assorted regimes, the prison had changed very little. Some buildings were added while others collapsed and a few walls were repaired here and there, but that was about it. From the terrible reign of the Turks to the rise and fall of the Ottoman Empire, Khalid Amr Ubaydah remained largely unchanged, a seemingly permanent part of the mountain, occasionally noticed, then forgotten once again, and over the years mostly ignored.

Yet always the prison had been put to use. And Saddam Hussein was its most recent master.

Housed inside Khalid Amr Ubaydah were a curious mix of thugs, murderers, overly ambitious generals, Shiite Malus, and boisterous intellects from the ruling party. Nearly half of the four hundred prisoners were Kurd leaders and military officers who had had the misfortune of falling into Hussein's hands. Several prisoners were members of the presidential family—two son-in-laws and a distant cousin. They rotted away in their cells, waiting for their turn to die. Being members of the royal family brought no special favors in Khalid Amr Ubaydah, where the prisoners walked the halls in silence, bent over at the waist, forbidden to speak, forbidden to raise their heads, forbidden to even look upon the military guards who ruled over them.

Odai Hussein's four guards pushed the warden's door open, nearly tearing it from its hinges as they thrust themselves into the room. A look of surprise and anger filled Major Al-Sidiqi's face as he looked up from a pile of papers, an unspoken curse hanging in the air.

Then his heart nearly stopped. He immediately sprang to attention as Hussein strolled into the room and positioned himself in front of the desk.

General Odai Hussein cleared his throat and extended his hand. The major ran from behind his desk and dropped to his knees. He took Hussein's hand in his own and lightly brought down his forehead to touch the back of the general's fingers.

Hussein left his hand in the grasp of the soldier, then slowly pulled it away. The major stood up and squared his shoulders. Hussein looked him straight in the eye. The major averted his stare, dropping his eyes to the floor. Tradition forbade him to speak until the son of the *Sayid Rais* had spoken to him. Hussein glanced around the office again, then, flicking his fingers toward the major, bade him to sit himself down. Major Al-Sidiqi hesitated long enough for the general to take a seat at the long wicker sofa, then dropped quickly onto his chair.

Two of the guards positioned themselves at the door while four others posted themselves in the outer office. Out in the hallway, the major could hear a commotion as the general's entourage began to spread through the halls of the prison.

Inside the office, a deep silence fell. So far, not a word had been spoken. The major's initial wave of panic subsided for a moment, then suddenly washed over him again. Whatever the purpose of this visit, he knew that his entire career, indeed, maybe his very life, lay in the balance of what transpired over the next few moments.

The general sat up, pushing himself against the back of the sofa. The wicker softly creaked.

"So, you are the warden of Khalid Amr Ubaydah?" he said. It was a statement more than a question.

"Yes, *Sayid*. This is my post. It is my pleasure to serve."

Hussein slowly nodded as he looked around the room once again. The major sat ramrod straight in his chair, his heart nearly bursting through his chest.

What could he want? Why was he here?

And then it hit him. Like a snake's poisonous venom, the dread began to pump in his chest.

Hassan Rahamani Hussein. Omar Farouk Khitib. Husbands of the president's beloved daughters. They were here. The general had come for them. And if they were to be pardoned, then certainly his life was over, for the torment and pain they had suffered at his hands would be immediately repaid upon his head.

The major pulled himself to his feet, extended his hands and then offered, "General, if you will come this way, I will lead you to them."

Hussein's dark eyes tightened for just a moment. "Take me to whom?"

"Hassan Rahamani Hussein, sir. And Omar Farouk Khitib. They are here. Are they not why you have come?"

The general grunted. "No major. They are not my concern. I care not about those who are already dead. There is another man I have come here to see." The general leaned forward and whispered his name. Major Al-Sidiqi stepped back, a look of relief spreading over his face. The crack of a smile crept across his thin lips. He turned and led the way to the door.

* * *

The prisoner sat huddled in the far corner of the cell. Shrunken from dehydration, his skin darkened with filth, he gently rocked from side-to-side in a barely perceptible motion. Strands of black hair lay matted about his head, a thin burlap cloth covered his scrawny body from his chest to down below his knees. Around his neck was a thick block of wood. It was black and round and at least two feet wide and six inches thick. The wood had been sawed in half, whittled out to make room for his neck, then placed over his shoulders and nailed back together again, leaving his head protruding through the block like a guillotine rack.

The prisoner's name was Rahsid Abdul-Mohammad. He was thirty-two years old. As owner of a small export firm on the outskirts of Amman, he had often traveled between that city and Baghdad. He was Jordanian by birth, but had been a frequent visitor to Iraq and had married an Iraqi woman from Kirkuk. They had four beautiful children, and only recently had moved to Iraq. He had been in Khalid Amr Ubaydah for two weeks, having been convicted of conspiracy against the holy leader Saddam Hussein by consorting with known foreign spies. His family still did not know what had happened to him.

And today he was scheduled to die.

And though he hadn't been to the United States for at least eleven months, he possessed a current Jordanian passport and a visa to enter the states.

The prisoner Rahsid Abdul-Mohammad didn't hear the men coming. With a sudden clang, his cell door opened, rolling back on its hinges. A dim shaft of light entered the room and cast shadows across the brick walls. Struggling from the weight of the block of wood, he pushed himself to his feet before either of the guards could enter the room, knowing they would beat him at the slightest provocation. The guards pushed forward, grabbed him by the arms and twisted him around to face the back of the cell. Holding his arms, they wrapped a thin wire around his wrist, cinching it tight until it cut into the skin.

"Come, criminal. The sun is rising. The spirits are waiting to take you away."

Rahsid Abdul-Mohammad lowered his head and began to cry. With a grunt of disgust, the guards turned him around and pushed him through the open door and into the hall.

It was then the guards saw the approaching general, along with their commander, Major Al-Sidiqi. They immediately sprang to attention along the prison wall, leaving the prisoner to stumble to the floor. General Hussein strode up to the guards, who remained rammed against the stone wall. Looking down, he studied the prisoner who lay on his side, too weak any more to stand on his own.

"Abdul-Mohammad." The prisoner looked up, twisting his neck in the block of wood.

"Abdul-Mohammad," Hussein said once again. "How would you like to live?"

FORT DETRICK, VIRGINIA
2137 LOCAL TIME

The CIA director's limousine was waved through the front gate of the Army post. His driver pulled along the main boulevard until he read the sign that directed him left. The car approached a massive and windowless building, the United States Army Medical Research Institute of Infectious Diseases, or USAMRIID. Exterior lamps, hidden in the shrubs and recessed into the grass, illuminated the building with a flood of yellow light. Hordes of insects swarmed round the bulbs in a frenzy of self-induced confusion. The heavy smell of lilac drifted across the thick grass, sweet and musky in the warm spring air. A light breeze rustled the oaks and tall pines. To the west, a band of storm clouds was beginning to rise, bringing the promise of imminent rain.

The limo pulled up to the front of the building. Michael Crosby stepped from his car where General Davis Beck was waiting to receive him.

"Sorry I had to wake you," the general apologized as Crosby climbed out of his car. "But this is something you need to see for yourself."

The director nodded, but didn't respond. The two men walked into the building without talking. Inside, the air was cool and dry. Bright lights hummed overhead, reflecting their light on the army-shined floor. Two security guards stood watch, peering from behind a booth of bulletproof glass.

Beck and Crosby were met by a three-star general and two colonels, all of them dressed in their laboratory attire—white smocks, disposable pants, and blue throw-away shoes. Only the army rank on their name tags identified who they were. After a set of curt introductions, the army three-star lifted his arm to direct the visitors. The men walked down a wide hallway, through two sets of double doors, then descended a steep flight of stairs.

It took the men almost forty minutes to go through the security and decontamination procedures. At the end of the process, General Beck and Michael Crosby found themselves alone in a room crowded with chrome utensils, oxygen bottles attached to expandable hoses, plastic-covered computers, and white, tile walls. A soft hiss sounded in the background from the over-pressurized air. Beck walked to the far end of room, where he stared through a huge Plexiglas window.

Michael Crosby followed him over. Beck turned and pointed to a lower part of the glass.

On the other side of the window sat an animal cage. It was made of thick Plexiglas and was perhaps six feet long and four feet wide. It was sealed off from the environment and self-contained, with hoses and filters providing clean air.

Inside the cage, a rat paced back and forth, running and scratching and spitting saliva. The animal moved recklessly about, pawing at its face and smashing its head into the glass. Its eyes were mucky with huge drops of drying blood, its ears were caked in red goo. Its mouth was open, its bare teeth shining in the light. Occasionally, a pink tongue would dart from the rat's open lips to lick the sides of his mouth.

Crosby took a quick step away from the glass. The general didn't move. Crosby glanced at the general, then turned back to the cage.

The rat suddenly stopped running. With a tight squeal, it rolled over again and again before coming to rest near the center of the cage. The rat whirled once, then held perfectly still. For a long moment it didn't move. Then, eyes wild and darting, it suddenly stood and turned to stare at the men. It lifted its right paw up to its mouth and bit clean through to the bone. Shaking its head violently from side to side, it tore the front paw from its arm. It chewed only once before swallowing it whole, then began to race around the cage, holding its bloody stump close to its chest.

Crosby closed his eyes in horror and quickly turned away. "Where did you get the culture?" he asked.

"From one of the pilots' blood. The virus was still active. Every piece of human remains was infected with the disease. They were time bombs of sickness, just ready to explode. We are very, very lucky that we cordoned off the crash site. It is hard for me to tell you how crucial that was."

"And you're certain it's the same virus as the sample taken from the Iraqi biological facility last summer?"

"Absolutely sir. Saddam is our man. Like the virus taken from the Iraqi lab, this agent is also a genetically engineered pathogen based on the enterovirus, a submicroscopic infective agent composed of DNA and RNA strands that replicate inside living cells. But while the nucleic acid sequence is nearly identical, clearly this variant is stronger and much more aggressive. Its incubation period is as short as three hours and the fatality rate appears close to ninety percent."

"And when was the rat infected?" Crosby asked.

General Beck glanced at his watch. "It was sometime late morning. Maybe twelve hours ago."

"And this isn't unusual? The fact that the rat contracted the disease. That is something you have already seen?"

"Michael, every rat, every dog, every chipmunk and squirrel, every warm-blooded mammal that has been exposed has come down with the disease."

The director cursed silently under his breath.

"Yes. It's that bad, Michael," the general went on. "I'm not exaggerating. So far, we are at 100 percent."

"And are all—are all the infections as aggressive as this?"

"No, not all. Most of the infected animals simply break out and die. A few live for several hours. Only about ten to fifteen percent exhibit the symptoms that you have just observed. But those who do become extremely violent. Almost like in the advanced stage of rabies. They go wild. They lose all fear. They attack anything that stands in their way. I was in here earlier this evening. Saw a rat go after a forty-pound monkey. Literally tried to chew him to pieces. The monkey died within hours, though whether it was from loss of blood or the virus, we really don't know. But in the larger sense, what does it matter?"

The director passed a shaking hand over his eyes as he turned away from his friend. A horrible image emerged in his brain. He pictured a trail of rats, wet, and stinking with death, crawling up from the sewers and squealing their way down New York City streets, crawling into . downtown apartments and occupied beds.

And it was real. It was here. It was knocking at their door.

Turning to the general, Crosby announced in a desperate tone, "Okay, you've showed me. I want to go." He turned and began to walk to the door.

The general didn't move. "Wait, Michael. You also need to know how the rat was infected." The general glanced into the cage where the rat was now hunched, sitting in a pool of blood, its chewed-off arm hanging limply at its side. Its tongue rolled slowly across its wet lips as it stared dismally at the men.

The director turned to face the general, who wet his lips and explained. "Mosquitoes," he said as he stared at the cage.

"Mosquitoes?" Crosby gasped.

The general nodded his head. "Mosquitoes and flies can spread the disease."

THE WHITE HOUSE, WASHINGTON, D.C.
2350 LOCAL TIME

Michael Crosby was standing near the corner of the president's desk, a red binder rolled up in his right hand. His black skin glistened with a dew of light sweat. His jaw was set, his jowls tense. "Mr. President," he began in a desperate voice, "it would be impossible for me to over-state the threat. It is simply our worst nightmare come true. Hussein doesn't know . . . he must not know how dangerous the virus might be. They don't have the labs, or equipment, or computer models to predict how far this could go. He and his scientists-thugs have thrown some-thing together, played a gruesome game with nature, without consid-ering the ultimate end. They think that they have a weapon they can control. But they are wrong, sir. They are wrong, and they don't even know."

"If he is successful, if he releases the virus in any major city, it will make a nuclear attack look like a minor inconvenience. I'm not exag-gerating, sir. It could be that bad."

President Brooks leaned forward and folded his arms in an effort to hide his trembling hands. His lips were tight, his eyes burned with rage and frustration. A tiny reading light was on over his desk, casting long shadows across his white face. He forced himself to swallow, then took a deep breath, while listening to the director of the CIA.

Crosby went on, caught up in emotion he could not bottle inside. "Sir, to even estimate the casualties boggles the mind. In the event of an attack on U.S. soil, unless we were able to immediately—and I mean immediately—quarantine the area, the virus would spread. USAMRIID estimates that as many as ten million people could die."

"Let's say he contaminates the water here in the city. Before the end of the day, perhaps half a million people are dead. The city panics. Everyone runs. The airports and railways shut down. The roads and highways in every direction are jammed with contaminated beings. The virus begins to spread its wings. The sickness shows up in other cities by dawn. It spreads along the entire east coast before we could even take the first step. It would spread, it would grow, and we really don't know—we simply don't know what the outcome might be."

Lightning flashed outside the window. The thunder immediately cracked and rolled overhead. A bitter wind blew through the white columns that lined the veranda of the White House, blowing down with cold gusts from the low clouds that had rumbled in from the west. None of the men paid attention to the storm which was pounding the district with marble-size hail and biting rain.

"And you really believe he will use it?" the president asked. From his voice, it was obvious that he had his doubts.

"Sir," Crosby was emphatic, "he has spent the last decade trying to evade our inspectors. He has spent an unbelievable amount of energy, money, goodwill, and time, all in an effort to develop this weapon. He has sacrificed more than two hundred billion in oil revenues by refusing to comply with the UN resolutions. Why would he do that? What purpose would it serve, if he had no intention of developing a weapon and putting it to use?

"And we already have the attack on Air Force One. What more evidence could you possibly want?"

"And you don't think he realizes the danger?"

"No, sir. We do not. He just doesn't realize what he has stumbled upon."

The president slapped his hands on the top of his desk. "But he developed the thing, Michael! He did all the testing! How could he not know?"

"Sir, in most other agents that have ever been tested or developed, the virus has always been extremely short-lived. You infect the host. The host reacts. The host dies, and that's it. It wouldn't go any further than that. Only those who were directly exposed to the weapon were ever endangered.

"But not this one, sir. We are certain this virus can jump between species. It migrates through other carriers—birds, pets, rats, and mice. Even insects—mosquitos and flies. Like the plague that killed a third of all Europe, this virus lives on, taking on a life of its own. In addition, the pathogen is virile enough to spread through normal human contact. A sneeze, a touch, a kiss, or a handshake. Any contact at all, even being in the same room, is all that is required to spread the disease. A victim coughs on his hand and then opens a door. Every individual who touches the doorknob over the next hour is doomed. A little boy is bitten by a mosquito while walking to school. That afternoon, his entire kindergarten class is vomiting blood on the floor. An infected individual strolls into his office and sneezes over the donuts and coffee. By night, the entire office is dead.

"And while we are just beginning to understand this monster, there is this much that we know. We don't have a cure. We don't have a vaccine. We are naked. Totally exposed."

The president stood and walked to the window. "But what about a delivery system?" he asked. "How could we be in this position? For years now, you and everyone else have been telling me that he wasn't making progress on developing a delivery system for his weapons of mass destruction. From the day I took office, you have always assured me of that. How many times have you promised that we have bottlenecked the technological migration that would allow him to develop the rocket motors and targeting systems with sufficient accuracy and range."

"Sir," the CIA director explained, "it is extremely important that you separate a military from a civilian objective.

"If Saddam wants to destroy our army divisions that are dug in out there in the sand, then no, he doesn't have a weapon. With our detection devices, hardened bunkers, chemical-biological protective gear, and early warning systems, our troops could easily withstand a biological attack if initiated under battlefield conditions.

"But if his objective is to inflict civilian casualties, if his objective is political and not military, if his objective is to inflict psychological, emotional, and moral damage by killing a huge number of noncombatants, then the delivery system for such a weapon could be as simple as a bar of soap, a can of spray, a cup of contaminant in a water supply. No intercontinental missiles systems are needed. No aircraft with special bombs or missiles. Nothing. None of that. Just a man and a vial of liquid. Just a man and a simple can of spray. Easily concealed. Impossible to detect. Our models estimate—" the CIA director cut himself short.

"Well, sir, I've already told you. And there isn't a bloody thing we could do. Not a single bloody thing you can do. Not until we have located and destroyed the weapons facility. That is the single most important objective we now have. It's critical. It is the only way to remove the gun from our head. Unless we do that, unless we are capable of destroying the biological weapons facility, then we stand here as sheep lined up for slaughter. But to find the facility, we will need the girl."

The president suffered for a moment in silence, then slowly nodded his head. He turned and walked toward Crosby, a grim determination on his face. "Go get her," he commanded. "Use any available means. Hopefully she will help us. If so, that is great. But this is a time when we won't take no for an answer. Don't back down until she has agreed."

WILLIAM AND MARY SCHOOL OF LAW, WILLIAMSBURG, VIRGINIA
DAY FOUR (FRIDAY)
1153 LOCAL TIME

The man was tall, with brown hair and piercing blue eyes. He sat alone, watching the crowd while pretending to concentrate on his book. Every so often he would glance at his watch. At eleven-fifty, he put his book away and trained his eyes on the building. Three minutes later, she stepped through the wide double door, her class on tort reform having come to an end.

He studied the girl from the safety of the crowded student terrace, some thirty feet off to her right. As he watched her move through the crowd, he sucked in his breath. Though he had seen several photos of her, he still wasn't quite prepared. She was beautiful. Exquisitely beautiful. Perhaps the most beautiful girl he had ever seen and for a moment he almost forgot why he was there.

She walked with her head upright and looking straight ahead as she made her way through the crowd. She was dressed in a white blouse and a perfectly tailored blue skirt. White sandals covered her feet. Her hair, cut to just above her shoulders, was black and shiny as glass. Her skin was dark and smooth, her face accented by high cheekbones and huge, sparkling dark eyes. Her neck was thin and extraordinarily long. She was tall, perhaps just under six feet, with graceful fingers and long, slender legs.

But her smile was the thing that was making him stare. It wasn't the artificial smile of a beauty contestant, all glossy and tight and cracking at the lips. This smile was delicate and round with soft lips and white teeth.

He tried to picture her as a child, starving in the mountains of northern Iraq. Even now, he could see an ache in her eyes—as if she had seen things, she had heard things, she had felt things before. Looking at her face made him wish he could just walk away and leave her alone.

As Aria McKenzie Cutter walked by the terrace, the man grabbed his backpack and fell in beside her, just another student walking in the crowd. She pretended not to notice him as he matched her stride. He cleared his throat. She kept her eyes facing forward and quickened her step, which forced him to pick up his pace. The crowd of students began to thin as they made their way toward a parking lot on the west side of the campus.

Finally, the man turned to Aria and said, "Excuse me, Miss Cutter, but may I have a word with you?" His voice was proper and soft, his accent obviously British.

Aria slowed. "How do you know my name?" she questioned cautiously.

The stranger smiled knowingly. The truth was, he knew almost everything about her. Her phone number. Her birthday. Her address and car. He knew that her last name had once been El-Kutrte. He knew she had been in the U.S. only since she was seventeen and that she had almost nine million dollars stashed in various banks, money that had been hidden away by her father. He knew she spoke Arabic and lived by herself. He knew more about her than she ever would have guessed.

Turning on his best smile, the man answered her question. "Oh, you know, it's a small campus," he said simply. "Small law school. Lots of people know you. It wasn't hard to find out your name."

Aria didn't stop to talk. This guy was nothing new. She had been hit on by many guys before.

"And your name is—"

"Johnathan," the man said. "Johnathan Blair." He turned to Aria and smiled. "Actually, my full name is Johnathan Churchill Blair. It's a rather long name I know, but then I didn't choose it."

Aria stopped in her tracks. Slowly, she turned to the stranger. "Johnathan Blair. Funny, I once had a friend, or I should say my father had a friend, a very dear man, who had the same name."

The man looked in her eyes as he smiled again. "Yes, I know," he said. "Your friend was my father."

They walked into the tiny coffee shop and sat down. Johnathan ordered black coffee. She asked for peppermint tea. Half a dozen students milled around them, exchanging notes and complaints about professors while griping about the misery of a summer semester. Overhead, a hidden speaker blared out the Moody Blues' "Tuesday Afternoon," the sympathy sounding tinny through the cheap, sunken speakers. Aria dipped the bag in her tea, her eyes sullen and somehow unexpressive. Inside, her stomach churned and rolled. A sense of depression and anger seemed to completely enfold her.

After all this time, she still reacted the same way.

Johnathan studied her for a moment as he sipped at his coffee. "How well did you know my father?" he asked.

Aria lifted her eyes and stared at the wall, a look of sadness falling over her face. "Not well," she responded softly. "I can barely recollect him from our days in London. There is a scene in my mind, hardly more than an impression, of he and your mother coming over for dinner. It seems you were there too, but I really can't be sure. We both would have been what—less than five years old.

"Mostly I recall him once we were back in Iraq. After the war, things were very hard for us. Living in the camps, I mean. It was winter, and the mountain was bitter cold. Your father brought us blankets. Once he snuck a doctor past the guards to look after my mom. He would come fairly often to consort with my father. They would talk until all hours of the night, whispering near the flaps of the tent. But by that time he had little energy to pay me any attention beyond an occasional pat on the head. I guess he had more on his mind. But I knew, even then, even as a very young girl, I knew that he was a lifeline for my father. For more than a year, he was my family's only hope."

Johnathan rolled the coffee around in his cup, swirling it up to the edge. Aria studied his face for a moment. "I owe my life to your father," she added slowly. "You know that, don't you? He did everything he could for us. I will always be grateful."

"Yes," Johnathan replied. It was all he would say.

Aria avoided his eyes as she studied the crowd. Shifting in her seat, she focused on him again. "Johnathan," she said. "I want to know why you are here. There is something you want. I can see it in your eyes."

Johnathan studied his coffee as he nodded his head. "I'm sorry, Aria," he said, his voice soft and yet firm. "But yes, you are right, there's a reason I'm here. You see, like my father, I too work for MI-5. I'm currently on assignment up at Langley. They are the ones who asked me to come down here. They thought that I should be the one to approach you. They felt it best if what I have to say came from a friend. Someone who is familiar with what you've been through."

Aria's face flushed with anger and her eyes narrowed just a bit. Johnathan watched her intently, waiting for her to speak. Aria slowly leaned over and lowered her voice.

"Let me get something straight." She pointed a finger at his face. "I want you to know right here and right now. If this has anything to do with Iraq, anything at all, then I want you to leave me alone. I won't even talk of that place. No. Not ever again."

Blair's chest muscles tightened as he stared at the table. Reaching into his shirt pocket, he pulled out a small photo and passed it to the girl. Aria glanced at the photo but didn't pick it up. A tiny shudder ran down her spine.

It was a picture of her family, taken back in Iraq, so many years and lifetimes ago. Her parents smiled brightly behind the two little girls with black hair and identical smiles. The oldest girl was about ten, the other maybe four. The little girl was sitting on the lap of her sister as her mother and father posed behind a white wicker chair.

Aria studied the picture as it lay on the table, still refusing to pick it up. Neither of them spoke. Then, with a gentle touch, Blair reached over and touched Aria's hands. Turning the right hand over, he studied the palm. It was still there. Several tiny, white lines, no wider than a thread, ran through the center of her palm. It was a scar, almost healed, but still easy to read and probably would be for the rest of her life.

He studied the three letters for just a moment. SKE—Shannon Kelsy El-Kutrte. The initials of Aria's little sister, the girl in the photo who was bouncing on her lap.

"We need you, Aria." Blair was honestly pleading. "It is so important. Please. We need your help."

WILLIAMSBURG, VIRGINIA
0337 LOCAL TIME

Aria McKenzie Cutter lay on the top of her bed, the sheets kicked in every direction. A gentle breeze blew through the open window, cooling her body despite the humid and sultry air that rolled in from off the ocean and up the Chesapeake Bay. She could smell the musky waters of the Rappahannock River, a salty and brine-laden smell that made the air thick and heavy to breath. It was very quiet and very dark, the only light in her room being the bluish digital alarmclock that sat on top of the wooden bedside table.

For the thousandth time, she turned her head and checked the time. She closed her eyes and pushed her head against her pillow, frustrated and angry, wishing only for sleep. She was tired of waiting. She was tired of the dark. She only wished daylight would come.

She lay in the darkness thinking, reminiscing, suffering again in the past. The memories washed over her, forcing sleep from her eyes and drawing out the long night. The feelings were as painful as any time in her life. As she stared up at the darkness, the vision ran through her mind, hurtful as on the night it was real.

The mountains of northern Iraq are some of the most barren and inhospitable in the world. The wind seems to blow at a near constant gale, howling down from the high peaks that define the border between Iran and Iraq. There is very little vegetation, for the mountains are dry, the only moisture coming as snow during the bleak winter months. The foothills sit like huge mounds of rock, rolling and jagged hunks of granite leading out to the desert. Above the foothills, stretching north and east, the mountains rise up to above twelve thousand feet, barren chasms of rock, dry cedar and scruff.

It was 1992 and the Gulf War had been over for just under six months. Just long enough for Saddam to turn his anger on his Kurds.

Huddled along the mountains' crevices, crouched in the narrow valleys at the base of the peaks, were thousand upon thousands of Kurdish refugees. Most of them were camped in the open, bracing themselves against the wind, fighting desperately just to survive. A few of the lucky ones huddled inside makeshift tents, uneven fragments of burlap and canvas sewn together with fishing line or thin steel wire. It was winter and the snow seemed to come every night, frozen crystals descending from the clouds that towered overhead. The refugees' days were spent scouring the hills for something to eat besides the bark of scrub oak and the bitter thistle grass. Almost as great as the need for food was the need for some means to stay warm. But there was no food. Not on this side of the mountain. And the wood had long before been collected and burned. Even water was scarce and oftentimes killed for, the only source being the meager streams that dribbled along the craggy ground.

To the south of the refuges were the brutal Iraqi soldiers. They lay at the base of the foothills, waiting, their guns trained on the camps, held back only by the threats of the coalition forces that patrolled the skies overhead. To the north of the camps, on the other side of the high mountain passes, lay Iran, an enemy for the past thousand years. Turkey lay to the west, another bitter opponent of the Kurds, and they were already busy moving their small army toward the border, hoping to keep the exploding refugee population at bay.

It was a desperate and miserable situation. Thousands had already died. Many more thousands would. And the only hope for those who remained on the mountain rested in the flights from the American transports. Dozens of C-130 cargo planes flew over the camps every day, dropping food and supplies in huge wooden crates suspended under black and orange parachutes. And while the supplies kept the people from starving, that was all that they did. They didn't provide shelter, heat, medicine, or peace.

Huddled among the mass of starving Kurds was an Iraqi named Abshel Omar El-Kutrte. He was there with his wife and two young daughters, ages thirteen and seven. At one time, Abshel Omar El-

Kutrte had been one of Saddam Hussein's most trusted advisors. The son of an early sultan, educated in the finest schools of Great Britain, married to an English woman, El-Kutrte had been recalled from England soon after Saddam's rise to power and anointed to the position of finance minister. Over time, El-Kutrte had proven to be an invaluable asset to the isolationist cabinet that surrounded Hussein. For more than ten years, he had been one of the Iraqi leader's vital links to the West.

But as Hussein had taken on a more and more militaristic and authoritarian posture, El-Kutrte had fallen from grace. To begin with, he was in the awkward position of being a Christian in a society of Islam, and married to an infidel at that. These two facts, coupled with his constant pleadings for a more democratic process, his stance against the senseless war with Iran, and finally, his adamant opposition to invasion of Kuwait, had finally proven more than Hussein had been willing to bear. The final straw came when El-Kutrte had been accused of sympathizing with the Kurds. Then, like so many others before him, his fall from grace had been brutal and absolute. Once welcome to walk the halls of the presidential palace, once a member of the highest positions of power, within hours of the whispered allegation, he was exiled to the mountains of northern Iraq. "Let the man be with his loved ones," Hussein had proclaimed in disdain. "Send him away to live with the Kurds!"

Within hours the family was gone, forced to leave behind every possession.

That night, they found themselves as beggars among the Kurds, already hungry, frightened, and cold. But because they weren't Kurdish, they were outcast from the group—pariahs even among one of the most desperate groups of people in the world.

It was the greatest irony of El-Kutrte's life that he would die among those he had only sought to help. In Hussein's mind, it was a sentence even better than execution, for it was just as deadly, but the suffering would be more bitter and prolonged.

At the time, El-Kutrte's oldest daughter, Aria, was little more than a child. Yet she spent nearly eight months of her life watching her family wither away as they starved on the side of the hill.

On the day that it happened, half a dozen U.S. transports had made their daily drop, cruising slowly through the sky as they passed over the Kurds. As the Iraqi army troops watched the American aircraft on their radar, a rumor made its way through the ranks. The U.S. was dropping military supplies to the Kurdish rebels. Guns, ammo, and even small tanks were falling in crates from the skies. And though the Iraqi generals knew the rumors were not true, they didn't really care. They had been itching for a reason to enter the camps, and finally the reason had come.

That night, just after sundown, just as the temperature was dropping to zero, the Iraqis entered the camps amid a barrage of gunfire and rocket-propelled grenades. Shooting at anything that moved, they went after the refugees. Amid shouts of laughter, they destroyed the entire camp. To the soldiers it was only a game. They weren't killing people, they were just killing Kurds.

At the first sound of gunfire, Aria's father had pushed her and her little sister through the flapping door of their tent. "Run!" he had screamed to them. "Run!"

Aria and her little sister scrambled up the side of the hill, followed by their struggling mother and father. Aria turned to wait for her parents. Shannon ran on and was soon lost in the darkness as confusion and chaos swarmed all around.

Aria and her parents found refuge under a small outcropping of rocks that formed a shallow cave. There they stayed, huddled together, while the Iraqi troops stormed around them, terrified not so much of the men as they were for the missing little girl. Finally, the soldiers climbed into their trucks and made their way back down the winding roads that led off the side of the mountain.

Aria's father immediately began searching for his missing daughter. Her mother was more panicked than she had ever been. "Find her," she pleaded to her husband. "You *must* find her, Abshel."

The man scrambled back to their tent and grabbed the only warm blanket the family owned. When he found his daughter, she would be freezing from the cold and he needed to have something he could use to get her warm. He wrapped the blanket around his shoulders, then scrambled off into the night, desperately calling her name while feeling his way among the rocky trails and begging God to help him find his little girl.

Aria helped her mother back to the camp, where she repitched the fallen tent and wrapped her ailing parent once again in the thick canvas bag to help keep her warm.

Finally, just as the sun pinkened the eastern horizon, after what seemed like an eternity of darkness, Aria's mother fell asleep. As the sun broke over the mountains, the camp slowly came to life. Aria listened to the commotion around her as the refugees started the ugly task of cleaning the mess and burying their dead.

And then she heard it. Off in the distance, the sound rolled toward her, making its way through the thin mountain air. She immediately recognized the sound of his sobs. She looked out of the tent to see her father stumbling toward her, his face caked in mud, the empty blanket hanging from his arms.

For six days, Aria and her father searched. They scavenged every inch of the camp. But Shannon was never seen nor heard from again. Three days after they quit looking, Aria's mother passed away in a heap of starving and delirious, burning flesh. Thereafter, Aria's father began to wither as he slowly lost his will to survive. Months went by in a blur of exhaustion and hunger.

Then Aria's father heard from Johnathan Blair. There was a chance he could get Aria over the border. Aria's father didn't hesitate even a second. Though the journey would be difficult and incredibly dangerous, he knew it was the only chance she had to survive.

But Abshel refused to even consider leaving the camps. "I need to be here," he told his oldest daughter. "I need to be here in case your little sister returns." And though it was a lie, it was a lie he could live with. Somehow it brought him a sliver of peace.

The bandits were standing at the tent, impatiently waiting, when Aria told her father goodbye. She put her arms around his drooping shoulders and listened to him cry, then touched him on the side of the cheek. Turning, she began to make her way up the side of the hill, knowing she would never see her father again.

The swallows that had nested outside her window began to stir. Aria rubbed at her eyes and glanced at the clock. Not quite 5 A.M. Swinging her feet to the floor, she sat up on the side of her bed, her bare legs cool against the soft cotton sheets. She sat for a long while without moving. And as she watched the sun rising, she made up her mind.

As she lifted the phone and dialed the number, an ancient thought kept rolling around in her head.

An eye for an eye, and a tooth for a tooth.

Or in this case, a son for a daughter.

CENTRAL NEVADA DESERT
DAY FIVE (SATURDAY)
1300 LOCAL TIME

Charlie McKay stared through the dusty window and across the barren desert to the unnamed mountains in the distance. Rising above the sagebrush and sand, the set of nearly barren peaks jutted upward at a vertical angle. Outcroppings of granite and sandstone mixed with the thin forest of knotted cedar to give the range a rutted and broken texture. Charlie scanned his eyes across the tops of the peaks, then down to the white desert floor. Reaching out, he wiped a thick film of oily dust off of the window and glanced upward, looking for the sun, hoping to get some assistance on gaining his bearings. Judging from the shadows, and knowing that most of the Rockies ran north and south, he guessed he was facing northeast, but it being midday, it was hard to tell.

Charlie was standing in an ancient aircraft hangar, a holdover from the last world war. The cracked cement floor was covered with oil stains and grease, and a pile of old aircraft tires filled the far wall. The hangar doors were closed and locked, as they had been for the last twenty years. The hangar was huge, at least eighty feet high and two hundred feet deep. Inside the hangar, it was dim and gloomy, the only light being a single square of sun that filtered through Charlie's window, and a series of bare lightbulbs that hung overhead.

Charlie peered to his right, out to where the sand gave way to the ancient lake bed, its sun-baked surface packed and smooth as cement, an effective, if improvised, runway. Thirty yards across from his window was another old building, a squat wooden structure with evenly spaced windows and a small outer porch, typical construction of the old Army Air Corps. A narrow path, well-worn and hard-packed though long-ago used, ran between the old barracks and the hangar.

Craning his neck, Charlie peered across the desert, searching for any indication of the underground compound that he knew was there. But all he saw were the mountains and sagebrush. No fences. No roads. No guard towers. No modern-day buildings. Nothing. It was an absolutely perfect disguise.

The guard beside him cleared his throat. "Sir, have you seen enough?" he asked. Charlie turned to face the guard, a young sergeant with hulking shoulders and short-cropped hair. The sergeant blinked as tiny beads of sweat dripped into his eyes. The temperature inside the old hangar had to be well over one hundred degrees and he was anxious to get back down underneath. Charlie turned to the sergeant and nodded his head.

"Yeah, guess I've seen about all there is."

The sergeant wiped his arm across his eyes. "Not much to see, is there captain?" he offered. "Kind of neat, ain't it?"

Charlie nodded his head once again. It really was. Like something out of a science fiction novel.

Originally designed in the early eighties, the underground facility known as the Bat Cave, was primarily used during the design and final testing of new weapons programs and top secret projects that had to stay out of the public eye. The Aurora supersonic, super-secret spy aircraft was housed somewhere in the Bat Cave, or at least that was what Charlie had heard. In addition, he knew that there was some kind of stealth aircraft in test. He had seen it roll out of the underground bunker on the night they had first arrived at Groom Lake. It must have been some kind of unmanned fighter, for it was tiny and unbelievably fast. It took off almost like a rocket and disappeared quickly into the thin mountain air. In addition, there where many parts of the facility in which he was forbidden to go. And the number of people in the compound—men, women, military, civilian contractors, and DOD personnel—was far more than he would have ever guessed. Though they passed in the halls and ate the same meals, rarely did they speak to each other. It was just easier that way. To keep to the personnel in your project. To mind your business and not ask too many questions.

Turning from the window, Charlie walked toward an old tool bin that was positioned along the far wall, a huge and creaky boxlike structure with the words NO FLAMMABLE MATERIALS painted in red across the front. Pulling back one of the narrow doors, he stepped inside. The guard quickly followed and pulled the door shut behind them.

As the door clicked and locked, a dim light automatically turned on and the back wall lifted away to expose a narrow, winding staircase. Charlie let himself through the small doorway and, grabbing a hold of the side rails, descended the stairs two at a time. The guard stopped to pull the wall down behind him before following McKay down to the coolness of the subterranean compound.

Up in the hangar, the hidden security cameras continued to pan across the inside of the building. Four miles off in the distance, and completely hidden under an outcropping of rock, two guards scanned their binoculars across the horizon, watching the desert that spread to the west.

Later that night, Charlie and Killer flew. It was a simple sortie, not much more than a quick hop through the bombing range. They took off shortly after three in the morning and landed just before sunrise, the jet touching down lightly on the surface of the ancient lake bed.

After debriefing the mission, Charlie went as quickly as he could to the life support room to shower and get out of his clothes. He hung up his helmet and G suit and placed his survival vest on the hook inside an oak locker. Like usual, he was drenched in sweat and his flight suit hung like a wet towel around his waist. Stripping to his underwear, he grabbed a huge, white cotton towel and turned to the shower, just as Killer walked into the room.

"We better pick it up there, Prince Charles. It's getting late," Killer said as he walked to his locker. Charlie nodded but didn't reply. He knew that by now the sun would be rising over the mountains and the desert would soon be searing with heat. But of course, he would see nothing of the day. Only the white cement walls of the underground compound.

"Have they let you talk to Linda?" Charlie asked as he stepped into the cool shower, lifting his voice to be heard above the flowing water.

"Nope. Not a word. Not a single word. Pisses me off. Locking us up, cutting us off from the rest of the world. All I want to do is hear her voice. Maybe thirty seconds talking to the kids. Just want to let them know I'm okay. It's a stupid rule to quarantine us like this. They should cut us a little bit of slack."

Charlie pushed his head under the water and let it roll down his face and over his body. It was alkali and sweet with iron, but he didn't care. It was cold and wet and it felt very good. Grabbing a bar of soap, he called out to Killer.

"So what do you think? Why are we here?"

"Don't know," Killer called back. "Colonel Wisner was saying some things about the CIA and Southwest Asia. But it's only rumors so far. I wouldn't be surprised if they held us here until Christmas, then suddenly changed their minds and let us go home. You know. The ol' '*Fire! Fire!*—oh wait, sorry—it was just a cigarette. Everyone, back in your seats' kind of thing. So I guess we'll see. But I don't think we're going anywhere anytime soon."

Charlie listened, then passed his head again under the water. There wasn't much to say. Killer was probably right.

KIMISK, EXTREME NORTHERN IRAQ
0755 LOCAL TIME

The herdsman had never seen anything like it before. The bridge had been completely destroyed. The old rotten timbers had been blown into pieces, shattered by the force of the explosion. The larger beams now lay in the bottom of the forty-foot gorge, the smaller pieces already having been washed away by the narrow river that ran down below.

For the past fifty years, the old timber-and-nail bridge had been the villagers' only connection to the world that lay on the down side of the mountain. Until they rebuilt the bridge, they were completely cut off, which the herdsman considered not to be such a bad thing. It wasn't like they had any good reason for contact with the rest of Iraq. But still, there were occasions when they needed to go into Amadiya, or even all the way down to Erbil. So the bridge would have to be rebuilt. And it was going to take some time.

The villager thought back on the Iraqi army troops he had seen sneaking through the forest and wondered again why they had blown up the bridge.

The Iraqi studied the river once again, then saw something he hadn't noticed before. There, near the water, it sat on its hind legs. It was fat and bloated with a slick skin and red eyes. Looking closer, he became more alarmed. The creature was staring and following him now, matching his movements with blood red eyes. In the afternoon sun, he could see the glint of its teeth. The bloated rat began to scratch its way up the side of the bank. It pawed at the wet earth, then let out a sick cry.

The villager was startled by the sound. After forty-three years in the mountains, he had never heard such a noise. And the rat was bigger than any he had ever seen before. He watched for a moment, then turned to walk back to the village, anxious to get away from the bridge.

The rat hesitated, then pulled itself over the top of the bank. After looking around, it began to follow the man, all the time hiding itself in the thick grass of the ditch that paralleled the road leading into the village.

KARACHI, PAKISTAN
0910 LOCAL TIME

Despite the black hair dye, four weeks' worth of beard, and his best efforts of maintaining a tan, he was awkwardly white and obviously an American huddling uncomfortably in a state of Islam. Everything about him—his clothes, his cologne, his money, and his manner—screamed of arrogance, pride, and conceit, all disgusting sins in the eyes of a Muslim. He sat at the cafe amid glares of contempt. But after four months of being in-country, he no longer noticed the stares.

He sat quietly at the sidewalk cafe watching hordes of three-wheeled taxies, British jeeps, decrepit trucks, wagons, and mules weave their way through the crowded streets. Occasionally a roaring motorcy-cle or small donkey-towed wagon would use the sidewalk as an addi-tional traffic lane, forcing the pedestrians to wind through the cafe tables as they pushed on down the road. The travelers would brush and jostle him as they passed by, but the American didn't seem to mind. Leaning back in his seat, he scanned the morning paper as he sipped at a warm cup of tea.

Across the street from the crowded cafe, an old Pakistani sat on a wooden crate next to a cage full of chickens. A rusted bicycle lay at his feet. A bright Pepsi sign was pasted to the wall over his head, right next to a washed-out movie poster of Sylvester Stallone. Occasionally the Pakistani would lift his arms and wave around a freshly plucked chicken to the pedestrians. A toothless woman, dressed in black, stopped and offered some money. The two haggled with adamant gestures. The woman frowned. The man shrugged his shoulders. A deal was made. The chicken was taken in exchange for the cash. Reaching into the cage, the man extracted another victim and, after a flurry of lice-infected feathers and blood, was soon waving another featherless bird in the air.

After ten minutes of scanning the paper, the American, a bio-chemist on contract to the Pakistani government's immunization lab, lifted himself from the table and moved across the street.

Walking toward the Pakistani, he could read the fear and tension in the man's face. The old man seemed to cower against the brick wall as the American approached, his black eyes constantly darting around. The American stopped and studied the chickens, then, selecting a young hen, waited as the Pakistani went to work. Glancing around, he searched the faces in the street, then lowered his face to the old man.

"What is it, Nadin?" he asked in a low voice, his Arabic awkward and broken.

"My son," the old man replied. "He sends me word. From the mountains along the Iranian border. It is very bad. It has happened again. And I am afraid."

The American looked the old man straight in the eyes. "What are you talking about?" he asked in a whisper.

"Another attack. Up along the border. Look north. You will see for yourself."

The American scanned the street. A Pakistani policeman, really a soldier, caught his eye from across the busy road. Slinging his Russian-made rifle over his shoulder, he began to make his way through the crowd, pushing to the American's side of the street. The American reached into his pocket and extracted some coin.

"Look north?" he pressed. "Where? What do you mean? Tell me! We haven't much time!"

"They talk of many deaths," the old man went on, ignoring his questions. "Rumors of something—something—I don't know. But I fear they have offended even our God."

"Listen to me, Nadin," the American hissed as he dropped the money into the wide-mouth jar on the crate. "You must find out! What are we looking for? What do you know? Please, it is very important."

The old man threw the plucked chicken onto a piece of yellow newspaper. "No," he muttered in anger. "I have done what I can. Now it will be up to you."

The American began to whisper again. The Pakistani moved away, pushing himself back from the small table, looking anxiously down the busy street as the policeman drew near. The American took his wrapped chicken and hurried into the crowd, never looking back.

Half an hour later, the CIA agent encoded his message and data-burst it up to the sky, where it was passed to a satellite hovering over Greenland, then on to another drifting over the eastern coast of the U.S. Within an hour, Langley had been informed of everything their agent had learned, which was just enough to scare them into action.

An urgently arranged meeting was held between CIA leadership and the director of the National Reconnaissance Organization. Despite his efforts to resist them, the director was finally convinced. Within minutes, a KH-9 photo reconnaissance satellite was moved slightly to the north of its original orbit. Forty minutes later, the CIA knew what the chicken man meant.

NATIONAL RECONNAISSANCE
CONTROL ROOM
WESTERN VIRGINIA
1900 LOCAL TIME

It was a face of death, stiff and pale, and even from the depths of space, crystal clear in its vulgar detail. The body lay in a heap, glazed-over eyes, thick with hazy scum, stared blankly from the sunken face. Tight lips spread across two rows of uneven teeth in a grimace of pain. A dark trickle of blood, dried black in the thin mountain air, oozed from each of the nostrils. The steady canyon wind had blown tiny drifts of sand up against the top of the head and through the thick black hair, evidence the body had been laying in the gutter for at least several hours. As the audience watched, a six-legged bug, black and shiny, crawled across the bridge of the dead man's nose and disappeared under his cheek.

The captain squirmed in his seat and coughed.

"Pull back," the colonel said, ignoring the emotion in the younger man's eyes. The captain didn't move, but stared at the screen as the bug appeared once again, making its way across the dead face to settle on a gaping eyeball. The captain blinked twice. The room was deadly silent, the cooling vents humming softly in the background. The black and white image filled the huge screen as thirty pairs of eyes stared at the display.

"I said pull back," the colonel repeated.

The captain shook his head in a barely perceptible motion, then reached forward to the keyboard that sat on the center of his console and typed in a series of commands. The image faded momentarily, then appeared once again, slightly more clear than before.

The screen shimmered with a thirty-by-thirty-meter cut at a barren street. Squat adobe buildings with pine roofs and tiny windows lined both sides of the road. Planted along the street were half a dozen posts, thick and round and about seven feet high. Several bodies hung suspended aside each log, ropes drawn tightly around the thin necks, bare feet suspended just inches above the ground. The colonel counted quickly. Eleven hangings in all. All of them young bearded men. The camera panned twenty meters to the right. An old pickup, rusty and weather-beaten, became the focus of the screen. The door was open, but no one was inside. A pair of crushed legs protruded out from under the truck, just aft of the left front tire. Behind the truck, half a dozen bodies sprawled across the unpaved street. A dead dog lay next to his master. A young women stared up into space with unseeing eyes, her brown hair blown back from her sun-worn face. Under her arm was a bundle of flesh that used to be her child.

Nothing appeared to be moving. Indeed, there appeared to be no life at all. No vegetation, no trees, no animals. Nothing. Even the wind appeared to have died, leaving scattered pieces of trash and an occasional dry leaf stranded in the middle of the street.

The captain glanced at his console controls to where a digital read-out counted down. "Fifty seconds, sir," he muttered, relieved to have something to look at, some kind of distraction to pull his attention away from the bodies on the screen.

"How long until the bird comes around again?" the colonel asked.

The captain reached up and lifted a red folder from the top of his console and quickly flipped through the pages. They were looking through the KH-9, a low-orbit bird. It was revolving around the globe, fifty-six miles above the surface of the earth. And although it circled the earth several times a day, it was not on a perfectly circular orbit and so wouldn't pass over this exact site for another nine hours.

The captain looked up from the binder. "Not until this evening, sir. Nineteen-fifteen local. But it will be dark in the target area by then. There'll be no moon tonight and, from the looks of it, we'll get little, if any, artificial lighting in the area. So our bird may be there, but we won't get a look. We'll have to wait until the next pass at"—the captain did some math on a piece of scratch paper—"tomorrow, oh-four-fifteen local."

The colonel turned to the young lieutenant two consoles over. She stared at the flickering screen with a blank look on her face. She was young and pretty and very near to being sick. She stared in a daze, focusing on a dead child. She had a little one at home, about the same age.

The colonel raised his voice to get her attention. "Lieutenant King." She quickly turned in his direction. "Are the tapes running? Are we getting this for later review?"

"Yes, sir."

"How much have you got so far?"

She quickly glanced at her console. "The last ninety-seven seconds, sir. From the point just after we switched over to the Micon lens."

The colonel pulled at his chin and turned to the captain.

"How much longer? When do we lose the image?"

"Twenty-four seconds, sir. The cameras are right at their limit now. As you can see, the slant-angle range is already beginning to distort the picture."

The captain nodded his head at the screen, then glanced up and asked, "What about it, colonel? Can I speed up the bird? We need to get her back to orbit velocity. We'll suck up twice as much fuel if she slows down any more. That won't make the guys out at Vandenburg happy."

The colonel hesitated as he glanced around the room. As he did, a stirring mental image emerged in his mind.

He pictured the satellite circling over the globe, serene and steady. He pictured it tracking along, flowing in orbit, passing through space without so much as a whisper. From the satellite's position, the earth was a most beautiful thing, its deep blue oceans, brown deserts, white clouds, and jungle greens sparkling brightly against the blackness of space.

For twenty-seven years, the colonel had peered at the earth through the eyes of his birds.

And never had he seen anything that hurt and scared him like this.

The seconds passed and the satellite moved out of visual range of the target. The image faded and suddenly disappeared. The occupants of the room seemed to breathe a collective sigh of relief.

"That's it, sir," the captain explained. "We lost it. The bird is too far to the east. We'll have to pick it up again in the morning."

The colonel didn't respond as he walked to the back of the control room. Every eye followed his movement. Eight technicians and six officers waited, thinking there had to be something to say. The colonel paused for a moment, then slowly turned around. The captain leaned forward in his chair. An overhead speaker softly hummed, crackled once, then fell silent again. Without a word, the colonel turned and walked from the room.

THE WHITE HOUSE
2015 LOCAL TIME

"So it's worse than we feared," Brent Hillard mumbled as he laid the stack of eight-by-ten black-and-white photographs on top of the desk.

Michael Crosby, Director, CIA, nodded his head as he looked at his friend.

"Tell me about the village."

Crosby began to explain. "The location is Kimisk, a small Kurdish village in the extreme northern mountains of Iraq, twenty-three miles directly south of the Turkish border. The town is so small, it's not even on our maps. Population of about two hundred people, more or less. Mostly herdsmen. Fairly neutral population, no known association with the PKK rebel forces, nor the Turkish invaders. The town has no tactical nor strategic value. It is too isolated and remote. And extremely high, above ten thousand feet. The photos were taken from one of our satellites early this morning. One of the KH-9s we have dedicated to Iraq since the end of the war."

Crosby stared at the photos for a moment, then picked up a red binder and lowered his voice. "He was testing the virus, Brent. You know that. He was testing it in real world conditions. Look at the photos. Read the report. It makes me sick. When I look at those bodies and think back on that rat, it nearly makes my skin crawl with fear."

For a moment the two men sat in silence, each of them deep in thought as a sense of foreboding seeped into the room. A grandfather clock ticked slowly away, marking the passing of time. Brent Hillard coughed and adjusted his huge frame against his chair, then pushed back a lock of gray-black hair to help cover the bald spot on the top of his head. Crosby picked at his teeth with the tip of a pencil. Hillard let out a huff, then glanced toward the only window in his office, a long rectangular piece of glass that faced out onto the gardens. It was late evening and the shadows outside were beginning to lengthen and spread eastward across the deep-green White House lawn. He noted that the traffic on Pennsylvania Avenue was beginning to thin, which, were he going home for the night, would have been welcome. But as it was, it really didn't matter. He would be at work until long after dark. And that was if he went home even at all.

Hillard rubbed his hands across his face and massaged the side of his head, then leaned forward to his desk once again. "Get you anything, Michael? Beer? Coffee? Perhaps a quaalude?"

Crosby smiled. "No thanks. I brought my own. But a glass of Coke would be nice. A real big glass. With lemon. And lots of ice."

Hillard leaned forward, pressed a button on the side of his phone and asked for a coke and a beer. Within a few minutes, a White House attendant entered the office from a side door, carrying a tray with the drinks and a plate of Buffalo wings, salsa, and chips. He set the tray down on a small coffee table and turned and walked from the room without so much as looking at the men.

Crosby pushed himself up and made his way to the sofa as the smell of spiced barbeque and jalapenos filled the room. He picked up the Coke and drank a long swallow, then grabbed up a couple of wings. As he stuffed one into his mouth, it occurred to him he hadn't eaten since breakfast. He knew the spicy food would bore another hole in his stomach, but he really didn't care. It seemed everything he ate now caused him indigestion.

Hillard watched his colleague tear into the food, then picked up the report and read through it once again, making tiny notes in the margin as he read.

DIRECTOR'S EYES ONLY
TOP SECRET (special background)
REPRODUCTION BY ANY MEANS IS UNAUTHORIZED
STORE AND DESTROY IN COMPLIANCE
WITH NSC REGULATIONS

SAMPLES OF THE SUSPECT AGENT TAKEN FROM KIMISK, HERE CATALOGED AS BILAB # 22, HAVE BEEN PROCESSED AND ANALYZED BY DOD FACILITY (U.S. ARMY CENTER FOR HAZARDOUS DISEASE CONTROL, LANDSTUHL, GERMANY) WITH AUGMENTED ASSISTANCE OF CENTERS FOR DISEASE CONTROL AND PREVENTION (CDC, ATLANTA, GA).

INITIAL ANALYSIS INDICATES AGENT IDENTICAL TO THAT FOUND IN REMAINS OF AIR FORCE ONE VICTIMS, I.E. A GENETICALLY ENGINEERED DERIVATIVE OF THE ENTEROVIRUS.

VIRUS APPEARS TO CIRCULATE THROUGH THE BLOODSTREAM TO RAPIDLY ATTACK TARGET ORGANS, ULTIMATELY CONCENTRATING AT THE BRAINSTEM RESULTING IN CENTRAL NERVOUS SYSTEM DYSFUNCTION, HALLUCINATIONS AND MENTAL INSTABILITY.

SYMPTOMS MAY VARY FROM INDIVIDUAL TO INDIVIDUAL BUT INCLUDE: RAPIDLY PROGRESSIVE VISUAL IMPAIRMENT RESULTING IN BLINDNESS, PROGRESSIVE SHORTNESS OF BREATH DUE TO ACUTE RESPIRATORY DISTRESS SYNDROME, BLEEDING FROM EYES AND NOSE, AND SEVERE NAUSEA. FINAL CAUSE OF DEATH IS THE RESULT OF EITHER CEREBRAL HEMORRHAGE OR CARDIOVASCULAR COLLAPSE. ANTICIPATE MOST VICTIMS WILL NOT SHOW SYMPTOMS FOR APPROXIMATELY 4–6 HOURS AFTER EXPOSURE, DURING WHICH TIME THEY WILL ACT AS INFECTIOUS CARRIERS OF THE DISEASE. ONCE SYMPTOMS BEGIN TO DEVELOP, DEATH WILL OCCUR APPROXIMATELY 20 MINUTES TO TWELVE HOURS LATER.

ALTHOUGH AGENT IS MOST EFFECTIVE WHEN INTRODUCED THROUGH RESPIRATORY SYSTEM VIA AIRBORNE DROPLETS, IT IS ALMOST AS DEADLY WHEN INTRODUCED ORALLY OR VIA ENVIRONMENTAL FOMITES, I.E. DOORKNOBS, EATING UTENSILS, HANDRAILS, ETC.

AGENT APPEARS TO REMAIN **VIABLE AND INFECTIOUS** IN BLOOD AND TISSUES OF DECEASED HOST FOR SEVERAL HOURS FOLLOWING DEATH.

AGENT IS **EXTREMELY** CONTAGIOUS. CARRIERS **WILL** INFECT OTHERS THROUGH NORMAL HUMAN CONTACT.

AGENT IS **EXTREMELY** TOXIC. DEATH FROM EXPOSURE IS ESTIMATED TO BE NEAR 90–93 PERCENT.

NO KNOWN VACCINE IS AVAILABLE.

NO KNOWN ANTIDOTE.

EPIZOOTIC EVENT (I.E. ANIMAL EPIDEMIC SPREADING THE VIRUS THROUGHOUT HUMAN POPULATION) CONSIDERED EXTREMELY LIKELY.

CURRENT U.S. CHEMICAL/BIOLOGICAL PROTECTIVE GEAR IS SUSPECTED TO BE **VULNERABLE**. VIRUS POTENTIALLY ABLE TO PENETRATE COMMONLY USED BIOLOGICAL PROTECTIVE MASKS.

URGENT—REPEAT—URGENT NEED OF FURTHER STUDY.

AWAITING YOUR INSTRUCTIONS.

LARSEN SENDS

END OF REPORT

Brent Hillard dropped the report in his lap, unable somehow to let it out of his grasp. His heart beat with the power of a drum, pushing the blood through the veins in his neck and thumping at the back of his head. He glanced once again over to Michael Crosby, who was dropping a glob of salsa onto a chip. Funny, he thought, how different men dealt with stress. The way he was feeling, the last thing he wanted was food.

Pushing up from his chair, he made his way over to the coffee table, picked up his beer, and wiped the beads of sweat off the rim before taking a sip. Swishing the brew around in the back of his throat, he plopped himself down in a chair opposite the CIA director.

"How many Israeli commandoes died after the mission?"

Crosby lifted his face and brushed a napkin across his mouth as he thought. "Seven, I believe. Could have been eight. I'd have to check. Either way, the Israelis are pissed."

"And none of them died fighting their way in or out?"

"No. Not a one. At least to hear the Mossad tell it. But once it filters through them, well, who really knows?"

Hillard nodded. He immediately understood what Crosby meant. Israel was a supportive and important ally, especially when it came to security concerns in the Middle East. But they were also extremely secretive. They liked to work on their own and they considered virtually everything a national secret. And the excursion to the village had been their idea. The U.S. didn't even know that they had gone in. At least, not until the mission was over and the Israelis had collected the air and soil samples. And analyzed them. And realized how incredibly dangerous they were. And that they had no clue what the deadly agent was.

Then, suddenly, the U.S. was again their best friend, for they realized that they needed its help. And the situation was, at least in their eyes, as dangerous and threatening as any of the past fifty years.

Crosby took a quick bite and then continued. "You know the village was attacked yesterday morning. The Mossad knew of the attack within hours. A couple of their Kurdish informers passed them word very quickly. They had identified it as a biological attack as long as ten hours before we got the satellite photos. But still, they didn't tell us. Really pisses me off."

Hillard nodded his head, but didn't respond. Crosby swallowed hard, and then went on. "Soon after learning of the attack, our friends over at Mossad decided to send in some men. Gather some information for themselves. The mission went like a piece of Swiss clockwork. The Israeli team helicoptered in from one of their Special Ops camps across the Turkish border. In and out in less than two hours. They encountered no one in the target area. The village was completely deserted. All of the soldiers were wearing protective clothing. They used our CBSs—" the NSA's face clouded over and Crosby stopped to explain. "That's 'CBSs,' as in 'chemical-biological suits.' Best protective clothing in the world. Designed to protect our soldiers from an enemy chemical or biological attack. Well, apparently the suits didn't do a very good job. After returning to their camp and beginning the decontamination process, a couple of the men fell suddenly sick. Within minutes, several were dead. Within an hour, a good part of the team was gone."

Crosby paused to chew, then belched and sat back in his seat. "Guess it scared the devil out of the Israelis," he concluded. "Within hours, they had transferred the samples to our army lab in Germany. The report pretty much fills in the rest."

Hillard sucked at his cheek and said, "Pretty gutsy, them going in like that. So much for the integrity of national borders."

"Yeah, they certainly took a risk," Crosby agreed. "Both from a strategic and tactical point of view. Had one of the choppers gone down, or worse, had they been forced to leave men behind, it would have been very ugly indeed. Israeli commandos on Iraqi soil. Islam would have been up in arms.

"But the critical nature of the matter speaks for itself. The Israelis are afraid. Maybe even more so than we."

"What about the hangings?" Hillard wondered aloud. "That's one thing I don't understand. Remember the pictures? There were multiple bodies hanging in the streets. That doesn't seem to make any sense. If it was a bio attack, why did the Iraqis hang some of the men?"

Crosby reached out and pulled the secret report from the NSA's hand. Flipping over the red, front cover, he pointed to the center paragraph on the page:

AGENT APPEARS TO CIRCULATE THROUGH THE BLOODSTREAM TO RAPIDLY ATTACK TARGET ORGANS, ULTIMATELY CONCENTRATING AT THE BRAINSTEM RESULTING IN CENTRAL NERVOUS SYSTEM DYSFUNCTION, HALLUCINATIONS AND MENTAL INSTABILITY.

"Looks like sometimes the victims go crazy," he explained. "So some guy, perhaps the commander of the local militia, gorked out and spent his dying moments meeting out justice to his paranoid fears. With the dead and dying all around him and his skull leaking puss and blood into his brain, who knows what the poor guy was thinking. But apparently, this thing—this BILAB # 22—has a way of making some of its victims go batty before it renders final death.

"At least that's what my analysts are telling me. And I would bet that their diagnosis turns out to be very close. But of course, only time and further testing will tell."

Brent Hillard turned to stare out the window, which had darkened to a mirror from the deepening shadows outside. He mused for a moment, then turned back to his friend.

"Tell me about the project," he asked. "Who's been heading it up? I mean other than Saddam. We know he's the ultimate power. But he must have assigned someone to direct the operation? Developing such an effective biological weapon is a huge undertaking. And yet they did it despite an international effort to see that exactly this didn't occur!

"Think about it, Michael! They've developed what is apparently one of the world's most potent bioviruses, even while the UN sanctions were still in effect. They did it despite daily inspectors. Despite international monitoring. And a worldwide embargo. And despite constant surveillance flights over their skies.

"Of course, we helped them by letting them screw around with our inspectors. But still, simply designing and implementing the deception and security concerns must have taken an incredible effort. So, yes, I would like to meet the man who directed the project. Meet him and shake his hand, then put a gun to his head."

"You know who the Israelis think it is, don't you?"

Hillard slowly nodded his head. "Odai. The Butcher's son."

"What do you think?"

"Odai? No. No way. At least not acting on his own. Saddam is the man calling the shots."

Crosby took a napkin and wiped at his nose. Reaching into his pocket, he took out a fresh pack of cigarettes and thumped the crisp cardboard on the end of the table. Lifting the package, he smelled the tobacco inside. Hillard raised an accusatory eyebrow. Crosby stuffed the Camels back into his shirt.

"And—have we heard anything from the girl?"

The CIA director paused. "Apparently she's doing okay. She's in the compound. They're trying to get her ready. But I don't know—"

As he focused his eyes on the far wall, a look of despair, almost bordering on sadness, softened the deep lines in his face. "It is a terrible thing we are asking," he muttered. "I mean, after all, she is a civilian. And a girl her age. There's no way to warn her of the danger she'll face. And she'll be on her own. I think it's crazy. And wrong. And maybe even illegal."

The room was very quiet. It was a long time before Hillard replied in his deep voice. "I understand how you feel. My daughter is about her same age. She was over last night. Spent some time hanging around with her mother. And as I watched them talking, as I thought about our plan, I found myself asking again and again if we are doing the right thing. And you know what? I went to bed without any answer. And woke up this morning wondering the same thing.

"And that's not all," he concluded. "There is something about this whole thing. It just doesn't feel right in my gut. There's something we're missing. An element we have not yet considered. What we are seeing doesn't fit what we've seen in the past, and it makes me uncomfortable that we're forging ahead. I'm telling you, Michael, there is something we're missing. And until we figure it out, we're just pissing in the wind."

The two men stared at each other. Crosby didn't know what to say. Truth was, he didn't agree with his friend. He considered the matter fairly simple and straightforward. He shifted in his seat while Hillard stared at the floor.

"There is something there." Hillard was now almost talking to himself. "I'm very sure. The pattern isn't logical. It doesn't make any sense."

Crosby waited for a moment. Hillard finally looked up. Another moment of silence passed between the two men. "So what do we do now?" Crosby finally asked.

"I don't know," Hillard answered. "I guess we better go talk to the boss."

THE WHITE HOUSE
WASHINGTON, D.C.

"Judas priest, this is sickening," the president muttered, more to himself than the men in the room. Reaching out, he picked up a picture, a close-up of a dead body in the early stages of decay, graying with rot and lying in a dust-covered street. There was a quiet knock at the door to his left, the door that connected the Oval Office to the office of his chief of staff. The president ignored the knock. It sounded once again, somewhat louder. The president didn't move. The knocking went away. The president dropped the photo on the table and looked at his advisors.

He directed his anger, his voice was sharp and clearly now in command.

"I want to ask you all something," he demanded. "Is there any man on this earth, anyone at all, who has demanded and received more of our attention over the past decade than Saddam Hussein? No. No one. Not Yeltsin. Not Kim Jong II. Not Deng. No one. We have half our air force flying over his country. A third of our navy has spent most of a decade sweltering in the heat of the Persian Gulf. And why? So we'll know what he's doing. So we know what he thinks. And in doing so, we have learned from this man. We know him now. We know how he works. And though he is a fox, this much I know to be true: There is always—absolutely always—a reason to the things he does. He is getting ready to act. Of that I am sure. He is a cat now, and he is hunting. And gentlemen, we are the mouse."

"Mr. President," Hillard began, "if we overreact, it will only make things worse.

"We have the attack on Air Force One, that is true, and that will have to be dealt with in time. But the attack on Kimisk is something very different, and I'm not certain we can tie the two together. It could be that his motives for the assault on the village were separate and completely unrelated to us. Perhaps the rebels *were* using the mountain settlement as a base camp. That would very well explain the attack. It is also possible, sir, that it was some type of accident. But to take this event and draw the conclusion that he is getting ready to instigate biological warfare—well, sir, frankly, that just might not be true.

"As you said, Mr. President, we *do* know this man, and if he has one priority—if he has one central tenet, it has always been the goal of self-preservation. And he knows we would destroy him. He knows we would bring him down.

"Remember, Mr. President, in many ways this BILAB is nothing new. We know he has possessed weapons of mass destruction since before the Gulf War, yet he never has chosen to use them except for a few isolated attacks on the Kurds.

"So, sir, I would ask you to be cautious. It will serve no purpose to stir up the pot. Let's let things settle down while we sort through the facts, then see what develops from there."

The president looked Hillard straight in the eye. "No, Mr. Hillard, I will not wait and see. The potential for disaster is simply too great.

"I want you to step up our security in the region. Draw me up a plan of military forces we can send and get the deployment orders in my hand. The *Kennedy* is scheduled for cycle out of the Gulf. Cancel that. Keep her on station. And I want more intelligence. More reconnaissance and satellite overflights. I want to know every time that hairy ape even goes to the bathroom. I don't want him to move without me knowing when and how.

"And I want the team ready. I want them ready to go. Do you understand? I don't like being the mouse!"

17

Odai Hussein drove to the meeting site with a small caravan of his most trusted personal guards. The procession of security forces wound its way slowly through the desert with their headlights off. The nearly full moon illuminated the fine sand like a moon over snow, and the drivers hardly needed their night-vision goggles to see as the two cars and single truck made their way along the sand-packed road.

The automobiles drove through an open gate and came to a stop under an huge wooden storage hangar where an unusual mix of military trucks and Mercedes were already parked. Odai Hussein studied the empty building for a moment. He rolled down the window, listening and smelling the air. He waited in silence for a full sixty seconds, then suddenly pushed himself out of the car, grunting an order for his guards to stay back, and walked toward the nearly hidden cement frame.

The Iraqi leader was walking through the remains of an old army storage facility, one of the many that had been destroyed during the war. Over the past few years Odai had frequently used the site to run his covert campaign against the northern Kurds and their PKK army— utilizing it as an interrogation site for captured soldiers, a planning site with his generals, or as a meeting place with Kurdish spies. It was not unusual for him to be here. But as he approached the underground bunker for the second time in three days, he knew he was pressing his luck. His father closely monitored his whereabouts, and though he had hand-selected the guards that came with him, still he could never be assured that one of them would not report his activities to the president of Iraq.

Still, the moment was pressing. He had to act. And the bunker offered privacy and discretion, things that were nearly impossible to find.

Odai bounded down the cement stairs and into the bunker, where his senior military leadership stood at rigid attention around the old wooden table. Odai dispensed with the formalities and ordered the men to sit down. The six men rustled stiffly into their seats.

"My brothers," he began, choosing the more intimate term than the traditional greeting of *rafeek* or "comrade." "The time has come. Tonight I will speak to you freely. Tonight, I will tell you what I intend to do."

Odai nodded his head toward a bearded general, who immediately stood and walked toward a small door in the far wall. The general unlocked the door and pushed it back, then barked out an order.

Rahsid Abdul-Mohammad uncertainly entered the room. He was clean shaven and dressed in a new suit and fine leather shoes. His hair had been cut in a neat and conservative style. His nails were manicured, his lips glistened with gloss, and he smelled of expensive cologne. The former prisoner turned to face Odai Hussein and bowed deeply at the waist, then lifted his eyes to stare at the wall, half a foot above the Iraqi leader's head.

"Convict Abdul-Mohammad," Odai asked, "to whom do you owe your life?"

The prisoner bowed his head. "To you, my *Sayid*."

"Who granted your pardon?"

"You did, *Sayid*."

"And you know your mission, do you not?"

The former prisoner nodded his head.

"And what will become of you if you fail?"

Rahsid lowered his eyes to the floor. "I will die, sir. As will my family."

"And where is your family now, convict Abdul-Mohammad."

The prisoner's shoulders heaved as he took a huge gulp of breath. "You have them, my *Rais*. You have my wife and four children."

"And should you fail in the simple task I have given you, what will I do with your children?"

The small man heaved once again. "You will burn them, my *Rais*. You will skin them alive, and burn them. Then feed what remains to your dogs."

Odai smiled and nodded his head. "I love my dogs, you know that don't you, convict Abdul-Mohammad?"

"Yes, my *Rais*. I know that you do."

"You will not fail me then. Can I be assured?"

The prisoner vigorously shook his head. "No, *Rais*. I will succeed. Never will I fail you or my family. It is a simple thing you have asked. So yes, sir, I will succeed."

"And, convict Abdul-Mohammad, should it ever appear that you are going to be detained or questioned by the U.S. police, or should it ever appear that you are in jeopardy of compromising the security of this mission, what are you then going to do?"

The prisoner lifted his eyes and stared at the wall. "You have fitted me with a cap on my lower tooth," he explained. "It is filled with a concentrate of cyanide liquid. Should it ever appear that I have failed in my mission, I will crush the cyanide cap and send my soul on to Allah. Dying a martyr guarantees a home in His paradise, along with the promise that my family will live."

"That is right," Odai smiled, then nodded his head toward the door. The convict bowed and retreated once again into the back room.

Odai turned to his generals. Pushing himself away from his chair, he began to explain.

"The convict Abdul-Mohammad is leaving for New York tonight. He has a visa. He speaks acceptable English. He has been to the U.S. several times before. Getting into the country will be easy for him.

"After arriving in New York, he will drive down to the American capital. When he checks into his motel, he will find a package waiting. It will take him no time to plant the devices. One simple chore, and he is gone. He will be out of the country before the canisters are even put to use."

Odai nodded to the bearded general, his chief of staff. The general stood up and went on to explain, picking up where his superior left off.

"Two days ago, the American press announced that the funeral for the former president and vice president will be held simultaneously at the National Cathedral in Washington, D.C. Because they want to allow time for the foreign presidents and dignitaries to attend, and because"—the Iraqi hesitated for half a second, his face lighting up with a smile—"because the autopsy and accident investigation have taken several days, the service will not take place until Wednesday. Four days from now. Allah has been gracious in giving us time.

"None of you should be surprised to learn that virtually every significant leader of the American government will be at the funeral. Members of the American congress will be there, along with their entire supreme court. Senior military leaders and administration officials will be there as well. All of them will be inside the cathedral, jammed in such a small space. And of course, the president will be speaking at the service. It is a once-in-a-lifetime opportunity to kill them all in one shot."

The general paused and turned toward Odai Hussein. "It was a brilliant plan, my *Rais*," he said in deep admiration. "It was brilliant from the very start. Killing Bush and the vice president to bring them together, thus creating an opportunity for us to kill all the others at once. Your stratagem is as dazzling in brilliance as the noonday sun. When we strike, it will be with a guaranteed result. We will kill the entire nest of serpents with one bold and final stroke. If ever our God has sent one to guide us, his hand is clear in the plans you have laid."

Odai stared at the general without moving or speaking.

The general turned back to the waiting men and went on. "At the same time the attack is taking place on the U.S. leadership in the National Cathedral, we will hit other targets throughout the city as well. In addition, we will release the virus among the concentration of U.S. forces at Saudi's Prince Sultan Air Base. As you know, my brothers, since the bombing of the Khobar Towers, the Americans have concentrated their forces in this single spot, out in the desert near the town of Al Kharj. To bring their troops together in one spot, to fence them in at one focused location—well their reasoning boggles the mind. It will make our work very easy and again, I recognize Allah's will in this matter. He has delivered the enemy into our hands."

The general turned toward Hussein, then quickly sat down. Every eye in the room was now focused on Odai. He listened for a moment to the near-perfect silence, trying to catch the sounds of their breath. He studied his generals for a moment, then rose from his seat.

"Our time is near, my brothers," he announced. "Our time is very near. For the past generation, the Americans have dictated misery to us. Since the end of the war they have fouled our country like the stench of rotting flesh. And why? So they would have excuse to deploy infidels on holy land in order to guarantee cheap fuel for their business.

So that they could profit from the continued sale of arms to our enemies.

"For endless years we have begged them to lift the sanctions that have caused so many of our children to die. We have begged them to allow us to sell oil, the only asset that we have ever had. For years and years they have stood with their foot on our throats. And all we have ever asked, is when will it end? We have appealed to their humanity. We have begged for release, yet our pleadings have fallen on only deaf ears. And meanwhile our children continue to die.

"And now we have power to act. Which carries an obligation to act. It is our duty. And it is Allah's will.

"The virus will be dispersed at the Washington National Cathedral. Within a day, the leadership of the United States will be dead. At the same time, we will strike at other locations throughout the capital, as well as their military forces stationed here in the Gulf. By the end of the week, the great nation of infidels will be headless, heartless, and without any power. At that is the time when Islam will be reborn."

The group of men murmured with excitement, their eyes flashing bright at the thrill of it all. They glanced at each other with nervous, eager smiles. Only the minister of state security shifted uncomfortably in his seat. He stared at the table, then turned toward Odai, a knowing and worried look clouding his face. Odai leaned forward in his chair as an invitation for the minster to speak. The minister slowly nodded his head. "My *Rais*," he began, his voice reverent and soft, "what about the bodies at Kimisk? Do you not think the Americans have seen? With their satellites and reconnaissance aircraft, it seems that they know everything."

Odai studied his face with a look of disdain. "The bodies are being taken care of tonight," he snapped. "They are being gathered up even as we speak. And though I had to wait a few days for the bodies to cool, I do not believe the Americans will know. Kimisk is an extremely isolated location and in an area they have no interest in."

"And your father?" the minister then asked with great hesitation. "Does he know? Does he approve of your plan?"

Odai's eyes narrowed and gleamed black and cold as a snake's, his face darkening from some unseen power. "My father knows," he nearly hissed. "My father knows all. His is after all, my *Rais*. He is my leader, my father, the president of Iraq. He knows of my doings. And be assured, he commands.

"Now go. Carry out your orders. But keep this in mind. My father is not your concern."

IRBIL MOUNTAINS, NORTHERN IRAQ

Morning was just starting to glow when Odai Hussein positioned himself behind the small outcropping of rock and lifted the binoculars to his eyes. In the distance, from the center of the pit, the smoke was just starting to rise, lifting black and oily in the dry desert heat. Barrels of diesel fuel had been prepositioned along the sides of the open hole that had been carved out of the sand. As he watched, workers cut into the sides of the plastic barrels and rolled them into the pit, adding more and more fuel to the fire.

Hussein studied the scene from the safety of two miles as the bodies were dragged from the back of the open-bed trucks and stacked in loose piles. Three huge bulldozers with enormous front blades began to push the piles of corpses toward the open flames. The bodies tumbled into the pit and were immediately consumed by the fire.

As Odai Hussein watched, a dry smile spread across his thick lips. He chuckled just a moment, a tiny rustle in his chest. He didn't know why, but there was something about it. The bodies tumbling into the pit, rolling over each other, arms and legs flailing around in awkward and uneven motions. It was grotesque he would admit, and yet comical in an absurd kind of way.

Mongrel Kurds, he laughed to himself. Even in death, they had no esteem.

The young Iraqi general watched for several more minutes. The flames seemed to leap higher as the bulldozers pushed in the dead, 285 bodies in all. The light wind suddenly shifted, turning the greasy smoke in the Iraqi's direction. As the stench filled his lungs, he smiled once again, then turned away from the fire and made his way toward the waiting car.

As he hobbled his way across the thick sand, he couldn't help wonder. What if the Americans knew? What would they do? What if they had any idea?

As Odai worked his way back toward his Mercedes, his bodyguards, members of the Amn-al-Khass, moved quickly into position to surround and protect their charge. Turning with their master, they followed in step, their eyes always moving, the barrels of their submachine guns glinting in the dim morning glow, shining black under the pits of their arms.

As the group moved through the sand, one of the men held back, slow to turn away from the flames that burned in the distance. He stared at the fiery pit with a hurt in his eyes that was as real and piercing as the burn of the sun. Though he didn't weep, his eyes misted over and his head hung low against his chest. The pain that he felt was the pain of a father who was watching his world disappear.

And from this one man—from this one Iraqi soldier, personal bodyguard of Odai Hussein—from this one broken heart and this single instance of suffering would rise the pivot upon which the world would turn.

BOOK TWO

War is an instrument of national policy.
Victory in war is not measured by casualties inflicted,
battles won or lost, or territory occupied,
but whether or not political objectives were achieved.

—*Air Force Doctrine*
Document 1 (September 1997)

A man who has a son has life's greatest treasure.

—*Shakespeare*

CENTRAL NEVADA DESERT
DAY SIX (SUNDAY)
0336 LOCAL TIME

Charlie McKay was wakened by a push on his shoulder. The room was dark. Only the light from the hallway shining through the open door illuminated the side of his bed. Colonel Wisner pushed once again and Charlie rolled over.

"Captain McKay. We need you in the main conference room."

Charlie glanced at the clock. He had been in bed for less than four hours. Passing his hands over his face, he tried to wipe the sleep from his eyes.

"What is it, sir? What's going on?"

"Get dressed, Charlie. We have a meeting in twenty-five minutes. Got a visitor here from D.C., and he doesn't seem to be in a very good mood."

Charlie rolled onto the side of his bed and passed his hands through his hair, which bristled at the top of his head. Colonel Wisner waited for him to get his bearings, then moved silently toward the door. "I'll wake up Captain Bennett. You get dressed. Meet us in the main conference room at four."

Charlie yawned as he nodded, then froze on the side of the bed, unmoving, his body slowly coming to life. Wisner reached up and turned on the overhead light. "Let's go, McKay. This isn't someone you want to keep waiting. Take a shower. Get some coffee. Drop some ice down your pants. Do whatever it takes to spruce yourself up. Just be in the conference room in twenty-five minutes."

Twenty minutes later, Charlie, freshly shaved and dressed in his flight suit, walked into the conference room and plopped into one of the wooden chairs around a huge, polished oak table.

Two minutes later, Killer entered the room. "Hey," Killer muttered as he dropped into the chair next to Charlie's. Charlie didn't smile as he nodded in return.

"So where is Wisner?" Killer asked as he looked around the room. "And why are we here at"—he glanced at his watch—"three-frigging-fifty-six in the morning?"

"I don't know. Maybe the colonel couldn't sleep."

Killer yawned and stretched his back just as Colonel Wisner walked and made his way to the head of the table.

"Good morning, guys. I know its early, and for that I apologize. We are starting early. We'll be working late. It's just going to be one of those days. But before we begin, there is someone here to see you." The colonel paused and looked to the back of the room. Charlie glanced to where he was looking. A young lieutenant was standing at the door. The lieutenant gave a quick nod and Wisner snapped himself to attention. "Gentlemen," he barked. "The Chairman of the Joint Chiefs of Staff."

A four-star general strode into the room, followed by his personal aide and two army colonels. Charlie nearly fell over as he jumped from the chair to stand at attention. He shot a quick look toward Killer, who had jerked himself up and was standing ramrod straight.

General Beck walked to the podium at the front of the room. Colonel Wisner turned and snapped a salute. "General Beck, good morning, sir. These are the officers I have selected."

The general turned to look Charlie and Killer in the eyes. "Very well, Danny. Take a seat." The colonel nodded and stepped toward an empty chair near the head of the table, which he stood by, but didn't sit down.

General Beck positioned himself near the center of the room, his hands behind his back, his eyes gray and sullen. He studied Charlie and Killer, who remained at attention. Not a sound could be heard. The general cleared his throat. "Please be seated," he said in a soft and yet commanding voice.

A soft rustle filled the air as the officers settled into their chairs. Charlie looked toward Killer, who returned a look of surprise. A hush of electricity seemed to hang in the air. A shiver ran down the center of Charlie's back. His stomach muscles tightened and his hands started to sweat. For the very first time, Charlie began to understand just how important this mission would be.

General Beck folded his arms across his chest. "Captain McKay, Captain Bennett," he began. "Colonel Wisner said it was early. I guess that depends on what you have been doing for the past four or five hours. For you it's early. For some of us, it's late. Either way, you can rest assured, I didn't assemble you here at this hour to add drama or emotion to our meeting. The simple fact is, I only have a few hours to spend with you. I have to be back in D.C. by early morning. But I wanted to talk to you and explain the situation myself.

The general paused and studied the flyers once again. He glanced to one of his aides as he collected his thoughts, then went on. "Several hours ago I left a meeting at the White House with the president and the national security team. At the end of the meeting, the president made a decision that will affect both of you. That's why I am standing here this morning. I'll be asking for your help."

"You know, of course, that four days ago Air Force One went down with former president Bush and the vice president on board. The press is reporting that we still have not determined the cause of the downing. That is not true. We know. We know the men were killed and we also know who killed them. And if that were the worst thing I had to tell you, I wouldn't be standing here this morning. But the news gets much worse, I fear."

The general went on to explain, talking for over an hour. Charlie and Killer sat in silence while he showed them the slides from the village. They saw for themselves the devastation at Kimisk. They saw pictures of the dead Israeli commandoes, the blood seeping from their nostrils underneath the thick lenses of their protective biological masks. They read the report from the lab. And for the first time in their lives, they heard of BILAB #22. They saw a short video clip of a rat in a cage, bouncing off the walls and eating chunks of its own flesh. Then another of infected mosquitoes biting a pair of monkeys, which within the day, were found to be dead.

"You can see, gentlemen," General Beck concluded, "that it doesn't take a Ph.D. in the obvious to know that he is getting ready to use the weapon. The test on the village was not just some wild hair. He wanted to know how the virus would spread. And he has proven already that he isn't afraid to use it. The problem is, we don't know where and we don't know when. It might be next week. It might be next month. Or it might yet be a number of years. But either way, it doesn't matter. We are not going to wait.

"The president has committed us to destroying the biological weapons production facility. We will use any and every available means. We would have done it already, except for one thing. You see, we don't yet—"

"Know where it is." Charlie cut in.

The general studied the young officer for only a moment, then slowly began to shake his head. "Yes. You are right. We don't know where it is. And that is why I am standing here today.

"There are perhaps only three men in the world who know where the production facility is located. One of them is Odai Hussein. He is going to be your target. You and your team are going to go into Iraq and bring the son of the butcher out alive. You will extract him out of the country and turn him over to us. Then we will take care of the rest. After a few hours with our doctors, we will know where his weapons facility is."

"But sir," Charlie said as he wiped his hands over his eyes. "I don't mean any disrespect, but have you gone completely nuts?"

Killer leaned over and kicked Charlie's leg. Charlie's face turned red as he shifted uncomfortably in his seat. "I'm sorry, sir," he muttered. "That was a poor choice of words. What I meant to ask was, are you—I mean—" Charlie shot a pained look toward Killer, who stared at the general, refusing to help bail out his friend.

Charlie stammered again. "What I mean, sir, is we are fighter pilots, not Navy Seals or the Delta Team. If you want us to kill him, well I think we could talk. If you want us to go in and blow his brains out, well that would be cool. We could scatter every presidential palace into shattered brick and blowing dust.

"But sir, what is this? You want us to go in and bring him out! I'm sorry, sir, but I guess that I don't understand."

The general shot a knowing look toward Colonel Wisner, then walked closer to the table until he was towering over Charlie. He looked down at the pilot and squared his huge shoulders, then placed his hands on his hips.

"Captain McKay," he said simply. "You should have let me explain. Then I think you will agree, we have come up with a plan."

The general cleared his throat, then went on to explain. Twenty minutes later, Charlie was shaking his head.

"Wow, that is so—cool," he said in amazement. Killer nodded his head to agree. "And the team is in place?" Charlie asked the general in awe. "The team is there, in the covert camp set up in southern Iraq?"

General Beck quickly nodded. "The CIA has been operating out of there for the past two or three years. Absolutely no one knows. Not the secretary of the air force, not even my staff. It is called Cobra Camp, and the choppers will stage out of there. The army Deltas checked in just a few hours ago."

Charlie's head was swirling. It was a daring and dangerous plan, a completely different box than he had been in before.

And he loved it. He was anxious. He was ready to go. He stole a quick glance to Killer, who sat with a questioning look on his face.

"But why Odai?" Killer was asking the general. "Why are you sending us after the president's son? I mean, we're not talking about some bedouin out in the desert. This is the military leader of Iraq, a man who half the Middle East already wants to kill. The Israelis, Iran, along with half a million Kurds—all of them would give anything to get the man dead. And that is to say nothing of the threat that comes from within his own walls, for his internal rivals can be found everywhere. Is it any wonder he moves like a cat in the night, sleeps in underground bunkers, and has tasters for his food? He travels only in armored limousines in a convoy. No one knows where he stays. No one knows where he lives. Surely there is someone else, perhaps one of Saddam's generals, who would be easy to snatch, but still could give us the information we need?"

"Captain Bennett, you bring up a good point and no doubt what you say is true. It would be much easier to get someone else. And it is possible they would have the information we need. I say possible, but not very likely.

"We could go after one of Saddam's generals. Or perhaps a senior member of his internal security staff. But were we to do that, we would have no guarantees, for it is likely that even they have not been informed of the exact location of the biological lab. Remember, captain, we're not talking about a huge facility here. It could be as small as an underground gym. Perhaps not larger than a few thousand feet square. A biological laboratory is much easier to conceal than a nuclear weapons facility. It is easier to work with, the components are readily available, and the research nearly impossible to detect. And with security as tight as it has been, it is certain that they have compartmentalized the information to the nth degree.

"Let us not forget we are talking about Saddam Hussein. He trusts his son, and no one else. He's been burned by traitors too many times before, which is why he put Odai in charge of his army. And with the constant threat of a coup, and nearly yearly defections, he will keep the location of this, his most secret program, very, very tight. At this point in time, we consider the location of this biological facility to be the world's most guarded secret.

"We will only get one shot at this, so we have to make certain that we get the right man. To destroy the biological production facility, we have to know precisely where it is. And I truly believe there are only two men in the world who can give us that information."

"But why don't we just blow his bloody brains into China?" Charlie asked. "That seems like a logical plan. You know he brought Air Force One down. It would seem to me that alone gives us justification. I say we make Baghdad glow like a cheap neon light!"

"No, Captain." Colonel Wisner cut in. "At this point, the last thing that we want is to alert Saddam Hussein. If we were to punish him now, before we can locate and completely destroy the biological weapons facility, he will put it to use. If he ever senses that we're onto him, he will act. And remember, Charlie, there's little consolation in destroying Iraq if it pushes him into using the weapon. If the virus is released, no matter the outcome in Iraq, we are the losers. It's as simple as that.

"So we have to pretend that we don't know what's going on. The press has been told we're still investigating the crash. Hopefully that will buy us the time that we need. And if we stall, for even a few days, that will give you time to go in and bring out the target. Then perhaps, we can turn this thing around."

"I don't know, sir," Charlie started to say. "I think you should do it. Nuke the maniac if you have to. Just go in and—"

The general abruptly raised his hand and Charlie fell silent. "Captain McKay," he said dryly. "It is really this simple. Until we find the production facility—until it is destroyed—Saddam Hussein is dealing the cards."

Charlie sucked on his cheek, then looked across at his friend. Killer sat on the edge of his seat, his face flushed with sweat. Colonel Wisner remained by the corner of the table, his blue eyes burning as he pulled at his chin. He glanced over toward General Beck, who moved away from the table.

"General," Charlie said, his voice now tired and more withdrawn. "How are we going to identify the target? How will we know it is him?"

"Frankly, captain, we are still working on that. But we are hoping to bring in a little help. She is someone who knows Baghdad and can operate in the country. The only question is, can we prepare her in time?"

"And how much time will we have, sir?"

The general studied the officers with a tight look on his face. "You are leaving later today. A transport will be here tonight to take you over to Saudi. We won't give the order to act until some time after the vice president's funeral. Until then, you will stay at Prince Sultan Air Base, just outside of Al Kharj."

19

CENTRAL NEVADA DESERT
2205 LOCAL TIME

Charlie McKay and Al Bennett spent most of the day locked inside the conference room, surrounded by aerial charts, intel papers, and mission planning cards. Huge satellite photos of central Iraq were taped across the front of the room. A blow-up of Baghdad was pasted on another wall, with the presidential palace, government headquarters, military compound, and royal family residence circled in red. A huge map of Iraq, with its major roads, cities, military installations, airports, and army positions, had been taped to the opposite wall. Blue and orange symbols were slashed across the map to identify the position of the Iraqi fighter bases, triple A, and missile sites. By early evening, they were finished mission planning, at least as much as they could with what little information they had. The remaining details would have to wait until they were over in Saudi. Charlie wearily pushed his papers aside. He had been working since three in the morning. He was tired and ready to do something else.

The transport wasn't due to arrive until nearly ten in the evening and so Charlie had several hours to kill. He packed his bags, which didn't take long, then wandered on down to the facility library. He was dressed in a pair of baggy plaid shorts, an oversized T-shirt and white tennis shoes without any socks. It was his free time. He was dressed to relax.

The library was crammed with books on high metal shelves, most of them technical manuals of one sort or another. *The Effect of*

Induced Drag on Velocity, or *Mobility and Warfare.* None of them were likely bestsellers, but then it was a library with a fairly technical pool of readers.

Like everything else in the Bat Cave, the almost-deserted library was sparkling and new, with the finest amenities a government contract could offer. The cement walls were pasted over with gray sound-absorbing fabric, the floor covered with a thick blue rug. Paintings and pictures of aircraft hung suspended on the walls. The neon bulbs put out a dazzling light and were set to a timer to dim themselves to a subdued glow when the unseen sun set outside. Huge plants and green ferns dotted every corner. A musky cypress tree was set to one side, its dark red vase collecting the cool water from a dripper that ran over. A digital calender hung over the front door, displaying the date and time.

Charlie found a small table with a desktop computer. Logging onto the Internet, he started reading the news.

Aria Cutter sat alone on the side of her bed. She dropped an old news magazine onto the mattress beside her, sat back, and looked at her watch. She was bored and anxious and tired of staring at the walls. Two days before she had been helicoptered out to the compound. Since that time, she had remained in her room. The CIA escort had been subtle, but clear. "It would be better if you were to just stay here," he had told her. "Most of the compound areas are classified above top secret. We don't want you to get into trouble or wander off where you shouldn't be found. You might find yourself on the floor, with a nine-millimeter pressed against your head."

"I'll check on you when I can," had been his parting words.

Since then, her escort had shown up only to bring food. Seven-thirty, twelve noon, and five in the evening, just like clockwork, he brought the meals to her room. He was polite, but distant, and it became very clear that he considered his escort duties an intrusion to more pressing chores. Aria had tried without success to engage him in conversation. After the first few visits, he said very little.

But Aria wasn't one for watching reruns on television. She was bored and frustrated and wanted to leave. She had stayed in the room for as long as she could. Standing now, she turned and made her way to the door.

Charlie didn't notice when she entered the library. For a while she stood with a questioning look on her face, waiting for a librarian to emerge from behind the small desk. Then she saw the sign:

This is a self-serve library.

Please return the books where you found them.

Honor code system, please.

Looking around, she glanced toward Charlie and studied the back of his head, then stepped over to his table with a determined look on her face.

"Excuse me."

Charlie lifted his head. He looked at her face. He looked into her eyes. His heart skipped a beat and then slammed in his chest. His mouth went suddenly and mercilessly dry. He started to speak but the words didn't come. She was the most beautiful thing he'd ever seen. Her hair was pulled back and tied with a ribbon. Her face was dark, her eyes glimmered in the light. She was dressed in a set of government-issue fatigues that hung ridiculously loose across her small frame. She was tall and perfect and surely the center of the world. She stood there, her arms folded tightly across her chest.

Charlie snapped to his feet. "Aaah, can I help you?" he stammered.

"I was just wondering," she began, smiling at his eagerness. "I'm kind of new here and was hoping to occupy myself with some reading. But, well,"—she glanced quickly down at her military fatigues—"despite my attire, I am a civilian. So I was wondering, is it okay if I'm here? They told me not to go wandering off. But I got kind of bored, and so I ended up here. So what do you think? Will they mind, or is it okay if I stay?"

"Oh, I'm certain it's okay. They wouldn't mind at all. Stay as long as you want. I'll vouch for you if they say anything." Charlie extended his hand. "My name is Charlie McKay."

Aria took his hand and shook it. "Hi, Charlie. My name is Aria Cutter."

Charlie smiled again and pointed to a seat. "Want to sit down?" Aria looked around the room, which by now was completely deserted. "Well, I guess I'll have to. There doesn't appear to be anywhere else to sit."

Charlie laughed as they settled in their seats. Aria sat down and crossed one leg in front of the other. She studied Charlie for just a moment and then said, "So, Charlie, what do you do?"

"I'm in the air force," he said. "I fly the F-15."

"Really! That must be exciting." Aria sounded genuinely interested.

Charlie nodded his head, but flying was the last thing on his mind. He stared at the girl. He wanted to talk about her. Clearly, she was the most fascinating thing in the world. He thought for a moment, unable to think of something to say. An awkward moment passed in silence before Charlie finally spoke.

"There aren't many civilians in the Bat Cave, Aria. So what brings you here?"

Aria turned and glanced down at the table. "That is a difficult question to answer," she said.

Charlie knew immediately not to ask any more. It was a professional courtesy that he owed. In a place like the Bat Cave, certain things were better left unsaid.

Aria seemed restless as she turned to stare at the pictures and bookshelves. She stared at the plants on the floor. She pushed her back against the hard wooden chair, then brushed a strand of hair from her eyes. "Do you know what I would really like to do, Charlie Air Force?"

Charlie looked up and shook his head.

"I would really, really like to get out of this compound. I miss the earth. I miss the sun and the wind. From the time I was little, I have adored the outdoors. I thought that, after a while, the claustrophobia might go away, but if anything, it seems to be worse. So I would love to slip outside. Even if just for a moment. That's what I would really like to do."

Charlie gave a sudden smile. "Aria, my dear, you have found the right guy. Come with me. I'll take you outside."

"Really, Charlie? How? We are prisoners here. That much I can see."

Charlie pushed himself up from the chair. "Aria, miss civilian, you better come with me. The sun is just beginning to set."

20

CENTRAL NEVADA DESERT
2248 LOCAL TIME

Charlie led Aria out of the library and down a green hallway, past the maintenance wing, and out to the gym. From there he took a right turn that led through a series of yellow double doors, then down a dimly lit hallway that appeared to go on almost forever as it faded away in the low, yellow light. It had a shiny cement floor and bare cinder block walls. Every twenty feet, huge red letters were painted on the floor.

RESTRICTED ACCESS
NO ADMITTANCE

Aria pointed to the warnings. "It wasn't my intention to get myself arrested, Charlie."

Just then Aria saw the shadow of a man walking toward them from the far end of the corridor and immediately froze in her tracks, unsure of what to do. The man emerged from the shadows, a gray-haired colonel in camouflage fatigues.

"Good evening," he said as he passed the pair. Then, stealing a quick look over at Aria, he nodded to Charlie and smiled. "It's beautiful out. You'll enjoy it, I know."

Charlie looked at Aria and smiled. Relieved and assured, she turned and led the way down the hall. As they walked Aria realized they were climbing very slightly uphill. Charlie tried to explain where they were.

"I was up top once," he said. "Got to look around for a bit and noticed this small hill, maybe a mile south of the hanger. There was a dirt road leading off to one side and an old building dug into the side of the hill. Figured that was where the service elevator and air shafts would be. So I did a little exploring around. Didn't take long until I came upon this hallway and found a way up. I was feeling particularly proud of my discovery. Very James Bondish. Come to find out half the complex knows about the service access. Here I thought I was Joe Spy, when all I had to do was ask, and almost anyone would have been willing to tell me. Seems people come out here for everything from having a smoke to laying in the sun. The facility commander knows, but so far she hasn't cut off access. I think she understands that people need to get out of the ground. Otherwise, we'd turn into moles. At any rate, as long as people stay close and remain hidden in the trees, they're apparently willing to let us escape once in a while."

Aria nodded her head as they walked together down the hallway. At the end of the tunnel they rounded a corner, passed through a pair of double doors, then up a narrow and brightly lit set of stairs.

There they encountered the huge locking doors, which could only be opened from the inside. After pushing their way through, Charlie grabbed an old steel rod that was lying nearby and used it to prop the door open. As he did that, Aria surveyed her surroundings. They were in the corner of a small wooden building. It smelled of old oil and had a dust-covered floor. Ancient, rotting timbers held up the swaying tin roof. Charlie led them to the far wall, where a small door stood on dry hinges. He slipped through the door and passed outside. Aria followed to find herself under a canopy of swaying pines. Looking up, she could barely see the sky. Twenty feet to her left, the terrain fell sharply away to the desert. Charlie walked to the ledge to look out through a hole in the trees. They were facing west, with the desert spreading out before them and the smell of pine and sage filling the air. The wind was sweet and dry, the horizon just turning pink.

Charlie plopped himself on the ground. Aria settled herself down beside him. Together they looked out on the desert and the scene of the brilliant setting sun. For a long time, neither of them spoke, just listened to the wind moving through the tall trees.

Charlie picked up a small rock and tossed it down the hill. Aria turned to face him and asked, "So Charlie Air Force, tell me, where are you from?"

Charlie didn't answer for a moment. "I actually grew up here in the West," he finally said. "On a ranch in the mountains of western Wyoming. Star Valley it is called. It sits near the base of the Teton Mountains. Absolutely the most beautiful place in the world. But the winters are brutal and the summers too short. My father took off when I was nine. Eight years later, my mother remarried and moved down to Texas. Her husband—he's okay, but we don't see eye to eye. I miss my mom. She's changed. Don't see her much any more."

"So what do you consider home, then?"

"Wherever the air force sends me, I guess. I really think I can be happy almost anywhere. I've lived in Europe and the Far East and all over the states. Seems that one spot is as good as another."

Aria watched him out of the corner of her eye. "Do you enjoy flying?"

Charlie stared at the desert as he answered. "It's the most fascinating, challenging, and thrilling job in the world. There's just something about being in the air. Sometimes, when I'm out there, I just shake my head. The things that I've seen. The things that I've felt. It is hard to make someone understand. 'And they pay me to do this,' I sometimes say to myself. It really is something I love."

Charlie tossed another rock as he continued. "One time we were out over the Atlantic on our way to Europe. It was the dead of night and Killer and I were—"

"Killer?" Aria interrupted.

"Killer, he's my backseater," Charlie explained. "My navigator. You know—the other guy who flies with me in my jet. His real name is Alex Bennett. He's also my best friend. And one of the most decent and honest men in the world."

"So who did he kill?" Aria wondered with a smile.

"Killer." Charlie laughed. "Oh no, you've got the wrong man. He's harmless. He wouldn't kill a fly. He picked up the nickname Killer on the first day he arrived on base. Seems he was driving his wife around, looking things over, driving through the base housing area, when he ran over the wing commander's poodle. Squashed the furry little creature right into the ground. The general's wife nearly died. Killed their poor little Fifi. Really—that was the dog's name. Fifi. That was what we called Al for a while, 'Fifi.' He hated it, of course, so then we tried 'Squash.' Then 'Assassin, the Great Poodle Killer.' But that was too long, so we settled on 'Killer.' And that was the nickname that stuck."

Again, the two sat in silence. The sun settled and then finally disappeared. The east wind picked up and rustled through the trees as the temperature started to fall. Soon it would be in the 50s as the high desert lost all of her heat.

Charlie glanced over in Aria's direction. She appeared to be lost in thought.

"So, what are you thinking?" he asked her.

She hesitated just a second and then said, "It reminds me a little of my home."

"And where would that be?" Charlie wondered, though something told him it was someplace far away.

Aria stared at the night, thinking to herself. She lifted her arms and linked her fingers in her lap. Finally, she told him. "I'm from Baghdad," she said.

Charlie lost his smile and a knot constricted in his throat. Baghdad! No! She was the girl!

Colonel Wisner had spoken more than once about a girl. Someone who knew her way around Baghdad. Someone who could operate on her own. Charlie's first thought was that it must have been some kind of mistake. It was crazy! All they would end up doing was getting her killed!

He glanced toward Aria, who was staring at the ground, poking at the dirt with a pencil-sized stick. She turned and looked at him, hoping he would understand. He stared at her face, but didn't respond. He could see something there, something she had been trying to hide. She was frightened already. Even now she was scared.

"Baghdad, really—well that is a surprise." It was the only thing Charlie could think of to say.

She slowly nodded her head. "That was my childhood home, except for the time that my parents lived in London. But at that time, I was a very little girl. We moved back to Baghdad when I was about five."

"So, Aria," Charlie muttered. "You're the one. You're going in."

"And you must be one of the pilots."

"Yes. I'll be flying the F-15."

Aria smiled in the dark. "I thought that might be so," she said. "When you told me that you were a pilot, I had a bit of a feeling."

"So, you're the one who is going in?" Charlie repeated. "You're going in to help us find Odai? You're the one who will lead us to him?"

Aria slowly nodded her head. "Yep. Charlie. I already said it. I'm the one. Kind of gives you a great sense of confidence, doesn't it. I can see it in your eyes."

Charlie shook his head. "No, Aria, it's not that. I would feel the same way about anyone. But especially you. It just doesn't seem right. I don't see how. It just doesn't fit."

"Well for one thing," she answered, "who else have you got? It's not like the CIA has hundreds of undercover agents wandering around in Iraq, all of them with access to Odai. And remember, Charlie, I spent a good part of my childhood literally roaming the halls of the Presidential Palaces. My family had, at least at one time, a very personal relationship with Hussein. I went to school with some of his children. I spent weekends with them at their retreats in southern and eastern Iraq. I speak fluent Arabic and though it has been several years, still, I am very comfortable in the environment. And though I am somewhat fair skinned, for my mother was British, still, I can easily pass as a local. As well I should. I *am* a local girl.

"You see my father was one of Hussein's most trusted agents . . . "

And with that, she began to tell her tale. Charlie sat there spellbound as he listened to the story of her life. And, for reasons she did not understand, Aria wanted to tell him it all. Perhaps it was the isolation of the desert. Perhaps it was the dark of the night, which by now was hiding their faces in gloom. Perhaps it was because she felt desperate and alone, a feeling that she had lived with for most of her life. Perhaps the secrecy of the bunker had bound them in ways that she didn't understand. But whatever the reason, she told him things that she had never told anyone else. Things about her childhood. Things about her past. About her family. And living in Baghdad with Hussein's younger children.

She ended her story at the camp, when her family was banished to the mountain. It was there that her voice trailed off.

A half moon shone from behind their backs. The night was peaceful and calm. For a long time Charlie didn't know what to say.

"And your family now?" he finally asked in a quiet voice, though he suspected he already knew.

Aria hesitated as she stared at the stars overhead. "All of them gone. They never made it out of Iraq. Hussein saw to that. He utterly refused to let us move across the border. Even in the camps, we were under constant surveillance from paid informants he had among the Kurds.

"One night, nearly a whole battalion of Republican Guards raided the camp. Hundreds of refugees were killed. My little sister ran away, trying to hide from the soldiers. Though we searched for days, we never saw her again. Soon after, my mother passed away. My father then contracted with some bandits to get me out of the camps. Once I left, I never heard from him again. I spent about two years in London before immigrating here to the states."

Charlie was absolutely stunned. His idea of courage had just shifted. But still, there was one thing he didn't understand.

"But Aria, why? Why are you going back? How did they convince you to do that? Is it because you want revenge?"

Aria was slow to reply. "You know," she said, "I had to think about that myself. And it took the last couple of days to come to the answer. At first, I wanted to get him. To hurt him like he has hurt me. But that's not how I feel. That is no longer true. I have turned my back on the anger. It's a poison I spit out.

"So I guess I am going because they asked me to go. Like I said, who else do we have? Beyond that, I am now an American, and having lived without freedom, believe me, I know what that means. It is a blessing I will never take lightly.

"But there's another reason I haven't told anyone about.

"It was late at night when my father turned me over to the bandits. Three of them came to our tent. They spoke with my father. There was an exchange of harsh words until he finally convinced them to get me out of the camps.

"I didn't even have time to pack any of my things, although you could have put every possession I had inside a little backpack. But the bandits wouldn't wait. They were scared and anxious to go. I grabbed my coat and a few other things, then turned to say goodbye to my father. He took me aside, pulling me into a corner of the tent, and whispered his final instructions to me.

"He told me about some money he had hidden away, as well as papers of importance he had sent from Baghdad. He told me where they were and how to get access to them. He reminded me of my parents and our family name. And as he spoke, I finally realized that I would be the last one. I would be the only member of my family to survive.

"My father's greatest regret was the death of our name, which he saw fading away like a wisp of smoke on the mountain. So he made me swear to name my daughter after my little sister. He wanted her name to be a part of this world. He wanted her name to be uttered every day. It was his way of knowing she would not be forgotten.

"So I promised my father, then the bandits took me away. And that was the last time I ever saw his face."

Aria lifted her hand. Charlie saw it in the light of the stars. He reached out to touch her slender fingers. She turned her palm over until he could see the tiny scar.

"An *Intafada Shee'mir*," she explained, tracing the white lines on the palm of her hand. "An ancient family tradition, the sign of a most solemn vow. Few will ever understand what this promise still means to me. And how could they understand? How could I ever explain? But it symbolizes the joys and the family I had taken from me.

"Now I have a chance to go back there to assist in the mission. But I'm also going back to find out if my sister is alive. And if she is, I'll find her. I'm bringing her home."

Charlie sat on the hillside, considering what she had said. He stared at the darkness, then turned to the girl. "You've never heard from your sister since that night on the mountain?"

Aria reluctantly shook her head.

"No letters? No correspondence through extended family or friends? Nothing about her at all?"

"Nothing."

"But still, you really think she is alive?"

"Yes, I know that she is. Somewhere in Baghdad, I'm certain."

Charlie studied her in the dim light of the moon. Her face was calm, but her eyes were determined and fierce.

Aria shifted against the side of the hill. "I know she is out there. I can feel it in my heart. I have felt it since the night she was lost on the mountain. And though there isn't proof, and though it defies my own reason, still I know what I'm saying is true."

21

CENTRAL NEVADA DESERT
0015 LOCAL TIME

The enormous C-5 lumbered down the runway, its massive turbo-fan engines whining softly in the night desert wind. The aircraft was so huge it nearly seemed to hover in place as it finally lifted into the air, its enormous wings bowing upward just slightly as its wheels lost contact with the cement. Powerful vortexes ripped off of the tips of the wings and descended to swirl the ground with tiny tornadoes. The gear came up with a solid *klunk* in the belly, then the nose pitched up another two degrees as the transport began a gentle turn to the east.

It was nearly dark inside the cavernous aircraft. Yellow lightbulbs burned every twenty feet along the bottom deck, where huge crates of equipment and machinery were strapped to the floor. The list of parts and supplies was a full hundred pages long. In addition, the aircraft carried nearly a quarter million pounds of fuel. It was an impressive, if not unusual, load for the jet. The C-5 would be landing in Saudi in just under twenty-four hours.

On the top deck, above the cargo, two long rows of airliner seats stretched most of the length of the aircraft. Almost all the seats were empty. Charlie and Killer were stretched out along the front row. Colonel Wisner was sitting midway back. Two dozen security forces and maintenance personnel were scattered throughout the rest of the compartment.

As the aircraft climbed into the air, the cockpit crew dimmed the lights to a sullen glow. Captain Bennett stretched out in his seat, stuffed a blue pillow under his head, and immediately went to sleep. Charlie sat alone in silence for almost an hour in the dark. There were no windows, so there was nothing to see. He glanced back at Wisner, who was sitting near the aisle, working on a laptop computer. The silver-blue screen bathed his face in a pale light. He looked up and saw Charlie, but didn't respond. Turning back to his work, he continued typing at the keys.

Charlie turned around to face forward again. Above the noise of the aircraft he could hear Killer snore. He felt the nose of the transport push over just a bit and then the throttles came back as the pilots leveled off at thirty-five thousand feet.

After a few minutes, Killer rustled in his seat and opened his eyes. Charlie leaned over and raised his voice just loud enough to be heard.

"Did they let you call Linda?" he asked.

Killer shook his head. "Nope. They wouldn't patch me through. They gave me all sorts of reasons why they wouldn't let me call. Security. Afraid of what I might say. They didn't want her scared. You know how it is."

Charlie nodded his head. He wasn't much surprised. "We'll be back in a week or two, you know."

Killer looked over and nodded his head. "That's what I'm thinking. I hope we are right. She hates it when I go and she doesn't know when I'll be back. It just adds more stress to the whole situation. After all these years in the air force, you would think we would just accept it. But it doesn't get easier. In fact, it gets worse. I'm telling you, Prince Charles, those orange groves with my family—I can hear them calling my name. I'm thinking that the time has now come. This will be my last trip. Pretty soon you won't be calling me captain. A simple 'Mr. Bennett' will do."

Charlie pushed himself out of his seat and crossed the aisle to sit next to Killer. "Listen to me," he said. "I know what you're feeling. But now isn't the time to go mushy on me, okay? We have a mission to do. The most significant and challenging mission of our lives. Nothing we will ever do will compare in importance to this. Think of what we're laying on the line here. Think of that, Killer. Don't think of home."

Captain Bennett turned to stare Charlie straight in the face. "Listen, buddy, I know what's at stake, and believe me, I'm focused. As focused as a laser. Have I ever let you down? It was simply a moment of whining. That is all. Nothing more. I am not distracted and I am not preoccupied with thoughts of home.

"But that doesn't change what I said. I've been thinking about this for the past five or six months, and I just feel like the time has now come."

Charlie slowly nodded his head and moved back over to his side of the aisle. Killer punched at his pillow and went back to sleep.

Charlie closed his eyes and lay still for a long moment, then shook his head, stood up, and went looking for Aria Cutter.

He found her sitting alone in the very back row. She must have been the first passenger on, for Charlie had not seen her board. He stood in the aisle, bracing himself against the seats as the aircraft bounced gently through the air. She was leaning against the cabin wall with a thin blanket over her shoulders. In the dim light, she appeared to be asleep.

Charlie watched her for a moment. Her eyes remained closed, and so he felt he could stare. As he watched her dark features, her thin face and black hair, he became absolutely certain of one thing. Aria Cutter was the most beautiful woman in the world. She was stunning in absolutely every way. She was intelligent, courageous, and deeply sincere, and no matter what happened to him in the future, having known her for even the short time that he had had changed him in a fundamental way. He felt lucky to have spent even a few days with the girl. His life had shifted in a way he couldn't explain. No doubt, she had captured his heart.

Yet there was something about her. Something distant and reserved. He could see it in her eyes and the way she would reach out for his hand. He knew there was a part of her that she could never explain, and it saddened him to think of it now.

Charlie stood in the aisle and stared at the floor, dreaming of things that would most certainly never be. He stood there and swayed with the rhythm of the aircraft.

"Charlie," she said, "do you want to sit down?" Charlie looked down to see her smiling up at him and immediately dropped into the seat. Neither one of them spoke as they sat in the darkness, then Aria turned and placed her head on his shoulder. He gently leaned sideways to smell the fragrance of her hair. Together, they both fell asleep.

* * *

Seven hours later, the air force C-5 passed a civilian jetliner as it crossed the Atlantic on its way to New York. Flying in the opposite direction, Delta Flight 1869 passed just three miles off to the south and two thousand feet above the air force jet. It passed the C-5 in the darkness. Neither of the aircrews knew the other was there. The trans-Atlantic jet routes were as busy as any in the world, so it wasn't surprising when the jets passed so closely together.

Inside the cabin of the jetliner was the former Iraqi prisoner, Rahsid Abdul-Mohammad. He sat in the business class section, where he could spread out and enjoy the ride. But it was apparent from his face that he wasn't relaxed. He sat forward in his seat with his eyes open wide, though they were lined with dark circles and red from a lack of sleep. He was staring out the window as the night passed outside. Occasionally, he would see the glimmer of ocean as the clouds broke away underneath, but mostly it was only the blackness, which matched the feeling in his soul. He was tired and edgy and in fear for his life. And the thoughts of his hostage family filled his head with such dread that he found it hard to even think.

Looking down, he read his travel itinerary once again, then did some quick math in his head. He would arrive in New York by early morning. He would spend the next twenty-four hours in the city. By noon on Sunday he would be on his way to D.C. It would take him about six hours to drive south to the District. He would check into his motel and get the package. By Monday morning, his work would be done.

Then he would reverse his route and drive up to New York City once again. Thirty hours later, after delays in Frankfurt, Cairo, and Amman, he would finally be back in Iraq.

Charlie and Aria were digging their way through an early-morning breakfast of pancakes, scrambled eggs, dry toast, and warm orange juice. They had been awake and talking for the past couple of hours, mostly about basketball, for they both were great fans. Aria was in love with the Pacers. Charlie was a huge fan of the Jazz. After a rather heated discussion, Aria finally consented that Rodman was an embarrassment to the game. Then they discovered a mutual love for classic rock from the sixties. "My mother had all these old records," Aria explained. "She had brought them over from England. I would listen to them over and over again. Since I've been here in the States, it's the only music I like." As they nibbled at their food, they began to play a little game, quizzing each other on the great bands of that time.

"Okay, okay. I've got one," Aria said. Lowering her voice, she began to softly sing.

"Layla—you got me on my knees, Layla—"

"Derrick and the Dominoes!" Charlie called out.

"What year?" Aria challenged.

"Sixty-seven," Charlie shot back.

"Ooh, you're good," Aria teased. "You clearly know your sixties. You probably don't realize how much I like that in a man."

Charlie glanced over. "Did you know Eric Clapton wrote that song on the back of a grocery sack?" he lied.

Aria giggled and nodded. "Of course. Everyone knows that!"

They laughed through a couple more bands, then leaned back in their seats. Several minutes passed in silence before Charlie leaned toward her and asked, "So tell me Aria, why did you decide to go into law?"

Aria cocked her eyebrow toward Charlie. "You're not going to tell me any jokes about female lawyers and pit bulls with lipstick, are you?"

"Well, I don't know. I guess that would depend on whether you had heard it before."

"What's the matter?" she protested. "You got a thing against lawyers?"

"Hey," Charlie feigned. "My commander in chief is a lawyer. And you know how us military types feel about him."

"Well, I guess that answers my question," Aria said.

"Heck, I love lawyers," Charlie countered. "Litigation is the American way. But somehow or another, you just don't seem the type."

Aria pressed her lips together and thought for a while. Her voice became serious as she began to explain. "I guess it had something to do with my father. He had a doctorate from the London School of Economics, but he always wished he had gone into law. Of course, once he got back to Baghdad, it didn't matter if he had an education in pig science. Few of Hussein's advisors are educated men, and those who are are never really trusted. Being members of Saddam's ruling Tikriti clan or the Baath party are the only things that matter to Hussein, and my father was neither one.

"Yet still, he felt there was honor in the law and saw it as a potential counterweight to Saddam's ruling power. Of course, he was wrong. But he was an idealist at heart, I guess some of his naivete rubbed off on me.

"So when I thought of my future, I really never considered anything else. Now, is that a good enough reason—I don't know? But so far, I have enjoyed it, and I think it will work out."

Charlie nodded his head. It was a good enough reason to him.

"So what about you?" Aria asked. "Why did you decide to fly? What made you decide to go into the air force?"

"It's funny," Charlie answered. "Killer and I were just talking about that, trying to figure it out ourselves." Charlie nodded to the front of the aircraft where he could barely see the top of Al Bennett's head. "Did you know that Alex comes from a very wealthy family? His father owns half of central Florida, I think. Has thousands of acres of orange groves. Al could get out right now and never have to work again, his family has that kind of money. Or he could live a very pleasant life, working with his brother in the groves."

"He must really love flying," Aria offered.

"Yeah, but it's much more than that. He came in the air force out of a deep sense of duty. He never needed the money, and his dad thought he was nuts. But he did it because he felt it was the right thing to do.

"But he's growing tired now and thinking more of his family. He says this is it, and I'm really going to miss him. It won't be the same for me when he leaves."

Aria lowered her eyes to stare at her hands, then leaned toward Charlie. "Hey, Charlie Air Force, can I ask you something?" Charlie immediately nodded his head.

"It is kind of a personal question," she added. Again, Charlie nodded in reply. Truth was, he couldn't think of a thing that he wouldn't be willing to tell her.

Aria turned herself in the seat and positioned her body a little closer to his shoulder. A strand of black hair fell to the side of her face. She reached up and brushed it away. "Charlie," she asked, "have you ever been really scared?"

Charlie thought of the first night of the war, sitting inside his jet as it flew toward Baghdad. "Yes, Aria," he said. "There have been times I've been scared."

Aria shifted her weight so she could lean against the armrest, then placed a single finger against Charlie's knee. "Charlie," she said, "I want to rephrase the question. I'm not sure that scared describes what I mean. I guess I want to know if you have felt gut-wrenching fear. A fear so real that it numbs you inside. A fear that goes beyond the simple dread of dying?"

Charlie swallowed hard. He immediately knew what she meant. He nodded his head as he answered her question. "When I finished pilot training, they kept me there as a FAIP. That's air force lingo for First Assignment Instructor Pilot. In other words, my first job after pilot training was to stay on as an instructor, teaching new students to fly the T-38.

"The T-38 is a small fighterlike aircraft. It is designed with the student sitting in the front cockpit. The instructor pilot sits in a cockpit behind.

"One day I was with a new student. Lieutenant Sammy Larkin. Good guy. Good student. Good stick. One Friday afternoon we were doing a low-level navigation sortie. That's where we practice flying very low and very fast while navigating through the hill country of central Texas. It was late in the day. The sun was low and we were just coming up on this little lake. We were maybe five hundred feet off the water, skimming across the gray waves."

Charlie's voice started to fade and he lowered his head.

"We were traveling very fast, maybe just over five hundred knots, when we hit a bird. The accident investigation board would later determine that a three-and-a-half-pound crane had hit square in the center of the front canopy, just two feet in front of Sammy's face. You don't know the force that such a bird has when it strikes your aircraft at five hundred knots. It becomes a projectile, like the shot of a cannon.

"When the bird hit the front canopy, it exploded the Plexiglas into a thousand shards. Pieces of the bird and Plexiglas blew into the front cockpit, striking my student in the face and chest. Glass and flesh and pieces of bird blew back, breaking the thin sheet of protective Plexiglas that separated my cockpit from his. And then came the blood. It seemed like a river of blood, red and flowing, swirling round in the wind, washing and splattering back over the cockpit, making it impossible for me to see.

"I immediately jerked the aircraft up and away from the ground and pulled back the throttles to slow down, at the same time turning for the nearest base. I remember screaming into my mask, calling out Larkin's name, asking him if he was okay. When I lifted my blood-stained visor, I could see him move around in his straps, but he didn't answer. From the back cockpit, all I could see was the top of his helmet, which was bobbing around in the wind, bouncing off the back of his headrest and falling down against his chest."

Charlie's voice mellowed to an almost monotonous tone. He was talking, but hardly saying the words. He was looking away, staring at the seat in front of him. Aria noted the hesitation in his voice. She noted the tremble in his hand. She leaned sideways half a foot and lowered her face against his chest. Charlie reached down and put his hand near her hair, but didn't touch it as it fell across his lap.

"What happened, Charlie?" Aria asked, though she was certain she already knew.

"We continued to slow down," Charlie answered. "And as the aircraft slowed, the noise and wind began to die away. After the initial blast of air, the cockpit became far more quiet. And then I could hear it. The gurgle in his mask.

"A piece of Plexiglas had hit Lieutenant Larkin just under his jaw, cutting through nearly to his neck. In addition, the bird had crushed his whole face. He was leaning forward, unconscious, bleeding to death. His mask, which was still attached to his face, was rapidly filling with blood. He was actually choking to death, drowning in his own blood. And through the headset, through the microphone in his mask, I could hear him gurgle. I could actually hear him as he choked on the blood. It was horrible. The most horrible sound. Unlike anything I could ever explain.

"We were only a few minutes from San Angelo's Airfield. I radioed ahead for emergency service. I lowered the gear and flaps and prepared to land, all the while crying into my mask, pleading with him to hold on. I only needed a few minutes to land. I could see the runway. I could see the rolling fire trucks and ambulances with their swirling lights. But the gurgle and choking became more and more faint. Once, I heard him moan. It sounded painful and so far away. And then his breathing grew distant until I could hardly hear it at all. He coughed a couple of times, then I didn't hear any more.

"Minutes later, we were on the ground. The emergency crews had him out of the cockpit before I could even unstrap. They hauled him away in the ambulance before I was even out of the jet. But it didn't matter. I knew he was already dead.

"I wandered over to the side of the runway and threw up until I fell down. I remember kneeling in the grass, looking down at my hands, which were covered with blood. I wiped at my face, which was covered with goo. Then I leaned over and threw up once again.

"Then I just sat down in the grass and watched the emergency crews work. They were trying to hook a trolley up to my jet so that they could pull it off the runway. It seemed they had all forgotten I was there. So I sat by myself. It was probably not more than a few minutes, but it seemed as if years drifted by.

"I sat there alone, hearing in my mind the sound of his gurgled breathing . . . I sat there alone, wondering what I could have done. How could I have let it happen? How would I face his wife? What was I going to say?

"He was my student. He was dead. I felt I had failed."

Aria looked up and touched Charlie on the side of his face. "Charlie," she said with a quiver in her voice, "can you see? Do you understand that that's how I feel? I feel the weight of the world is crushing me down. I feel weak. And utterly alone. I don't fear for myself, I have faced death before. But this other thing—this terrible responsibility that has been given me. I don't want it. I can't carry it. I'm afraid that I'll fail.

"And what will we do then? What if I fail? What if I go into Baghdad, but don't find Odai Hussein?"

22

PRINCE SULTAN AIR BASE, AL KHARJ, SAUDI ARABIA
DAY SEVEN (MONDAY)
0810 LOCAL TIME

Prince Sultan Air Base is tight and compact, and though as hot, dry, and miserable as any place on earth, it is also a marvel of engineering and planning. Brilliance born from desperation, the base sprung up in the desert nearly over night. Within hours of the bombing of Khobar Towers in Dhahran, a bombing that brought about the deaths of nineteen American airmen, the men and women of the United States Air Force were ordered to evacuate the city and move to the desert. Over the next few weeks, the tent city at Prince Sultan sprang up, tight and inhospitable, but extremely secure. Indeed, to the five thousand air force personnel who lived there, it was more a prison than a city. Few airmen were ever allowed off the compound and the gate guards were always alert. Eighty miles out in the desert, it sits in what the Saudi's refer to as the "Empty Quarter," the vast nothingness of sand that even they didn't want.

Prince Sultan is a sprawling city of tents, wooden sidewalks, makeshift roads, cement bunkers, guard towers, and multiple runways surrounded by snarling wire fence. Inside the tent city, thick, black electric cables snaked their way through the sand. Metal signs are posted at every sidewalk intersection to direct newcomers through the maze of identical tents and rolling barbwire. Fine gray sand, light as talc, hangs suspended in the air, and the only change of weather is when the sandstorms blow through; huge, black, rolling monsters that fill the entire western sky while pushing across the desert with a blast of biting wind. Most of the permanent structures are out near the main runway, along the east side of base. Rows of squat cement buildings house a significant percentage of the airfield's seventy combat aircraft inside air-conditioned and hardened concrete bunkers, testimony to the fact that, though the airmen are important, the aircraft are more tender and so require better care.

The C-5 touched down with a screech of rubber tires and taxied toward a huge iron hanger. A bus was already waiting to carry the passengers away. The security personnel and maintenance troops gathered their gear and climbed down the portable stairs that had been positioned along the rear of the aircraft.

Colonel Wisner indicated for his team to remain in their seats. For the next hour, they remained in the aircraft, long enough for the cargo to be unloaded from the lower deck. Then, the giant C-5 was finally towed into the hangar. With its tail sticking out the rear, the doors were rolled closed until they almost touched the transport's delicate skin. A team of air force security specialists then swept through the building. They turned down the lights and evacuated nonessential personnel. Colonel Wisner watched it all from the front of the cockpit before he pulled a cell phone from his canvas attache case and made a quick call. He spoke for just a moment, all the time nodding his head. With a flip, he closed the phone and dropped it back in his bag. "Guess we're ready," he said. "Let's get out of here."

Aria followed the three men as they made their way through the crew compartment and out the crew door. Descending a tiny ladder, they stepped out onto the sparkling-clean hangar floor. Colonel Wisner led the way toward a pale blue minivan. They tossed in their gear and climbed in, the colonel at the wheel. He drove out of the hangar through a small back access and began to make his way along the flightline road.

Charlie glanced toward Aria, who was staring quietly out the window, then glanced through the glass at the expanse of desert spreading for unending miles in every direction. The powder-brown sand rolled into dunes like enormous waves in a sea that, over time, moved across the horizon. He watched a flight of F-16s taking off, their afterburners crackling the air. He glanced down the flightline, at the rows of aircraft and huge brown tents. He watched the expression on Aria's face as the desert rolled by, knowing she was thinking of her childhood home. After several minutes, she turned to him with awe in her eyes, then laid her head back and looked away once again.

"Where are we going, sir?" Killer asked as Wisner drove toward the south end of the flightline.

Wisner glanced into his rearview mirror. "I'll take you guys to your bunker where your aircraft is waiting. You can give her a look over, then we'll go over a few things when I return."

"And Aria?" Charlie asked with a hint of concern. "Is she going to be staying with us?"

The colonel shot a look toward Charlie. "Of course not."

Charlie looked toward Aria, who was watching the colonel. "Okay," Charlie said, "but where will she go?"

The colonel looked in his rearview mirror. "Aria, I received word just before we got off the aircraft. You'll be leaving for Baghdad today. We've arranged transportation with the diplomatic convoy. They're waiting for you to arrive."

Charlie watched Aria's shoulders sag.

The van pulled up to a neatly trimmed, low brick building. Colonel Wisner jumped out and stepped to the back of the vehicle, where he opened the back door and reached in to grab Aria's bag. Killer slid open the side door and stepped into the heat, which was suffocating and dry as white bone. Charlie slid out of his seat and held the door open for her. Aria hesitated just a moment, then stepped out of the van and followed the colonel toward the building. A persistent northwest wind—the Shamal—blew at her face and stung her eyes with flying grains of fine sand. She lifted her hand to protect her eyes from the wind and the sun. Her walk was unsure, and she slowed just a bit. The colonel didn't notice, for he never turned around. Approaching the front door, Aria stole a quick look back at Charlie, then smiled and whispered goodbye.

NEWARK INTERNATIONAL AIRPORT
JERSEY CITY, NEW JERSEY
0614 LOCAL TIME

Rahsid Abdul-Mohammad stood in line, waiting with the group of passengers to pass through customs. He held a worn leather briefcase in one hand, his folded suit jacket in the other. He appeared to be disinterested as the line slowly moved forward to the customs booths. Rahsid moved along until he was the next person in line, all the time chanting a prayer in his head.

An immigration agent lifted her arm. Rahsid stepped forward and quickly placed his passport papers onto the counter.

The woman examined his passport. "Good day, Mr. Abdul-Mohammad."

Rahsid smiled weakly and nodded his head.

"And what brings you to New York, Mr. Abdul-Mohammad?"

"Business," he replied simply. "I trade Middle Eastern art. Persian rugs and paintings."

The woman turned to his papers once again. "And Mr. Abdul-Mohammad, can you tell me, how was your flight today?"

"Oh, it was fine. Long, but most comfortable."

"And I see that you came in on the Delta from Frankfurt. How was your flight into Frankfurt? Did you fly Delta from Dubai as well?"

The Arab's mind went suddenly blank. He swallowed once and thought, but he couldn't remember. Was it Delta? Air France? Or Lufthansa? And why was she asking? Why did she care?

"Oh Allah," he thought with a sickening thump in his chest. Was she suspicious? He thought quickly of his children. His heart pounded again, his throat went horribly dry. The woman stared at him with an impatient look, apparently unaware of the confusion inside. The Arab swallowed again, then finally said. "Lufthansa, ma'am. I flew in on Lufthansa. I flew from Dubai on the German connection into Frankfurt, then transferred to Delta from there."

The immigration agent stared at him for a moment, then made a note on his passport and stamped it twice. "Well, Mr. Abdul-Mohammad, I hope you enjoy your stay in New York. And I hope you packed an umbrella. It will be raining by later tonight."

The woman dismissed him with a sweep of her hand. The Arab turned and moved through the turnstile, toward the long customs lines.

Before she allowed the next passenger to come forward, the passport agent picked up the phone that was suspended behind the counter, tucked away down by her knee. She dialed a number and voiced her concern, then began to describe what Abdul-Mohammad was wearing as well as giving a general description of the man. Then, placing the headset back into its cradle, she motioned to the next person in line.

* * *

After checking through customs, Abdul-Mohammad walked through Newark's concession area on the lower floor. The airport was just as he had remembered, a splash of pastel greens and blues desperately mixed and thrown on the walls in an effort to make the old terminal building look modern and new. He glanced through the dirty glass to the greasy tarmac and beyond to the Manhattan skyline.

Abdul-Mohammad walked up to a bagel stand and ordered a Coke and a sandwich, then carried his food to a small corner table. From where he sat, he could look out on the open food court and watch newcomers as they rode the escalator down. He studied the crowd for a full twenty minutes as he ate the sandwich and sipped at the Coke. He scrutinized the faces, trying to memorize clothing, shoes, glasses, and hair, anything at all that would make them stand out in case he ever encountered the same person again. If he were being followed, he wanted to know. If he were under suspicion, it would change the whole plan.

Satisfied, he stood from the table, hoisted his carry-on over his shoulder, made his way outside, and hailed a cab.

"Midtown Hilton," he called through the half-open Plexiglas that separated himself from the cabbie. The driver dropped the beaten, yellow Olds into gear and pulled away from the curb with a jerk.

Several hundred FBI agents are assigned to counterterrorism duty in New York City. There they have the impossible task of monitoring the whereabouts of suspected spies, industrial snoops, extortionists, saboteurs, and foreigners with any terrorist affiliation. And while they spend most of their time watching suspected agents from the UN staff and the embassies of unfriendly nations, they also have the unproductive and completely monotonous assignment of monitoring the thousands of suspect travelers that are booked through the city's three major airports.

The FBI van pulled into position four cars back from Rahsid's yellow cab. As the cab made its way toward the city, the van remained inconspicuously in the main flow of traffic, never moving too near and always remaining in the middle lane. Inside the van, veteran agent Pisco was sitting on the passenger side, eating a loosely wrapped sandwich. The rookie agent was driving the van. He nervously searched the road up ahead while continually checking his rearview mirror.

"Why are we trailing him?" the rookie asked again.

Pisco swallowed another wad of meat and cheese, then wiped a thin napkin across the side of his face.

"Nothing big really. Routine trail more or less. Customs had a question about his transfer from Dubia. It wasn't enough to stop and question him, but the new security procedures require us to at least check him out. It'll turn into nothing, I'm sure. But anyway, we need to give you some more time behind the wheel to practice your observation procedures. So just keep on him and see where he goes."

The rookie nodded, eyes focused on the cab up ahead that was winding its way into midtown Manhattan.

Rahsid Abdul-Mohammad pushed himself out of the cab in front of the midtown Hilton while the driver jumped out to open the trunk. Abdul-Mohammad took the light garment bag and handed the driver thirty bucks, then walked quickly into the Hilton. The FBI van watched from fifty yards up the street, having passed the cab when it had suddenly pulled over. The two agents watched the foreigner with an uninterested look, then picked up their log to note the time and what had occurred.

The senior agent studied the Arab as he moved quickly through the glass doors, then turned to the rookie and said, "I'll have some guys come over from the United Nations detail. They can keep an eye out for him later on. But for now, there isn't a whole lot more we can do. Besides, this guy is harmless, I am willing to bet. He doesn't have the demeanor of your typical terrorist. This is a loser that we can ignore."

The rookie nodded faithfully as he agreed with his boss. He concurred. But then again, what did he know?

The blue-gray van pulled away from the curb as the agents turned their attention to more pressing business. Later that day, another team was assigned to monitor the hotel, but though it made a real effort, it had a lot going on, and so never got around to making a visit to the Hilton.

The Arab passed by the Hilton's crowded counter and proceeded to the rear of the almost-full lobby. For the next thirty minutes, he waited while constantly checking his watch. He put on the air of a businessman who did not like to be kept waiting, then picked up his carry-on and briefcase and walked out the side door. Stepping out onto 54th

Street, he raised his hand just slightly and immediately hailed another cab.

"Take me to Times Square," he announced. "I just want to look around. Then maybe down Broadway and through the Garment District."

The driver nodded his head. He didn't really care where the guy wanted to go, so long as he paid cash when he stepped out of the cab.

Twenty minutes later, Abdul-Mohammad found himself on the corner of 10th Avenue and 51st Street. The Pontiac Motel was just down the street. He pushed himself from the cab and walked the half block to the motel.

He strode toward the counter, where he found his room to be waiting. He checked in and asked for any messages, then turned to go up to his room. But before he left the lobby, he walked to the pay phone near the restaurant. Dropping in a quarter, he dialed an international number, then listened carefully as the call was put through. He spoke just a moment before he hung up again and immediately took the elevator to the sixteenth floor.

COOTER SEVEN FOUR
OVER THE SAUDI DESERT
2130 LOCAL TIME

The lumbering aircraft, a highly modified and very expensive C-130 turboprop, rolled into a shallow bank as it approached the Iraqi border. The darkness merged perfectly with the empty desert of the Jebel Shammar, making it impossible to discern any horizon. The pilots kept the aircraft at 20,000 feet, circling in a wide arc on the Saudi Arabian side of the border. They had been in the air for just over six hours. They would stay airborne for another two, until their relief had joined up to release them. Then they would fly back to Dhahran, where another crew would be waiting, ready to go.

There would never be a gap in the coverage of the airborne listening post. Their orders from the Pentagon had been precise and direct: Keep a Listening Bird in the air.

The specially equipped turboprop aircraft was jammed with no less than thirty different radio antennas and receivers, designed to pick up and monitor every possible means of communication. In the back of the cockpit, two dozen intelligence linguists sat huddled around their monitors, headsets pulled tightly over their ears, their eyes either closed or lost in a faraway stare as they concentrated completely on the sounds their receivers picked up.

In the third console back was a young lieutenant named David O'Brian. He was focusing his attention on monitoring calls that were made over Iraq's long-distance phone lines.

As the voice crackled in his headset, the lieutenant lifted his head. The transmission was a relay from a cell phone, which was interesting by itself, for there weren't that many in Baghdad. As the voice came through, speaking in Arabic, the lieutenant listened carefully, pressing his headset even closer to his ears. And then he heard the name. His heart suddenly jumped in his chest. Then he heard it again. The caller was speaking to Odai Hussein.

The lieutenant's eyes flashed in surprise. The caller was either careless or not very well trained, for most every Iraqi agency had long before learned that cell phone relays could be monitored from the air. The caller should have been far more cautious. He should never have used the actual name.

The young officer immediately lifted his hand to turn up the volume and checked that his record light was on. Motioning to his supervisor, he began to take notes on a yellow legal pad.

The conversation was brief, lasting less than three minutes. As the line went dead, the lieutenant's computer switched his receiver back into scan mode. The supervisor reached up and plugged his own headset into the lieutenant's communication chord. The lieutenant rewound the tape, then pushed the play button. The two men listened, then rewound the tape and listened again.

It was a curious and vague discussion, one that was broken with multiple unfinished sentences and partially completed words. Something about "it being delivered." Then something else about "the hotel" and "checking the package." The entire conversation was ambiguous, which of course only caused them to wonder. What was the caller really trying to convey?

"You sure it's Odai Hussein?" the supervisor asked.

"I think so, sir. I have heard his voice three or four times before. But of course, only the voice analyst back at Dhahran can tell us for sure."

"And you think the call was placed from an overseas location?"

"Yes sir, I really do. The fact that it came through the switchboard in Al 'Aziziya indicates it was an overseas call. At least that is the pattern we have seen in the past."

"Okay," the supervisor said. "See if you can triangulate the geographical source of the caller and receiver cells."

"I've tried, but no good, sir. Project 858 you know."

The supervisor nodded his head. Project 858 was the Iraqi agency responsible for electronic eavesdropping and countermeasures. They were staffed by close to one thousand technicians and analysts at six different locations throughout the country. All international calls, both incoming and outgoing, were eventually routed through their headquarters at Al Rashedia, just north of Baghdad. With their scramblers and decoders in place, it was virtually impossible to track any particular call and trace it to a single location.

The supervisor listened to the tape once more and then said, "Alright, data-burst the message down to intelligence at Dhahran. Let them take a listen and see what they think." The lieutenant didn't look up as he knowingly nodded his head. The supervisor watched the young officer work for a moment, then without further comment, moved back to his post.

The lieutenant sent a copy of the message on to Dhahran, then decided to take another crack at tracing its source.

For the next ninety minutes he worked at his console, using a highly classified and extremely sensitive computer program to work through the geometry and math. Several times during the painstakingly detailed process, he interacted with a satellite positioned over his head, quizzing it for additional information. The computers attempted to refine their estimates, but were blocked and confused again and again. The lieutenant became more intense, and even once thought that he might have broken through. His pulse nearly doubled and his fingers grew cold. Then the computer reset as the scramblers kicked in.

But he was almost there, he could feel it in his bones.

The lieutenant swore to himself and slapped the worthless computer printout into the burn bag, then turned back to his console to try once more. Time slipped by as he worked at the table. But despite his best efforts and perhaps eighty million dollars worth of hardware, he simply could not crack the code.

Though he was angry, the lieutenant was also impressed. The boys down in Project 858 were doing a pretty good job. He had tried every tool the United States had to give him, and still came up short.

But there was something there. Something important. He could sense it in the tone of the call. Though he had tried to sound calm, the caller was far too intense. And hesitant. And very unsure. Something was going on, the lieutenant was sure.

In frustration, he pushed the work off to one side and stood from his console with an awkward strain. His back was stiff and both of his legs had lost feeling. They began to tingle uncomfortably as he stood up to walk around. He glanced at his watch. Less than fifteen minutes to go before the aircraft would be turning south for base.

The lieutenant swore once again, then decided to put the problem away. He would be back in the aircraft very early in the morning. Maybe if things were slow, he would try to trace the call once again.

23

PRINCE SULTAN AIR BASE
AL KHARJ, SAUDI ARABIA
1150 LOCAL TIME

A group of United Nations weapons inspector support personnel was scheduled to fly out of Prince Sultan Air Base to Baghdad within less than two hours. The White House intended for Aria to join with the group. Each of the nineteen United Nations personnel had already been issued passports, visas, as well as a photo ID that would guarantee diplomatic immunity.

However, while it was true that the U.S. could slip Aria in with the UN group, such an action went against every grain of international diplomacy, as well as several laws and the UN's own charter. Had the State Department known, they would have never approved. Had UN leadership known, they would have gone through the roof. The action was, by necessity, a well-guarded secret. Only a few men in the world knew what was going on.

Even Colonel Wisner wasn't sure how Aria was going to get into Baghdad. At this point he was only following orders: take her to the passenger terminal at Prince Sultan and deliver her to her next charge.

As Aria followed the colonel into the small passenger terminal at Prince Sultan, she noted the multinational group of inspectors milling around. Colonel Wisner pressed his way through the crowd to a small room in the back of the lobby where he knocked twice, then pushed the door back and held it for Aria to step inside.

A British officer stood from behind a small metal desk and walked toward Aria, summing her up with a glance as he made his way across the scuffed tile floor. Reaching into his breast pocket, he brought out a small stack of papers.

"Your papers," he said in a matter-of-fact tone. "Don't lose them, or you'll never get home."

Aria glanced at the folders in her hand, then thumbed through the passports and diplomatic card.

"My name is Major Austin," the man continued. "I'll be your escort today. Your instructions are simple. First, follow me. Do as I say, and don't talk. We'll be traveling with some TCNs—that's Third Country Nationals. The UN employs representatives from all around the world, but don't assume that just because they are with us today that they are our friends. So watch what you say, and don't wander very far.

"Second, I do not want to know why I have been tasked to get you into Iraq. It matters not, and it should not be explained. Not to me. Not to them," the Brit nodded his head out toward the lobby. "Not to anyone until you meet up with your escort in Baghdad. Finally, remember this Aria, for this is *very* important. From now on, consider no one, and I mean no one, your friend. You can now count the people you trust on only two fingers. Me, and your handler in Baghdad, who you will refer to as Osman. No one else is to be trusted. No one else is your friend."

Aria stared at the British officer with a closed and frightened look. Then her eyes narrowed some and her shoulders squared a bit. The instinct for survival, the gut feeling, the fear and the hatred, were once again beginning to emerge in her chest. She swallowed hard, then looked the Brit straight in the eye. "That will be fine, Major. Now where do I go. I need to change clothes, then let's get out of here."

Three hours later, Aria and the Brit were landing in Baghdad. The delegation was loaded into a convoy of pickup trucks and open jeeps. With their Iraqi escorts in the lead, the convoy began to wind through the suburbs of Baghdad toward the UN compound on the south side of the city. They crawled through the streets, the escorts always taking their time, in a long snail of closely packed vehicles.

Midway through the journey, the convoy reached a cement barricade that had been placed across the street. A dozen armed guards waited behind the barricade. The leader of the escort, an Iraqi colonel in desert fatigues immediately began to argue, protesting the inconvenience and delay. The guards held their ground until they received further orders. The members of the UN delegation began to crawl out of their vehicles and stand around in the suffocating air as they waited for approval to pass through the security check. Aria stayed in her truck and kept her head down. After half an hour, the Iraqi colonel prevailed and the delegation was waived on through.

Such delays were not uncommon. The inspectors had long ago come to expect them as part of the Iraqis' efforts to slow down their work. Such irritants were the lesser part of a much larger pattern of harassment, intimidation, and abuse. It was the Iraqis' way of reminding the inspectors who was in charge. It was a way of reminding them that the charade of an all powerful and knowing UN was a myth that was accepted only in the nations of the naive. Inside Iraq, the UN personnel were treated for exactly what they were—foolish paperpushers who at no time had hindered the Iraqis' weapons development in any way.

After the barricades were lifted, the delegation continued to snake its way through the city. Twenty minutes later, it arrived at the compound, passed through the opened gates, and moved safely inside.

Aria was allowed to stay in the compound only until it grew dark. All afternoon, she remained locked in the British officer's tiny office. It was dusty and cramped and unbearably hot. Mid-afternoon, he brought her a meal and a set of used clothes. He stayed with her while she ate, though he didn't say much, seeming preoccupied with some unspoken problem. Aria ate what she could, though her stomach was in knots, then drank a full quart of water. The British officer gathered her tray and quickly left. Aria curled up on his couch and tried to go to sleep.

At a quarter to nine, just after sunset, the Brit came for her again and led her to a dry hedge along the back wall. A low hole in the wire had been cut along the back fence. On the other side of the hole, a filthy alley led off toward a refugee camp. It was growing dark. She could smell urine and rotting decay. The officer studied the alley for a long moment while Aria stood at his side.

She was dressed in a worn *thob*, or flowing black robe. Her feet were bound up in old leather sandals. A veil of gray cotton material was draped over her head and wrapped under her chin. She had pulled the veil around her cheeks until it nearly covered her eyes. Under the *ghutra*, her hair had been tied back with a set of tiny metal pins that were popular among the poorer women of the city. Looking her over, the Brit slowly nodded toward her feet, which just barely showed under her robe.

"Spit on your feet and rub in some dirt," he said. "You don't look like a local girl. Your feet are far too soft. They should be cracked and dry. But there isn't a lot you can do about that now, so at least try to hide them under some mud and dust."

Aria did what she was told, then stood up once again. The British officer nodded with some satisfaction. Reaching into his pocket, he extracted her travel papers and Iraqi ID, along with a small wad of dirty and well-worn Iraqi dino notes. Aria handed him forged United Nations passports, which he traded for the money and false Iraqi ID. Aria tucked the new set of papers under her robe. The last thing the Brit handed her was a small wicker basket that had been covered with a sheet of faded, yellow paper. The smell of fish lingered heavy in the air. Aria grabbed the basket and lifted the paper to see the fish underneath. The Brit touched her shoulder and then pushed back the wire.

"Remember," he said, "the number of people you can trust is about to be reduced to just one. After you pass through this gate, I can't help you. With the papers in your hand, you are now an Iraqi, unless, of course, they identify you as a spy.

"So be careful, little darling, and think before you speak. Now head to the market. Curfew is at nine-thirty, so you only have forty minutes to make contact with Osman. Go to the bakery. He will come looking for you there. Good luck and be on your way."

Without a moment's hesitation Aria bent over and slipped through the hole in the fence. She made off into the night, merging quickly with the darkness of the alley.

The British officer watched her go with a face of concern. He closed his eyes to the darkness as he listened to her footsteps fade away, then pressed his lips tightly together. A deep sense of frustration and anger welled inside him and he cursed his superiors once again.

The girl was taking a horrible chance. And unless he was mistaken, and he dearly hoped that he was, Iraqi intelligence would soon be hot on her trail.

The delay at the checkpoint had made him very suspicious. He had seen the photographers on the roofs of the nearby buildings and the Iraqi intelligence officers hidden behind the guardhouse walls. He had expressed his concerns to his superiors at the first opportunity, asking if he should let the girl go in. After waiting all afternoon, his orders came back from MI-5. The U.S. had made its decision. Send the girl in. Her mission was not to be delayed.

The Iraqi intelligence photographers had taken several hundred photos of the waiting delegation as it had milled around the barricades at the checkpoint. Though Aria had remained in the truck, the windows had been rolled down and her photo was taken at least two dozen times.

Late that evening, at about the same time that Aria was slipping through the hole in the fence, the photographs finally came back from the processing lab. Each of the photos of the delegation was then separated, identified, and matched against a list that had been preapproved and coordinated with the UN Inspector General. The photographs were then added to the incredibly detailed dossiers that the Iraqis kept on all UN personnel.

When the Iraqis couldn't match Aria's photo with any name on the list, General Aziz bin Al-Saud, the director of the Iraqi Special Security Organization, the man who was directly responsible for evaluating and controlling every threat that involved Saddam Hussein, was immediately called in. The general studied the photos for several minutes. It was extremely unusual. The UN always played by the rules. Unless they too didn't know who she was.

The girl looked almost Iraqi, with her slim features, brown skin, and black hair. But there was something more. A tinge of uncertainty and fear in her eyes. The general could see it in the way she held her head and the tightness of her lips. He had seen the look a thousand times before, and he knew this girl had something to hide.

The general turned to his assistant and issued his commands. A call was made to the United Nations central office in Baghdad. A British officer was assigned to handle the call. After several minutes of discussion, he informed the Iraqi that the girl was an assistant to the senior inspector.

"I would like to meet her then," the Iraqi general said. "I would like to have a look at her papers. We do not have her on our manifest list. Until she is cleared, her presence in our country is a clear and inexcusable violation of the agreed upon charters."

"Yes, yes, of course. I will arrange a meeting. How about Thursday morning?"

"How about now!" the general demanded.

And that was when the excuses began.

Which was what the general suspected he might hear. Within minutes of hanging up the phone, his security forces slipped into gear. An alert was put out through the massive Iraqi security machine. A photo of the girl was sent to every local precinct and intelligence service. Before early morning, several thousand Iraqi soldiers and police were on the lookout for the girl.

THE CAPITAL
WASHINGTON, D.C.
1510 LOCAL TIME

The president was meeting with key congressional leaders inside the senate majority leader's office. The members had grown very restless and demanded a briefing on what the administration had learned about the downing of Air Force One. By no means did the president intend to tell them the truth. Not all of it, anyway. Not now. Not until the mission to Baghdad was over.

Twenty minutes after getting underway, the meeting was interrupted by a soft knock on the door. A senate aide answered and let Brent Hillard slip in. The national security advisor motioned to the president, who excused himself from the table. Every eye in the room followed the two men as they made their way out onto the office patio, a huge stone veranda with chest-high, sculptured walls. The patio was on the north side of the Capitol Building and from where the men stood, they could see the entire mall. The president stayed close to the building, not venturing far past the doorway, careful, as always, not to expose himself for very long periods of time.

Hillard leaned against the white stone and lowered his voice. A dark frown fell over the president's face as Hillard explained.

"The girl is being sought," he said. "We were first alerted by our man in the UN delegation. The Brit. The colonel we have worked with before. He felt there was a good possibility that Miss Cutter had been photographed at one of the checkpoints in Baghdad. At the time, we considered it a very remote possibility and considered the mission still worth the risk. Since then, we have intercepted no less than six telephone conversations between various security organizations within the city. They are after her now."

Brooks cursed under his breath, then looked quickly away. "Will they find her?" he asked with a snarl in his voice.

Hillard hesitated before he answered. The truth was, he really didn't know. "Hard to say, sir," he finally offered. "Baghdad is a large city and she won't be long on her own. Once she makes contact with her handler, they will hide her away. But, as you know, Iraq is as tight a police state as any on earth. They have more internal security agents than men in their army. You can't walk a block without encountering soldiers. You can't drive across town without being stopped at least twice. So if she panics at all, this whole thing will crash down on our heads. But if she is careful and cautious, she will probably make it."

The president turned from his advisor and stared to the west, looking past the grassy mall to the Lincoln Memorial beyond. His face remained stoic. Hillard stared at his friend.

"Sir," he said, "there is something more. The Iraqi military forces have been moved to their highest state of alert. The Republican Guard has been ordered out of their garrison positions. The Border Security Forces are on battlefield watch. Every missile, every radar, every air-to-air gun appears to be waiting, as if attack were only hours away. Every SAM site around Baghdad is pointing to the south, toward our bases in Kuwait and the Saudi Arabian border. Even worse, the six Iraqi fighter squadrons at Shithatha and Al Musaiyib have been recalled, rearmed, and refueled. They have twelve MiG-29s and eight SU-27s, sitting on runway alert.

"Saddam knows we are coming, and he is preparing for us. This report of an American spy has pushed him to the edge. I don't know what he's thinking, but clearly he is assuming the worst as he waits for a retaliatory strike.

"And with them looking for the girl, and his military waiting, the odds of mission success have gone straight down the tubes. We have to consider our options, in case it's a failure. Get our eggs out of this basket before it crashes to the ground."

24

PRINCE SULTAN AIR BASE
AL KHARJ, SAUDI ARABIA
1900 LOCAL TIME

"Gentlemen, we are talking about what we call MOOTW, or Military Operations Other Than War. The rules are different, the intensity is the same. Your lives will be just as much on the line. And the outcome may be even more important. We will not entertain the option of failure, for the price we would pay is simply too great.

"And I don't need to tell you," Colonel Wisner went on, "that a series of eighteen separate miracles has to take place in order for this operation to work. The timing has got to be perfect. Not five seconds off. Not two seconds off. The timing has got to be perfect. Each of you knows your position and individual responsibilities, but I want to go over the mission one more time."

Wisner was standing before a mix of U.S. Army and Air Force pilots. The tiny briefing room, which was settled deep within the Special Operations Command building, was packed. The army crews were wearing shoulder patches identifying them as Apache pilots, men who were privileged to fly the most deadly attack helicopter in the world. The Air Force Special Ops crews were from the 1st SOW, or Special Operations Wing, out of Hurlbert Field in Florida, which flew the MH-60 Nighthawk, a highly modified and extremely sophisticated helicopter that was used for covert insertions and extractions of special operations forces behind enemy lines.

Charlie and Killer, the only fighter pilots in the group, stood in the back of the room, watching and listening intently. Wisner stood in front of a dry-erase board, where little blue, yellow, and red symbols had been drawn to represent the various aircraft in the formation. Turning to a map on the side of the board, Wisner traced his finger along a black line that represented the primary highway leading south out of Baghdad toward the southern city of Basra. The road followed the Tigris River through the marsh beds of Amara and on to the peninsula at Shatt-al-'Arab, where green barley fields and date groves struggled under the scorching heat of the sun.

Wisner rested his finger at a spot on the map where the highway intercepted the small town of Kut. "This," he said, "is where we will take him.

"We expect that, once things are tight back in D.C., once the memorial service for our fallen leaders is over and the president has had some time to review, that he will authorize us to strike at the target. As some of you know, Odai Hussein, code name Spider from here out, is scheduled to meet with his southern commanders next Thursday, as in five days from now. We anticipate the meeting will drag into the late afternoon. If he follows the pattern he has set in the past, he will wait until nightfall to travel back to Baghdad.

"Between now and then, our agent in Iraq," the colonel paused for a moment and glanced toward Charlie, "will hopefully have planted the transmitter that will identify the target to you. If not, we will roll back the mission until she has a chance to complete her job. I don't think it will take much more than a week. Maybe ten days at the outside. But once she has planted the beacon, we will have only three days to act. That's all the battery in the transmitter is good for. So we need to be ready. It could happen any time.

"Once the transmitter has been activated, it will send a one-time, hour-long signal to our communications satellite hovering over the Gulf, giving us just enough time to get a rough estimate of the target's position. After that, the beacon will switch to low-power mode in order to save its battery power. Once we get the initial signal, the choppers will launch out of Camp Cobra in the rebel-held territory in southern Iraq. The F-15E, call sign Hound, will launch approximately seven minutes later. Each aircraft and chopper will hit their refueling point and top off their tanks, then rendevous at the orbit point.

"As you can see from this map, there is a small series of bridges leading into Kut." Wisner pointed to the trestle symbols along the highway. "This is where we will set up the Kill Box. This is where we will take out Odai's convoy, trapping him between a char of burning military machines. Once we've destroyed his protection, we'll take him alive, plucking him from the desert like a rat from a cage.

"Once Odai's convoy has crossed the first bridge on the highway, Hound will attack, coming in from down this narrow valley. The Strike Eagle will take out both bridges, one in front and one behind, essentially trapping the convoy between two holes in the road. The Eagle and Apaches will then turn on the convoy. Once you get to within three miles of Odai's vehicle, you should be able to pick up the low-power signal from the beacon, which will enable you to identify which car he is in. You will then kill every other truck and armored personnel carrier in the convoy, which should totally eliminate Spider's mass of bodyguards and security forces, while at the same time leaving him completely unharmed.

"We have allowed three minutes for the Apaches and Strike Eagle to take out the security vehicles. The air force Nighthawk choppers, with their Delta Force teams, will be on target exactly three minutes after the first bomb explodes. All they expect to see, gentlemen, is a bunch of smoking holes with Odai sitting like a sheep in the middle. The Delta troops will then move in and get him. Once he is aboard the chopper, Hound One and the Apaches will clear a way out for them as they make their way back toward the border in southern Kuwait."

The colonel paused and looked down to review his stack of notes. "As for the tactical threats we will be dealing with, we have basically three. First, there are these two surface-to-air missile sites at Kut and on this mountain ridge." Again Colonel Wisner jabbed at the map. "The U.S.S. Lexington, which is steaming off the Kuwaiti border, has been tasked to take both of them out with Tomahawk cruise missile attacks. They will attack the SAM radars when you push out from your orbit point, which should be enough time to cover your ingress route.

"The second threat we are concerned with is the fighters staged at Al Mosaiyib. Once the Iraqis get word that the SAM sites at Kut have been taken down, you can bet they'll launch their alert jets in anticipation of an all-out attack.

"Which brings me to the last and probably most dangerous threat you will encounter, that being the shoulder-launched SA-7 Grail. Every armored personnel carrier, or APC, in the convoy will be carrying several of these and there is no way to ensure that some grunt on the ground won't pop one of them on your trail. However, if the

Eagle and Apaches do their job, none of the APCs will survive and the choppers should be able to approach the target without fear.

"That's how the real mission will go. Of course, for tonight's practice sortie, we will be operating in the North Saudi Range. The fighters out of Riyadh will be acting as Iraqi aggressors. The Electronic Range squadron has already positioned three simulated surface-to-air missile batteries to act as the Iraqi threats. Finally, the army will be operating some of their remote-controlled vehicles for us to use as our targets. As you can see, we have gone to great lengths in order to simulate the real-world conditions, so let's wring as much training as we can from this sortie. It will likely be the only practice you get."

Colonel Wisner glanced at his watch, then surveyed the men once again. "I guess that's it," he finally concluded. "Flight lead, Capt McKay will now go over the communication plan, ingress route and escape routes, deconfliction altitudes, and threat calls."

Charlie made his way from the back of the room and began his briefing. Fifty minutes later, he was wrapping it up.

"Okay," he said. "We are going to go try this tonight. And as the colonel said, it will be the only time we have to practice this, so please guys, let's not screw this up. Before we go, are there any other questions?"

The room was silent for a moment before an army captain raised his hand and directed his question to Colonel Wisner, who was standing near a front corner of the room. "Sir," the captain said, "I have only one real concern. How is your agent going to make contact with Odai Hussein? How is he going to plant the transmitter? I mean, what is this agent of yours going to do, walk up to Odai, hand him the transmitter, and say, 'Excuse me, but would you mind carrying this around with you? And maybe keep it pointed toward the sky. Here let me show you, hold it up over your head—yeah, like that. Thanks. That will be great.'" The sarcastic edge in the captain's voice barely masked his fear and concern. Every eye in the room turned toward Colonel Wisner. The captain hesitated a moment before finishing what he wanted to say.

"Sir, in my mind, planting the transmitter is a fairly impossible task. Yet if your agent is not successful, our mission is doomed.

"So level with us, colonel! Are you even sure that it can be done?"

Charlie glanced over to Colonel Wisner, who slowly shook his head. "That's not something that you need to be concerned with," he said.

The captain pushed, not willing to be put off so easy. "I understand, sir. But we are the ones hanging it on the line here. I'm not asking for details, I just want to know that we have a reasonable expectation for success. Can you assure us the target will be there, the transmitter will work, the equipment on our aircraft will pick up the signal and that it will allow us to sort out the target without killing him or getting our own tails shot off?"

Wisner shot the captain a deadly scowl. "I'd like to remind you," he snapped, "we are here to defend democracy, not to participate in it. Your orders are clear. You will do as I say. And if you're asking for promises, you're in the wrong business. In war, you see, there are no guarantees."

DAGGER ONE FLIGHT
OVER NORTHERN SAUDI DESERT

Capt Charlie McKay pulled his jet into a hard left turn as he glanced back over his shoulder. The familiar pull of the Gs pressed him down in his seat and narrowed his vision as he craned his neck to the right, searching for the enemy fighters, knowing they were there even though they had not yet been seen. Instinctively, he tightened his abdomen muscles and pushed against the strain of the G-force to keep the blood from draining from his head. His anti-G suit filled with high-pressure air, swelling tightly around his legs and stomach, giving him something to strain against as he racked the Strike Eagle around.

"Where are they, Killer?" he pressed his backseater. "You know that they're there! What have you got!"

The F-15 crew was trying to hide from the American fighters that were acting as aggressors, protecting this piece of sky.

"Radar's clean, man! I'm telling you I don't think they've seen us. They're still forty miles off to the south. If we stay down low, I think we're okay."

"I don't know, Killer," Charlie shot back. "I'm not the sharpest knife in the drawer, but I'm telling you they will find us if we loiter here very much longer."

Capt Bennett grunted as he lowered his head and adjusted his radar out to maximum range. He agreed with Charlie. The bandits were there. They had to be there. And it was his job to find them. But still, his scope was clean.

Charlie scanned the night sky, which was dark as black velvet. The barren Saudi desert held very few ground lights and only a quarter moon filled the sky. He could barely make out the deep shadows of the high terrain that was passing by on his right, a nine-hundred-foot peak that rose out of the barren terrain. Off to his left and far in the distance, was a dim patch of white, a pale shadow in the night where the salt flats spread out toward Wadi al Batin, a rough washout that was at least ten thousand years old.

Charlie sat with his hands in his lap. The fighter's terrain-following computers were flying the aircraft, keeping the jet exactly three hundred feet above the ground. His radar and forward-looking infrared systems continually scanned ahead of the aircraft, picking up the small hills and gorges of the rough desert, then feeding the raw information through a series of computers that actuated his flight control systems to keep the aircraft just above the ground. Using the terrain-following system was the only way he could fly in darkness. It was much too dark and he was far too low to safely fly the jet at this speed.

Charlie glanced at his watch. Only two minutes to go. He glanced off to his right once again, peering through the darkness. He could just make out the crest of the Arma Plateau, which jutted out of the desert six miles to the east, its summit just slightly darker than the backdrop of black sky. The rest of his formation was on the other side of the plateau. The helicopters, four army Apache gun ships and four air force MH-60 Nighthawks, were also circling in the darkness while they glanced at the clocks, waiting anxiously for the moment to go. Crammed inside each of the Nighthawks, stuffed between the Gatling guns and bins of ammunition, were the army Delta Forces. One team in each chopper. Six men in each team.

Charlie glanced at his engines and weapons displays, then checked the time. "Almost ready," he announced to Killer. "How are things looking back there?"

"Great. Radar is tight. INS has less than a tenth of a mile of drift. Every-thing's ready to go."

Charlie glanced at his watch as he counted the time. "Twenty seconds," Killer announced from the back. Charlie racked the fighter into a tight left-hand turn and pointed himself to the push line. The fighter, heavy with weapons and missiles, vibrated gently as he pulled it around. Charlie rolled out heading west and then pushed up his throttles to military power, just below the afterburner range. The fighter immediately pounced forward, pushing him back in his seat. Ten seconds later, at exactly 2000 hours, they passed over the hold line and headed in to the target.

The helos were already far ahead of them, for they had been holding much closer to the bridge. In addition, Charlie had been the last one to push. But still, because of his greater speed, he would be the first aircraft to reach their objective. Charlie's fighter spewed a light yellow flame as it screamed low across the desert. As he rounded the north side of the plateau, he immediately picked up the choppers on his radar.

"Got friendlies down low. Twelve miles. One o'clock." It was Killer who had made the call, his voice calm in Charlie's helmet.

"Two spots in the HUD," Charlie shot back. "We'll come up on their east side. Should pass over them about five miles out from the target. We're looking good. The timing's just right."

"Yep," Killer responded. "Now if the bandits will just leave us alone."

The exhaust from the choppers' engines was beginning to show on Charlie's infrared display, blotches of glowing, white heat. He studied the screen for a moment to distinguish the two separate formations of helicopters. The four Apaches were out in front. They were flying so closely together it appeared their blades were overlapping on his screen. They flew in a single V-formation, the leader in front, then one on his left and two on his right. Three miles behind them were the Nighthawks, slightly slower and not packed quite as tightly together. All of them were low. Very, very low. Charlie estimated they were no more than twenty-five feet above the rocks and brush of the desert. It was an amazing sight, watching them run in to the target, mere floating blobs on his infrared display.

In the back cockpit of the fighter, Killer was studying his own screen, looking for the target on his radar. He moved the radar around, panning its pencil-wide beam across the desert. He could see every oil rig and tree, every rock and jagged break in the desert floor. The first target, a narrow steel bridge across a deep gorge of rock, was very easy to find. It stood out like a mass of green, the reflected energy of the steel burning dark on his screen. Glancing very quickly at his weapons display, he noted the distance to the target. Thirteen miles. He checked the time. Seventy-one seconds. He checked his arming switches. Green. Armed. Ready to release.

"Coming up on sixty seconds. Confidence check complete. I've got the bridge at twelve o'clock, just under twelve miles now. We'll take out the two bridges, then hit the back side of the convoy as we come around on the second pass."

"Rog," was all Charlie said. He was watching the flight of helicopters. They were moving toward the road very quickly. He glanced at his airspeed. Five hundred eighty knots. More than six hundred and forty miles an hour. He was screaming up on the choppers from their six o'clock, and was now less than two miles behind them. He reached down and keyed his mike.

"Hound is ready and in position," he said, broadcasting over the HAVE QUICK encryption radio. His voice was slightly choppy from being scrambled, but still easily understood.

"Roger, Hound. You have the lead," the leader of the helicopter formation replied.

Charlie clicked his radio twice, a signal that he had heard and understood what the Apache pilot said, then watched as the group of helicopters disappeared underneath him as he passed two hundred feet over their heads.

Inside the lead Apache, the pilot looked up. He could see it, but just barely, a twin set of tiny circles, the white-hot exhaust from the jet's two Pratt and Whitney F100-PW-220 engines. The circles flew directly overhead and passed out in front of him, then quickly disappeared. The fighter was now in position. Looking down, he returned his attention to his own weapons display.

Charlie was just inside eight miles to the target. The heat from the convoy would soon start to show on his screen. He glanced at his infrared display, but nothing was there. No convoy. No line of ground vehicles. No glow of hot engines or warm, rolling tires. He scanned his HUD. They were right on course. He studied the radar image of the bridge on his screen. He checked the timing one final time, turned the aircraft half a degree to the right, then returned his eyes to the infrared display.

And there they were, small blobs of white. Growing pinpricks of heat on his IR display. He counted them as they emerged on his screen. One—two—three—four and then five. He studied the white outlines of the trucks, trying to determine which vehicle held the target. He glanced at his time-to-target display. Just over five miles to go. He should start to pick up the beacon in the next ten or twelve seconds. He glanced at the radar. The convoy was just under a half a mile from the first bridge. It was going to be close. No, it was going to be perfect.

"Twenty seconds," Killer snapped. A dim light glowed on Charlie's display. It read "WPN ARMED." Charlie nodded his head. "Target captured. You are cleared to release."

Almost immediately there was a bump and a *whoosh* from the aircraft as both of the two-thousand pound, satellite-guided bombs were ejected from their rails on the fighter's wings. The Strike Eagle bobbed just a little from the reduction of weight. The two bombs glided in to their target, taking their guidance from the group of satellites that spun over their heads. Four seconds later, there were two huge, rolling, white-hot explosions. And that was it. Both of the bridges were gone, crumpled into broken and smoldering spans of hot metal, they lay in disjointed pieces at the bottom of the gorges they had spanned. Charlie snapped the fighter in a tight combat roll to attack the convoy from behind.

He glanced at his radar, looking for the overlap of the beacon to tell him which of the trucks or autos Odai Hussein was riding in. And there it was, just coming into clear focus, a tiny pulse emitting from the second car on the road.

It was working! A shiver ran down Charlie's back as he jammed on his mike. "Spider's in Bravo!" he nearly screamed over the radio. "I say again, target is the Bravo automobile!"

"Roger! Roger! We've got him," the lead Apache pilot called back. "Flight, copy! Bravo. Confirm and respond!"

"Bravo." "Bravo." "Bravo." The other three Apache pilots called back, each in turn, confirming they understood where the target was on the road.

Charlie pulled the aircraft even tighter around to approach the convoy of vehicles from the south side of the road. He was just moving into position when he saw another explosion in the night. The helicopters weren't waiting for Charlie. Even before he could bank the fighter around, the Apaches had fired the first of their missiles. As Charlie turned his head over his shoulder, the night exploded again with a searing white light, then settled into a warm orangish glow as the first truck in the convoy exploded into flames. As Charlie watched, another missile was fired. He saw it leave the Apache with a white spurt, then disappear as it trailed to the target. With a sudden blast, the third troop carrier also burst into flames and then rolled violently onto its side.

Captain McKay was now rolling out toward the road. He turned the fighter to run at the narrow strip of pavement at a forty-five degree angle, giving him more of a cut at the APC on his HUD. Again, he and Killer went through the familiar routine.

"Target in sight," Charlie called.

"Confirm target in sight. I've got a good radar picture. We'll take out numbers four and five—it looks like number four is maybe thirty meters behind the truck Spider is in."

"Roger, I've got it. Okay, you are cleared to engage."

The pistons on the weapons carriers slammed down once again, dropping the two bombs off of their wing-mounted rails. The aircraft fluttered in the airstream as the bombs dropped away, shaking Charlie just a bit in his seat. Squinting his eyes, he waited for the blinding explosion. *BOOM. BOOM.* The blast rattled the night as the weapons exploded into the targets and tore the vehicles and road into a million pieces of black asphalt, molten metal, and flying rock.

Glancing back over his shoulder, Charlie studied the single truck that remained. It was a small APC, almost surrounded by fire. The APC didn't move. There was nowhere to go. The Nighthawks were now beginning to move in.

The choppers had landed, blowing dust and sand out before them as they set down next to the road. Within seconds, the Delta Force Teams were out of the choppers and scrambling through the darkness, their night-vision goggles making it very easy to see. The Apaches hovered nearby to protect the unarmed Nighthawks, their all-weather, night-vision equipment searching the road for any enemy soldiers.

In less than thirty seconds, it was over. The Delta Teams scrambled back to their choppers and shoved a bag full of sand into the back. Inside the canvas bag was the tiny transmitter. They had it. The target was in hand. The Hawks immediately lifted into the air. The choppers turned as one big formation, the Apaches surrounding the Nighthawks as they flew back to the west. The helicopters made their way across the desert, again at low level.

Pulling back hard on the stick, Charlie threw both of his throttles into full burner and climbed into the air. He wasn't concerned now with trying to conceal his position. The target was burning. The enemy knew he was there. It took him less than twenty seconds to climb to ten thousand feet, where he rolled inverted and pulled the nose of the fighter down to the horizon, then rolled upright once again. As he was setting himself up in a shallow turn, Killer armed up the four air-to-air missiles. Their mission had now changed. Their purpose now was to protect the choppers down below from the fighters that would be scrambling from the north.

But the fighters didn't show up. They formation slipped through the night, unseen and undetected. The desert slid silent and empty below them. Yellow and white stars burned overhead.

Twelve minutes later, the mission came to an end as the formation crossed the simulated border.

Colonel Wisner was waiting when Charlie entered the debriefing room. Charlie smiled at the colonel, then nodded his head. "It went perfect, sir. A near perfect plan. If the real mission goes anything at all like tonight, I think that target is as good as in the bag."

The colonel didn't smile. He had too many concerns. And one lucky night didn't guarantee success. Besides that, when it was all said and done, the success of the mission hinged on Aria Cutter, not some cocky pilots and their million-dollar machines.

BA'QUBA HIGHWAY
NORTHERN BAGHDAD

Eight hundred and ten miles north of Charlie's position, and about the same time he was talking with Colonel Wisner, a soldier was working at a frantic pace, breathless and covered with sweat, the dim moon reflecting the beads of perspiration that rolled off his heavy brow. Desperately pulling the parachute across the sand, he reached into a canvas bag and pulled out the iron rods, using them to stake the parachute material in place. Scrambling through the sand, he spread the material out and then cut it into the required design.

It only took him twenty minutes to have the signal in place. When he was finished, he studied his work for only a moment, using a small flashlight to illuminate the material, then turned and ran down the shallow incline toward the road that lay two hundred meters in the distance. Jumping into his car, he looked back to ensure the parachute signal could not be seen from the road. Satisfied, he started the engine and pushed on the accelerator, then sped away into the night.

25

BAGHDAD IRAQ
2105 LOCAL TIME

Aria walked down the alley at a deliberate pace, not giving any indication of feeling unsure, not hesitating despite the darkness. Broken glass crunched beneath her sandaled feet, for the pathway was cluttered with waste and debris. Steel frames and old boots, rotting cloth and torn burlap bags, anything that could not be rebuilt or burned for fuel lay strewn across the weed-infested alley. The path darkened as she moved away from the dim lights of the UN compound until, half a kilometer away, it brightened again as she approached one of the many dilapidated neighborhoods of the city.

Aria emerged from the alley without stopping, turned right on the road, and headed west. Watching the doors of the old stone and mason apartments, she counted down the building numbers. Three blocks later, she turned south once again. The bus station was a half block ahead.

Every wall and corner of the station near the King Faisal Bridge, both inside and out, was lined with venders and merchants pedaling their wares. The smell of sweat, fresh cotton, and incense permeated the air. On the outside of the station, along the east wall, tucked between the terminal entrance and maintenance garage, was a small food market. Like everywhere else in the city, the AMAM Secret Police, or Amn-al-Amn, with their black berets and white armbands, monitored the faces in the crowd.

Aria pulled the dark veil closer to her face and moved through the darkness toward the market, her stomach in knots, her eyes darting around. The streets were less busy now, with curfew coming on. Up ahead, she could hear the clamor of a small crowd at the station. She glanced at her wrist to check the time, then caught herself. Of course, she did not wear a watch. Baghdad women didn't monitor the time. With sullen eyes, she lowered her head and pressed on to the market, anxious to merge with the crowd. The weight of the fish basket pulled on her arm. A huge multicolored bus, noisy and belching blue diesel fumes, rushed by, not more than a few feet away. It slowed to bounce over a hole in the street, then accelerated once again as the driver pressed on. A tan army jeep came down the road in the opposite direction. Aria glanced up to see it, her heart skipping a beat. Very quickly, she lowered her eyes. The army vehicle passed by, the soldiers staring straight ahead. The smell of the market reached her nostrils. She quickened her stride as the lights came into view.

Minutes later she was walking among the local Iraqis. She listened intently to their talk, the sing-song rise and fall of their voices, as they gossiped and haggled in their native tongue. She felt the heat of the summer night and the familiar taste of light sweat on the edge of her lip. She smelled the deep aroma of the fish, baking bread, and Turkish coffee. The memories of her childhood swept over her, saturating her senses. And for one terrifying moment, she felt like she had always been here. Like she had never left Iraq with all its desperation. Like this was all that was real and all that would ever be. Her hands began to tremble and her knees weakened a bit as the fear, and emotion flooded her brain.

She stopped in the middle of the crowd and looked quickly around.

Where was Osman? Was he watching? Did he see her? Was he even there?

Aria avoided the urge to stare at the faces. She avoided the urge to look all around. She began to mingle again with the shoppers, careful to avoid close body contact, knowing she did not yet have their smell. She worked her way to the fruit stand and began to feel the apples, then selected half a dozen and placed them on the worn-out counter. The vendor, a small, white-haired man with brown teeth and leather hands, watched her place the fruit on the table. Around the corner, two AMAM Secret Police emerged and worked their way through the crowd, which parted like a flock of scared chickens before them. Aria glanced at the police, then quickly looked away. Reaching under her robe, she extracted some money to pay for the apples.

"Where you from?" the vendor asked in a weary voice, after noting the softness of her hands.

Aria nodded toward the street. "Across the river," she replied in Arabic, her native language coming back easily and gracefully to her tongue. "In Risafa."

The old man studied her a bit, then slowly shook his head. "No," he said. "I don't think that is true."

Under her veil, Aria's eyes didn't change. Glancing to her side, she looked for the AMAM police, while holding back the terror that was building deep in her soul. Turning to the vendor, she lowered her voice. "No, *bey*," she said, using the Persian term of respect that was common among the locals that lived along the Iraq/Iranian border. "It is true. Risafa is my home."

"No, sister, you are not from Risafa, for I have lived there for the past sixty years. I know the people in Risafa, and I do not know you."

Another wave of fear washed over her. Her voice stuck in her throat. She didn't know what to say. She quickly sorted the money and handed the Iraqi a couple of dino notes, much more than the apples were worth. The vendor looked with surprise at the two dinos, took the bills in both hands, a gesture of the gift being too heavy to hold, then backed away from the table and dropped the money into his bag. Aria kept her eyes looking downward as she listened to the thumping boots of the approaching police and pulled her veil cloth closer to her face.

The two guards were now close enough that they could easily pick up their voices. She glanced sideways, down the brick and mortar walkway, toward the end of the market. The crowd was growing thin, the last bus already having departed. One of the soldiers turned to the other, then motioned toward the girl with the apples. They both turned to stare, taking her in, for the shawl didn't hide all of her beauty. Aria caught their eyes, then swallowed hard, her throat tight as a drum. The vender approached the table once again. Aria's mind was racing as she glanced again at the guards.

"Sister, how long have you lived in Risafa?" the old man asked.

"Not long, *bey*. I came down with my father from Qal'a. He is—" Aria's voice trailed off. "I should say we are one of the Dhanna." Aria looked with shame to the ground.

The man frowned and took one step away. The Dhanna—a soldier from the Mother of Wars. A prisoner of the American *Kalb*, or American dogs. One of the failed army officers who had shamed the *Great Rais* by ordering his troops to surrender to the American pigs.

Such men were now doomed to suffer the official hate and contempt of their country. They were not to be trusted. They were not to be friends.

Aria studied the floor a moment longer, then went on. "My father lost his legs in the war. I am caring for him now. We hope to see a doctor at the government hospital. We have been so long seeking treatment. But still we are hopeful. One day, the sun will rise on my family again."

The old man nodded his head, though he didn't believe it. It would never happen, not while he was alive. Aria took the apples and placed them on top of her basket, careful to keep them separated from the oily fish. Under her robes, she took a deep breath, then turned around to face the guards and walked by them as quickly as she dared. She didn't look back, so she could not see them watching as she made her way back down the walkway that led through the bazaar. As she walked, she listened closely to know if the guards followed her. Only after thirty seconds of not hearing their footsteps did she let out a deep breath of air.

The Kurd moved through the market slowly, his every movement calibrated to mesh with the crowd. He was young, perhaps no more than nineteen or twenty, and small for his age. His face was soft and babylike, his shoulders slim and round. He looked no more threatening than a child or old woman, which was exactly the way he wished to appear. Contrary to his outward appearance, the Kurd was a cold-blooded killer, and a member of the PKK, the Kurdish Workers Party, since he was thirteen. He was a warrior in both heritage and training, a direct and proud descendent of the great twelfth-century Kurdish warrior Saladin. The young man had spent the past seven years waging guerilla warfare against the Iraqi military in northern Iraq. A veteran of eight guerilla attacks, he had spilt the blood of two dozen men.

And he would kill the girl too if he had to. Protecting his cover was far more important than any mission she had. He didn't know why she was here, and he really didn't care. To him, it was just another job, no more or less important than all of the others in the past.

He watched her for several minutes, taking in her movements, her walk, the graceful flow of her hands. He watched and listened as she talked with the fruit vendor. He followed her as she made her way toward the far end of the market. Glancing over his shoulder, he saw the AMAM guards. Approaching the corner of the bus terminal, he quickened his step and moved up behind her. He didn't slow down as he brushed her left shoulder. "Follow me," he said with a whisper in her ear.

Aria watched in surprise and relief as the man strolled out of the market and onto Alwazia Street. A car pulled up and he quickly climbed inside. She followed just three steps behind him. The door was still open and she didn't even pause before dropping into the back seat. The interior was dark and she couldn't see his face as he lifted the gun to her head.

CIA HEADQUARTERS
LANGLEY, VIRGINIA
1410 LOCAL TIME

The CIA director leaned forward, resting his arms on the desk as he passed the black-and-white photo to his waiting friend. The Israeli, a small man with white hair, took the picture and placed it carefully in his lap while extracting a pair of wire glasses. He studied the photo for several seconds in silence. Looking up, he carefully dropped it onto the desk.

"What do you think, Shamir?" Michael Crosby asked. The Israeli sat back and studied the wall, his forehead curled into rows of wrinkled skin. He thought for a moment, then picked up the photo once more.

"When was this taken?"

The director looked at his watch. "About four hours ago."

"And the location?"

"Thirty kilometers north of the city. On one of the alternate and lesser used highways that leads up to Ba'quba."

"And is this the first signal you have seen?"

"Yes," Crosby lied. Of course he wouldn't tell of the others. To admit their inability to understand and heed the prior warning was not a conversation he wanted to get into today."And it was taken with one of your satellites, am I correct in assuming?"

The director didn't reply. Truth was, the photo had come from an unmanned aerial drone called a Rapture, one of the half dozen remote-controlled spy and reconnaissance birds that the U.S. was now constantly flying over Baghdad. But he didn't explain this fact to his fellow intelligence friend. Where the picture came from shouldn't matter to him.

The head of Israeli intelligence waited for a reply, then when he could see that none would come, returned to stare at the photo. It was remarkably clear, as if taken from a very low-flying aircraft. It showed a small highway cutting through the sand, a nearly perfect straight line of asphalt and cement. On one side of the highway, maybe two hundred meters off in the sand, was a strange and inexplicable sight. Someone had taken a wad of black cloth and stretched it out as a signal. It showed a rough figure eight, maybe ten or twelve feet across. Inside each circle of the eight was a two-foot black dot. To the north side of the figure was another strange symbol—a small square set inside another.

The Israeli immediately recognized what each signal meant. And though he didn't say, he also had a very good guess of why the two were together.

He looked up to Crosby, who was studying him closely.

"You know what the two signals represent, don't you Shamir?"

"Yes, of course. The modified figure eight was the symbol your American pilots used during the Gulf War as a signal of distress. As I remember, when a pilot was shot down, he was to take his parachute and cut it into strips, then stake them into the sand in a rough figure eight as a signal to your rescue forces."

The American slowly nodded his head. Even though the signal had been a highly classified secret, he was not surprised the Israeli knew. He nodded to the picture and raised his left eyebrow. "And the box within the box. Do you know what that is?"

"Of course, Mike. It is the symbol that represents the Amn-al-Khass, the elite Palace Guards, personal bodyguards of Saddam Hussein and his family."

The American leaned forward in his chair. "So why do we find these two signals in the sand?" he wondered. "And why in the world are the two put together? It is a question we have been asking since this picture came in. I was hoping that you might have some insight into the matter. That perhaps you could give us some help."

The Israeli didn't smile as he tossed the picture on the desk. "Michael," he said in a nearly apologetic tone. "There is something that perhaps I should have told you before."

The Israeli unconsciously lowered his voice, having decided to tell the American the truth.

"There is an Iraqi that we have been watching for the past dozen years. When he was a young man, before all this ugliness began, he married a women whose mother was a Kurd. This was a terrible secret he would have never disclosed, for to do so would mean certain death to his family, as well as an unauspicious and equally violent end to his career. Such a breach of judgment would not have been overlooked. Being one of the Amn-al-Khass, personal bodyguards to Saddam and his family, it would have certainly been viewed as an outright betrayal.

"Now, as you can see from the signal, it appears he will play. This may be an opportunity to crack Odai's tightest circle of guards. You've got to contact this Iraqi. It may be your best hope."

PRINCE SULTAN AIR BASE
SAUDI ARABIA
2315 LOCAL TIME

The Iraqi sat in his water truck and watched from the side of the road as the single F-15E was towed into the hangar, the bright lights of the aircraft parking area made it easy to see. Along the outside of the bunker, a total of eight Apache and Nighthawk helicopters sat quietly on the ramp, their rotors tied down, a full load of Hellfire missiles strapped under the Apache's stout wings. It was a little unusual, the choppers and single fighter being together. Something he had not seen before. For a moment he considered making contact with the *Sayid* Odai, then just as quickly reconsidered and changed his mind. He wasn't on an observation mission. His mission was far more important than that.

He thought of the container tucked away under the floor of his truck. He had only seen it once, and even now did not know what it was. But his orders were simple. Drop the silver container inside his water tank before delivering his supply of fresh water to the base in the desert.

He glanced at his watch. Less than forty-eight hours to go.

NEW YORK CITY
1700 LOCAL TIME

Rahsid Abdul-Mohammad lay on the bed in his hotel. The room was growing dark. The television was on, but the sound was turned down. The image on the screen caused a flicker of light to cast mystical shadows around his room. Outside his window, a siren sped by, a fire truck rolling out of the station that sat one block to the north. Rolling onto his side, the Arab sat up and checked the time.

He pushed himself from the bed, walked to the sitting room table, reached into his briefcase, and extracted the neatly typed paper, a list of clients he intended to call. Holding the paper carefully at the corner, he stepped into the bathroom and stood at the toilet. Opening his fly, he urinated over the list. As he did, a message began to show through, written in a thin Arabic scrawl. The former prisoner placed the paper on the edge of the tub and read his instructions from the general. As he read the words, his face grew stolid and his fingers grew cold. Standing, he weakly made his way back to the bed.

BA'QUBA HIGHWAY
NORTH OF BAGHDAD
0300 LOCAL TIME

The reconnaissance drone flew slowly over the parachute signal at three thousand feet. It was dark, the sliver of moon just twenty degrees above the crest of the desert horizon. The black aircraft hummed quietly in the night, unheard and unseen from the road down below. The small, funnel-winged aircraft was flying just above stall speed, making just over sixty miles an hour. The satellite data-link conveyed every image from its sensors in real time back to the mobile control booth at Incirlik, Turkey.

The pilot stared at his flight-data screen, flying the drone exactly as he would a regular aircraft. He had a readout of his instruments and engine performance, as well as his navigational equipment and status displays. He turned the drone to fly into the wind and watched as his cameras searched the desert below. He was surrounded by half a dozen technicians and photo-interpretation specialists, who were all intently studying their own critical displays. The technicians adjusted the sensors and cameras to search the area with optical, radar, and infrared sensors.

The road was deserted. The closest human was twenty miles away, tucked behind the perimeter fence of the Ba'Quba compound. The senior officer studied the screens, then gave his command. "Fly right over the signal and drop down to fifty feet."

"Yes sir," the lieutenant replied. He rolled the drone over onto her left wing and pulled back the throttle to let it descend. As the remote-controlled aircraft approached the signal in the sand, the senior officer began to count down.

"Ready—ready—ready—*now!*" he shouted as the drone passed directly over the chute. The controller to his side immediately pulled down his switch, illuminating a red light on the console.

Under the belly of the drone, a small bundle released into the air and dropped quickly toward the gritty desert. The black canister fell directly onto a white piece of parachute, then began to roll south, following the path of the drone for twenty feet before coming to rest at the edge of the sand.

If the Iraqi who left the signal ever came to gather it up, the canister would be hard to miss, for it glistened black and shiny against the colorless desert. Inside he would find a message directed to him, explaining very clearly what the U.S. needed him to do.

The real question was, would the man ever come back? What would he consider more dangerous—leaving the signal out where it would eventually be found, or returning to the signal to gather it up, thus taking the chance of being observed once again?

Inside the control room, the men were evenly split. Half thought the Iraqi would return to the signal. Half thought he would never show his face at the spot again.

26

BAGHDAD, IRAQ
2I20 LOCAL TIME

Aria stared at the gun, a look of disbelief in her eyes. The Kurd nudged the muzzle half an inch closer to her face. In the front seat, the driver pushed on the gas. The Renault sped into the night, bumping across the ruts in the road and banging Aria's head against the low roof of the car.

"Who are you," the Kurd sneered in Arabic. "What are you doing in Iraq? Tell me before I kill you and throw you out to rot in the street!"

Aria's hands trembled uncontrollably as she gripped the basket in her lap. Her eyes almost closed as she started to pray. Under her veil, her chest rose in fear, a feeling of betrayal sweeping over her body. She stared at the gun, the blue steel shining dimly in the light, and wondered desperately where the plan had gone wrong?

The Kurd slid toward her and reached out to pull the cotton veil away from her face. Aria turned to look into his eyes. He stared at her, an awkward and surprised look on his face.

"Answer my question!" he cried after a moment's hesitation.

"My name is Asrar Rahmani," Aria began, her voice almost a whisper. "I live in the city, just south of here. I was only coming into the market. My father is hungry. The fish. The apples—" Aria nodded toward the basket that was sitting on her lap, afraid to move anything more than her head. "I came to the market because we needed some food—"

"Lying daughter of a dog! If you were only out shopping, then why did follow me into this car? And where is your father? I want you to take me to him!"

Aria's head slowly dropped until it was touching her chin. "Who are you?" she whimpered. "Why are you screaming at me? I only came to the market because we needed some food."

"We needed some food." The agreed upon code. It was the second time she had said it. Perhaps he didn't hear.

The Kurd didn't react. The car sped through the city. Taking side roads and alleys, it avoided the road blocks that clogged the main arteries of Baghdad. The driver watched his rearview mirror as much as the road. There was no one behind them. They were not being trailed. He nodded and grunted the news to the Kurd.

The Kurd studied Aria, then lowered the gun and shoved it under the seat. Turning toward the front of the car, he nudged the driver on the shoulder.

"I think she is alright," he said in Kurdish.

The driver looked back through his rearview mirror at the girl. "Yes, she matches the description. She is the one. Tell her now to be calm."

The Kurd turned to Aria, his face still unfriendly but less threatening now. "Okay. That is over. Relax. It's okay."

Aria looked up, her face flushed with anger. She saw that the Kurd was no longer holding the gun. If she felt some relief, it didn't show in her eyes, which flashed with each light that passed by outside.

"Why did you do that!" she demanded. "I followed procedures. I am wearing the agreed upon clothing. I had the basket. The code. I did everything they told me to do. It was pointless and cruel to treat me that way."

The Kurd didn't hesitate to shake his head. "No, my sister. We could not take a chance. What if you had been delayed and questioned. What if you had fallen under suspicion and been interrogated by unpleasant means. The AMAM would turn you into a sputtering fool in a matter of seconds. And after breaking you down, they would have used you as a trap, hoping to capture us all in the tangles of their web. What I did was simple procedure, so get used to it, sister. Life is hard and unpleasant out here on the street."

Aria studied the Kurd for moment, then nodded her head. The car continued to make its way through the city, though more slowly now. It turned and doubled back, then took a series of left-hand turns so as to drive down the same street again. Finally, it came to a four-way intersection, then proceeded straight ahead.

They were now traveling through the south ghetto of the Khalid District, a mass of dingy apartments, fabric-covered windows, and brick shops; a surreal mixture of ancient stone buildings stuffed between rusting aluminum shanties. Hordes of people and domestic animals seemed to live in agreeable ease. Glancing out the window, Aria watched as a short-haired mongrel chased a family of geese down the street. She watched as a group of children, dirty and thin, played wall-ball against a rutted, brick building, their game illuminated by a single dim bulb that hung overhead. She listed to the sounds of the traffic, the honking horns and sputtering engines as drivers accelerated among the people and debris, each of them trying to finish their errands before the restrictions of the curfew set in. Aria then turned to the stranger. "Where are we going?" she asked.

"We have borrowed a small apartment for a couple of days. One of our brothers from Algiers. He owes us a favor. We'll be safe there."

The car began to slow. It turned down an alley hardly wider than the car, then through a back street and around a high cement wall before pulling into a dark and dusty garage. The driver got out to pull the garage door down. The metal door clanged downward on its chain. "Come with me," the Kurdish gunman commanded, climbing out of the seat.

Aria pushed open her door and followed the man inside the building. The apartment was dark. The Kurd turned on only one light. The driver disappeared up a set of narrow stairs. Aria heard him unlock a door, then silent footsteps as he positioned himself by the front window. The Kurd turned to Aria and motioned for her to sit down.

For the next two hours they sat on the floor, eating rice and hot beans while mentally prodding each other. As the darkness grew, and the night air turned cool, each exposed their own motives just enough to show they were real: just enough to build a narrow bridge of trust between their two worlds.

"I only have to get close enough to touch him," Aria whispered as she stared at the Kurd. "Just close enough to pin the transmitter into his clothes. His hat, his lapel, the hem in his jacket. Anything will do. The transmitter is so small, it will be very easy to conceal. But I have to get to him. That is the key."

The Kurd had been watching her closely throughout the entire conversation. It had been only a matter of minutes before he had been taken in. Her beauty, her voice, and her quiet determination had broken down the barriers that normally would have kept him on guard. He liked her right off. She was a rebel at heart. She was loyal, determined, and clearly very smart.

But there was also something more. Something he didn't want to say. Something about her that troubled him now.

He studied her out of the corner of his eyes as he shoved another wad of dark bread into his mouth. "Will you show me the transmitter?" he asked through a mouthful of food.

Aria hesitated, not knowing if she should, then reached into her hair and extracted one of the decorative metal barrettes. Turning it over, she pulled it apart, snapping a tiny metal pin away from the back. She studied it for a moment, then placed it on the floor between her and the Kurd. Carefully, he reached out and picked it up, holding it close to his face.

It was a straight piece of metal, shiny and black, just under two inches long and no thicker than the lead of a pencil. One end had been filed to the sharpness of a pin. The other was smooth and round, with a small indentation that allowed it to snap into place on the back of the barrette.

"You can see," Aria instructed, "it was designed as the clasp on my barrette. I put it in my hair and snap it shut. There is no way to tell what it is. But I am told the transmitter will work for up to seventy-two hours and transmit far enough to be picked up from an aircraft or satellite."

"And what will they do, once the transmitter is in place?"

Aria shook her head. "I don't know," she lied.

"And why are they so interested in Odai Hussein?"

She shook her head and lied once again. "I don't know. They wouldn't tell me. There was no need to know and they felt the less I understood, the more protected I would be."

The Kurd nodded his head, though he had already guessed. The slaughter at Kimisk was well known among the rebels. He chewed another piece of bread. His throat bobbed as he swallowed. "So your only purpose is to get close enough to Odai to pin this key piece of metal on his clothes?"

Aria nodded her head.

"And how will you do that? How will you get near?"

Aria didn't answer. The Kurd nodded his head. "Are you a whore then?" he asked, though he knew she was not.

Aria stared at the floor, a stricken look on her face. "There are other ways," she said simply. "I have papers that identify me as a member of the Turkish press. A small but pro-Muslim newspaper operating out of

Adana. The Turkish embassy, despite their objections, and without knowing why, has been convinced to forward a request for an interview. So far, Odai has been very willing to share his views with the pro-Muslim world. His office told us they would provide an answer by the end of the week."

The Kurd raised an eyebrow, apparently completely unconvinced. "You'll never see him," he said. "He'll never even get near. Credentials with the press, pro-Muslim or not, will not allow the kind of access that will get you to him. Ten minutes on the phone is as close as you'll get. If it were that simple, Odai would already be dead, with a line of pseudo-journalists lined up outside his office door.

"You are clinging, my sister, to a ship full of holes. I am more than surprised that they sent you out here without a more feasible plan. I consider you as having little chance for success."

Aria thought for a moment, then lifted her eyes to meet his. "We didn't have any time to set up anything else. The mission is urgent and there just wasn't time. So what should I do? Just say forget it and leave? We don't have other options! I am the only hope that we have."

The Kurd nodded his head. His eyes softened in the darkness as he finally understood. The two sat in silence. It was growing late and both of them were now feeling very tired. The Shamal continued to blow, scattering dry leaves and walnut shells across the red-tile roof. Aria listened to the wind for a moment, a familiar and haunting sound. It reminded her again of the winter on the mountain.

The Kurd watched her, then leaned back against his chair and said, "You know that I will not be able to help you. My instructions were to bring you here. To help keep you safe. To assist if I can. But as far as getting you to Odai Hussein, I'm afraid I will be little help. I'm not capable of operating here in Baghdad. We have no operatives or system here in the city. Coming here myself was a horrible risk, more dangerous than many of the assault missions I have been on. Much as I would like to, I will not be able to help you. By and large, you understand, you will be on your own."

Aria nodded her head. She already knew that was true. "I understand," she said. "But there is something else. I am seeking some information. Something very important to me."

The Kurd lifted his head, waiting for her to go on.

"I have a little sister—"Aria began to explain.

The Kurd immediately pushed himself off the floor. "I knew it," he cried, throwing his hands into the air. "You are the spitting image of her. I knew it the first time I saw your face in the car. It scared me almost, I thought for a moment you were her. Yes, I knew your sister. I knew her very well."

Aria didn't move. She felt as if she had been kicked in the chest. Her breath became shallow, her throat tight and dry. "She is alive, then?" she whispered with tears in her eyes. "Please—please tell me it is true. Tell me she is alive!"

"Oh, yes." The Kurd smiled. "She is very alive. I haven't seen her for years, but I know where she lives." Aria stared without talking. The Kurd went on to explain. "I knew your little sister when we lived in the camps, before she was taken away. But what was that now—going on almost four years."

"You knew her," Aria said, reaching out to the Kurd, as if touching him would help to bring her sister close. "You know her. Oh yes. But where is she now? Can you take me to her? Please, I am ready to go. I want to see her right now! I'll give you all that I have."

The Kurd looked away, his face clouding with concern. "I cannot do that," he said matter-of-factly. "It is not possible. It can't be done."

"What? But why? What do you want?"

"Nothing, sister. I am not holding out. I am cruel and greedy only when I have interest at stake. But your little sister, there is something about her. Something you obviously don't know."

"What is it? What is it you know?"

"Aria, your sister is working for us. She's been with the rebels since she was a little girl. Several years ago, she was forced into service as a house-maid for the Iraqi security minister. Ever since then, she has been working for the underground resistence. She is now our ears and eyes within the ministry office. And her cover is so deep that I could never make contact. They would never allow me to jeopardize the communication system she has. It would put her in danger. Surely you can see that."

ALONG THE TIGRIS RIVER
220 MILES SOUTH OF BAGHDAD
2151 LOCAL TIME

The American helicopters came in low up the river. Only the whine of their engines and slap of their rotor blades gave any warning of their approach. There was a moonless sky and a partial overcast helped to block out the starlight, leaving the night very dark, which was exactly why the chopper pilots had chosen this time to go. All of the helicopter's external lights were off, making them virtually invisible in the night. Inside the cockpits, the pilots used infrared cameras and night-vision goggles to maneuver along the banks of the river. They followed the slow, muddy water, barely above the tops of the trees, keeping their choppers always pointed in a northwestern direction.

After taking off from Camp Doha, the American outpost in extreme northern Kuwait, the formation of six AH-64 Apache attack helicopters and four MH-60 Pavehawks had initially headed south. Following the sandy coastline along the Persian Gulf, they flew well out of range of Iraq's most powerful search radars. The formation then turned to the east and headed out over the water. After sixty miles, they began a gentle turn back to the north. Approaching the Shatt-al-'Arab, the marsh-laden peninsula that marked the southern border of Iraq, the choppers dropped to only ten feet off the water. They pushed up their speed and made their best time for the river.

For almost forty minutes they flew up the Tigris, penetrating more than one hundred miles into southern Iraq. At a bend in the river, they began to slow down. The river sat low in a steep and narrow valley. Fifty-foot walls of rock and brush passed above the helicopter pilots' heads. On the east side of the river, a goatherd's camp had been set up. Passing over the camp, they saw the prearranged signal, a goat that was tethered along the south side of the fence.

Six of the choppers—two Pavehawks and four of the Apaches—separated themselves from the other choppers in the formation and set up for their approach. Seconds later, they were hovering in the middle of a wet, grassy field used to protect the goats from the heat of the day. The other four choppers circled once, then continued to fly up the Tigris, acting as a decoy in case the formation was being watched by Iraqi search radar.

As the landing helicopters settled into a hover, a line of camouflage netting moved back, pulled against the side of the hill by a series of long hydraulic arms. The choppers moved under the nettling, and quickly shut down their engines. The mesh netting was immediately moved back into place, completely concealing the helicopters under a wrap of tan, brown, and gray. Less than five minutes after the sound of their rotors had first beat the air, the river valley was quiet once again.

The lead chopper pilot unstrapped from his seat and climbed out of his narrow cockpit. Every piece of clothing he wore was black; his flight suit, his gear, even his leather holster and gun. His face and neck were covered with black camouflage paint. His eyes shined in the darkness, red and sullen beads of white against a flat and featureless face. Pulling his helmet up over his sweat-covered hair, he shook off the tension of the low-level flight.

A CIA man was waiting. The intelligence expert extended his hand. "Welcome to Camp Cobra," he said with a smile.

The pilot didn't answer as he took a quick look around.

OFFICE OF THE CHAIRMAN OF
THE JOINT CHIEFS OF STAFF
THE PENTAGON, WASHINGTON, D.C.
1405 LOCAL TIME

The chairman was standing by the side of his desk, anxiously waiting for the call. The secure line softly buzzed. He jammed the receiver to his ear.

"The choppers have been moved up to Camp Cobra," Colonel Wisner announced, his voice scratching and broken through the satellite phone.

General Beck nodded his head. "Any sign of detection?" he worriedly asked.

"Nothing, sir. No hostile indicators at all. Despite the Iraqis' heightened state of alert, the choppers apparently got into the camp without being detected. The decoys returned without incident as well."

"How about from our side?" the general pressed. "Have we been able to keep this thing under wraps? Are you getting any indication of any security leaks? The last thing we need is for this thing to get out."

"Sir, I believe that we have it under control. The number of men who are aware of this mission could be counted on one hand. As you know, even the secretary of defense has been kept in the dark. The security around this mission is almost without precedent. If we can keep it under wraps for the next two or three days, I think that is all that we'll need. "

The general grunted into the phone."Keep me appraised," he demanded. "I want to know every move. And call me as soon as you talk to the girl."

27

Lieutenant David O'Brian, the communications specialist, was back at work inside the C-130 aircraft by five the next morning. Once again, the eavesdropping aircraft circled over the north Saudi desert. For the next two hours, the lieutenant hunched over his console, concentrating his efforts on tracking the phone call that Odai Hussein had received the night before. It was a work of frustration, and the time passed very slowly. Just as he was about to give up in disappointment, his computer broke through. Several minutes later, it spit out the location of the man who had initiated the call.

The lieutenant plotted the coordinates on his map, then frowned as he considered his mistake. He checked the computer printout and plotted again. His pencil pointed to the same spot on the map.

He wiped his sweating hands across the front of his face, then commanded the computer to run the numbers again. The computer spit out the same estimation.

The phone call had come from a satellite over Greenland. A satellite that was used exclusively for calls originating along the east coast of the U.S.

Lieutenant O'Brian nearly choked as he called out across the floor.

"Mr. Churchill, I need to see you. Churchill, get over here, *now!*"

His supervisor strolled with some urgency to the lieutenant's side. The lieutenant pointed to the map, explaining as fast as he could, then handed him the computer printout, which he studied without saying a word. The supervisor read through the figures, then dropped the sheet on the floor.

"How did you get through the scramblers at Project 858?" he asked, unconvinced the lieutenant was right.

"I was able to pick up some of the bleed-over. They were using a skip-code, much like their secure radios, where they take the incoming call and break it into nano-second pieces, then rebroadcast portions over different frequencies at a very fast rate. Simple technology, but as you know, very effective. Once I started to get a handle on the code they use to coordinate the skip frequencies, I was able to detect enough bleed-over to pinpoint which satellite was used."

The supervisor took another look at O'Brian's notes. He had to be sure. He had to be 100 percent certain before he could report this finding back to Dhahran.

After several minutes of study, the supervisor was convinced.

Odai had a man inside the U.S. A man he was controlling. His agent was in place. The words Odai had used began to repeat themselves in his mind.

"The package is there, waiting for you at the hotel."

Without a word the supervisor ran to the communications board and dialed a number to the command post in Dhahran. Within minutes, the White House switchboard was accepting a call from the commanding general in Saudi Arabia. Minutes later, the president had been notified.

BAGHDAD, IRAQ
1020 LOCAL TIME

Aria slept through a good part of the morning, still tired after a restless and fearful night. She pushed herself out of her bed and made her way into the shower, then dressed and sat down on the floor. Listening, she could hear voices and footsteps down the hall. The Kurd and his lieutenant were already awake. She listened to them talking, but couldn't make out what they said. Leaning toward the door, she listened again. The two men were talking in Kurdish. After a few moments of whispering, they went quickly upstairs.

Aria stood up and locked her door, then sat down once again and pulled the now-empty fish basket out from under the bed. Fingering the hidden latch, she lifted the false bottom to reveal the flat cavity that was hidden underneath. There lay the tools she would need for the mission. Very carefully, she extracted the tiny satellite transmitter. It only took her a moment before she had it hooked up, for her days of training were few, but very intense. She unfolded the silver, umbrella-like antennae and connected it to the main unit, then snapped her tiny earpiece connector into its socket. Shoving the earpiece into her right ear, she reached over and turned the radio on, then waited for the unit to synchronize itself to the satellite that spun overhead. After several seconds of static, her status light turned from red to amber, then finally to green. She immediately clicked down on the mike.

"Mother, Dhanna is here," she said simply. Her words were scrambled and data-linked to the satellite in a half-second burst of encrypted static and noise. The message was sent so fast that the source could never be traced, nor the message copied or intercepted in any form.

She waited, expecting a several second delay. It surprised her when the voice immediately came back.

"Say status, Dhanna." The voice was urgent and tight.

"Contact complete. Dhanna secure."

"Copy, secure. Dhanna, stand-by to receive your new instructions."

The radio went silent. Aria frowned. It was not what she had expected to hear. She was only calling Mother because she was supposed to check in. And what did they mean, "new instructions"? What did they want her to do? A sinking feeling grew in the pit of her stomach. A new voice then came through her receiver, more urgent and demanding than the one before. Aria hesitated as the sound of Colonel Wisner's deep voice filled her ear.

"Dhanna," he began. "You are to attempt to make contact today. Repeat, it is extremely important for you to contact the target today."

Aria's face turned pale as a sickening feeling came over her body. A rush of blood flowed to her head and an immediate pain thumped at the back of her neck.

She hesitated, then pressed her transmitter switch. "Negative Mother, unable. Negative contact today. Let me wait to hear word from the Turkish consulate. The interview is our best chance of success. It's important that we stick with the plan."

She released her microphone and waited for her words to be scrambled and data-burst through the sky. Colonel Wisner came back, his voice calm, but demanding. "Dhanna, I repeat. You are to attempt contact today. We have evidence of imminent use. Repeat. Imminent use. We fear he will go into hiding. Things are unraveling at a dangerous speed."

"But how?" she replied. "What am I supposed to do?" The panic and anger were clear in her voice.

"Ask Osman to help you get to the presidential palace. There is an Iraqi colonel there, a member of the presidential body guard. His name is Colonel Samih Bakr Hajazi. He will help you get to the target."

Aria didn't reply. She knew it wasn't that simple. Even with the colonel's help, how would she get to Odai? And how would she find the colonel? She didn't even know where to begin.

A long moment passed. The radio hummed in her ear. When she didn't come back, Mother queried her again.

"Dhanna, confirm you understand your instructions."

"Yes," was all Aria was able to say.

"Report as soon as you can then. Make contact. Use any and all means available. Use your best judgment. We trust you to do the right thing." With a soft click and quiet buzz, the radio hum turned to static as Mother shut the satellite link down.

Aria stared in a daze at her unfamiliar surroundings. She reached up and wiped her hands over her eyes, then pressed her fingers at the back of her neck. Inside, her heart was racing. There were so many questions! So much that didn't make any sense! Why were they pushing up the mission? What was the danger that she didn't know? The whole conversation left her completely confused.

She glanced at the window, where the curtain was only half-drawn, the sky sheening silver in the dry morning heat. She glanced at the clock. Twenty-five after ten. Time was pressing her now. She needed to go.

She was just sitting up to fold in the satellite antennae, when there came a sudden knock at the door. She quickly stood up and walked over to release the chain. The Kurd immediately burst into the room. "Quickly," he cried. "Get your gear. We have to leave."

"What! But why? What do you mean?"

The Kurd turned to the girl, a look of anger and pain in his eyes. "Whoever set up this operation ought to be strung up," he shot back. "Your people are obviously a bunch of incompetent fools! The mission has been screwed from the time you stepped foot in Baghdad."

Aria stood there, unmoving, unsure of what to do. The Kurd

surveyed her equipment and reached down to help her put it away.

"What?" Aria muttered. "What do you mean?"

"We have a military scanner. We can monitor their radios. For the past twelve hours they have been looking for you. They even have pictures. You face has been shown everywhere. The AMAM soldiers at the market remembered you from last night. They reported that you were picked up by two men driving a rust-brown Renault. And now they are checking every flat within a mile radius of this place, for some informant also reported seeing our car. There are a dozen road blocks out and we are in real trouble."

Aria glared at the Kurd with a dumbfounded stare. She opened her mouth as if she would speak, then pushed her hand up to cover her face, her hands trembling against her mouth. The Kurd stared at her in a moment of suspicion, as if she were the one he would blame, then bent to gather the equipment that was still strewn across the floor.

"Quickly, Aria," he said. "We need to go. We need to clean out any trace of our visit, then set out on foot. We will leave the car here. They are looking for it. If we try to get out of here in the Renault, we wouldn't get more than half a mile before getting picked up. With the roadblocks out, we don't have any choice but to walk. We've got to get away, get out and melt into the crowd, get some distance between us and the house."

"That is foolish," Aria stammered. "In the middle of the day—when they are looking for us! What are we going to do, run from house to house? Hide behind garbage cans? We won't last five minutes.

"We should stay here," she concluded. "It is safer than being out on the street."

The Kurd was now shoving Aria's gear into the bottom of the old wicker basket. "Look," he sneered, his patience now running thin. "You do not know the AMAM. This isn't like New York or Chicago, or wherever you live, where you can just shut your door and hope they don't get a search warrant. The AMAM will search every building, and the first place they will look is the garage. They will find our Renault. They will then rip the flat into pieces. Nothing will be left intact. We could not hide here! We would be immediately found!

"So we must get away, find a place to hole up or disappear. We cannot stay here, and seconds now count."

Aria thought for a moment, then nodded her head, convinced now that what he said was true. Quickly, she kneeled to help gather the gear. Taking the pieces of the satellite radio, she lay them carefully under the false floor in the basket, stowing them in the molded Styrofoam container that was hidden under the fish-smelling wicker. After sealing the basket, she stood up and looked around. Grabbing her *ghutra*, she draped it over her head and wrapped it under her chin before lifting it to cover her face. The long, flowing cotton fell over her shoulders and down both sides of her back. She slipped on her sandals and grabbed the fish basket, then began to move toward the door.

"No," the Kurd shot out. "Don't take the basket. Leave it in the garden, along with the others. If they find you with it, they will tear it apart."

Aria turned around, a determined look on her face. "I'm taking it with me," was all she said, her voice deliberate and composed.

"No, Aria, leave it here. At some point, you are going to be stopped. At some point you are going to be questioned. Clever as it is, the false bottom is no stroke of genius, and is almost certainly going to be found. And when they spill your radio across the ground, then what are you going to say? So I want you to leave it. It doesn't matter anymore."

Aria unknowingly tightened her grip on the basket. "No. I am taking it with me. It's my only hope. The only thread that connects me with the outside world. And remember, I still have a job to do—"

"*What!*" the Kurd stammered. "What do you mean, job to do? You no longer have cover! You haven't any hope. The only mission you have is to get yourself out of the country, something that in itself will be almost impossible to do. So what are you thinking? Your mission is through."

Aria turned away from the Kurd. "No," she said simply. "You don't understand. You don't realize what is at stake. If you knew—if I only could tell you—you would know that I still have to try."

The Kurd hesitated just a moment, a desperate and sad look on his face. He started to speak. Aria quickly cut him off. "Osman," she said quickly. "I will have to go on by myself. We are splitting up now. Staying together would be very foolish."

The Kurd stared again as he considered what she said, the look in his eyes betraying his surprise. She seemed so determined to strike out on her own, and it was not at all what he had expected to hear.

"No, Aria," he shot back. "Stay with me. It would be better if we were together. If we can make our way to the bus station, we might still get out of here. And once we get to the northern territories, we will be among friends. That is where I will be able to help you. So stay with me. I am your only hope."

Aria took a step toward the Kurd and reached out to touch his arm. "Osman," she said as she studied his face, noting the coal blackness of his eyes. "I am grateful for your help. You know that I am. I would not have come even this far without you. But we need to separate ourselves. They are looking for three persons, two men and one girl, so traveling together is the last thing we should do. I'm not going north, and there is nothing you can do for me here. By your own admission, you know that is true."

The Kurd thought for a moment, then nodded his head. "What are you going to do then?" he questioned.

Aria studied the street, which could be seen through the half-open blinds of the bedroom window. Her face drew tight, her forehead wrinkling into creases. He watched her eyes as they narrowed and burned.

With a sudden turn of her head, Aria made up her mind. "I have an idea," she said simply. "Something I have thought of before."

The Kurd watched her a moment, not knowing what to say. Shrugging his shoulders, he decided not to press any further. He glanced at his watch, then turned from the girl. "Let's go then," he muttered as he moved toward the door.

"Osman, wait. There is something." The Kurd came to a stop.

Walking to the bedstand, Aria picked up a pencil and paper. Writing quickly, she scribbled a note in Arabic, then folded the paper into a tight, little square. With a pause in her voice, she took half a step toward the Kurd. "Osman," she said, "can I ask you? Can I beg you to do something for me?"

With a barely perceptible motion, the Kurd nodded his head.

"Please." Aria was begging now, with tears in her eyes. "Find my sister. Give her this message for me." Aria passed the folded piece of paper to the Kurd. "These are directions to a barren lot on the outskirts of the city. It is far off the main road, not more than three kilometers from here. Tell her to meet me. Tell her I will be waiting for her tomorrow night at exactly seven P.M. Will you find her, Osman? Will you tell her for me?"

"Yes," he muttered. "I will try. I do not know how, but yes, I will try."

Aria reached out to touch the Arab's leathery hand. "Help her if you can. She will need you. It is asking so much, I know. I have no right to beg this of you. But if you can help me, if you can do this one thing, if you can get her to this spot, I will take her from there. And I will never forget you. I will always remember. But my gratitude is the only thing that I have to offer."

The Kurd stared at the folded piece of paper. With a sigh, he shoved it deep into his pocket, then quickly turned for the door.

"Let's get out of here," he muttered. "Every moment that passes is one we will need."

They stepped from the room and out into the dim hallway, where Osman's lieutenant was waiting for them, anxious and fretting. Osman approached the front window and pushed back the blind to study the street that passed in front of the flat, which was crowded with shoppers and children and dogs. No soldiers or policemen were in sight, and only an occasional car weaved its way down the narrow drive. He shifted his body to study the other side of the street.

"What about the back way?" Osman asked his lieutenant.

"There is nothing there," the other man replied. "Beyond the back wall, it leads out to an open field, then through a schoolyard and down to the market. It is barren and not well-traveled, and we would draw attention to ourselves by going that way. We would be better to stay near the street, out in the crowd and along the main alleys."

The Kurd pointed to a Fiat not more than forty meters down the road, which was parked in front of a small vegetable market.

"What do you think?" he asked his companion.

The man studied the car for a moment. "I can do it," he replied matter-of-factly. "Four or five minutes is all it would take."

"Alright, that's what we will do." Turning to the girl, the Kurd started to say, "There is a bus stop not two kilometers from here. If you follow—"

Aria cut him off. "No matter. I won't be going there."

The Kurd paused, a wondering look on his face. He thought about arguing, but knew it wouldn't do any good. Reaching out, he took her hand. "Little sister, be careful," he muttered.

"Thank you, Osman," was all she replied.

Turning to his companion, the Kurd pulled back the door.

The two men stepped out of the flat and onto the street, neither one of them turning to look back. Aria stood by the open door.

Seconds later, they were approaching the Fiat. Osman walked around to the driver's side door. A black sedan approached from the south side of the street, driving recklessly up the narrow road. It slowed only slightly as it passed the two men. As the sedan moved on, Osman reached into his pocket and pulled out a locksmith pin. Seconds later, he had the driver's door open. Climbing in, he reached over and unlocked the passenger side. The other man jumped in and immediately disappeared under the dashboard, where he went to work to hotwire the car. The street was busy with shoppers and children at play. A man with a donkey and cart of firewood clanged his way from a side alley, the donkey's bell ringing noisily down the narrow street. A group of three women emerged from a small shop and walked toward the Fiat. Aria involuntarily sucked in her breath. The women passed the car and hurried down the street, laughing and calling to each other. Osman remained in the car, a disinterested look on his face.

Aria watched from the deep shadows of the narrow, tile-covered porch, waiting for the women to pass by while praying the Fiat would sputter to life.

It was then that she heard the sound of the approaching truck. It came down the road at a slow and deliberate pace, its powerful engine rumbling heavy and low. Immediately, her instincts came alive. The truck was traveling too slowly, and she knew that was wrong. A deep-brown army deuce came into view, making its way bullylike down the crowded street, scattering chickens and children before it. The blood in Aria's veins started to rush to her head. She stepped carefully back into the house and pulled the door behind her, leaving it open just enough so that she could watch.

The sound of air-brakes hissed through the desert air, then the *thump* of a slamming truck door.

"You! There! Step out of the car!" The voice was harsh and angry. Aria slid further back behind the almost-closed door and held her breath, all the time straining to hear what was said.

"I say you, swine! Out of the car!"

Aria moved forward and peeked through the wedge of sunlight to see a single soldier standing near the front of his truck, which was positioned alongside the Fiat. She saw the black beret and thick armband. AMAM. The soldier was staring at Osman and motioning angrily with his hands, commanding the Kurd to get out of the car. Osman sat unmoving in the front seat, a confused look on his face. He lifted his arms to show his hands, a gesture of obedience but also confusion. The soldier took another step toward the Fiat. Osman glanced quickly down at his feet. The soldier stopped and lowered his weapon. Aria watched for a moment, knowing Osman and his lieutenant were through. It wasn't until then that she made her decision.

Quickly, she stepped out of the house and onto the street, walking deliberately toward the soldier. Reaching up, she pulled the veil away from her face, exposing everything from her eyes to her neck. She shot a quick glance toward Osman, who was staring at her with a look of panicked disbelief. He lifted his hands to motion her back, then started to get out of the car. Aria walked toward the guard, a determined look on her face. Time seemed to freeze as she closed the gap between them. Aria stared at the soldier, who looked up to check the approaching girl. The Kurd didn't move, frozen now in his car, both of his hands gripping the black steering wheel. The soldier studied the girl with a puzzled stare. Quickly, all too quickly, she pulled the shawl over her face and looked away, drawing even more attention to herself. The recognition slowly spread across the soldier's dark eyes. Aria turned and looked down the street, moving behind the street peddler and his donkey cart full of wood.

The soldier lowered his gun to his hip, knowing that she was the girl. Inside the car, the Kurd didn't move as he realized Aria's intention of sacrificing herself. Pointing the gun skyward, the soldier stepped away from the Fiat and toward Aria. The Kurd let out a horrified groan and raised his face toward the sky. The Fiat sputtered once and then caught with a purr. The soldier ignored it as he followed the girl.

"You! Woman! Don't move," he screamed in Aria's direction.

At that moment Aria started to run. Lowering her head, she sprinted down the street, dodging between baskets and barrels of food. The soldier set out after the girl, the barrel of his rifle bouncing against the side of his hip. Osman sat for one stunned moment, then pushed on the gas. The soldier didn't look back as the car sped away.

Aria glanced over her shoulder to see the Fiat disappear, then stumbled over a huge sack of rice. The soldier was on top of her in less than an instant, shoving her head into the rough cement and jamming her arm behind her back. Aria let out a cry of pain. The soldier jerked her arm once again. Reaching over, he called into the radio microphone that was clipped to his shirt. Moments later, half a dozen other soldiers arrived. Screaming at each other, they bound Aria and threw her into the back of the brown army truck.

THE WHITE HOUSE
0505 LOCAL TIME

General Beck left his office and nearly ran down the hallway, then took the elevator down to the White House Situation Room. The president was waiting, along with the rest of his security staff. The lights were dim and subdued, the room illuminated mainly from the backlit maps on the wall. The general took his seat around the huge oak table, along with the rest of the national security staff.

In the background, along three sides of the room, were chairs for the myriad aides and assistants, communications specialists, and military advisors. A group of technicians manned a bank of ringing phones. Another group monitored a row of computers. The status of United States military units around the world blinked from a display overhead. On a huge silver screen to the right, a computer-generated image displayed the location of every seaborne aircraft carrier, fighter squadron, and bomber wing. Along the near wall, a row of televison screens showed various newscasts from major cities around the world, with translations in English captioned at the bottom of the screen.

Brent Hillard, the NSA, sat near the head of the table. His eyes were sour, his face tight as stone. As General Beck sat down, the NSA turned to the president and began to review the SITREP, or Situation Report.

"As you can see, Mr. President, the national security team is finally assembled. In addition, your new vice president is also accounted for. He departed Miami just over an hour ago and is expected to touch down at Andrews in the next thirty minutes. He has agreed to lead the delegation to Europe and the Middle East. They should be on the ground only long enough to refuel and receive your instructions. He will depart for Europe no later than noon.

"Our present status, Mr. President, is this: Our military and civilian forces have been moved to THREATCOM ALPHA, our highest state of antiterrorism alert. That is not at our discretion, sir, but an automatic response to the situation. Our command and control checklist requires moving our forces to ALPHA status. However, sir, should you deem it prudent, you can at any time decide to back our forces to a lower state of readiness."

General Beck immediately lifted his hand. "Sir, recommend maintain present status. We can look at it again as the situation develops."

The president nodded his head to concur.

The NSA went on. "Sir, the B-1 squadron has been tasked. It is preparing for the mission, which will launch sometime tonight.

"State has been in touch with the heads of each of our primary allies. We have advised them what you intend to do. But as of yet, we have not been in contact with"—Hillard glanced down at the notes he had scratched on the red checklist—"the presidents of Russia, Poland, Canada, and—"

Brooks abruptly cut him off. "Russia! You haven't got a hold of Chernigov yet!"

"I'm afraid not, sir. Apparently he's boar hunting somewhere on the southern Crimean Peninsula. At least that's what they are telling us. I think it's at least equally likely that he's holed up in the Ukrainian sanatorium once again.

"At any rate, we have been in communication with the prime minister and expect to get through to the president within the half hour."

The president leaned back in his chair. "Okay," he replied. "What about nations in the Middle East?" The president turned quickly to his secretary of state. "What about it, Patty? What did the Israelis say?"

The secretary was very quick to answer. "Sir, I have been assured by Prime Minister Shalev that they will sit tight. Though, like us, they have increased their state of readiness, he has promised to make no provocative gestures or statements.

"But I have to tell you, sir, the Israelis are very, very concerned. It would be hard for us to underestimate how dangerous they perceive the situation to be. The prime minister is seeking for your assurance that—"

"Listen to me, Patty," the president interrupted. "Get Shalev on the phone. Tell him to stay out of the way. Tell him that we will not leave him hanging. Surely he knows us better than that.

"But tell him this too. If he escalates tensions in any way, if he seeks to take advantage of our situation, then I will screw his head to the wall. The last thing we need—the last thing I need—is to worry about the Israelis muddling the waters of this stinking sewer."

The secretary nodded her head. The president went on. "Now tell me, madam secretary, when will the Iraqi foreign minister be here?"

The secretary nodded toward the door. "He's here, sir," she said. "He was in New York at the UN headquarters. We summoned him as soon as we heard. He is waiting upstairs in the White House. We could go up there, sir, or I can summon him if you'd prefer."

"Get him down here," the president ordered.

Five minutes later, Mr. Abdullah Abbas, the Iraqi foreign minister, was escorted into the command center by a young marine. The soldier led him into the room, then turned crisply and walked back out the door. The Iraqi stood in dismay, wondering what he should do. With nervous and darting eyes, he glanced at the faces that were now staring at him. A sudden hush fell over the room. Every eye watched as the foreign minister stood awkwardly near the door, searching for an understanding face in the crowd.

The secretary of state leaned forward to whisper into the president's ear. "Sir," she muttered, "shouldn't we step into the conference room? It would be more private. And easier to talk."

"No." The president shook his head. "What I have to say can be said in the open."

The secretary didn't move for a moment, then slowly pushed herself up from her seat. The Iraqi caught her eye as she rose from her chair. She walked forward and motioned for the Iraqi to come. The two walked toward the head of the table, where the president was waiting. The president stared coldly as the Iraqi approached. Extending his hand, the minister questioned in a hurried and accented voice.

"Mr. President, what is the meaning of this? Why have you summoned me at this hour of the day?"

The president cut the minister off. "Save your questions for later. While you're here, I want you to shut up and listen to me."

The Iraqi minister's face hardened. It was not at all what he had come to expect. "Mr. President," he said, "I'm afraid that I do not understand."

"Mr. Foreign Minister, let me get straight to the point. We know—

we have absolute proof that Saddam Hussein is directly responsible for last week's downing of Air Force One."

The Iraqi's face tightened into an incredulous frown. "Mr. President, that simply is not possible. You know that—"

"I want you to know," the president quickly went on, cutting the minister off in mid-sentence, "that I consider the downing of Air Force One a flagrant act of war. I consider it as hostile an action as we have ever in our history endured. It was as egregious as the attack on Pearl Harbor. Far more dangerous than any Russian missiles in Cuba. Indeed, Mr. Minister, I have already determined that mere words can't adequately convey what a despicable thing you have done."

The president paused and left his phrase hanging in the air, the intended threat subtle, but nonetheless clear.

The Iraqi squared his shoulders and lifted his chin. "But, Mr. President, it is a vicious and unbearable lie. I can assure you with every fiber of my soul, that my president, the great leader of Iraq, had absolutely no knowledge of the aircraft downing—"

Brooks cut in for the last time. "Mr. Abdullah Abbas, we know that it was Iraq who instigated the attack. We have direct and irrefutable proof of your president's culpability. Indeed, we have been watching and listening for several days now. And the link to Hussein is perfectly clear.

"In addition, Mr. Foreign Minister, we know of the attack at Kimisk. We know that Hussein used a new biological weapon. And we know he has been speaking with and giving orders to an agent here in the States."

The foreign minister's face clouded over. A look of genuine disbelief showed in his eyes. "No, Mr. President, that could not be true. Surely you don't really believe what you said!"

"Yes, Mr. Abdullah Abbas, that's exactly what I believe. And now let me tell you what I want you to do. I want you to creep back to your nation and give Hussein this message for me.

"First, and this is *very* important, I want you to tell Hussein that if he so much as flexes a muscle, if we have any hint of any terrorist activity in our country, if we even smell an intent to use the biological weapon, your nation is finished, Mr. Minister. It will no longer exist. We will wipe Iraq off the map and leave a radiate hole in the desert so hot it will glow for the next thousand years. I am completely serious, Mr. Minister. I will wipe Iraq off the earth.

"I'm telling you now that a flight of fully loaded B-1s will be airborne within hours. The aircraft will meet up with fighter escorts and set up in an orbit just south of Cypress, less than a forty-minute flight out of Baghdad. There they will wait for my word. And they will go, Mr. Minister, they will blow you away. You. Your president. Your country. One flight of B-1s is all it would take. So tell Mr. Hussein to put his bio-weapon away. That is the single most important thing you will tell him today."

The Iraqi took a step back from the president, then turned as if he would leave. The president stopped him with a raise of his hand. "I am not finished, Mr. Foreign Minister," he said.

"I also want you to tell Hussein that we demand an immediate and unconditional disclosure of each and every one of your nuclear, biological, and chemical sites, so they can be targeted and completely destroyed, once and for all. No more screwing around with UN inspectors. No more hassling or yanking our chain. No more secreting biomaterial in a warehouse or bunker, then calling it a Presidential Palace. No more broken promises to the UN. After all these years, we are weary of it.

"Third, and this is also important. I want Saddam Hussein to step down. I want him to relinquish his power. I will give him seven days to organize a transition. Seven days to choose a replacement and step aside. But that is all. Seven more days of Hussein is all I will endure.

"We have an air force jet waiting at Andrews to fly you to Iraq. Now go. Meet with your president and tell him what I said. I will expect an answer by the end of the day."

The Iraqi scowled with anger as the bile rose in his throat. The demands went so far beyond insulting, it was an affront to even consider the words. He lifted a finger and stabbed back at the man.

"Mr. President," he said, his voice firm with conviction. "You can sit here and bully. You can sit here and make threats. But in the end, it will do you no good. And are you so blind to the fact, Mr. President, that you are the one who has continued with this insistent and never-ending harassment of our people, killing our children with your mind-less embargo, starving our mothers in the street? If you had not cut off the import of food and medicine, the most basic of needed supplies—if you had not ripped out the heart of our people by cutting us off from a world we need to survive—if you had not crippled our nation and left us one hundred billion dollars in debt—if you had not fouled the soul of Islam with your presence in Arabia, all in an effort to feed your raging pride, then perhaps this event would not have happened. I have to feel that you share in the blame."

President Brooks' face turned crimson as he stared at the man. A moment of dread passed between them before the president said, his voice quivering and barely under control, "I am tired of talking to you, Mr. Abdullah Abbas. I have told you what I want you to do. Now go. Your aircraft is waiting."

The minister steeled his eyes on the president, then turned to stalk from the room. But before he could go, the president called out to the man. "B-61, Mr. Foreign Minister. Do you know what that is?"

The minister didn't stop, choosing to ignore the president's words. He was insulted and angry. He had no use for the man. And, yes, he knew what a B-61 was.

IRAQI PRESIDENTIAL MOBILE COMMAND CENTER EASTERN SUBURB OF BAGHDAD 1450 LOCAL TIME

The trailer looked like any other semi as it bumped along the street. It made its way slowly through the city, attempting to blend in with the autos around it, nothing more than a silver and black semi-trailer en route to some unnamed warehouse or industrial center.

The back of the trailer had been converted into a mobile command post, with a long conference table and enough chairs to sit twenty men. In addition, the trailer provided all of the necessities to keep the Iraqi president hidden and impossible to locate, but never out of touch. Underneath a false ceiling, the trailer bristled with an array of communication antennas. The walls were both sound- and bullet-proof. A tiny hutch provided refreshment and the back wall could slide forward to provide a compact, but still comfortable, bedroom. Cool air blew down from the overhead vents. A small fan whirled from the front of the room.

Saddam Hussein stood at the head of a mahogany table, with his ministers and generals around him. The table ran half the length of the trailer. Not all of the men sat at the table. A few were relegated to the back of the room, where they sat staring uncomfortably at the floor. The president's bodyguards stood in each corner, their weapons armed and held in the ready position.

The president turned to a general who was standing near the front of the room. A thin piece of rope had been stretched around his neck and looped at the back of his belt before being wrapped around his hands. Saddam thumped a nightstick against the palm of his hand.

"Tell me!" the president screamed. "Tell me, where is my son?"

Hussein took a step forward, his voice suddenly calm and under control, though his eyes burned with anger. He leaned toward the petrified general. "Tell me, Abbu," he almost whispered. "Tell me, what have you done?"

"Sir," the general stammered. "I swear by everything holy, I do not know. I do not know where Odai is."

Hussein lifted his arm and brought down the stick, catching the general square in the face with a sickening thud. Blood splattered across the near wall, like dots of red paint. It splashed across the face of the nearest minister, who didn't dare reach up and wipe it away.

His nose crushed, the general wavered, then dropped to his knees. A trail of blood began to run down his chin and drip onto the gray carpet. The president raised his arm once again, holding it near the top of his head, then grabbed the general by the hair and lifted his face. "I want to know, you traitorous coward! Who authorized the attack on the village? And what have you done with my son? Where have you taken him? What have you done?"

The general began to open his mouth. The president jerked on his hair. "The truth, my brother, and I let you live."

"My *Rais*," the general whimpered. "Never in my life have I attempted to deceive you. Never in any way. You are the chosen. I live and die by your orders. Believe me, *Rais*, I wallow in devotion."

"Then tell me."

"Sir, I have not seen him. I do not know where he is. I swear to you, I have no idea."

The stick came down once again, striking the general across the right ear, splitting it nearly in two. The man fell to the floor, then rolled onto his side. The president nodded to one of his bodyguards who immediately reached down and lifted the general, dragging him up on his feet. The general's head bobbed, his neck muscles incapable of holding its weight.

The general didn't wait to be asked another question. "*Sayid*," he muttered. "It was your son who ordered the attack on Kimisk. He used his own people. He didn't even discuss it with me. And now, he has gone into hiding. I haven't seen him for almost two days. But I know it was him. He didn't hide his intentions."

The president's face burned with rage. He lifted the stick once again. "You lie," he screamed at the top of his lungs. "You lie, every one of us knows it was you."

"No, *Rais*. It had to be Odai."

The stick came down at the base of his neck. The room filled with another sickening *crunch* as the vertebrae were crushed under the blow. Again, the general's body dropped to the floor. He lay without moving while Hussein paced back and forth by his head, occasionally brushing his boot through the general's hair.

No one moved. No one breathed. The air hung heavy with fear and the impending death of the man.

The president looked down at his general once again, staring into his eyes to make sure he was still conscious. Hussein moved his head from side to side. The general followed his movements with flickering eyes. "General Abbu Nedal-amal," Hussein said. "You have lied to me again. You have shamed us all, General Abbu Nedal-amal. You have shamed us all with your lies."

"No, my *Rais*," the general was able to mutter. "It is you who have shamed us. It is you and your son."

The words hung in the air. Hussein stopped in his tracks, then looked to the guard. A single shot was fired. The general was dead.

The room sat in horrible silence. Each of the men, each of the ministers and generals, stared at the president with fearful stares and broken hearts. Each of them knew that it could have easily been them. And worse, they knew the general had spoken the truth.

WASHINGTON, D.C.
1137 LOCAL TIME

The former prisoner Rahsid Abdul-Mohammad checked into the Reston Holiday Inn for only one night. By early morning, he would be back in New York. After signing for his room, he asked if there was a package for him, and was relieved when the clerk handed him a small air-freight box. He noted the return address and postmark. The parcel had been sent from the Federal Express office at Madrid's international airport.

Taking the package up to his room, Abdul-Mohammad placed it over the heat vent and turned on the heat, having been instructed to keep the package warm. He undressed, showered, then went out for something to eat.

After returning to his room, he carefully opened the package, where he found three small, silver canisters. They were round and metal, about the size of a ruler, with electronic timers and tight rubber seals. He glanced at his watch, then picked the canisters up and headed out to his rental car.

It was a forty-minute drive through the city. The first place he went was the National Cathedral, where he followed a group of German tourists inside. He gawked at the cavernous structure for an appropriate amount of time, then made his way to one of the bathrooms. He sat in a stall until the bathroom was empty, then quickly went to work.

It took only seconds to push the first canister through the baseboard air conditioning vent. When it popped open to release its deadly vapor, virus-infested air would be forced through the entire cooling system. And it would take only one part virus to one billion parts air.

The next stop Abdul-Mohammad made was to the George Washington Park, located just off the Potomac River in downtown D.C. He strolled through the park for several minutes before finding an appropriate spot. Deep in the forest, thirty yards back from the river, was a muddy and moss-covered drainage pool, surrounded by brush and grass up to his knees. Reaching down, he set the timer, then slipped the second container just barely under the mud. In thirty-six hours, the canister would open. Soon after, dead animals would litter the ground. The flies and mosquitos would carry the virus from there.

Returning to his car, the Iraqi made one final stop, at the city's main water purification facility. There he planted the third canister in the city's water supply, something that proved very easy to do, for he simply had to throw it over the fence. There was no security. No guards and no checkpoints. It took less time than he had even been briefed.

The Iraqi then made his way back to the hotel, where he made another quick international call, confirming to his master the job was now done. He was surprised at how much detail the *Sayid* wanted to know, insisting on being told the exact whereabouts of the three canisters in the city. Abdul-Mohammad told him everything, describing the locations with precision and detail. Apparently satisfied, the Iraqi leader had simply hung up the phone, leaving Abdul-Mohammad listening to a harsh dial tone.

* * *

Sitting at a desk in a private villa on the outskirts of Baghdad, Odai Hussein sat back and smiled. The prisoner had done well. He would let his family live.

Between the infestations at the cathedral, the city water, and the park, the disease would reach what his scientists considered critical mass. From that point on, there would be no chance of containment. Twenty-four hours after the canisters opened, perhaps half a million people would be dead, including every government official who attended the vice president's funeral.

And it wouldn't end there. The virus would be just getting started.

DYESS AIR FORCE BASE, TEXAS
0610 LOCAL TIME

The phone started to ring. It took him a moment to rouse himself, for Lieutenant Colonel Jake "Mad Dog" Chambers was a very deep sleeper. On the fourth ring, he finally rolled over and fumbled with the receiver before placing it next to his ear.

"Ya, what is it?"

"Sir, is this Lieutenant Colonel Chambers?"

"Ah—yes it is," Chambers replied in a thick voice, though his brain was now bursting awake.

"Sir," the voice went on. "This is the Wing Command Post. General Summers is holding to speak with you."

Chambers immediately rolled onto the side of his bed and turned on the nightstand light. A short burst of adrenaline pumped through his body. His wife rolled over, then sat up with a start. Chambers rubbed at his eyes and reached for a pencil and paper.

Half a second later, the general's voice broke through the line. "Mad Dog, this is General Summers."

"Yes, sir."

"How you feeling Jake? Are you awake? Do you need me to give you some time?"

"Ahh, no sir, I'm awake and feeling just fine."

"Good. Okay. Here's the deal, Jake. Our wing has been tasked with a LONGBOW mission. I have the execute order in my hand."

The general paused to let his squadron commander think. He

wanted to make sure the lieutenant colonel had time to digest this information before he told him what he wanted him to do.

After several seconds of silence Lt Colonel Chambers replied, "Yes, sir, LONGBOW. I understand. I will be right in."

"No, Mad Dog," the general replied. "I want you to fly it. You'll be the mission commander. You'll be formation lead. So I want you to stay home for the next twelve hours or so. Get some sleep if you can, though I understand if you don't. But at any rate, I want you to rest. Be in here at exactly eighteen hundred tonight, and when you come, come ready to fly."

Lt Colonel Chambers felt a shiver run through his body. He quickly brushed his hand through his dark hair as he listened to his boss on the phone. His wife also felt the light shudder in his back, and immediately became concerned. It had been her experience that early morning phone calls weren't ever good news.

"Okay, sir," Chambers replied. "I will stay here in crew rest. I'll be in at six P.M."

"Good. The other members of your flight are also being notified. You'll have Snake and Dingo. And probably Clancy. Should be a pretty good crew. Colonel Harris, your ops officer is already in here at the command post. We'll take care of all the pre-mission planning. All you have to do is show up and fly."

"And the jets, sir?"

"Your B-1s are being loaded even as we speak. Just go back to bed. Like I said, rest if you can. Sleep all through the day, for it might be as long as a thirty-hour mission. Crew show time is eighteen hundred. Briefing at eighteen-oh-five, you'll have about an hour to go over the plan. Take off is scheduled for nineteen-fifteen, local. And tell Cindy you won't be coming home tonight."

AIR FORCE TWO
OVER THE NORTHERN ATLANTIC
1610 WASHINGTON TIME

Ted Hardy, the new vice president, had enjoyed the position for less than seventy-two hours. He sat in the huge reclining chair near the front of the aircraft. He shifted in his seat, then glanced at his watch, which showed just a little after four in the afternoon. Reaching down, he set the time ahead by five hours. He was due to touch down at

Heathrow by midnight, London time, just under three hours away.

He turned across the aisle toward Michael Crosby, who was resting his huge face in his hands while staring gloomily down the wide center aisle. For the past five hours, the two men had been sitting together, trying not to keep each other awake. But though the flight from D.C. had been generally quiet, neither had relaxed enough to get any sleep, something they would regret since they had to work through the night.

As the vice stared at Crosby, a telephone chimed lightly in the armrest next to the cabin wall. A swirl of butterflies danced in the vice president's chest.

"Yes," the vice president answered

"Ted, it's Andrew," the voice on the other end called out. The satellite link buzzed and the encryption system added even more static, making the voice seem weak and very far away.

"Yes, Mr. President. What is the word from Hussein?"

"Haven't heard anything from him yet. Not a word."

"Okay, Mr. President. And what about the girl?"

"She's been advised of the situation. But we haven't heard back."

There was a slight buzz as Air Force Two cut through a high wall of cirrus clouds. The moisture in the freezing vapor built up static on the aircraft's skin, causing a noisy electrostatic discharge. The president waited a moment to let the static noise pass, then continued, "I've got the times for you, Ted. Are you ready to copy?"

The vice president grunted and picked up his pencil, then reached down and opened a black leather folder. "Okay, sir. I'm ready."

The president began. "The B-1 squadron has been notified and will depart Texas at seven-fifteen P.M., central. They will be in the area by early in the morning."

The vice was scribbling the numbers in the chicken scratch he called writing while he listened to the president on the phone.

"Okay, sir," he said when the president quit talking. "I have that. Now has State worked out an appropriate schedule?"

"Yes, Ted. The people here will pass it on to the flight crew and your staff, but basically, this is what we have planned. You will meet with the British prime minister there at Heathrow. The German chancellor will meet with you there as well. You will describe for them our intentions. Reiterate that the B-1s will *only* attack if we have cause. They are not on a preemptive mission. However, should we find any evidence that Saddam is bent on using his biological weapon, tell them to look out, for we will not hold back.

"After briefing the chancellor and prime minister, you will travel on to Cairo, then swing up to Israel. Your final stop will be with the king in Saudi. By tonight, you should have had opportunity to hit all of the main players. Those you can't brief personally, we will brief on the phone. And remember, some of them will try to persuade us to take another course. To them, I have this reply: We are simply advising them of our intentions, not asking in any way for their support. Do you understand, Mr. Vice President? I am absolutely determined in our cause."

The vice nodded and muttered agreement into the phone.

"Once you finish your briefings, you will return immediately," the president concluded. "I want you back in D.C. as soon as you can."

DYESS AIR FORCE BASE, TEXAS
1900 LOCAL TIME

As Lt Colonel Chambers stepped off the crew van, he was met by a wall of blistering, dry air. It was summer in west Texas, and though it was getting on in the evening, the temperature on the aircraft parking ramp was still above one hundred degrees. The colonel began to sweat underneath his Nomex flight suit, tiny drops of perspiration running down the sides of his ribs. He and the other members of his flight stepped off the bus, threw their flight gear over their backs, stuffed foam plugs into their ears, and began to walk toward their jets.

The three B-1Bs stood dark and menacing at the end of the ramp, amid a blaze of maintenance lights and armored jeeps. A squad of security forces guarded the jets. The airmen stood rigid and serious, braced against the blustering prairie wind, unmoving as they guarded their charges. Their M-16s were slung in the ready position as they suspiciously watched the crew unload their gear from the bus. The B-1s' engines were already running, their horrible whine shattering the air. A crew chief was standing next to each of the aircraft.

As Mad Dog approached his aircraft, the crew chief turned to salute. The colonel was loaded with gear, so did not salute in reply. The chief jogged to the colonel's side and leaned forward to yell into his ear to be heard above the sound of the engines.

"She's ready, sir. All set to go."

The colonel gave a quick thumbs up, then nodded to the crew, who quickly disappeared inside the rumbling jet.

Mad Dog climbed into the pilot's seat and began to strap in. The other pilot, Captain Rattle, who everyone called Snake, began to climb into the ejection seat beside him. They slipped on their helmets and tightened their seat straps. Behind them, just aft of the bulkhead, the two Weapons System Officers were doing the same thing. It would take several minutes for them all to get settled in. Colonel Chambers was just strapping a checklist around his left thigh when he heard an awe-struck call from the back.

"Look at that guys!" the WSO called out. He sounded astonished. And a little bit scared.

The colonel stopped short and didn't move. His mind shut down for a second before starting again. He immediately knew what the WSO was talking about. He glanced over at Snake, then keyed his microphone switch.

"What you got there, Clancy? Which bay are they in?"

"This is so unbelievable. I mean, as many times as we have practiced, I never thought—I swear I never thought I would actually see this!"

For a moment the crew didn't respond. A quick vision flashed in the colonel's head. What they were doing had been done only twice before. Only twice in the history of man.

He shook his head. "Okay, Clancy. Enough of the Alice in Wonderland stuff. We've got a mission, so let's not get too excited. Now tell me, which bay are they in?"

The WSO was studying his computer display, which indicated the location and status of each of their weapons. He stared at the screen for a long moment more, before keying his mike once again.

"Intermediate and aft bay, sir," he shot back, a now determined edge in his voice. "Bottom station. Right where they should be. "

"And confirm they are B-61s?"

Another short pause, and then, "Yes, sir. B-61s. Five low-yield nukes. Two hundred kilotons each."

Mad Dog didn't move as the reality hit him. Despite the heat, a cold chill ran down his spine. He reached into his calf pocket and pulled out a squeeze bottle of ice water and took a long drink. His stomach tightened up as the water dropped into his gut. Again, he glanced over at Snake. The captain was waiting, studying the look on his face. Mad Dog Chambers sipped at the water once more, then jammed it back into his leg pocket.

Reaching for the control stick, he nodded his head. The captain keyed the radio mike.

"Dyess ground, Bat One to taxi. No flight plan. Due regard." The B-1s had not, and would not, file a flight plan. No one needed to know where they were going tonight.

Chambers began to push up the power before the ground controller replied. "Bat One flight, clear to taxi. Your choice of runway. No need to contact tower. You are cleared to take off."

Chambers twice keyed his radio switch, an unspoken reply that he had heard the controller and would comply. The massive jet began to move slowly forward. Three minutes later, it lifted into the air, followed quickly by the other two wingmen.

The three B-1s would not take the most direct route to the hold point over Cypress, but instead one that would allow them to stay over international waters, a necessary precaution to conceal their position. For the next thirteen hours, they would make their way over the Atlantic to the Straits of Gibraltar, then through the Med to a point on the southern tip of the island. A convoy of fighters would then meet the B-1s and take up protective positions above their wings.

The formation would then descend to five hundred feet and wait in its orbit to hear from the Man.

PRESIDENTIAL PALACE
BAGHDAD, IRAQ
0100 LOCAL TIME

Odai Hussein slipped into the darkened office. The drapes were pulled over the enormous round windows. The room was heavy with smoke and the smell of deeply oiled wood. A small reading lamp on his father's desk was the only illumination in the room. Saddam Hussein was leaning back in his chair, his eyes closed, his arms clasped across his thick chest. The younger Hussein pushed back the huge double doors and silently entered the room, accompanied by two of Saddam's personal guards. The guards posted themselves at the door. Odai made his way across the thin Persian rug, the ancient floorboards creaking under the weight of his step. Saddam listened to his approach, but didn't open his eyes.

"My son," he said, his voice thick with despair. "Come in. Sit down. I am relieved you are here."

Odai did as his father told him, positioning himself on a squat wooden couch on the side of his father's desk. The president swiveled his chair and opened his eyes. He turned to his son, his face dull and lifeless. After several hours of thought, he had decided what he would do. Odai looked at his father and locked onto his eyes as Saddam wearily pushed himself up in his chair.

"Odai," he said, his voice heavy with grief, "you are my son. My only son. I have in-laws and bastards and children I deny. But really, in it all, I had only you.

"For thirty-seven years I have nourished you. For thirty-seven years you brought hope to my soul. For I believed from the day I first held you in my hands, that it was you who would carry this nation when I was through.

"But now, my son, what am I to do?"

Odai didn't move. His eyes remained fixed on his father. "My *Rais*," he began. "You left me no choice. You have squandered a power that was not yours alone. It was mine. You said it just now. My legacy is inseparable from the life that you lead. I am burdened or lifted by the things that you do."

"But Odai," the president slowly replied. "All that I have would have been given to you. You did not have to steal what was already yours. You have betrayed me for something you already owned."

Odai quickly stood up and took two steps toward the desk. "What, my father, would you have left me? What thing of value would I have owned? You are the one who betrayed me, my father. Look what you've done to my birthright! What value is it to me now? You have shamed us. You have shamed all of Islam. You are lower than the dogs that roam through the market, for even they find an occasional home. But not you, my father. Not you, and not I. We are outcast among our brothers. Among even our friends. I have watched it for so many years now and it chills me to the bone.

"How many thousands of our children have died of starvation because of the U.S. embargo? How many women? How many men? We suffer from hunger, sickness, and disease. And when will it end? What do we have to do? When will they leave us alone!

"You have failed us, Father. Failed me. Failed them. The hate in my heart nearly drives me insane. But now, after years of watching you drive us into the ground, now I will have my release!

"Respect comes from power. Power comes from fear. Millions of Americans are soon going to die. Who knows how far the virus will spread? They will be without leadership and quarantined from the world. In a matter of hours, they will be on their knees. My father, how can you not see the beauty of this plan?"

The president remained almost lifeless, sitting still as a vulture. He had already resigned himself to killing his son. And though a certain part of him regretted the thing he must do, another piece of him was actually content. Now he was anxious to pull the trigger himself. It would be the only honorable thing he could do.

He nodded toward the younger Hussein. "Odai," he said, his voice now determined and clear. "I just had a talk with the foreign minister. He was rushed back here on an American jet. They have American bombers over Cyprus. Do you have any idea what you have done?"

Odai sat in the dim light without responding. Saddam lowered his voice and went on. "I feel that I should be the one to do it. Somehow it is important to me. Like a man who must kill his favorite dog, a dog who has become old and useless and in constant pain. It would be cowardly of me to command someone else. Another could do it, but that would be wrong. I was hoping that you would understand."

Odai came forward to lean against the edge of the desk. "Father," he narrowed his eyes and sneered, "there is so little about you that I understand. But in this matter, I know what you mean. Indeed, I feel the same way myself."

Odai turned toward the two guards, who immediately pulled their guns from their tight leather holsters. A flash of panic shot through Saddam's weary eyes. Odai nodded his head toward his father. Three shells were fired in just under a second. The first one entered Saddam's skull just below the bridge of his nose, splattering brain matter over the wall. The other two entered his throat and his chest. The president of Iraq fell out of his chair and was dead before he even hit the floor.

The acid smell of burned powder drifted through the room. Odai Hussein stood for a moment, staring down at his father. A dark pool of blood, almost black in the dim palace light, began to grow in a near-perfect circle on the hardwood floor. Leaning over, Odai kicked the body, satisfied the job was now done.

30

OVAL OFFICE
THE WHITE HOUSE
2037 LOCAL TIME

At 8:37 in the evening, the telephone in the Oval Office buzzed gently. The president was sitting behind his desk, staring at Brent Hillard, his NSA. The room was quiet, the two men wallowing in anxious, if unspoken, thoughts. Brent Hillard sat near the left corner of the president's highly polished, cherry desk, staring at a pitcher of water and the thick slices of lemon that floated among the chunks of ice. Outside the heavily draped windows, the low sun had pushed the shadows to the east. The smell of Havana Royals wafted heavy in the air, the blue smoke hovering over the president's brown leather chair.

The telephone buzzed once again. The president glanced at his national security advisor as he lifted the receiver to his ear.

"Yes, Monica, what is it?" he asked simply.

"Sir, I am holding a call for you from Iraq. The watch supervisor at the com. center has passed it up to me."

The president sucked in a quick breath of air. "Who is it?" he asked tersely.

"The caller has identified himself as President Hussein, sir. Voice verification is not possible, but we have confirmed that the call has originated from the Tigris Presidential Palace."

The president paused for a moment. His eyes narrowed slightly and his heart skipped a beat. For just a moment, he felt completely unprepared. He had never once spoken with the man. Though he had attacked the nation of Iraq on no less than three separate occasions, a series of aerial attacks that ranged from a few Tomahawk cruise missiles to a full week of aerial war, and though he had on innumerable occasions stood to declare the president of Iraq as the single greatest threat to mankind, still, at no time had he ever spoken with the man. At no time had they met or shared written correspondence. At no time had they ever spoken on the phone.

As the president pressed the telephone receiver to his ear, tiny beads of sweat popped out on his forehead. He impatiently wiped them away. "Go ahead—put him through," he said.

"Coming to you now, sir," the switchboard operator replied.

President Brooks leaned forward in his chair to hit the speakerphone button, then nodded to the NSA, who immediately picked up a pencil to take notes on the conversation to follow. In the background, and only on the White House end of the line, a soft beep toned every ten seconds, advising the president that the conversation was being recorded in the communications center downstairs.

There was a slight delay as the call was transferred to the president's desk. The president cleared his throat. "This is the president," was all he said.

"Mr. President, this is Odai Hussein." The caller pronounced his words with exaggerated precision. The president was surprised. He had expected to hear an interpreter's voice, knowing Saddam refused to ever speak English.

"Yes, well—where is your father? I thought I would be speaking with him."

"Mr. President," Odai replied. "It is very important that we speak. We have critical matters to discuss."

"I'm going to ask you one more time," President Brooks said flatly. "Where is your father? I won't talk through a spokesman. I will deal only with him."

A moment of silence passed before Odai Hussein replied. "Mr. President, I want you to know that neither I nor my generals, my ministers nor my people, had anything whatsoever to do with the incredibly hostile and dangerous situation in which our two countries now find themselves. Whatever has happened up to this point, whatever grievance or ill will that has passed between you and my father— well, I just want you to know that it is now over."

"What do you mean?" The president's voice was low and intense.

"When you say it is over, what do you mean? What are you saying? Where is your father?"

"Mr. President, my father is—unavailable. No, let me say that again, for I want you to know the truth. My father is dead. He was killed early this evening. The commanding general of the Republican Army, acting under my direct authority, has taken control of the elite Palace Guards. The foreign minister Abdullah Abbas and several other ministers were also killed in the struggle. Earlier this evening, I dismissed my father's entire cabinet and senior military advisors. Many will face trial for high treason and crimes against the state. I am in control now. The mantle of authority has been officially passed."

The president wiped his hand across his eyes in an urgent motion of final understanding. His face began to pale as he glanced toward the NSA, who sat stoic in his seat, his pencil dangling limply between his fingers. Neither of the men looked at the other, both of them momentarily lost in their thoughts.

Saddam Hussein was dead. Another man had taken his place.

For how long now had they sought such outcome? For how many years had they worked for this day? How much effort and how many lives had been sacrificed to bring Saddam down?

And now that it had happened, what were they supposed to do?

On the other end of the line, and half a world away, Odai Hussein was almost smiling. He sat alone in his father's office, the darkness of the night fully around him. The room still smelled of gunpowder and blood. The President of the United States took another deep breath. Odai listened as the man sighed into the receiver. And with that, he knew. The Iraqi then knew. This was a man that he could control. The president's hesitation said far more than words and Odai was an expert at detecting weakness in another.

Sitting in the gloom with the telephone pressed to his ear, Odai felt a quick thump in his heart. He considered it the most thrilling moment of his life. It was a feeling of power he would never forget.

Again, Odai smiled in the darkness and then went on, not waiting for the president to gather himself. "Over the past forty hours," he explained quickly, "as the gravity of the situation began to unfold, as we discovered the atrocity at Kimisk and the link to Air Force One, as we received confirmation of our worst suspicions from Minister Abdullah Abbas, I realized that the very fate of our nation was hanging by the most delicate thread. And I was faced with a horrible decision. A decision I must live with for the rest of my life. You and the world may question my methods. That is fine. I can live with that. I did what I did, I would do it again. Someone had to bring an end to this madness.

"And so I am saying, Mr. President, that we have reached a critical junction. A time when all mankind looks to us, while holding their breath. A time when the smallest of words, the simplest gesture, can mean the difference between peace or a most horrible war. A war that would affect millions of people and forever change the history of mankind.

"So again, Mr. President, I want to be certain that you understand. I had nothing at all to do with what has transpired up to this point. And I have already taken the most tragic of steps. My father is dead. What more could you ask?"

The president didn't respond. The NSA didn't move. A moment of silence passed. "Alright, Odai—" the president finally started to say.

Odai quickly cut in. "Please, Mr. President. I believe that, under the circumstances, common courtesy would dictate that you refer to me by my title. I am the President of Iraq. I would therefore ask you to acknowledge the position I now hold."

Brooks hesitated and looked over to his NSA, who nodded his head slightly. "Alright, Mr. President," Brooks continued, a hint of sarcasm frosting his voice. "Tell me then, why have you called?"

"Mr. President," Odai went on. "I want you to know what I intend to do. As soon as the technical details can be worked out, I will make an address to my nation. An address that I am certain international news organizations and networks will carry live throughout the world. During this address, I will make these three simple points.

"First, that we, the nation of Iraq, accept full responsibility for the actions of our preceding leadership and will do everything in our power to rectify those who have been wronged.

"Second, that the criminals, those men and soldiers, including my very father, who were responsible for the actions that have brought us to this precipice, have already been punished.

"Third, and this is very important Mr. President, I will make the point that it would be equally treacherous for the United States to hold me or my people responsible for the sins of my father. It would be brutal and wrong to take action against this people when I have done everything in my power, absolutely everything in my power, in order to establish an environment of peace.

"I cannot change what my father has done. But he is gone now, and it is up to us to build on the shambles he left. So I am asking you, Mr. President, not to punish an innocent people for something over which we had no control."

President Brooks rubbed his palms against his closed eyes, an unexpected feeling of relief sweeping over his body. After a moment of silence, Odai's voice broke over the phone line once again.

"Mr. President," he said, "I have one more thing to tell you. Please listen. It's important and you haven't much time.

"You see, I have learned that my father has an agent. Someone with whom he was in contact within the past few days. Someone who is even now in position along the East Coast. This agent has orders to use the biological weapon. Now you must act quickly. There is precious little time."

PONTIAC MOTEL
NEW YORK CITY
2118 LOCAL TIME

The former prisoner Rahsid Abdul-Mohammad sat and listened very carefully. Someone was there, at the door. He lifted his eyes from his reading, his heart beginning to race in his chest. He listened, not moving, straining to hear. He glanced at his watch. Nine-eighteen in the evening. The hotel room was dim and quiet. He didn't move, concentrating on the sounds from the hall. He waited patiently while touching the tip of his tongue to the extended molar in his lower jaw.

Now the hallway was quiet. He lowered his eyes, his breathing and heart rate slowly returning to normal.

The door burst open with a horrible thud, breaking back on its hinges and slamming into the wall. The uniformed men burst into the room, their pistols drawn and ready, as the Iraqi struggled to his feet. Having been told by their window observer where the target would be, they crossed the room screaming in both English and Arabic for the Iraqi to drop to the floor.

Rahsid Abdul-Mohammad didn't move. He was simply too scared and startled to think. The helmeted men crossed the room in seconds, their guns pointed at his chest. Rahsid pressed himself against the far wall. He thought of his children. He thought of his home. Then he bit down on the tooth, cracking the thin enamel cover, then swallowed the bitter liquid and dropped onto the floor while placing his hands limply over his head.

As he flattened himself out, his chest was already growing tight. A burn in his lungs seemed to spread along his ribs and reach out with searing fingers to his heart. He rolled onto his back, his vision already failing, as the SWAT team stared down into his dying eyes.

THE WHITE HOUSE SITUATION ROOM
WASHINGTON, D.C.
2340 LOCAL TIME

Odai Hussein, the new president of Iraq, finished his address to the television world. Brent Hillard lifted his hand and pushed the remote to turn the television off. Odai Hussein's face flickered once, then collapsed immediately into a white diamond of light that sparkled from the center of the television screen. The president stared at the floor, lost in thought. His national security team watched him closely, but didn't interrupt.

After several moments, President Brooks looked up to face the men in the room.

"He was good, wasn't he? Very smooth and assured."

The others nodded to agree. "He was nothing like his father, that's for certain," Hillard replied. "Just watching him on camera, you could see the generational difference. One, a brutal clansman who was raised in the hills. The other, a spoiled tyrant who was raised in summer palaces and spent his time grooming himself for TV."

The president stared at his hands, then swore under his breath. "We really screwed up, not getting that Iraqi alive. That was extremely important! Maybe more than we know. We needed to talk to him! To hear him. To find out who he worked for and why he was here! There are so many blanks we don't have answers to. I'm telling you, gentlemen, this will reach up and bite us. I can sense it. I can feel it. I can feel it in my bones."

The other men nodded their heads to agree.

"I guess the bottom-line question is this," the president concluded. "Can we trust Odai Hussein? Do we accept that he had nothing to do with this mess? And if we believe him, what are we going to do now?"

PRINCE SULTAN AIR BASE
SAUDI ARABIA
0815 LOCAL TIME

The signal from Baghdad came through just after eight in the morning, a ten-digit symbol on the Iraqi agent's radio beeper. He immediately went to his water truck and slipped the silver canister inside the huge, stainless-steel tank. He activated the timer, just like he had been trained at the camp in Sudan, then slipped behind the wheel of the truck. Twenty minutes later, he was driving through the streets of Al Kharj, toward the American air base on the edge of the desert.

TIGRIS PRESIDENTIAL PALACE
BAGHDAD, IRAQ
0825 LOCAL TIME

Odai Hussein leaned forward at his desk and stared at the general. "So it is done, then?" he asked him, his voice wire-tight.

"Yes, my *Rais*, it is done. The prisoner Abdul-Mohammad has accomplished his mission. Now he is dead and they will never find out. And our man in Al Kharj has acknowledged the signal. He is heading toward Prince Sultan even as we speak. There is no way they could ever put a stop to it now."

Odai sat back and smiled. Even the general relaxed. It was a moment to savor. Odai pushed himself up from his chair and turned toward Mecca. In his mind, he muttered one of his prayers.

Allah is gracious. He grants justice.
The suffering years must all end.

Odai turned to his general, a look of relief on his face. "And when all this is over, when we have completed the attack at Prince Sultan and the city of Washington, D.C., we will still be able to blame it all on my father! To me that turned out to be the best part of this plan. We have positioned ourselves so we can always blame him. 'It was my father!' I will say. 'I had no knowledge of the plan!' And the American pigs will be left with this question: How do you retaliate against a man who is already dead?"

BOOK THREE

War is a complex and chaotic human endeavor.
Human frailty and irrationality shape war's nature.
Uncertainty and unpredictability—what many call the "fog"
of war—combine with danger, physical stress, and human falli-
bility to make apparently simple operations unexpectedly and
sometimes even insurmountably difficult.

> —*Air Force Doctrine*
> *Document 1 (September 1997)*

"Hi, Daddy. I love you.
This is Michael. I'm seven now."

> —*Telephone conversation welcoming home Major Michael Glendon,*
> *who had been shot down over North Vietnam in 1966.*

31

Aria lay huddled in the corner, waiting in fear. The cell was hardly more than a box, with a smooth cement floor and blood-splattered steel walls. The ceiling was not more than four feet high and the walls were close enough that she couldn't spread out her arms. And it was hot. Oh so hot. Well over 130 degrees. The air was dry and nearly impossible to breathe. She had long ago sweated away her body fluids and was now faint and weak from severe dehydration. Cramps knotted her legs. Her tongue was swollen and dry.

Every hour or so, the guard would stop by the thick sliding door and pull it back just enough to stare at the prisoner inside. With a grunt, the door would slam shut once again.

All through the hot day, Aria had been left in the cell. They left her to bake in the heat, knowing it would break down her will. Every time she heard footsteps, she expected the worst. But the day slowly passed and the guard didn't return. Eventually she drifted off to sleep. The heat slipped away and the cell became cool as night crept over the prison.

Early the next day, the heat began to build again. Then, just as the sun was climbing to its apex in the silver-haze sky, just as the box was reaching its maximum temperature once again, Aria listened as footsteps marched toward her cell. She pushed herself up, her legs cramped and burning in pain.

The guard slid the door open and stared into her cell. Aria looked up with sunken, dry eyes.

"I need to see Odai Hussein," she muttered, her voice raspy and dry. "I have a message for him. Why don't you understand!"

The guard allowed a smile, a crooked twist on his mouth. "Oh, yes, my little rat. I understand what you say. And you'll have your chance. Soon you will talk. You will tell me your message and your other crimes. And when I am finished, you will beg me to let you tell me more.

"So don't worry, little rat. When I'm ready, you'll talk. Then, if you still want, you can go see the master Hussein."

Aria pushed herself forward, moving slowly toward the guard. "Why can't I see him?" she begged. "Please, you don't understand!"

The guard watched her crawl toward him and shut the door with a slam. Aria listened to the footsteps slowly fading away.

The two men studied the girl on the television screen. The hidden camera was mounted in the near corner of the tiny cell, allowing a clear shot at the prisoner's face. The two officers watched and listened as the young girl spoke with the guard, her face white and ghostlike in the dim light of the room. They listened as she asked to speak with Odai Hussein, then turned and stared at each other.

General Aziz bin Al-Saud, the director of the Iraqi Special Security Organization, looked down on the colonel who stood at his side. "You idiot fool! How long have you had her?" he demanded.

The colonel nearly cowered. "Sir, the prisoner was arrested about yesterday-noon in the south ghetto of the Khalid District. One of my men captured her out on the street. Apparently she had no idea she was being sought, for she made little attempt to conceal herself. It was an easy apprehension. She put up little resistance.

"We brought her here and placed her in the holding cell. My intention, *Sayid*, was to follow normal procedures. We would let her bake for twenty-four hours, then begin the interrogation sometime later today."

The general took half a step toward the colonel. "Stupid fool!" he bellowed. "This isn't some street wench. Some petty thief or political whore! Don't you know! Haven't you read the reports! This girl is far more valuable for who she is than what she knows. She is an intruder, you fool, an American spy!"

The colonel stepped back and lowered his head. "Sir, I had no idea."

"It was in yesterday's bulletin," the general shouted in anger. "Hold her," he commanded. "Don't touch her. Don't talk with her. Keep your filthy guards away. Don't let anyone into her cell. I must speak with the *Rais* and see what he wants us to do. Until then, she is your charge. Keep her well, or by Allah, you will not live to see another day. I will return for her. Until then, the responsibility is yours."

The general turned and stalked from the room.

As the general made his way down the hallway, he was confused and unsure of what to do. Something was going on. Something terrible and dangerous. Something that had nothing to do with the girl. There were rumors flying around from his guards near the palace. The *Sayid* had not been seen and many of his ministers were gone. There was danger, he could sense it. He could feel it in the air.

The question now was, what should he do with the girl? Who should he talk to? Who should he tell?

Colonel Samih Bakr Hajazi, the senior member of the Amn-al-Khass, those hand-selected body guards of the presidential family, tapped gently on the door, then waited for the command that would allow him to enter. After several moments of silence, he tapped once again, something he rarely would have dared to do. But the matter was urgent, and he needed to see the *Rais*.

Listening intently, he heard Odai's voice calling out from the bowels of the office. "Yes, what is it?"

The colonel gently slipped the door open and let himself inside. Odai was standing behind the president's desk, staring intently out an open window, his hands folded neatly behind his back. He was listening to the wind as it blew across the desert. The office was warm from the blast of afternoon heat. But Odai didn't care. He loved the desert and the feel of dry air, the whispering wind, and the sun in the huge open sky.

The colonel approached his superior with an urgent stride, then positioned himself in front of the desk. "Sir, forgive me. I know it is an intrusion. But there is a situation that I believe you should be aware of."

Odai turned to face the colonel. With a nod of his head, he motioned for him to go on.

The colonel lowered his eyes to stare at the front of the desk. "My *Rais*, General Aziz bin Al-Saud has a prisoner. She was taken yesterday morning. She is being held now. And sir, there are indications that she is a spy. Apparently an American here on some kind of search and destroy mission."

"What are you talking about, Colonel Hajazi? Has General Al-Saud sent you to me?"

Colonel Hajazi hesitated just a moment. "No, sir. He did not send me. But what I have told you is true. He is holding a girl. An American citizen. And she is asking that she be allowed to speak with you."

Odai moved around the corner of the desk. "Where is this prisoner being held?"

"At the headquarters of the AMAM, sir."

"And why was I not notified sooner?"

"I don't know, sir. Perhaps the general could tell."

Odai thought for a moment. It was an incredible story. *If* it was true.

Turning to the colonel, he gave his instructions. "Bring her to me. And General Aziz bin Al-Saud as well. I want to speak to them both. Bring them to me now."

Forty minutes later, General Aziz bin Al-Saud was escorted into the president's office. Following the general was a girl.

Two guards were helping Aria walk, with a pair of strong hands under each arm. Her eyes were frightened, her lips dry and pale. She was dressed in prison attire, a thick, black robe with long sleeves and high neck. Struggling weakly, she staggered to match General Aziz bin Al-Saud's long stride. Her hands hung loosely at her sides, her fingers swollen and blue. The wire that had been wrapped around her wrists had been cut off only moments before she entered the room.

Tucked between Aria's fingers was a tiny steel pin. She had quickly pulled it from her hair when the guards had turned away. Tightly, she held it between her fingers and palm. The transmitter was ready to go.

As Aria entered the office, she pulled a deep breath. She willed her mind to focus for she had to be strong. With darting eyes, she scanned the enormous room. She saw the men waiting beside the huge desk. She saw the black leather couch and smooth marble floor. She saw the open window and felt the heat blow in from the desert. Looking behind the desk, she saw Odai Hussein. He sat like a ferret, his dark eyes unmoving and joyless beneath heavy lids. She avoided his stare, afraid to look him in the face. Her heart skipped a beat. She could taste her own fear. It seemed to settle upon her, overwhelming her senses and making her weak. Quickly, she turned her head to the right.

There, near the desk, was Odai's army beret, lying on the edge of a mahogany chair. Draped over the armrest was his desert field jacket. Underneath the chair was his thick leather briefcase. Any one of these items would conceal the pin.

It would only take a second. The opportunity was there, sitting just a few feet away.

General Aziz bin Al-Saud came to a stop near the front of Odai's desk. He stood at attention, his eyes staring straight ahead.

Odai glanced at the general with a look of disdain. Slowly he let his eyes drift to the girl. Staring into her eyes, he studied her face, then turned to the general again. Aziz bin Al-Saud began to explain. After two minutes, the general had told him everything that he knew. It was painfully little. The general trembled with fear.

"She came in with the UN inspectors?" Odai asked.

"Yes, sir. Of that, I am sure."

"And you know she is American?"

The general's voice was more hesitant this time. "I do not know for certain, *Rais*." I have not had the opportunity yet for interrogation. We were going to proceed with that later today."

Odai lifted his eyes, which were sullen and brown. "Apparently, General Aziz bin Al-Saud, you are too incompetent to achieve such a thing. A simple girl. A simple interrogation. Yet, here we are, a full twenty-four hours later, and still she is silent."

The general lowered his eyes and stared at the floor. Odai nodded toward the center pillar of the room, a smooth column of polished marble. "Leave her with me," he commanded. "I will do your job. Tie her to the pillar. Shove a rag in her mouth. Then bring me my stick."

PRINCE SULTAN AIR BASE
AL KHARJ SAUDI ARABIA
1400 LOCAL TIME

Prince Sultan Air Base was not completely secure. People had to eat. The aircraft needed fuel. Supplies by the truckload worked their way through the front gate. Even the water and ice came from miles away, shipped to the Americans on the backs of huge silver trucks from the salt-water distilleries near the border of Qatar. Service contracts had been extended. There was cleaning and digging and building to do. The TCNs, or Third Country Nationals, were the ones who did most of the work. Hundreds of Pakistanis, Indians, Koreans, Egyptians, and Syrians worked within the walls of the American compound.

And therein lay Odai's advantage.

Charlie McKay walked into the day room and dropped onto the couch, propping his white-stockinged feet onto a fabric footstool. Killer was the only other person in the room. Charlie's flight suit was unzipped half way down the front of his chest in the typical, if still frowned upon, alert style. Charlie glanced out the low window toward the flightline and endless desert. The mid-afternoon sun was burning the sky silver-blue, and he knew it was at least 110 degrees outside.

Charlie pulled down his zipper just a bit more and reached across the end table for his Coke. Sitting back in the couch, he glanced at the room's cement walls. The alert bunker was comfortable and Charlie's only complaint was that the rooms were a bit warm, a result of the air conditioner having to work overtime. But it was clearly much better than being on the other side of Prince Sultan, where everyone else lived in communal tents stuck out in the sand. At least he and Killer had their own rooms, great luxuries compared to what the others had to endure.

The television was on to some second-rate U.S. satellite feed. Charlie turned toward Killer. "So buddy, what's going on?" he asked.

Captain Bennet didn't turn away from the television. "Andy took away Barney's bullet. You know, the single bullet he let him keep in his pocket. This is a classic. I remember watching it as a kid."

Charlie turned his attention to the black-and-white image on the screen. He watched for a moment, his mind drifting away.

Over the past several days, a sense of gloom had been seeping upon him, a deep frustration he couldn't quite explain. He almost felt angry, and Aria was the cause. In his mind, he thought of the softness of her face; her dark hair, her smile and wide, expressive eyes. If he were honest with himself, he would have to admit that she was the only thing he had thought of for the past several days. For the thousandth time, he wondered where she might be at that moment. How was she doing? Was she safe? And would she make it to Odai Hussein?

Charlie turned toward Killer and leaned forward in the couch, "Al-babe," he said. "Can I ask you a question?"

Killer turned his face away from the television screen.

"It's this thing with Aria," Charlie went on. "I mean, you've talked with her. You two spent some time alone. You got a feel for what kind of person she is. Not exactly your James Bond type. I think we made a terrible mistake. She shouldn't have gone in there. Anyone could see she's in over her head."

"So what was your question, Charles?"

"I don't know. It just seems like, I don't know—"

"Hey," Killer asked, "do you really want to know what I think?"

Charlie nodded his head.

"I think you have several things wrong here, Charlie. For one thing, I think you have way underestimated Aria and her capabilities. She isn't some pushover, Prince Charles. Look at her life! Look what she's done! Look what she's lived through and what she has lost. She is a strong person, Charlie. Don't underestimate that.

"Secondly, don't forget her experience with the Kurds on the mountain. I think she learned a thing or two about how to survive.

"Finally, you should remember that she volunteered for this mission. She isn't going to Baghdad because she couldn't figure out a polite way to say no. She's doing this thing for the same reason as you or I. She feels she has to. It's as simple as that. She knows that we need her and she is willing to help."

Charlie studied his friend, but didn't reply. After a moment, Killer nodded absently toward the back door. "Where's Colonel Wisner? Haven't seen him around for a while."

"He was going over to the main base," Charlie replied. "Said he probably wouldn't be back until late afternoon."

Killer turned casually back toward the television screen. "Has he heard anything?" he asked, hoping Charlie would know.

"I know that he talked with Aria earlier today. Said she made it in country, but that's all he would say.

"But you know," Charlie continued, "I think he isn't telling us everything. Something is going on, buddy. He was on the satellite phone to D.C. and Europe for hours this morning. I was with him for a while, and he had to ask me to leave the room. Makes me nervous. I hate secrets. Secrets are never good news."

Killer nodded his head but didn't respond. Charlie watched the television for a minute, then got up and walked back to his room.

The three Americans had walked from the flightline through half a mile of sand to eat lunch at the central chow hall. Slipping through the wooden frame that acted as a door to the huge dining tent, they were hit in the face by a blast of cold air from the portable air conditioners that ran at full speed, cooling the tent to a tolerable level. The sweat on their faces was quickly blown away as they worked their way through the line to get to the food.

The young men ordered the main course, a mixture of pasta and meat that the cook called spaghetti, then sat at the nearest table. The youngest, a new airman, barely out of training, stood up and walked to a counter to retrieve two huge pitchers of water and ice. Returning to the table, he placed the water between the three trays, then sat down beside his new friends. The conversation, as always, centered around only two things: work, and getting back home.

The three airmen were jet-engine mechanics, a tough and demanding job, especially out in the desert. The blowing sand had a way of working havoc on the fighters' sensitive engines and they always had plenty to do.

But today was slow. Most of the day's sorties had been early morning go's and there was a six-hour gap until the night sorties took off. So instead of snarfing their lunch and heading out the tent door, they relaxed and took a little time to eat.

Forty minutes later, they were walking back toward the flightline. Saying goodbye to his fellows, the most senior of the men, a twenty-three-year-old sergeant named Billy Cross, turned and made his way across the scorching white cement toward the jet-engine building where he worked.

Five hours later, Sgt Cross was feeling funny. If it was a flu coming on, it was going to be a killer. His stomach was vicious and his skin felt like wet clams. The surprising thing was, it had hit him so quickly. One minute, it seemed, he was feeling just fine. Two minutes later, he swooned, hardly able to stand.

He stood at a high metal table, parts and tools spread out before him. He leaned against the table as his head started to spin. He was alone in the repair room and the only sound was his breathing and a small CD player that was playing jazz.

The sergeant let out a low groan as his stomach rolled into knots.

Inside his body, the virus was busy at work. After entering his stomach through the water in the chow hall, it had immediately attached itself to the base of his brain. It then spent the six hours multiplying like a fungus, spreading slowly at first, then seeming to explode, the cells doubling in number every ten or twelve minutes.

As the young sergeant leaned against the table, the virus attained critical mass.

His vision suddenly narrowed. The room seemed to darken, then roll on its side and turn instantly black. Cross fell to the floor and stared at the ceiling with eyes that could no longer see. A terrible swelling seemed to grow at the base of his neck. The swelling tightened and grew until it cut off the blood to his head. His breathing became short and he let out a scream, a gurgle in his throat, hardly more than a whisper. A fire burned from the back of his head, deep under the skin, almost as if from the center of his bones. The sergeant rolled onto his side in terrible pain, aware he was dying, but not knowing why. He thought of his family. He felt isolated and alone as the darkness engulfed him. He tried to call out, then let his head fall to the floor. The fire burned forward to claw at his eyes. Reaching up, he attempted to push back the pain, pressing his fingers violently against the top of his face. Though he didn't know, his hands were quickly covered with blood as the capillaries in his eye sockets ruptured.

Mercifully the pain began to give way as the tissue in his brain started to die from the lack of oxygenated blood. He couldn't see. He couldn't hear. He couldn't talk, feel, or breathe. He called out once more, a desperate cry for help, then lay back and sighed.

The sergeant was dead.

TIGRIS PRESIDENTIAL PALACE
BAGHDAD, IRAQ
1505 LOCAL TIME

Aria was cuffed with her face against the marble pillar, her arms pulled forward and wrapped around the smooth, polished stone. Odai had beaten her with the stick so many times across her legs that she was now completely unable to stand. She leaned against the pillar, her knees buckling in pain, her arms straining to hold up her weight.

Odai stood beside her with an oak stick in his hand. It was greasy and blood stained. It had been used before. He had beat her before he asked the first question, thinking he would save time by breaking her before the interrogation began. As he beat her, he had varied the power of each stroke, spreading the blows from her thighs to the middle of her calves, always careful not to break any bones.

"Tell me," he demanded, as he finally pulled the rag from her mouth. "Tell me, why are you here?"

"I have a sister," she muttered. "My sister. Please, *Sayid*, my sister is all."

Odai swore in her face, a vile insult to Allah, saliva spraying on her cheeks with each word that he sneered. "You're a liar! You're an American spy. You were smuggled into my country on the United Nations flight. We have photographs! Now why are you here?"

Aria lifted her eyes to stare in his face, then dropped her head to her chest. Odai grabbed her hair and pulled back her head. Studying her closely, he looked at the pupils of her eyes, noting the still-sharp glare of resistance.

Odai turned to Colonel Hajazi, who was standing by the door. The colonel took a step forward and asked once again. "Let me take her, *Sayid*. This is no work for you. Give me an hour with her, that's all I would need. Don't dirty your hands with this foul and filthy chore. Let me have her. You know I am only anxious to serve."

The president paused, studying the bodyguard with a curious and cautious eye. That was the third or fourth time he had begged to do the interrogation. Never had the colonel shown any interest in doing such a job, though the opportunity had been present many times.

Odai considered the colonel and then slowly shook his head. This one was delicate and it had to be done right. As an American, the girl was worth a great deal, and for that reason, he might let her live. But it also complicated the process, for he didn't want to leave any scars. So he would conduct the interrogation himself. Besides, it had been a long time and the truth was, he was enjoying himself.

Odai turned and walked to the back of his desk. Reaching into his pocket, he extracted a smoke and placed the delicate paper between his thick lips. Lighting the tobacco, he inhaled and sat down.

Aria slumped against the pillar, her eyes distant and faint, the glow of life veiled in a haze of pain and fear. She glanced over at the colonel, silently begging for help. The colonel watched her for a moment, then slowly looked away.

Odai Hussein's chief of staff was in the palace communications center when the message came in from their agent at Prince Sultan Air Base. The general read the transmission quickly, then looked at his watch.

After doing the math in his head, he swore under his breath. It was early. Far too early. Something was wrong. The American funeral was still more than two hours away.

But the virus was already taking casualties at Prince Sultan! That should not have happened for another couple of hours! And if the word got back to the States before President Brooks left for the funeral? If the Americans knew of the attack on Prince Sultan . . . ?

The general gathered himself, then climbed the narrow staircase leading up to Odai's office.

Odai remained in his chair, enjoying the last of the cigarette as it burned down to his fingers. He dragged on the smoke, pulling it into his lungs. He stared at the desert, knowing he would soon have to leave.

The virus at Prince Sultan had already been released. They would start to see deaths within a couple of hours, about the same time that the virus would be discharged in the American cathedral.

By then, he wanted to be safely tucked away in his underground bunkers. He was planning on taking a convoy into the desert, to a bunker seventy miles east of the city. It was not an easy trip. It would take several hours. There he would stay hidden for the next two or three days, until things had settled and the damage was done. He glanced at his watch. He would soon have to leave.

He dragged once again, then turned to the girl, wondering if he should just kill her. So many things were going to change in the next couple of hours. The whole balance of world power was waiting to shift. By early morning, this girl's mission would hardly even matter. Maybe he would just shoot her and get her out of his hair.

A moment of silence filled the enormous room as he fingered the ash on the end of his smoke. He heard a sudden knock against his private door and his chief of staff allowed himself in. He walked quickly toward Odai, then leaned down to whisper in his ear. Odai listened for a moment, then suddenly stood.

"Watch her," he called to Colonel Hajazi as he led the general out of the room.

Hajazi watched as Hussein left through the private door, then moved like cat toward the girl. Grabbing her head, he ran his fingers through her hair, feeling for the pin, praying it was still there. Lifting her face, he stared straight into her eyes. "Where is the transmitter?" he muttered in a barely audible breath. "We haven't much time."

"Who are you?" Aria whispered.

"I am Colonel Samih Bakr Hajazi. Now tell me where the transmitter is, and keep your voice low. There are microphones in virtually every room."

Aria studied the colonel, a mixture of hope and doubt in her eyes. She started to speak, then quickly turned away.

"Listen to me," the colonel breathed, lifting her face to look in her eyes. "I know who you are. I know what you're doing. I have offered to help, but my offer is thin. I won't risk my neck and we haven't much time."

"How can I trust you?" Aria muttered. "How can I know?"

"A number of years ago," the colonel whispered, "before it would have been considered a crime, before it would have meant death to my family, I married a women with Kurd in her blood. Several days ago, my wife had taken my children and slipped up to the mountain to visit her family. They were in Kimisk on the night that the virus was used. My entire family was killed. My wife. My two sons and daughter.

"Now I want you to tell where the transmitter is. And quickly, we haven't much time!"

An aide handed the message to Odai as soon as he walked into the communications room.

TO: WADI

FR: WADI V

1346/06/99encryptionALPHA< ALPHA

Water delivered. Timer activated.

Casualties have begun much earlier than expected.

Negative hostile report to Mother. Several survivors have slipped into the desert.

Await your instructions.

"So it has started then," Odai said as he placed the paper transcription upon the table.

"Yes, sir. It has begun. Apparently, when introduced through the water, the virus acts somewhat more quickly than we had observed. In our experiments with Iranian prisoners, we had never seen symptoms in such a short amount of time. And while there are a number of possibilities to explain the acceleration, I feel the most likely—"

Odai lifted his finger to cut him off. The general immediately fell quiet.

"Have there been any warning radio transmissions out of the base? Do you know if they have reported the attack back to D.C.?"

The general shook his head. "We cannot know for certain that the attack has not been reported, my *Rais*. There are ways of communication that we cannot monitor or decode. So while I don't think they have reported back, we really cannot know for sure."

"We need to move then," Odai replied, a cut of anger in his voice. "If the Americans were alerted—if they get word of the attack—then the president will act. I need to get down to the bunker. It is the only safe place to be. Gather your men. We need to leave now!"

* * *

Aria stared into the colonel's eyes, then finally made up her mind. "I stuck it in the sleeve of my robe," she replied. "It is there, near the hem at the wrist."

The colonel ran his fingers along the hem until he felt the pin under the fabric. In an instant, he had the transmitter in his hands.

"Punch it three times," Aria explained, her voice weak and strained. "That activates the battery and initiates the signal." The colonel pushed, but only slightly. Aria watched him with sunken eyes. "No," she explained. "You have to push hard. And twist while you push. You will feel a small detent that activates the battery."

The colonel did as Aria instructed. He felt the pin compress. Turning for the desk, he made his way for Odai's hat. He was just picking up the field beret when Odai burst into the room, followed by his chief of staff and two army soldiers.

The colonel looked up, too startled to react. Though his face remained passive, his eyes panicked with fear. Odai studied the colonel, then looked at the beret in his hand.

The colonel slipped the pin into the crest of the beret. Turning to Odai, he extended the cap. "Sir," he asked, "are you ready to go?"

Odai paused for a moment before crossing the room to take his combat beret. Turning, he placed the black cap on his head.

Nodding to his chief of staff, he said, "General, I want you and Colonel Hajazi to come with me. We will caravan south to the bunker. I'll ride in one of the Range Rovers. Both of you follow in one of the army trucks."

"And the prisoner, sir?"

"Bring her with us," Odai replied.

PRINCE SULTAN AIR BASE
SAUDI ARABIA
1615 LOCAL TIME

Charlie McKay was lying on his bed, almost asleep.

Someone slammed a fist against his door. Charlie bolted up in his bed as he heard Alex Bennett's voice. "Charlie! Oh please—Charlie, get out here, *now!*"

Charlie jumped from his bed and ran to the door. Throwing it open, he hurried into the hall to see Killer making his way up the stairs that led out to the aircraft hangar. Killer stopped for a second to make sure that Charlie was there. Motioning desperately, he ran through the thick double doors.

Charlie followed, running up the stairs three at a time, and pushed his way into the hangar. His F-15 stood in the middle of the cement apron, fueled and ready to go. The huge hangar doors had been rolled shut and locked, blocking out most of the light. The shiny floor glistened in the semi-darkness of the enclosed hangar. "Al? Al, where are you?" Killer was nowhere in sight.

Charlie took two or three steps toward his jet, then saw him standing at the small door that led out onto the flightline. Tears of fear and desperation glistened on his dark and stubbled cheeks. He was holding the door handle while yelling through a small window on the door.

"Sir, I can't do that!" he screamed. "I can't let you in."

Charlie sprinted toward Killer, his stocking feet slapping against the hard cement. As he ran, his throat tightened and his breath jammed in his chest. Something in Killer's voice scared him to the core. He raced up to the door and put his arms on Killer's shoulders. Killer was pulling on the door handle. "Stay back, sir," he was crying. "Please, you cannot come in."

Charlie turned to the small window, his face almost touching the glass. On the other side of the glass, only inches away, was Colonel Wisner. His eyes were blood red, his mouth wet with dark spit. A trickle of blood seeped from both of his ears. He was pulling on the door handle, trying to open it up.

"Please . . . please . . . " his voice was desperate and weak. "I'm dying! Please . . . let me in?"

Reaching for the handle, Charlie attempted to open the door.

"No!" Killer shouted. Charlie felt two hands clamp over his own. "Don't let him in, Charlie! Can't you see what's going on!"

Charlie shook his head, then pulled on the handle. Together, he and Killer were able to pull the door closed. Charlie reached down and locked it. The door was secure. Colonel Wisner pulled once again, then realized the door had been locked. Leaning against the glass, he let his eyes drift to the ground, a lone and forsaken look washing over his face. Clear teardrops emerged from the bloodshot blue eyes. "Oh my . . ." he muttered, his voice weak and thin.

Charlie stared at Colonel Wisner, a frozen knot in his throat. Killer fell back and leaned against the side of the hangar, then bent over to grasp at his knees. Charlie glanced over at his friend. Killer barely looked up, his face pale as gray ash.

"Did you get the other door, Alex? Is the building secure?"

Killer stared down at his hands, which were clenched into fists. "I saw him coming down the road," he mumbled. "He was . . . I don't know . . . wobbling and sick. I went out to help him. He started coughing up blood as he stumbled toward me. He looked at me, begging me to get him inside. I ran. Oh please, Charlie, what was I to do?"

Charlie ignored Killer's question. Reaching down, he grabbed Killer by the shoulders. "Did you lock the other entrance?" he demanded. "Tell me, Alex!"

Killer slowly nodded his head. "The building is secure. All the doors have been locked." Charlie turned back to the window. The colonel was still leaning against the glass, though his face and shoulders had slipped several inches toward the ground. He looked toward Charlie, his eyes growing dim. Their eyes met for a moment. Charlie didn't look away. "I'm sorry," Wisner whispered before dropping his head. "Get him," he then muttered. "Go and get him for me."

Charlie nodded his head, then turned toward Killer and pulled him to his feet. "We've got to get out of here," he commanded. "Now let's get on our gear! We might already be infected. It might already be too late."

"But where? Where will we go?"

"I don't know!" Charlie cried. "Bahrain. Tel Aviv. Maybe we can get up to Turkey. But we can't stay, Killer. If we stay here, we die!"

Captain Bennett nodded his head, then turned for the stairway. Together they ran down the steps to where their fight gear was stored.

Ten minutes later they were strapped in their jet. The canopy came down, sealing them inside their aircraft. The steel doors of the hangar began to roll back as Charlie ran through the checklist to start his two engines. Sitting in the rear cockpit, Killer began to bring his navigation systems on line. They worked very quickly. It didn't take very much time. The aircraft's right engine began to turn, a soft rumble and vibration working its way through the cockpit. The left engine started even before the first engine was stable. With a soft whirr, the two generators came on line. The internal gyros and aviation software began to spin up. The aircraft bounced on the cement as Charlie stirred his controls, the ailerons, rudder, and horizontal stabilizer jerking from one extreme to the other. The two crewmen talked to each other in barely recognizable code. In less than four minutes, they had completed almost eighty steps in the checklist. Charlie pushed up his throttles. The engine compressor blades accelerated to twenty-five thousand revolutions per minute, emitting a horrible whine. The fighter rolled out of the hangar with the canopy down, then sped without stopping toward the end of the runway.

Charlie didn't try talking to the tower. Aligning himself down the long piece of cement, he pushed up the power. The Strike Eagle accelerated, its twin afterburners spouting blue flame as it lifted into the air.

As the fighter approached the end of the ten-thousand-foot runway, it was only fifty feet off the ground. Charlie glanced at the airspeed indicator and was surprised to read only two-hundred knots. He was flying near the stall line and not gaining any speed. He shoved at the throttles, making certain they were both at full power, then released a tiny amount of back pressure on the stick, his fingers feeling the aircraft, sensing its every response, his body taking in every noise and vibration.

He watched through his HUD as the airspeed picked up, the fighter accelerating across the level ground. At three-hundred knots, the aircraft became more responsive. At three-fifty, it began to feel like a fighter again, crisp and anxious to snap at his commands. He pulled back on the stick. The fighter climbed into the air. Minutes later, they were passing through ten thousand feet.

It was then that they got a chirp from the Satellite Navigation Receiver, the special satellite beacon that had been wired into their jet.

Killer immediately scanned his navigation display. "Judas Priest," he cried out. Charlie's eyes narrowed as he studied his screen.

WHITE HOUSE
WASHINGTON, D.C.
0710 LOCAL TIME

The presidential motorcade pulled up to the White House, where the president was already waiting. Although the actual service at the cathedral wouldn't start for almost two hours, he had scheduled a private meeting with each of the families—half an hour to mourn with each of their kin. At 0730, he would meet with the former president's wife and three children. At eight, he would meet with his former vice president's family. The meetings would be private and personal, not public displays of affection. After these private meetings, the groups would file into the National Cathedral.

Even now, on the north end of the city, the cathedral was beginning to fill with foreign dignitaries and government heads. Justices, cabinet members, senators, congressmen, generals, and head executives were all scheduled to arrive soon.

The president watched from his private study as the line of cars moved into the White House's private, semi-circular drive. Four D.C. motorcycle cops were leading the way, their lights flashing blue and white in the dim morning sun. He noted the presidential car, which was stuck in the middle of the black limousines and Chevy Suburbans. A line of twenty-eight vehicles and thirty police escorts would caravan through the city to deliver the president to the chapel.

The president kissed his wife, then took her hand. Together, they walked from the office, making their way from the West Wing exit, waving solemnly to the silent reporters staked out behind a yellow barricade in the grass. A few shouted to the president, but he ignored them, a deep sadness dulling his eyes. He walked arm-in-arm with his wife to the presidential limo. The back door was open. They both slipped inside.

Brent Hillard was waiting. The president slid over, then pulled his suit coat from his shoulder and lay it across his lap.

Hillard looked up. "Good morning, Mr. President," he said.

President Brooks didn't respond. He glanced through the front window to see if the lead car was moving. The motorcade began to inch along. Picking up speed, it moved out of the driveway and into the street for the twenty-minute ride to the Washington National Cathedral.

"Mr. President, there is something I wanted to mention to you," Hillard said, his voice sounding much more calm than he felt.

"Yes, what is it?" the president replied, though it was apparent he was only half listening. The remarks he would make at the funeral service were weighing heavily on his mind.

"Sir," the NSA went on, "we received a message from our command post at Prince Sultan."

The president focused his eyes on his security advisor. The first lady looked away. "What kind of message?" the president snapped.

"Sir, it was a fragmented OPREP—I'm sorry, sir, that's Operations Report—from the base communications center. It was only half complete. It was cut off midway through. And the Pentagon has so far been unable to reestablish any communication lines with the base."

Leaning toward his NSA, the president focused his glare. "What do you mean, can't establish any com.? Why don't they just pick up the freaking phone!"

"It's not that easy, sir. The com. links to the desert are extremely limited, and this isn't the first time the lines have gone down. And our satellite down link is sporadic at best.

"But sir, I don't feel this is something we need to concern ourselves with right now. If something was going on—if there were some real crisis, I can assure you the commander at PSAB would find a way to let us know. We are due another report at noon. I'm certain the guys at Prince Sultan will have the problem figured out by then."

"Alright," the president said. "Let me know when they reestablish com."

Hillard nodded and smiled reassuringly, then turned to the window and scowled inside, angry at himself for not saying more. But he just couldn't do it. Not until he was sure. He wouldn't worry the president with the over-anxious concerns of a staff that had been getting far too little sleep.

But the NSA knew. Or at least he suspected. The problem at PSAB wasn't a simple issue of down communication lines. Indeed, a test of the lines showed they were working just fine.

So why wouldn't anyone at the communications center answer the phone?

Death hung like a fog on the village of troops. The virus had already made its way through the camp. Wails of fear and pain sounded in the dry desert wind. Soldiers kneeled in the street, doubled over in pain, as they clawed at their faces while gagging for breath. Officers bent at the waist and wretched out the lining of their lungs, then died in a pool of blood.

A few of the men, the less fortunate ones, didn't die as quickly as the others. As had happened in Kimisk, some went crazy from the virus, a delirium screaming inside their head. Roaming the camp, they shot at the demons and beasts they found lurking in shadows everywhere.

Within six hours, almost every soldier at Prince Sultan was dead. Those who survived escaped by running into the desert. By nightfall, not a living soul could be found in the camp.

33

HOUND ONE
OVER THE NORTH SAUDI DESERT
1649 LOCAL TIME

"It's the satellite receiver, Charlie! The beacon has been activated! I'm showing a pulse. It's intermittent and weak. But baby, no questions, it's there."

"Are you sure?" Charlie shot back. "It's far too early. A full couple days ahead of schedule."

"Who knows, Charlie? But look at what happened at PSAB. You said yourself that something was going on. Things have accelerated. Spinning out of control.

"So we don't know why it's activated, but this much is clear. She found him. The transmitter is on. The only question now is, what are you going to do?"

Charlie was already turning the fighter to the north. He jammed at the throttles, pushing them up to military power, stopping in the detent just below afterburner range. He felt the familiar push in his seat as the aircraft lurched forward and watched as his mach indicator climbed.

Killer settled himself against the back of his ejection seat and got down to work.

The rear cockpit, or pit, of the F-15E was surprisingly clean, almost completely lacking the clutter of switches, scopes, buttons, and dials that one would expect in such a complicated machine. Instead, four multifunction displays were lined up, each of them controlled by a side-arm controller, a relatively simple keypad device. Each of the four computer displays allowed the WIZZO to manage imagery, data, avionics status, target identification and designation, weapons status, flight control information, and communication, all with a touch of a finger, all while flying at two hundred feet and six hundred knots.

Killer flicked a couple of switches on his side-arm control grip to update his moving-map display, a multicolored screen that showed their progress along the ground. He checked the weapons status, then tuned his air-to-air radar out to eighty miles. Finally, he activated the satellite beacon, allowing his onboard computers to data-link with the orbiting satellite high over his head.

"Okay, Prince Charles, this is what I got. The satellite is getting the beacon at approximately 44.37, 32.96. That plots out to be about twenty, maybe twenty-five miles southeast of Baghdad. We won't get any information on heading or speed. The signal up to the satellite is just not strong enough, nor the software well-enough refined. In addition, the satellite is going to pass out of range of the beacon in only ten minutes or so. After that, we will have to find Spider on our own. But I have enough information now to at least get us close."

Killer punched a few of the buttons on his navigation display, then added, "Fly the heading marking. That will give us a pretty good intercept heading. I'll update it as we go along."

Charlie turned the aircraft seven degrees to the right and centered the tiny V on his Head Up Display over a bearing of three-forty-nine. Reaching to the center pedestal, he tuned in his long-range high frequency, or HF, radio.

"Cobra, Cobra, Hound One on HF." The radio crackled back, full of static and noise. The HF was great for long-distance communications, but extremely susceptible to the electromagnetic interference that was common in the desert. Charlie listened, then broadcast his alert message once again.

"Cobra, Cobra, Hound One on HF." He listened carefully as the radio squelched, then a faint voice replied, "Hound, authenticate with Bravo, Hotel."

Charlie waited, knowing that Killer would look up the proper reply in the top-secret code book that was stuffed in the classified mission-planning documents. Killer flipped quickly through the pages, running his finger along the multicolored matrix. After several seconds, he replied, "Sierra, Eight."

"Are you sure?" Charlie asked him.

"Sierra Eight. I got it right here."

Charlie repeated what Killer had said, speaking the words carefully into the microphone buried in his oxygen mask. He knew Cobra Camp would immediately cut him off if he didn't give the proper response. The location of the forward helicopter operating base was one of the most highly classified secrets in the military. The fact that the U.S. was operating warships out of a desert location in the rebel-held territory of southern Iraq would have been a great surprise to many, up to and including even the secretary of defense.

The two crewmen listened carefully, waiting to hear back from the camp. After several seconds of noise, the radio crackled again.

"Hound, go secure." Charlie reached over and synchronized his HF to the HAVE QUICK secure voice radio, which would encode and decode everything that was now said, allowing them to carry on a classified conversation.

Charlie keyed his mike once again. "Urgent, Cobra. Urgent. Mission to Baghdad is go. I say again, mission is go. We are in the air. ETA over target is—"

"Forty-one minutes," Killer shot from the back.

"Forty-one minutes, Cobra. Confirm."

The radio hissed with a noise that seemed to roll like a wave on the ocean, coming in strong and then suddenly fading away. Charlie reached down and turned the volume up a notch while scanning his eyes across the desert horizon. They were approaching the neutral zone, a buffer of barren thistle and sand that separated Saudi Arabia from Iraq. Soon they would be crossing into enemy territory. Glancing to his right, he studied the threat rings that were starting to slide down over his moving-map display, white circles that depicted the radar-detection zones, the area of space where he would be detected by Iraq's early-warning radar. He studied the map, then pulled back on his throttle and dropped the nose of the aircraft, allowing the fighter to begin a gradual descent.

The fighter started down. The radio crackled once again.

"Hound, authenticate again with Oscar Three."

Once again he and Killer went through the confirmation routine. It was tedious and irritating, but they both understood. Indeed, they had expected nothing less. It would have been foolish for the Cobras to launch with only a single confirmation. This was far too important to not be absolutely sure.

This time Killer was forced to pull out another plastic book, one from a previous communications security edition. That was smart, he thought to himself, as he tore open the plastic-wrapped binder. Cobra was forcing them to use two different authentication books, clearly determined to ensure the message wasn't a matter of a simple stolen code. Killer thumbed through the second authentication guide and gave Charlie the proper response. Charlie relayed it to Cobra, then added this final message.

"Cobra, it's us. You know that now. Now listen. We are approaching the Iraqi border and are descending to stay out of their radar-detection range. The target coordinates are approximately 44.37, 32.96, which is about twenty-five miles southeast of the city.

"Get your birds in the air. Get your birds in the air. We'll meet you. Good luck, and let's go."

Two hundred and sixty miles north of the fighter, buried deep in the marshes of the Shatt-al-'Arab, hidden against the east bank of the mighty Tigris River, the Cobra camp shot to life. Within minutes, four Apache attack choppers were spinning their rotors, their steel blades cutting with a whish through the air. The special operations MH-60s also began to spin up, even as the army Delta Teams scrambled on board. Hydraulic arms lifted away the desert camouflage nets that had been hiding the helicopters' location. With a blast of sand and powder, the choppers lifted into the air. Rolling onto their sides, they turned to the north. The lead pilots set their power for maximum speed. Flying only feet above the desert, the flight spread out in a loose V-formation.

The chopper pilots were extremely apprehensive. They were bats, night creatures—not used to flying in the light. They were trained and ready to fight in the nighttime. Like vampires, they hated the sun. It gave away their position. It made them easy to see. It took away all of the advantages of their multimillion-dollar avionics systems. The sun reflected off their windscreens like the flash of a mirror. Lumbering and slow, the choppers were easy to kill without a cloak of darkness to conceal their positions.

Inside the lead MH-60, the aircraft commander swore as he flew the powerful helicopter over a mound of rock and dead grass. He glanced at his radar altimeter, then swore once again.

They were going to Baghdad. To the heart of the den. They were going in broad daylight, losing the element of surprise. They didn't know for certain where the target would be. Some vague coordinates in the desert were all that they had. In addition, the Iraqi forces were already on alert. He glanced again at his map and counted the enemy threats. No less than eight Iraqi surface-to-air and triple A sites lay between the choppers and the target. And he hadn't even considered the Iraqi fighters at Shithatha and Al Musaiyib.

The pilot stared at the desert then slowly shook his head. What, he wondered, had happened to their plan?

HOUND ONE

Charlie allowed the F-15E to settle down to three thousand feet. As the fighter descended toward the sun-baked sand, it began to bounce on the heat-generated thermals. Charlie checked his threat display, then scanned his engine and avionic instruments before coming to rest on his total fuel gage.

"Got a little problem."

Killer sensed his sarcasm. "What's going on?"

"Been doing some math. Hate doing that—math in public you know—but as I see it, we won't have the fuel. Even with our drop tank, there is no way we're going to get all the way to Baghdad and get the job done, then return without some kind of air refueling. So I need you to get on the radio and try to rustle up some air-refueling tankers."

A moment of silence passed before Killer replied. "Who are you kidding, Charlie? Where are we going to get tankers? They were all back at Prince Sultan. All of those guys are dead. Whatever we do here, we do on our own."

AL AZIZIYA HIGHWAY
TWENTY-ONE MILES
SOUTH OF BAGHDAD

The presidential convoy moved quickly through the desert. It consisted of two army APCs, a covered troop transport, two black Mercedes, and two huge Range Rover all-terrain jeeps. Odai Hussein was sitting comfortably in the second Range Rover, the fourth vehicle in the long row of cars and trucks. He sat in the back with two of his most trusted guards, watching the sandy landscape at it quickly slipped by him. The convoy moved along as its best speed, the army trucks fighting to maintain their position in line.

Odai Hussein was heading to bunker 86A. It sat deep in the desert, twelve kilometers off the paved highway, accessible only by following a hard-packed trail through the desert. On the surface, there was nothing to give the location of the bunker away. No visible entry, no fences, no electric cables or telephones wires. Nothing surrounded the bunker but smooth and uninterrupted sand. In an extraordinary effort to keep the location of the bunker hidden, bunker 86A, like the other presidential bunkers, had been constructed by laborers who worked exclusively at night. The last step in the process had been to restore the area to its natural state, leaving no trace of construction behind. There were more than four dozen such bunkers scattered across central Iraq. The Americans knew the location of only two or three.

Odai kept glancing up at the sky, then checking the time. It was another thirty-three miles to the bunker turnoff, then a ten-minute drive along the bedouin trail.

In forty-five minutes, he would finally be safe.

The last vehicle in the convoy was a black army truck. Aria sat in the back seat of the huge all-terrain vehicle, her hands bound with thin wire, her feet tied with rope, a black hood pulled tight over her head. Her battered legs burned with every jolt of the truck. Her skin was raw and tender and bristled with pain. The bag over her head made it nearly impossible to breathe. She sat quiet and alone, no one paying her any attention.

And though she couldn't see, Aria was clearly aware of two things.

The vehicle she was in was the last truck in the convoy. She knew that from listening and cocking her head. She could tell from the sound there were no vehicles behind them. The only thing that followed was a soft rush of wind.

The second thing she knew brought icy fear to her heart.

When the attack commenced, as she was praying it would, the first and last vehicles in the convoy would be the first targets destroyed. The attack choppers would aim for the lead vehicle. The F-15E would aim for the last. It was the only way they would have to bring the convoy to a halt—by bottling it up between two burning wrecks. And they would have to stop the convoy if they were to get Odai alive.

And Aria knew the attack was drawing near.

HOUND ONE

Charlie moved around his forward-looking infrared sensor by toggling a coolie hat with his thumb. He called up his radar and armed the two AMRAAM missiles. His HUD told him everything he needed to know, allowing him to concentrate on flying the aircraft and scanning the terrain as it sped by under the nose of the aircraft.

He was flying at two hundred feet and almost six hundred knots. The barren landscape raced by at such an incredible speed that the sand flowed beneath the plane like brown, gushing water. Since crossing into Iraq, he had passed over only two towns, both of them isolated cinder block villages that served as markets and way points for the bedouin herdsman. Glancing over his shoulder, he watched a set of huts pass by in a blur of tin roofs and awkward corrals of goats and white sheep.

Facing forward, he adjusted his shoulder straps to tighten them up, pulling himself back against the ACES II ejection seat. The thick seat cover helped to cushion his back from the packed parachute and rocket motor inside.

"Target now estimated ninety-five miles." Killer announced calmly from the back. "We should be there in just under ten minutes. I'm guessing we will find him along the Al Azizya highway. That is really the only road in that sector. Unless he's off in the sand, four-wheeling his way through the desert."

Charlie studied his map display and nodded his head. He angled his chin to the left so that he could speak into his mask, which he had disconnected from the side of his helmet, allowing it to dangle from one strap near the top of his shoulder. "Agree," he replied as he studied the map. "We'll get to within fifty miles or so, then pop to four thousand feet and angle left. That will give you a chance to get a good radar picture. Finding him in the desert shouldn't be a big chore. The convoy will stick out like a ship on an ocean of sand. Once we find him, we'll duck down once again."

Killer grunted in agreement, then reached down to adjust his target acquisition radar to maximum range.

With a sudden chirp, the F-15's threat-warning radar began to sound in his ears. Both of the crewmen pricked up in their seats. Charlie's head began to swivel, swinging right, then turning left. He immediately began to scan the horizon, looking for bandits coming from out of the sun. As Killer glanced at his Tactical Situation Display, a knot of fear rose in his throat.

"Bandits!" he croaked. "Thirty-one miles—dead ahead."

Charlie kept his eyes out of the cockpit, while Killer stared at his radar screen.

"What have you got?" Charlie cried as he shoved his mask up to his face.

Killer studied his threat-warning display. "Slot Back radar. Two. Angels twenty-eight. Face shot. Range—now thirty miles."

Two MiG-29s. Altitude twenty-eight thousand feet. Coming right in their face. Range closing inside thirty miles.

Charlie scanned the horizon with a purposeful stare, searching desperately for any hint of the aircraft. It was always his first gut reaction to search with his eyes, a technique that had saved him more than once in his life. Like all fighter pilots since the First World War, he trusted his eyeballs before any electronic machine.

Focusing inward, he then studied the HUD and its radar display. He studied the two bandits, the two tiny, white spikes that were working their way toward the center of his screen. He studied the display for maybe three or four seconds, an eternity in the high speed world of aerial combat. In his mind he developed a four dimensional picture of exactly where the enemy was—how high and how far, what direction and azimuth, the speeds they were traveling and the element of time that would play out as the opposing aircrafts flew at mach speed toward each other. He determined what air-to-air missiles were most likely hanging from under the MiG's wings, along with their maximum effective range, and the best way to defeat them.

Charlie kept the F-15 moving forward, always pointing to the target, while the distance between him and the Iraqi fighters closed at an incredible speed.

He was faced with a decision, and he had only seconds to react.

He could pull the nose up and engage the enemy fighters, or stay on target and hope they didn't know he was there. If he waited and stayed low, he might slip by them in the desert. But if they found him—or if they already knew he was there—then he would be at a critical disadvantage, for the Iraqi pilots would be starting the battle with the clear benefit of having twenty-eight thousand feet of potential energy to use against him. And energy and power were the primary tools that allowed a fighter pilot to maneuver his jet. Speed and altitude were life. It was as simple as that.

Charlie considered a moment, then studied his fuel-remaining readout.

"Say distance to target?"

"Seventy-two miles," Killer shot back.

Charlie pushed the aircraft forward while he sweat in his seat, a trickle of perspiration running down the sides of his ribs. His mouth was bone-dry as he stared at his screen.

The Iraqi pilots were still heading directly toward him.

Did they see him? Did they have him? Did they know he was there? Or would he slip underneath them, hidden in the sands of the desert?

A sudden whine screamed in his helmet with a high-pitched squeal. At the same time Killer began to cry from the back. "Spike off the nose! They're looking for us, Charlie! They're locking us up!"

34

HOUND ONE
SOUTHERN IRAQI DESERT

Charlie slammed the fighter into a tight left-hand turn and threw both throttles forward against the stops. Twin afterburner flames burst from the tail pipes of the aircraft, accelerating it through the air. Charlie rolled the fighter up to eighty degrees of bank, then jammed the control stick into his lap, using the energy of his momentum to pull him around, turning to keep the fighters at maximum range. The onset of G-forces sucked his body into the seat and pulled at his arms, which now weighed eighty pounds each. His head sunk against his neck and his vision narrowed slightly as the fighter rolled into nine Gs. His anti-G suit inflated, the rubber bladder constricting tightly against his abdomen and legs. Grunting, he strained to keep the blood in his head. Over his headset, he could hear Killer strain against the Gs.

Charlie nudged the aircraft lower, heading toward a small bluff of rising sand, then rolled out on a heading that would keep the bandits off his right side. Punching a button on the top of his control stick, he dispensed triple bundles of chaff—the tiny, paper-thin streamers of aluminum that would help to hide the aircraft behind a wall of radar-reflective material. His eyes shot across the horizon as he frantically searched for the Iraqi jets.

Scanning his radar, he saw the fighters moving inside twenty miles. Just within range of their air-to-air missiles.

* * *

Twenty-eight thousand feet above him, and moving to fifty degrees off of his right, the two Iraqi MiG-29 pilots were watching the incoming fighter on their Russian-made, look-down, shoot-down Slot Back radar, one of the finest pieces of aviation equipment in the world. They studied the incoming aircraft, picking it easily out from the relatively smooth ground clutter of the desert. Their helmet-mounted infrared tracking system made following the F-15 a very simple chore. The laser range finder ticked down the distance to the target, a readout that was accurate to within just a few meters.

As the American fighter moved inside eighteen miles, the lead aircraft fired two missiles. The Alamo air-to-air missiles dropped away from the belly of the MiG, their rocket motors bursting white smoke in the air. The missiles wobbled for a fraction of a second, then moved away from the fighter, accelerating with breathtaking speed before dropping down toward the desert.

The second MiG pilot waited to fire until the first two missiles had disappeared. Then, with a quick burst of smoke, two Alamos also dropped off his rails, ignited, and streaked toward the American fighter.

The two Iraqi MiGs then split, one heading east, the other west. Watching, they waited for their missiles to explode.

"They're going offensive!" Killer cried from the back. "East, west! We've got to commit!" Charlie glanced at his radar to see the two fighters split up. A cold chill of adrenaline ran down the center of his back. He immediately knew what the fighters had done. Turning over his shoulder, he stared back to north, scanning high in the silver-blue sky.

And there he saw them. A stream of hair-thin contrails. Four long, fuzzy lines trailing white against the sky. The missile's ramjet engines heated the cool air at high altitude into a steady stream of white vapor. Like arrows, they trailed from the missile's exhaust, pointing directly toward the American Eagle.

A cold hand of terror wrapped around Charlie's chest. It squeezed him and held him, taking the breath from his lungs. Every muscle in his body wadded into a tight little ball. It was then that instinct and training took over.

"*missiles!*" Charlie screamed. "*four trails. three o'clock.*" Killer wrenched around in his seat to get a look over his shoulder. What he saw made his heart jump halfway into his throat. Four missiles! Not more than ten miles away!

Charlie hit the chaff button as fast as he could, leaving a thin wall of aluminum clutter behind him. Killer turned back to his console and ran his fingers over his keypad. "Twelve-eleven!" he called in a desperate voice from the back.

"What! No! Are you certain?"

"It's perfect!" Killer shot back. "We're lower than the Iraqis and the clear sky will bounce out multiple signals. It's our only chance!"

"*do it!*"

Killer quickly went to work.

Charlie leveled the aircraft and pushed the nose toward the sand. The desert rose up to meet them as the fighter leveled off barely fifty feet above the ground, a rooster tail of blasting sand trailing in their exhaust. Glancing over his shoulders, he watched the missiles collapse the tiny bit of airspace that remained between them. Again and again Charlie swore to himself as he stared at the incoming missiles. He would give Killer a chance, but not more than five or six seconds. After that, he would take evasive action himself.

Inside the rear cockpit, Killer was working with desperate speed, stroking his electronic-countermeasures keypad, commanding his computers to initiate the new jamming procedure that had been given the deceptively simple name of "Twelve-eleven."

The four Alamos continued toward the F-15. The two lead missiles were just over eight miles away, the second two trailing three miles behind them. They had a near-perfect angle and had just reached maximum speed. Their warheads had been armed and were set to proximity fuse. Impact with the fighter was only thirty seconds away.

Killer initiated the countermeasures system. A beam of electronic energy instantly emitted from the F-15's jamming pod, the most sophisticated and classified piece of equipment on the jet. It put out a barrage of electronic particles toward the incoming missiles, a computer-generated signal the Alamos couldn't ignore.

Suddenly the missiles' seeker heads saw multiple targets. Three—then five—and finally ten. Ten identical targets cluttered up their seeker relays. To the Alamos, the fake targets were indistinguishable from the real F-15. The pseudo targets began to split off in every direction, some climbing high while others stayed low.

Each of the Alamos' internal computers commanded an immediate change in course in an effort to sniff through the complicated electronic jamming. A wall of nearly impenetrable radar energy emitted from the nose of each missile. Nothing changed. The fake targets remained. The missiles fired a wall of energy once again. No good. The multiple targets continued to confuse and distract, flying wildly in different directions.

The missiles' seeker heads then became completely confused. Out of the ten targets, which one was real? Which one was the F-15 they were supposed to attack?

Charlie glanced over his shoulder to see three of the missiles trail off, following ghost aircraft that were tracking to the south. "Yes! Yes!" he cried into his mask. "Go baby! Drag them away!"

The final missile faltered before momentarily turning to the west, then reengaged to home in on his Eagle again. Charlie watched as the missile made a final turn for his aircraft. It was now only three miles away.

"missiles three miles!" he cried into his mask. He jammed on the stick, pulling it back onto his lap, hitting the chaff button three times as he climbed into the air. He heard Killer gasp at the sudden onset of the Gs. Charlie pulled on the stick, keeping it back in his lap. Within seconds, the fighter was pointing upward at ninety degrees, climbing skyward at thirty thousand feet every minute. More than five hundred feet every second it climbed. Charlie reached for the combat jettison button. It was time to lighten the load. He punched the drop tank, sending it and its remaining eleven hundred pounds of fuel tumbling and spinning through the air.

The missile scooped toward the desert, then began to pull up as it chased the Strike Eagle into the sky. Charlie craned his neck back, looking over his shoulder toward the ground, which was fading with astonishing speed. Killer was also looking back. Both of them searched for the enemy missile.

The Alamo's control fins steered the missile after the aircraft. Turning upward, the missile locked onto the American fighter once again. The fighter was now passing through fifteen thousand feet, the Alamo trailing just four thousand feet below. Charlie pushed his throttles forward. They were already at the stops. The aircraft was heavy with bombs and not accelerating in the climb. The missile gained very quickly, closing to within two thousand feet. Charlie nudged the fighter over and rolled to the right. The missile followed and closed to less than five hundred feet. Charlie's face drained of color as he bit on his lip. The missile closed and grew even larger, every detail showing in startling detail, its seeker head glinting white in the sun.

"Baby! Baby! Baby!" Charlie was stroking the jet, begging her to push upward with even more speed. The thought of ejecting never entered his mind—every fiber of soul focused on evading the missile. In the rear cockpit, Killer considered the option. His left hand drifted down to the ejection handle by his knee.

Charlie never took his eye off the missile, which was trailing a huge contrail once again. It was closing. And closing. Charlie rolled to the left. The missile followed as the fighter climbed through twenty-four thousand feet. Charlie sucked in his breath and checked the altitude readout, knowing—thinking—hoping he was right.

The missile puffed, then wobbled, then ran out of fuel. Like a rocket, it coasted upward in a long, graceful arch before slowly rolling its nose back toward earth. Charlie saw the missile hesitate. That's all it took to know it was done. The motor had burned out barely in time. Another two or three seconds and it would have taken out his jet.

As the missile floated upward, it suddenly slowed. Decelerating through five hundred knots, the self-destruct pin fired into the warhead in a desperate attempt to kill whatever was near, exploding the missile in a harmless ball of flame and black smoke, eight hundred feet below the American fighter.

Charlie didn't wait to see the missile self-destruct. He knew there were still enemy fighters in the air. Pulling on the nose of his fighter, he rolled back toward the horizon. The aircraft pulled level, but inverted in the sky. Charlie rolled it upright at just under twenty-six thousand feet. He was very slow, only two-hundred knots. As Charlie maneuvered the aircraft, Killer was working his radar, searching for the two Iraqi fighters in the sky.

It took him only a moment to find them. They had rejoined and were both flying north, accelerating quickly at seventeen thousand feet.

Charlie scanned his HUD to see the fighters running ten miles off his nose.

"I've got the radar," he called out from the front. With a flip of the switch, he took control of the radar and moved it to illuminate the bandits, then selected two AMRAAM missiles. Killer strained in his seat to look past the nose of the aircraft, trying to get a visual on the low-flying targets. Charlie pushed the Eagle's nose thirty degrees toward the ground in an effort to build up his speed. He designated the first MiG as his primary target. On his canopy bow, his "lock and shoot" light illuminated in a steady orange glow. He hit the launch button. Two missiles accelerated off the belly-rail that ran along his conformal fuel tanks. With a burst of white smoke and a clearly audible *whoosh*, the missiles trailed away, the Eagle accelerating downward behind them. Killer watched on his radar. The two MiGs began to split and turn. The first MiG went vertical. The other dived in a hard right-hand circle, a post-hole maneuver that took him spiraling toward the desert sand. Charlie slammed his radar into auto-guns, his fingers dancing over his control stick like a piccolo player as he commanded his jet to snag the second bandit with a heat-seeking missile. He punched a final button. Two more missiles fired away. Both of the MiGs were wildly jinking in a desperate attempt to break the missile's lock-on. They maneuvered left and right at max perform Gs. Killer could see their chaff reflecting on his radar screen.

The missiles continued to track straight for the targets.

The lead MiG was destroyed by the first AMRAAM Charlie had fired. The second missile trailed through the burst of wreckage in the air. The other MiG was killed by simultaneous hits from the third and forth missiles. Charlie and Killer watched as the two Iraqi fighters exploded in flames, black balls of smoke and yellow fire bursting out in huge mushroom-shaped clouds. They watched as pieces of wreckage began to fall to the ground. The twin fireballs rolled silently in the air only to collapse in on themselves and slowly disappear.

Without a word to each other, without any sign of emotion, the two American crewmen went back to work. Charlie immediately began to scan the horizon ahead while Killer swept the radar for other MiGs.

"What ya got?" Charlie asked, his voice empty and dry.

"Nothing. Not here anyway. I could search, but we would have to go back and look through each sector. It would take a few minutes. Is that what you want to do?"

Charlie glanced very quickly at the cockpit clock. "No," he shot back. "No time now. The choppers are approaching the target. We have only minutes to get there. And that's our priority. That is our mission."

Though Charlie couldn't see, Killer was nodding his head. "Rog, boss," he called back. "Give me a heading of zero-one-zero. Last known position of the convoy now—thirty-one miles. We're fifty seconds late. The choppers are going to beat us there."

Charlie turned and looked north. In the distance he could see it, a dark ribbon of road that cut its way through the drifting sand of the desert. Rolling the aircraft over, Charlie began to descend. Turning north, he glanced at his time-to-target display. They were just over three minutes away from the highway.

Reaching for his radio, Charlie dialed up the attack frequency and punched at his microphone switch. "Cobra, say time to target?" he said very quickly.

"Two minutes," the lead chopper immediately came back. "We've been waiting, Hound. Where have you been?"

Charlie hit the afterburners and accelerated toward the ground. "We're on our way, Cobra. We're almost there," he replied.

The aircraft accelerated quickly toward the dark ribbon of road.

"I'm starting to pick up a possible target," Killer called. "Yeah . . . this has got to be it. I've got a very solid radar return. Looks like six . . . no, make that seven, large vehicles in convoy. Twenty-eight miles. Right off the nose. And I've got a good return on the Apaches. They're hovering two miles south of the road."

Charlie looked at the radar. The choppers were just starting to come into view. As he approached the Al Aziziya Highway, he could see their dark silhouettes. They were spread out, line abreast, taking up combat positions. Charlie saw a quick jump on the altimeter as his aircraft sliced effortlessly through the sound barrier. He glanced at the mach indicator. Mach 1.12 and still climbing. He pulled back on the throttles. He would be there in time. He was fifteen miles out. The battle was about to commence.

Charlie hesitated a moment as he stared at the road. Lifting his eyes, he scanned across the horizon, searching the open sky from the surface up to thirty thousand feet. Glancing over his shoulder, he quickly looked back at his tail.

Something gnawed at him, holding him, drawing his eyes to the sky.

It was wrong. The Iraqi fighters were too quick to engage.

Their doctrine hadn't changed since the opening days of the Gulf War. They would never attack unless they outnumbered the Americans by at least four to one.

Yet these two MiGs had come at him without any hesitation. Their behavior went against everything Charlie had ever seen before. Never had the Iraqis engaged with just two-to-one odds. As his aircraft descended toward the convoy and the hot desert sand, Charlie shook his head and tried to concentrate on the mission again. But in the back of his mind, he was filled with a nagging self-doubt. They were there. Other fighters. He could feel it in his bones.

The two Iraqi MiGs followed him, flying at thirty thousand feet. They stayed behind the American fighter, but always kept him in sight.

AL AZIZIYA HIGHWAY
SOUTHERN IRAQI DESERT

Aria felt a sudden pull on the hood that had been placed over her head. With a jerk, the black cloth was pulled away. Colonel Samih Bakr Hajazi glared into her eyes, his face just inches in front of her own.

"Are they coming?" He sneered. "Are they coming to kill him?"

Aria squinted her eyes from the bright desert sun, unable to focus or see in the glaring white light. She didn't answer at first, then nodded her head. "They are coming," she nodded. "We are in very great danger!"

The colonel pulled out his knife and pushed the blade against her throat. "When! How! What will they do?"

"Attack choppers and aircraft!" Aria whispered in fear. Her voice was so weak the colonel had to struggle to hear.

"They are coming. Now! In the middle of the day?"

"They will come," Aria muttered. "You know that they will. They will come when they get the signal from the transmitter. Even now, the aircraft are certainly in the air." Aria glanced out her window, turning her eyes to the south, to the direction from which the attack would soon come. "You must help me," she said. "Get us both out of here."

"No," the colonel growled as he thought to himself. "We will stay. It is the best place to be. When they come—if they come—they will go after him. They have the transmitter. They will know which car to attack. We are safe, as long as we stay away from his car."

"N-No," Aria stammered. "You don't understand. They don't want to kill him! They want to take him alive! We are the target, not Odai

Hussein. This isn't an assassination. It is much more complex than that. Can't you see—they will kill everyone else in the convoy. They are using the transmitter so they can take him alive—"

Aria suddenly stopped, her voice trailing off.

She listened. She could hear it beating on the horizon. The sound of the choppers echoed through the empty desert air.

A white-hot flash of yellow and red blazed across the day sky. A visible shock wave burst outward, an exploding circle of pressure that moved across the dry earth like a tiny wave in the sea. The first truck in the convoy exploded up on its rear tires, then fell on its side in a ball of yellow flame. Pieces of bent steel and burning rubber blew out from the center of the fire. The following trucks in the convoy quickly slammed on their brakes. Aria turned to her window to see the fighter appear, a black dot that grew above the southern horizon. The nose of the fighter was pointing directly at her.

She sucked in her breath as her heart skipped a beat. She pulled her arms tight, tucking them into her chest. Every action and sound, every feeling and fear, seemed to come as if from a million miles away. Her heart seemed to slow as she stared at the aircraft, it's shiny gray nose glinting bright in the sun.

Charlie listened to the radios as the chopper pilot started to scream. "Tally! Tally! Cobra One has a good beacon. Target is in the number four car. Repeat. Target is in car number four." A half second of silence passed, then the frantic voice cried once again.

"Cobras have missiles away. Hellfires in the air. We've got the lead vehicle. Hound start at the rear."

Charlie acknowledged with a short "Rog!" in his mask, then turned the fighter toward the last vehicle in the convoy, a huge black army truck that lumbered forty yards in the rear. He was approaching very fast, but was still just over five miles away. The last vehicle illuminated brightly on his infrared display.

"Weapon armed and ready!" Killer called out from the back.

"Forty seconds!" Charlie replied as he flipped his weapons arm switch.

The colonel saw the F-15E as it flew over the desert. For a moment he stared, a look of awe on his face. Aria stared at the fighter, completely paralyzed with fear. If they didn't do something, they had only seconds to live. She grabbed her door handle and jerked it around. It was locked from the outside. She couldn't get out. She stared at her hands, which were still tied with wire. She shuffled her feet. The rope did not give way. With a cry she clenched her eyes tight. She lowered her head. She couldn't watch anymore.

She was about to be killed by one of her friends. One of the few men she had ever met who she thought she could love. He was daring and handsome and kind as a child.

She prayed for a moment that he wouldn't find out. She knew it would haunt him, and it wasn't his fault. Like everyone else, he was just doing his job. Battle could be so confusing. How was he to know . . .

The fighter bore down. The convoy was easy to mark. Charlie studied the attack choppers, which were suspended in the air, hiding behind a small of mound of sand and shale rock. Behind them, the MH-60s hovered just above the ground, anxiously waiting for their time to go in. As Charlie watched, another Hellfire was sent on its way. He could see its long, flowing tail as it guided toward the second vehicle in the convoy, an Iraqi APC. The troop carrier jerked forward, crashing through the burning wreckage ahead. The missile adjusted its track a few degrees to the right. Everyone inside the carrier had just under four seconds to live.

Charlie's radio beacon began to ping in his ears. A small blue dot began to flash in the center of his radar, pounding with a quick pulse from the fourth car on the road. Clearly, it marked Odai's position in the convoy. He was there. The end was seconds away. Charlie glanced at Odai's car, a huge black limousine. It was cranked sideways on the road, two tires locked in the deep sand.

At that moment Charlie felt his whole world stand still. Seeing the black car, he realized just how easy it could be. For a moment, he flashed back to the scene at Prince Sultan. His mind filled with an image of Colonel Wisner's desperate face, begging Charlie to help him, to let him open the door. He saw the colonel's blue eyes, rimmed with blood and tears. He could feel Killer's hand slap down over his own as together they closed the door on their friend. He felt the despair once again as Colonel Wisner turned away, his eyes dimming with sadness as he stared at the sand.

"Get him," Charlie heard Colonel Wisner's voice in his head. "Get him, Charlie. Go and get him for me."

Charlie suddenly nudged the fighter four degrees to the right. Odai Hussein's limousine slipped into his target box. His pipper settled in the center of the box, directly over the huge black sedan. A growling "lock-on" signal buzzed in his ear. The laser designator sent a beam of invisible light from his target pod to bounce off the top of the car. The beam of photon energy hit the limousine square on the roof. The two outermost bombs on his wings came to life, their seeker heads tracking down the beam of invisible light. The two bombs would hit in the exact center of the car.

He could kill him. He could do it. He could end it all now.

He lifted his finger and touched the button that would send the bombs on their way. He touched the small button, feeling it through his flight glove.

He could kill him. He could do it. He could send him to hell.

For another half second, he saw Wisner's crying, blue eyes. Killer looked up from his radar and started to scream into his mask. "No! Charlie! No!" Charlie hesitated a moment. "come back to the target!" Killer screamed once again.

With a shake of his head, Charlie pushed the vision away. A chill of adrenaline shot through the middle of his spine. He took a huge breath, then pulled the aircraft back to the left. For the first time, he noticed that he hadn't been breathing. His hand was wrapped like a vise on the top of his stick. He took another gulp of air and repositioned his fingers, forcing himself to block the image of Prince Sultan from his mind. He lifted his eyes to his Head Up Display and studied the last vehicle in the procession of cars. Once again, his target pipper settled over the center of the army truck.

"Ready!" Killer called.

"I got it!" Charlie replied.

The Strike Eagle shook with a sudden vibration. The two laser-guided bombs were released from their rails. They tracked toward the target, following the invisible beam that was striking at the top of the black army truck.

Aria felt a jerk on the rope around her legs. Opening her eyes, she watched the colonel hack at the chord. With his left hand, he reached over and pushed open his door. "Roll out!" he cried as he sliced with the knife. Finally, he cut through the last of the cord. The truck was rolling slowly forward, the driver unsure of what to do, when Colonel

Hajazi rolled out and onto the pavement. Aria pushed herself out and fell flat on the ground. Grabbing her by the arms, the colonel pulled her toward the side of the road. Aria scrambled and kicked backward, pushing away from the truck. Inside her ears, she could hear the strangest of sounds, a high-pitched whine, unlike anything she had ever heard before. Like the buzz of a motor or a thousand angry bees. She looked up to see the bombs whistling toward them. The colonel dropped into the shallow ditch on the left side of the road, pulling Aria into the dirt beside him. She fell on her face. The colonel rolled onto her back and covered her head with his arms.

The two GBU-15 five-hundred-pound bombs exploded exactly into the middle of the truck, blowing it nearly ten feet straight up into the air. A deafening explosion smashed into Aria's body, pressing her into the dirt as it shook the ground. A thousand pounds of over-pressure pounded into her body. Her eardrums nearly split. The air was sucked from her lungs. The world started to tumble, though she was laying in the sand, as the fluid in her ears started spinning around.

The four-wheel drive spun and twisted in the middle of the road, burning fuel shooting outward on thin fingers of fire. A deep, black smoke billowed upward, rising furiously from the heat of the fire. Aria felt a wave of scorching air passing over her body. Another explosion sounded thirty feet down the road as a third GBU exploded into another Iraqi truck. A thousand pieces of rock and hot steel passed directly over her head. She felt a sudden *whoop*. The colonel slumped against her back. She pushed against the colonel. His weight didn't give way. She pushed until he finally rolled over. A fragment of metal was protruding from the side of his neck.

The colonel looked up, an expression of surprise in his eyes. A look of pain and great sadness flashed across his dark face, then faded as the life began to seep from his body. He looked almost peaceful as he lay in the sand. He reached out toward Aria, pulling her near.

"He's—going to use the weapon," he whispered, his voice a mere gurgle as he choked on his blood. "Today—in D.C. That is—all that I know—"

Charlie strained over his shoulder. He watched without emotion as another bomb smashed into the last APC, sending it tumbling and spinning in a red fireball. He jerked the stick on his Eagle, pulling it into a hard, climbing turn. He skidded through a half circle as he

turned his fighter around. Halfway through the turn, the line of burning Iraqi vehicles came back into view. Five balls of fire were now scattered across the long road. He watched a lone army truck turn and lurch
through the ditch, then widely cut its way across the hot desert sand.
Its huge, underinflated tires spun up rooster tails of dust as it frantically
scrambled away from the fires. Charlie pushed his stick to the right and
his aircraft rolled over. With a flip of his finger, he armed up his gun.
He bore down on the fleeing truck as it ran across the sand. He pressed
on the trigger. A sudden vibration worked its way through his seat as
the 20 millimeter cannon spit out eighty-five shells, any one of them
powerful enough to cut its way through the truck or blow its sloshing
gas tank into a billowing fire.

Geysers of sand blew up from the desert as the individual shells
impacted the ground. The line of explosions stretched toward the black
truck. The vehicle weaved to the left, then cut back to the right. It
almost tipped over as the driver fought for control. Charlie fired another
two-second burst, then let off on the trigger and kicked on the rudder
to point his nose to the left. Another three-second burst and the truck
exploded in flames.

Charlie looked over his shoulder as they passed over the road.
Odai's car was still there. It sat alone on the road, the only vehicle that
was not burning.

"Choppers moving in!" Killer cried from the back.

Charlie turned his eyes once again to the burning truck in the sand.
Two Iraqi soldiers were scrambling away from the fire. Turning his
head, he watched the MH-60s as they moved into position. They
slowed to a hover near the side of the presidential limousine. The army
Delta troops were hanging from the open doors of the choppers. The
door gunners were mowing 50-caliber shells down both sides of the
road. Charlie craned his neck to see what the gunners were trying to
kill. He watched a body guard roll out of the presidential limousine,
only to be cut down in his tracks before he could lift up his gun. The
choppers settled very quickly, coming to rest near the road, blasting a
whirlwind of sand out from under their rotors. The first Delta Team
was set to jump out of the chopper. Charlie pulled his fighter up into
a tight circle at five hundred feet.

Had he been looking, he might have seen the glint of their wings.
But he was looking below him. And there was so little time.

The two Iraqi MiGs approached from the west, masking themselves in the glare of the now setting sun. They had planned their

attack as a visual-only maneuver. Neither of them activated their radar, which would have given them away, for the Strike Eagle would have immediately detected the signal emitted from the radar dish in their nose. And that would have given him a few seconds' warning. So they planned their attack using only their heat-seeking missiles. They moved in on the American fighter, silent as wind, their canted wings painting fleeting shadows across the dry sand.

At two miles, the lead MiG fired two of its missiles.

Charlie never saw the fighters. Had no idea they were there. He never saw the missiles tracking in on his tail, seeking the white-hot exhaust that scorched from his twin engine cores. The heat-seeking missiles didn't use any radar, so his radar warning receiver never screamed in his ears. At two thousand feet, the missiles locked on hard to the fighter. At that point, even had Charlie known, there was nothing he could have done.

The first missile impacted the left engine, flying straight up the tail. It got halfway up the exhaust before the detonator fired. Twenty pounds of explosives blew the aircraft apart. The impact was sudden and deadly. The Eagle fell from the air. The two engines were blown away from the airframe. Tumbling end over end, they fell to the earth. Four thousand pounds of jet fuel ignited behind them. The cockpit and airframe remained largely intact, though it spun like a top as it fell through the air. The explosion was powerful enough to tear Charlie's oxygen mask from his face. His head beat the side of the canopy as he tumbled through the air. His arms were pinned to his body, the air was pushed from his lungs. He tried to open his eyes. He saw nothing but black. The G-forces were pushing all the blood to his head. With a crack, his canopy shattered, blasting him in the face with tornado-force winds. The fighter twisted in a ball of broken steel and flames.

Instantly, Charlie became aware of the fire as his cockpit was enveloped in an intense wall of flame. He reached for his ejection handles half a second too late. Killer had already initiated an ejection of the crew, commanding both of their seats to fire them into the air. Charlie felt himself accelerate as his seat slung up the rails, the G-forces snapping his head to his chest. He felt a hot blast of wind, then a spine-wrenching jolt as his parachute billowed and snapped in the air.

For a long moment, Charlie hung motionless under his orange, brown, and white parachute, a gentle flapping of material sounding over his head. He hung there in shock, hardly knowing where he was, until the sound of the battle began to jar in his ears.

Below him, he could hear the crackle of fire. The acidic fumes burned his eyes as he passed through a column of smoke. He could feel the pound of the choppers' machine guns. Then he heard the roar of the MiGs as they screamed fifty feet over his head. The two fighters flew east for only two thousand feet, then turned sharply back toward the road while dropping low over the ground. He watched in silent horror as the two MiGs set up their attack. Without knowing, he screamed out a warning to the choppers. He saw two missiles drop from under the leading MiG's wing, then fire and track toward the first MH-60 on the road. With a flash, the chopper exploded in a white-hot ball of fire. The second MH-60 rolled backward from the force of the explosion and settled abruptly onto the loose sand. The second MiG turned its nose at the Apaches. With a low *brrrrrrrr*, it began to fire its gun. Within seconds, another chopper was blown into bits. The other Apaches took off, jinking and banking away. They accelerated to the south, fading behind a wall of greasy smoke. Charlie watched them disappear and wondered what he would do.

Glancing over, he saw Killer's parachute drifting slowly in the wind. His friend remained motionless as he descended through the air.

Looking downward, Charlie watched the desert come up to meet him. With a jar in his legs, he landed on enemy soil.

36

WASHINGTON NATIONAL CATHEDRAL
WASHINGTON, D.C.
0827 LOCAL TIME

The President of the United States sat in the front pew of the War Memorial Chapel, a dark, high-ceilinged annex to the Washington National Cathedral. An enormous stained-glass window stood watch over the two coffins, casting lustrous shadows across the side wall. The room was dimly lit, the deep mahogany furnishings and cold marble floor compounded the feeling of emptiness in the air. The families of the deceased were scattered in groups; talking, mourning, and crying with each other. The former vice president's wife stood by the president's side. She squeezed his shoulder, then moved slowly away to huddle with her children near the back of the chapel.

The president stared at the two caskets for a very long time. He had just added their names, written by his own hand, into the latest volume of the *National Roll of Honor*. Sitting alone in the pew, he lowered his head.

A huge wooden door swung open on well-oiled hinges. The cardinal entered the room, his robes sweeping the floor. The mournful sound of music drifted into the chapel from the Great Organ that was being played out in the nave. The ten thousand pipes played each note with great power and precision, the sound gracefully echoing off the high cathedral walls. The president looked up. The cardinal nodded his head. He then turned to the others and began to walk through the small groups, bringing them together with a gentle sweep of his arms.

Lowering his voice, he told them the service was about to begin.

The president reached into his breast pocket to take out a stack of three-by-five cards. For the last time, he reviewed the points of the eulogy in his mind.

At the rear of the cathedral, near the west portal, under the tympanum that depicted the story of the creation in stone, the steel canister lay hidden in the air vent in the small public bathroom. No one knew it was there. With a soft *whoosh*, the air conditioner pulled the air in through the vent before sending it through the coolers to circulate throughout the cathedral. Inside the canister's brain, the final electronic chronometer clicked on. It began to count down.

Sixty minutes to go.

AL AZIZIYA HIGHWAY
SOUTHERN IRAQI DESERT

Aria stayed in the ditch as the attack carried on. She stayed as low as she could, pushing herself into the sand, too terrified to look, too confused to even react. She lay without moving as the smoke filled the air. After several seconds of madness, the attack came to a halt. The sound of the choppers then grew loud in her ears. She lifted her head to peak over the top of the ditch. The MH-60s were coming to a hover over the road. They couldn't have been more than fifty yards away. She saw the army soldiers hunched at the door of the choppers. Glancing up the road, she saw a black limo in the sand. The back door burst open and a bodyguard jumped out. A harsh *brrrrr* filled the air as a door gunner fired. The Iraqi fell backward, his body rolling through the sand. The limo's door remained open, but no one else appeared.

Aria rolled onto her back, her mind in a panic. How could she approach the chopper without getting mowed down? The constant chatter of their machine guns made their intentions perfectly clear. Shoot. Shoot anything that moved.

Aria glanced down at her dark robe and struggled at the wire round her hands. She felt a sharp pain erupt from deep in her legs. She looked up once again to study the scene on the road, pushing her head just above the shallow ditch in the sand. The army vehicles burned and the smoke grew very thick. A constant buzz of machine gun blaze emitted from both of the choppers, the door gunners anxious to eliminate any threat from the ground. She saw two Iraqi soldiers run in a panic through the sand, twisting and turning as they scrambled for cover. One of them turned and pointed with his arm to the ditch. They were heading straight for her. One of them lifted his gun. They were only thirty feet away, when they were cut down in their tracks, their bodies sawed nearly in two from the power of the American guns.

Aria took a deep breath, then quickly made up her mind.

Forcing her hands over her head, she pushed herself up. Limping, she made her way to the chopper. "Help me!" she cried over and over again. Her voice didn't carry. It was far too noisy to hear.

The left gunner saw the figure emerge from the shadows of smoke that was billowing in thick sheets across the Al Aziziya Highway. Swinging his gun on its floor mount, he turned it to train in the center mass of the target. With a feather-light touch, he pressed against the trigger of his gun. He watched for a moment as the figure struggled through the thick smoke, waiting to fire only until he had a clear shot.

He hesitated a moment. It just didn't look right. There was something about it. He peered through the smoke. The target was moving so slowly. And it wobbled somehow. Then he saw that the target had raised its hands over its head. It was dressed all in black, like a rough-fitting robe. Clearly, this target was not an Iraqi soldier. But what else could it be? A bedouin herdsman? A shepard? What else could it be! A deep sense of grief, almost panic, washed over his body. Had civilians been hit? Had they been too loose with their fire!

The gunner watched intently as the figure emerged from the smoke. Then his lower jaw dropped. He squinted against the dry wind. It was a girl! A woman! And she was calling to him. She stumbled and fell. He didn't know what to do. She struggled to stand, her bound hands pushing her up.

"Cease fire!" he barked into his helmet-mounted microphone. "I've got a woman approaching on this side of the aircraft. She appears to be friendly. What do you want me to do?" The other crew members immediately turned in their seats.

Aria was still twenty yards from the American chopper. The door gunner let the barrel of his weapon drift toward the ground. Stumbling forward, she lowered her hands and started to run.

She had only taken two steps when the missile flew into the side of the helicopter, blowing it into a thousand pieces of charred and burning debris. The MiG screamed overhead, following after its missile. Pulling right, the fighter avoided the rising fireball.

Aria was blown backward from the force of the rising explosion.

The searing fire seemed to wrap her entire body with heat. Her ears nearly burst from the force of the blast. She stared in confusion as the chopper erupted in flames. She stared at the helicopter as it rolled onto its side, the core of the airframe burning in a bright, yellow fire.

Another explosion rocked from the center of the chopper as the helicopter's secondary fuel cell blew apart. A piece of burning leather flew out from the core of the fire. Aria looked down and gasped. A combat boot smoldered at her feet.

She gulped in horror, her face turning white as a sheet. Stumbling backward, she turned away from the burning machine. In the distance, over her shoulder, she heard the buzz of a gun, then dual outbreaks of sound as two of the Apaches burst into flames. She heard the MiG flying over, not more than fifty feet over her head. Falling to her knees, she began to whimper in slow, sobbing breaths. The sound of the fires seemed to grow in her ears. She could smell burning flesh. She wanted to puke. Bending over, she covered her head with her arms. With a start, she felt a firm grip at her shoulder. Whirling around, she looked up with unbelieving eyes. Charlie reached down and lifted her to her feet.

She shut her eyes, convinced that he wasn't real. Charlie supported her body as he leaned forward to her ear. "Were you in one of the convoy vehicles?" he asked in a trembling voice. Aria nodded her head. Charlie's face turned more pale. Reaching to his survival vest, he extracted a long combat knife. Working quickly, he hacked at the copper wire around her wrist.

"He's going to use it," she muttered into Charlie's ear. "He's going to use the biological weapon."

"He already has," he said in a voice thick with despair. With a jerk of his hand, he cut the last of the wire. Aria leaned weakly against him, grabbing his face to stare into his eyes. "No," she said. "You don't understand. Today. In D.C. Millions of people will die."

Charlie studied her eyes, then nodded his head. He was neither shocked nor surprised. It was the next logical step. No doubt, that had been the plan all along. And after the scene at Prince Sultan, he was beyond being scared. Nothing the Iraqi leadership could do would ever shock him again.

Looking up, Charlie saw the last MH-60 claw its way into the air. It sat in a hover, then began to move forward. Nodding toward the chopper, he pulled her by the arm. "Let's go," he cried. They both started to run.

Inside the last MH-60, the copilot was frantically searching over his head, looking for the MiGs who had just blown his buddies apart. The army Deltas waited fearfully by the still-open door. A second MiG flashed suddenly over the top of the chopper. Its shadow flickered like a ghost across the brown ground, its faint image jumping out from behind the thick wall of smoke.

"*Go!*' the copilot started to cry. "Get outta here, *now!*"

The pilot steadied the chopper, then added more power. The helicopter accelerated quickly across the blowing sand. As the door gunner peered through the smoke, he saw them running toward the chopper.

"*Hold!*' he cried. "I've got an American survivor! It must be Hound. And look, he's not alone!"

The chopper slowed, then immediately settled back to the ground. Charlie stumbled toward them, pulling Aria along as fast as her beaten legs could move. With his arm around her shoulder, he supported her weight. They approached the chopper, sand blasting into their eyes. The door gunner reached out and grabbed Aria's hand, lifting her quickly into the vibrating helicopter. Clutching at the gun braces, she dragged herself aboard, then clawed her way forward to the center of the chopper. Charlie helped push her in, then pulled himself up. The chopper immediately lifted again into the air and began to race across the desert floor. It hugged the earth, not more than a few feet off the ground.

The wreckage of the mission was soon left behind.

The gunner stared at Aria, not sure of what he should say. Aria lay without moving, a stricken look on her face. She wrapped her arms around her knees, her hands still trembling with fear, then lay her head back against the aft bulkhead wall. The army Deltas jammed together, making room for the pilot and the girl. The landscape passed swiftly, dust and sand filling the air. Charlie lay still for a moment, then pushed himself up to his knees. Crawling forward, he moved to the front of the chopper and positioned himself between the two pilots. "What are you doing!" he cried above the noise of the engines.

"Getting out of Dodge!" the pilot replied. He shot a quick look back in Charlie's direction. Charlie saw the fear and despair in his eyes. It was the look of one who was leaving dead friends behind. Charlie thought of Killer and shuddered inside.

"No," Charlie shouted. "We need to go back. We need Spider. And my WIZZO might still be alive!"

"MiGs," the pilot said, nodding frantically to the sky. "This mission's over. There's not a thing we can do!"

WASHINGTON NATIONAL CATHEDRAL
WASHINGTON, D.C.
0903 LOCAL TIME

The president and the first lady led the funeral procession down the long center aisle. The granite spires towered ninety feet over their heads. The main organ played, a solemn and beautiful sound. The nave was muggy, crowded, and uncomfortably warm. Not another soul could possibly have been packed into the narrow cathedral.

The families followed the first couple toward the front of the church. A half dozen television cameras broadcast the service to every corner of the world. As the president and family members slowly made their way down the aisle, the crowd respectfully rose to its feet.

37

SOUTHERN IRAQI DESERT

"Listen to me," Charlie screamed above the noise of the chopper. "I've got a friend back there. And he's probably alive! We're not leaving him behind! And we're not aborting this mission!"

The pilot didn't react. Charlie grabbed him by the arm. "We have to get Odai!" he cried once again. "You don't understand. We don't have any time!"

The helicopter pilot looked back, frustration and rage burning bright in his eyes. He wasn't afraid. But the situation was clearly out of control. The mission had failed. What more could they do? With a jerk, he nodded toward the hazy, white sky. "Listen to me, Hound. We all want to be heros. But you also have to know when its time to turn in your guns. We're out numbered and defenseless against those MiGs. Think of those soldiers sitting in the back of this chopper, then tell me you are willing to sacrifice their lives as well."

Charlie pushed himself even closer to the pilot. "Forget the fact that our lives are in danger. If we are killed, what is that! This is bigger than us all. We have to go back there or a million people will die! He's already used the weapon at Prince Sultan. Five thousand people— American soldiers—have already been killed today!"

The helicopter pilot stared at Charlie. "No—"

"Yes!" Charlie shot back. "I was there. We barely got out alive!"

"But the MiGs—" the pilot questioned.

"Forget them!" Charlie cried. "They're running out of fuel. And even if they don't, what choice do you have? He has planted virus canisters on American soil! We can't run. We can't leave. We *have* to do something. Now as the mission commander, I'm telling you to turn this chopper around!"

The pilot rotated forward in his seat. He watched for a second as the dry sand passed underneath him, the desert sliding quickly under the nose of his chopper. Turning, he glanced back at Charlie once again, then spoke into the microphone at his lips.

The six Delta soldiers began to stir in their seats, pulling their M-16 submachine guns up to their chest. The door gunners moved again to the fire positions and checked the long line of shells that fed from the ammo storage containers to snake into the bottom of their machines. Staying as low as he could, the pilot banked the helicopter around, turning back to the north. The fires on the highway slid back into view, multiple columns of smoke rising like black pillars in the hot desert air. The dark columns bent east as they rose above the desert, carried forward by the afternoon wind.

Charlie swallowed again, fear rising in his throat. Reaching down, he unstrapped his 9 mm pistol from his survival vest. He locked the safety and extracted the clip, counting the ten bullets inside. With a shove, he placed the weapon in his leather holster again.

Staring at a bluff of sand near the south side of the road, Charlie leaned forward to the helicopter pilot.

"How good are your marksmen?" he yelled above the noise.

The pilot spoke into his mike, talking over the intercom system with the Delta Team leader. Turning back to Charlie, the pilot called back. "Two hundred, maybe three hundred meters is all. They've got M-16s, not high-powered rifles."

Charlie thought for a moment, then pointed toward the rising bluff. "Make your way toward that bluff," he instructed. "There's a small wadi that runs from there to the road. I noticed it as I came down in my chute. Set down near the wadi on this side of the hill. If you stay low, the terrain will conceal our position. The wind and smoke will also help cover our approach."

The pilot nodded, then turned his chopper twenty degrees to the right. The sandy bluff grew larger as the helicopter drew near.

Odai Hussein was surrounded by six of his men, a combination of personal guards and elite Republican Soldiers. They were the only survivors of the aerial attack. He stood on the pavement in the middle of the road, the sun setting low on the western horizon. Looking up, he saw the MiGs circle over his head, then turn quickly to the west. Their job was finished. They were going home, critically low on fuel.

Odai lowered his head. The wind picked up, blowing grains of sand in his face. He was surrounded by fire, adding more heat to the desert. The smell of burning rubber and oil stung in his nose. Pieces of ash stuck to the sweat on his arms. The fires would burn for several hours, but Odai would be gone long before then.

He had already called, demanding reinforcements move in. The Third Battalion of the Republican Guards was less than twenty minutes away.

Until then, he would wait. But he wouldn't waste the time.

Odai moved to the American, hate and scorn burning his eyes. He dropped to his knees, staring the aviator straight in the face. Capt Alex Bennett was kneeling in a heap on the road, his left eye swollen shut, his upper lip spit nearly in two. He looked up at Odai, hardly feeling the pain of the beatings that had already broken one of his arms.

"Tell me!" Odai screamed. "I want to know how you found me! How did you track me! How did you know where I am?"

The implications of the assault had not been lost on the Iraqi leader. He had been betrayed, of that he was sure. Someone close to him had passed his whereabouts to the conniving U.S. And he wanted to know who. He would punish the man. The mere thought of treason had sent him into a rage. That fact that it had been someone close, someone that he had trusted, had clouded his thinking until he could not even speak.

Odai stared for a moment. Killer wobbled on his knees, his flight suit having already been ripped from his body. His bare legs burned against the searing heat of the road. A broken piece of bone protruded from the middle of his arm, the jagged edge of bone having ripped its way through the flesh.

Odai leaned over and screamed once again in his face. "Listen to me, you little American pig! I want to know right now, or I will kill you right here. How did you find me? Who told you where I am?"

Captain Bennett looked away, his lips cracked with dried blood. Odai nodded to the soldiers who were standing at his back. "Break his hands," he announced in a cold-blooded voice. "Smash all of his fingers."

A sergeant moved forward and grabbed Al's broken arm. Jerking it out, he pulled it away from his body. A second Iraqi grabbed him by the head, forcing him down and smashing his face against the pavement. The soldier then sat on the back of his neck. Another Iraqi moved forward with a hammer in hand, the only tool they could find in the trunk of Odai's car. The three soldiers worked together to pin Captain Bennett's wrist against the pavement. The sergeant lifted the hammer and brought it down with a crunch, smashing the bones and tendons in Killer's left hand. Killer let out a cry that seemed to echo in the wind. He cursed and pleaded and struggled to stand. Odai nodded to the sergeant. The hammer came down once again. Bennett bit through his lip, a fog of sheer anguish building up in his mind. He tried to block it all out. He tried to think of his home. He tried to think of his wife. He thought of his two little girls.

But nothing could keep the pain from boiling inside him as his hand was beaten into a pulp.

The MH-60 settled under a swirling cloud of sand. The wadi was narrow and steep, a mere wash in the desert from centuries of intense, if occasional, rain. Two of the six Delta Team members remained in the chopper. The others quickly scrambled out the right door and began to run toward the top of the gully, a crest of broken stone that lay two hundred yards in the distance. Charlie moved quickly toward the cabin door, then paused and turned toward Aria. She stared at him, an anxious and scared look on her face. Charlie smiled only briefly, then jumped from the chopper.

Charlie scrambled up the side of the wadi, bending over at the waist, using his hands to help pull himself up the side of the wash. Grabbing at the brush, he followed the elite army soldiers, who were already halfway to the crest. Three minutes later, Charlie dropped into position beside them. The men lay at the top of the wash, their heads barely peaking over the sand.

The Delta Team leader was staring through a set of flat-black binoculars. Looking out across the desert, Charlie saw they were even with the road. Squinting, he peered into the late afternoon sun. The burning automobiles smoked three hundred feet in the distance. Charlie watched as half a dozen human figures stood in a rough semicircle. Waves of heat rose over the baking sand, causing the faint images to shimmer in the distance. Scanning up and down the road, he looked for any sign of his friend. He looked across the horizon, searching for an orange-and-brown parachute. He studied the open desert, looking for the wreckage of his plane, which he found not more than half a mile to the south, a scatter of black pieces and silver-gray hunks of metal. Turning, he scanned from the wreckage to the north.

Charlie heard a sudden gasp. The Delta Team leader lowered his binoculars, then jammed them to his face once again.

"Oh, help him," he whispered in a dry and pleading tone.

Charlie reached up and grabbed the binoculars, shoving them up to his eyes. He saw the Iraqi soldiers staring at a heap on the pavement. He could see Killer's face, which was turned in his direction. Then he saw the hammer come down. He saw Killer cry out in pain, though the sound didn't carry. The hammer beat once again. Killer's eyes slowly shut.

A sickening fear rolled over Charlie's body. His breathing became heavy, a tight knot in his chest. His heartbeat nearly doubled, pounding the blood in his ears. Dropping the binoculars, he rolled onto his back, a thick wad of bile rising into his throat. Coughing, he slowly rolled onto his side.

"They got him!" he cried. "That's my WIZZO on the ground. Look at him! Look what they're doing to him!" Rolling onto his stomach, Charlie glanced across the hot desert again. "We've got to do something! Kill all of them, *now!*"

The Delta Team leader was already ordering his troops, his voice stern and commanding, but always under control.

"*do it!*" Charlie screamed.

Turning to Charlie, the team leader placed his hand on his arm. "Steady there, Hound," he instructed the captain. Turning to his men, he quickly barked out his final commands.

"Alright Deltas, the third—no, fourth man, the one in the simple black beret. That's Odai. Is everyone clear!" The soldiers nodded their heads, all the time looking down the sites of their guns.

"Acknowledge!" the leader demanded of his men.

"One's got him!" the end soldier replied without hesitation.

"Tally two!" another soldier called out. Each of the shooters acknowledged they had a bead on Hussein, the only Iraqi they intended not to kill. They then divided the enemy soldiers in a quick target selection. Extending their elbows, the six soldiers spread out to take aim.

"Ready—" the leader called as he settled himself in the sand. "Ready—take aim—fire on my command!"

* * *

"Oh please," Captain Bennett muttered in a soft and ebbing tone. "Oh please . . . I'll tell you. What do you want to know?"

Odai reached forward and grabbed the American by the thick of his hair. Jerking his face upward, he looked him straight in the eye. Killer struggled to breath as Odai pulled back on his head. "You know what I want." Odai sneered in his face. "You know what I want. Don't play stupid with me."

"If—you will just—let me up," Killer struggled to breath. The pain in his hand was more than he could ever describe. Every muscle, every tendon, every nerve, and every bone was burning in horrible fire. The pain in his arm was nothing compared to the pain in his hand. The nerves in his fingers literally screamed in his brain. He was only vaguely aware when Odai jerked on his hair once again.

"Listen to me," Odai commanded. "I won't do this fancy. I don't have any time. Not out here in the middle of the desert. This hammer is brutal and messy, but I don't really care.

"You know what I want. And you will tell it to me. The only question is, will you do it before I crush every bone in your body? Or will you tell me now, so that I can leave you alone?"

Killer lowered his eyes. "My name is Alex M. Bennett," he said in a voice as thin as a child's. "My—social security number is—"

"Do it again!" Odai screamed in a rage to his guards. The sergeant reached out for Killer's other hand. Pulling it down to the pavement, he lifted the hammer over his head.

The hammer came down with another horrible crunch, cutting clear through the flesh to make contact with the road underneath. Odai watched intently as Killer writhed on the road. Killer began a slow moan, a sad sound from deep in his chest.

As Odai watched, the emotion welled like thunder inside him. There was a hate and frustration he simply could not ignore. It swallowed him in an anger he could not control. Rushing forward, Odai grabbed the hammer from the guard. "I will do it myself!" he screamed in uncontrollable rage. "I will kill him. I will do it! I don't care if he's dead!"

Bending over, Odai brought the hammer down against the back of Killer's head, swinging wildly, again and again. Odai slipped into a vision of America dead, a vision he had dreamed of every night for the past dozen years. His mind slipped out of focus as he brought the hammer over his head. He thought of the desert and the attack helicopter that had mercilessly blown off his leg. He thought of his father and how his country had been brought to its knees. He thought of so many things that didn't make any sense, all of them due to American pride. But they would pay. *This* American would pay. It would end his life now.

After twenty seconds of exertion, Odai let the hammer fall to the ground.

Then he heard it, a strange buzzing sound in his ears, a funny vibration that whizzed at the side of his head. The first soldier went down, spinning backward in the sand, his knees buckling under the weight of his body. Another one fell, a three-inch hole in his chest. Another three dropped before Odai could scramble to his feet, his eyes wide in confusion, his mouth open in fear. He saw the helicopter rise out of the depression in the desert. He heard the final bullet slicing into the only soldier still alive.

The helicopter approached him in a blaze of speed and blowing sand. The jagged sound of thunder emitted from the two 50-caliber machine guns. The door gunners fired in a tight circle around him, blowing up geysers of rock and broken pieces of road, trapping him with nowhere to go. He saw two soldiers leaning from the side door, their M-16 submachine guns raised to keep him in their sights. Odai froze in his tracks. He didn't know what to do. The sand blew in his face as the chopper approached. He thought about running, but knew it wouldn't do any good.

He looked down at the air force captain who lay at his feet. A smile crossed his lips. At least this one was dead.

38

AL AZIZIYA HIGHWAY
SOUTHERN IRAQI DESERT

Charlie watched from the distance. The Delta Team fired almost as one. Six Iraqi soldiers were sent to the dirt. He turned the binoculars to Killer. His friend did not move. He held them tight against his eyes, the steel pressing hard on the bridge of his nose. He watched Odai stand as the chopper lifted up from the wadi, then turned again to look at his friend on the road.

He could see the blood. He could see the pinkish gray gore. And he knew that Alex Bennett was dead. His brother and comrade in arms. He stared at the body through the dry desert heat, then let out a cry that he couldn't control. Rolling over, he covered his face with his arms.

At that instant, Charlie McKay experienced a sudden and irrevokable change in his heart. Something inside of him crumbled and his character changed. A scar was gouged through the middle of his soul. Pushing himself up, he screamed, and then started to run. The Deltas followed, not knowing what else they should do.

Charlie ran through the desert, the other soldiers in tow. As he raced toward the chopper, his eyes clouded with tears. The loose pile of sand gave way under his feet. Falling, he rolled over, then pushed himself up and ran once again. He cried as he ran, groaning under his breath. As he approached the helicopter, he saw Odai Hussein. The Iraqi sat in the chopper, a sullen look in his eye. He sat on his seat, an arrogant smirk on his face. The two Delta soldiers who had stayed on the chopper had bound up his hands in thin plastic cuffs. They stood guard at each of the helicopter's doors, waiting for Charlie and the others to arrive. Aria knelt on the road, holding Killer's body in her arms. She had torn off a piece of her robe and wrapped it around his head. Leaning over, she whispered quiet words in his ear.

Charlie ran toward the chopper without looking at her. He didn't want to see. He had seen more than enough.

He stopped at the side of the chopper, staring at the monster inside. Odai glared at the pilot, his dark eyes gleaming under heavy lids. The two men stared at each other. Neither one of them spoke.

"You killed two of my friends," Charlie said in a frank and dismal tone.

Odai stared, unmoving, his face blank as dark glass.

"*You killed two of my friends!*" Charlie screamed it this time.

Odai slowly looked away and muttered, "They aren't the last Americans who are going to die." He glanced at his watch, then smiled once again. Five after eight. The canister in the cathedral would open in only twenty minutes' time. The other two canisters would open less than an hour after that. It was over. There was no way they would ever stop him now. Odai turned back to Charlie. "The time has come," he announced. "The time has come, and there's not a thing you can do.

"You can't kill me. You can't touch me. I'm the President of Iraq."

"No," Charlie muttered. "You are the president of nothing. You are nothing but a scum who defiles this earth."

"No," Odai replied. "You do not understand! And if you know what is good for you, then you'd better listen to me!"

Charlie moved forward so quickly, Odai nearly came out of his seat. Scrambling into the chopper, he cursed under his breath. The Iraqi backed away.

"No!" Charlie cried. "Now you listen to me! You killed two of my friends and five thousand U.S. soldiers. And I won't sit here and do nothing while you kill a million more!"

Odai shifted again, putting distance between the two men. His eyes flickered with fear, but his face remained calm. He recognized the determination and rage in Charlie's voice. And it scared him. He knew his life dangled on the edge. "Don't touch me," he cried. "There is nothing you can do! You're too late. So don't waste your time with meaningless threats."

Charlie moved forward and grabbed the Iraqi by the arms. Shaking him, he started to scream in his face. "Tell me where the canisters are! We know they are there! Tell me, if you want to live!"

Odai turned away, his face a blank and expressionless stare. Let the American rage. Let him threaten. Let him curse and let them all burn.

Charlie studied the Iraqi, then made a decision.

He would not wait. He could not wait. There simply wasn't time.

"Get in the chopper!" he screamed to the group of Delta soldiers. "Grab my friend. Get the girl."

Everyone scrambled on board. Killer's body was carefully placed inside the chopper. One of the soldiers took off his camouflage shirt and placed it over the top of his face, tucking the edges of the shirt underneath the limp body.

Turning to the two pilots, Charlie issued his command. "Take us up to fifteen feet." The copilot glanced back with a dumbfounded stare. The pilot nodded and the chopper lifted straight up into the air. Charlie turned toward Odai, who was looking out the door. His eyes opened wide when the chopper stabilized in a hover.

Charlie leaned toward the Delta Team leader. "Throw him out," he shouted loud enough for Odai to hear.

Odai turned around quickly, his face quivering in fear. "No—wait—what are you doing!" he cried. The solders moved forward. Odai grabbed at his seat railing, holding on for dear life, his fingers a white-fisted grip on the back of the steel brace. Aria looked away, casting her eyes to the floor. Two soldiers reached out and grabbed Odai by the arms. With a push, they shoved him out of the open cabin door. His falling scream lasted much less than a second.

Charlie looked out of the doorway. Odai lay in a heap in the middle of the road. He rolled over, dazed, but apparently unharmed. He pushed himself up onto wobbly knees and felt at the bruise on the back of his head. A stream of blood worked its way down the side of his cheek. He started to run, but then fell to his knees. The chopper descended again, landing not five feet from his side, the rotors beating with a dull and constant whomp. The same two soldiers jumped out and shoved Odai back inside. He sat in a daze as the chopper lifted again in the air.

"Take us up to thirty feet," Charlie shouted.

Odai started to cry. "What are you doing! You killers! I'm the President of Iraq!" The soldiers lifted him, pushing him to the open door. "Wait! Stop!" he cried. The soldiers rolled him over so that he was facing straight down. The chopper hovered gingerly, thirty feet over the road.

"Wait! I will tell you! What do you want to know!"

Charlie leaned down beside him and screamed in his ear. "Where are the virus canisters located? What time are they set to go off?"

"Tomorrow," Odai lied. "They are set in New York. In the subway. Near the UN headquarters building."

"You're lying," Charlie screamed.

"No, I swear," Odai cried.

"Throw him," Charlie instructed the guards.

Again, they threw him out. Again, they heard him cry, a muted scream that disappeared as he fell.

Charlie leaned forward as the chopper descended to the ground. Odai didn't move as it set down beside him. He lay in a broken bundle of flesh in the middle of the road. The guards climbed out and dragged the body inside. He was conscious and teary, gingerly holding his chest. His face was pale. His heart beat at the veins in his neck. He coughed and spit blood. There was damage inside. "I can't—breathe," he whispered. "My ribs—my shoulders. You're going to kill me, I swear!"

"You're right," Charlie said. "Take us up to one thousand feet."

The chopper immediately climbed back into the air. Straight upward it ascended, hovering over the road. The two turbine engines whined from over their heads as the chopper climbed quickly over the hot desert sand. Five hundred. Eight hundred. One thousand feet. The pilots held the chopper steady as they fought the high-altitude winds. They didn't really try to keep the chopper over the road. At this altitude, what possible difference would it make? Charlie leaned toward Odai, bending down by his ear.

"Listen to me," he sneered as he glanced at his watch. "This is the last time I will ask you. I know you have canisters that are set to go off. They will open today. Colonel Hajazi has already told us that. And I want to know where your biological facility is located. We have to know where it is so that it can be destroyed. Now tell me. Tell me now. Or do you not want to live?"

Odai winced, then turned away, his lips pressed tightly together. His shoulder was broken, as were half of his ribs. Intense and unremitting, the pain clawed at his mind. But the pain meant very little, he could put it behind him. Death was his fear. It was the other side he dreaded most. The terror of it was more real than any fear in this world. For he knew, deep inside, they would be waiting for him. In his mind, a vision opened, of the tormented souls waiting to touch and tear and send him to hell. *Johannom*, they called it. It meant the same thing. And he knew it was waiting. He had known that for years.

A deep shadow of doubt crossed in front of his eyes. The smell of death lingered near.

Would the American do it? Had he underestimated this man? Was he capable of ordering the death of another?

Odai turned toward Charlie and started to speak. Then with a renewed flash of hate, he suddenly changed his mind. Wetting his lips, he closed his eyes and slowly shook his head.

"Get rid of him," Charlie said. "Then let's get out of here. I never want to see this miserable country again."

The guards moved forward and grabbed ahold of Odai's arms. Pushing, they moved him to the very edge of the chopper. Odai screamed out in fear, completely ignoring the pain. He opened his eyes just long enough to see the desert below. The burning cars lay in the distance, like the toys of a child. The road cut through the desert. He could almost see Baghdad. A thousand feet up! A thousand-foot drop!

How long would he fall? How long would it take him to die? A minute? Two minutes? He really didn't know. What would it feel like? Would he splatter? Would his kin know who it was? Would he see the ground coming? Would he feel the pain?

Clawing, he grabbed onto the side of the chopper, holding onto the metal with his manicured nails. The fear was so real it shook his whole soul. He tried to cry, but there was nothing inside. He grabbed and pawed, but there was nothing to hold. The soldiers held him by only the boots on his feet, his upper body hanging completely over the side of the chopper. He looked over his head. The ground was so far below.

Charlie moved forward again and called above the sound of the rotors. "You will die here, you coward. And nothing will change. There will be no New World. No great Arab uprising. No embracing of Iraq as the new world leader. Just a pitiful man and his pitiful plan who caused so many innocent people to die.

"You will die like your ancestors, a mere bug on the rocks. None will mourn. None will care, except you and your god."

With a nod, Charlie motioned to the two Delta soldiers. Slowly, they began to let go of his boots. Odai slipped away, clawing at nothing but air. "I'll tell you," he screamed. "I'll tell you. I swear! The cans are in the cathedral. And the city water supply. I'll tell you exactly where they are. Just hold me. Please hold me! Please don't let go!"

Charlie dropped to his knees as the soldiers pulled Odai inside. Charlie knelt down beside him. Odai told him what he needed to know. The helicopter pilot was already working his satellite radio. He dialed in the classified frequency to the National Command Post in D.C. Charlie spoke with Odai for almost a minute, then shoved a radio headset over his ears, adjusting the microphone next to his mouth. In seconds, it was over. The command post had been notified.

Leaning back, Charlie sat against the side cabin door. Odai lay on the floor, his eyes tightly closed, his hands shaking at his chest. Charlie looked down at the man. The U.S. would try him for crimes against humanity, assassination, and murder. He would certainly die in an American prison. The only question was, when? Charlie knew it would take too many years.

The MH-60 banked right as the pilot lowered the nose. Gathering speed, it headed to the south once again, making way for the Cobra base in the foothills of southern Iraq.

Charlie sat exhausted. No one spoke. No one moved. Sadness seemed to permeate the air. There was no celebration. There was no reason to cheer. Charlie glanced at the body that was lying on the floor. He started to move toward it, when Aria crawled to his side. "Charlie," she begged him. "There is still something more."

WASHINGTON NATIONAL CATHEDRAL
WASHINGTON, D.C.
0920 LOCAL TIME

The Secret Service agents moved like lightning to the president's side. In seconds, they had him out of the cathedral and into the presidential limousine. Policemen and Secret Service agents moved through the chapel, rushing everyone out the main doors. A noisy fire alarm clanged from the walls overhead. The sound of sirens could be heard from the parking lot outside. District policemen began to sweep through the area, turning traffic and pedestrians away. The evacuation would continue until a three-mile clear zone could be established around the cathedral.

High overhead, two black-and-silver helicopters suddenly came into view. They didn't carry tail numbers or identification of any kind. Sweeping low, they landed on the west side of the cathedral, setting down on the courtyard of thick sandstone and brick. Orange figures emerged from both of the choppers, their Racal space suits shimmering bright in the sun. They were RATs, or Rapid Assessment Team members, elements of a highly trained and top-secret military organization who specialized in containing a biological attack. Like spacemen, they raced toward the west door of the cathedral, their huge, portable suits allowing them to enter without any fear. The detection equipment was wheeled inside. It only took moments to locate the canister of deadly virus. The chrome tube was dropped into an airtight container and triple sealed inside a biohazard air lock.

The canister's internal timer had just passed through the three-minute timer.

At the district's Number Three pump station, the water mains had already been shut off. The biohazard team arrived in gleaming new minivans behind an escort of wailing police cars. The team had donned their Racal suits as the caravan had been cutting through traffic. Another set of vans was already working its way to George Washington Park.

Within twenty minutes, the remaining virus canisters had also been found and contained.

BAT ONE (AIR FORCE B-1B BOMBER) OVER THE NORTH IRAQI PROVINCE OF KIRKUK

At 1447, Greenwich time, the satellite communications radio burst to life. An encoded message was sent to the B-1, providing the order to attack. After receiving the message, the crew replied, then authenticated the code. Withing seconds, the target coordinates were loaded into the aircraft's weapons computers. The huge bomber rolled out of its orbit and turned to the east, charting a course toward the central Iraqi desert.

Eighteen minutes later, the target was just coming into sight.

"Weapon armed and ready," the offensive WSO called out from the back.

Mad Dog, the pilot, reached down and lifted a red-guarded switch. "Ready in the front," he replied in as cool a voice as he could muster.

"Master control panel on," the WSO shot back. "Consent requested from the front cockpit."

Without hesitation, Mad Dog flipped up the switch. The two-man-consent policy having been complied with, the weapons computers immediately sent the final arming code to the B-61 nuclear bomb.

"Target now thirty-two miles," the offensive WSO announced to the crew.

The defensive WSO keyed his mike to report. "I've got nothing on any of my scopes," he said. "It looks absolutely clear. Not an aircraft in the sky. Not so much as an electronic peep from the ground. It looks like intel was right, not a missile or gun within a hundred miles of us now."

Mad Dog peered through the windscreen, then lowered his eyes to the weapons panel. Just over three minutes to go. The aircraft was traveling at just under supersonic speed. He reached up and pulled the throttles back just a hair, reducing his speed to six hundred knots. They were flying over the terrain at only two hundred feet. The setting sun cast long shadows across the brown sand. He stared at the desert, the scrub oaks and sparse juniper trees. He had no way of knowing the trees were as ancient as Islam itself, having survived in the dry foothills for the past twelve hundred years.

At sixty seconds out from the target, the two pilots placed the darkened window shields over their canopy panels to save their eyesight from any blast that might work its way up from the hole. At forty-five seconds, Mad Dog said a little prayer in his heart, assuring God that he meant no offense. At ten seconds from the target, the aircraft was still two miles away. The underbelly doors started to open, swinging back on their hydraulic arms.

"Two . . . one . . . *weapon away!*" the WSO called from the back. The aircraft shuddered just slightly as the doors closed once again. Mad Dog threw the heavy bomber up on her side, rolling her hard into a ninety degree angle of bank. He pulled on the stick and settled into his seat as the G-forces pulled them around. He pushed up the throttles into afterburner range and accelerated quickly through the speed of sound.

The B-61 blasted its way into the soft desert sand. It plunked into the loose soil with hardly a sound. The weapon was designed for just such a target, an underground bunker buried deep beneath layers of rock and packed soil. It was designed to penetrate through thick walls of cement, counting the rooms as it burst its way through a bunker.

The weapon worked as expected. It penetrated the desert until it reached the underground bunker, then worked its way to the center of the weapons-production facility, blasting through ceilings and floors to reach the heart of the underground laboratory.

Ninety-eight hundredths of a second after coming to rest, the detonation timer kicked in. A short burst of electricity flowed from the weapon's internal battery. A minor explosion took place in the center of the detonator, sending a supersonic shockwave toward the weapon's uranium core. The chain reaction of bursting electrons finally began. An incredible blast of two-million-degree heat burst from the center of the weapon, melting the bedrock and cement into walls of bubbled goo. The ground beneath the explosion buckled like waves on the sea. The shockwave rolled outward. The biofacility ceased to exist.

No radiation or light even escaped to the surface of the earth as the multiple layers of rock and broken stone caved in on the hole. It was in essence nothing more than an underground explosion. Few would even know that it had taken place.

SOUTHERN BAGHDAD

The MH-60 flew low over the desert. The lights of the city glowed like dim fires in the night. The chopper stayed low, barely over the sand. It approached the main intersection of the Al Aziziya Highway, then banked right to follow a small road that turned east. The chopper flew without lights. The gunners stood ready near their doors.

The MH-60 slowed, then started to descend, coming to rest in a field of junk and debris. A few Iraqi women watched as the helicopter set down in the field. They couldn't see the U.S. markings, for night had set in. Aria waited, terrified that she would not be there. She scanned the dark corners of the field, peering through the shadows as far as she could see. No one moved. It stood empty. It appeared no one was there.

Then she saw her running through the high, wild weeds. She ran toward the chopper, a tiny sack bouncing in her arms. Osman, the Kurd, was standing in the distance. Aria waved to the Kurd and mouthed a deep "thank you." He nodded, then disappeared again into the shadows of the night. Aria reached toward her sister, calling her on. The girl clambered into the helicopter, a look of panic in her eyes. Aria reached down to hold her, drawing her near. Together they fell against the interior cabin floor. The chopper lifted again. A soldier pushed the door closed. Banking into the night, the helicopter turned to the south.

Aria sat with her sister, holding her in her arms, their faces shining in the moonlight, glistening tears in their eyes.

Behind them, Charlie sat beside Killer's body. He swayed back and forth, rocking gently with the motion of the swaying helicopter. Tears too streaked his face. He didn't wipe them away.

EPILOGUE

The enormous C-141 transport drifted out of the sky toward the long cement runway. Its four engines spooled up just before it touched, slowing its descent to make a barely noticeable landing. The wheels touched down with a squeal of rubber and a wisp of white smoke. The aircraft slowed quickly to take the mid-field runway exit, then taxied toward the main terminal where the families were waiting.

There was no color guard to meet them. No band or marching parade. No thronging press or crowd of pushy television reporters. Though the bodies had been collected from the sands of the desert, no one would ever be told, not even the families of the dead, the truth of how their husbands, sons, and fathers had died. The details of the mission to Iraq would never be released. The choppers had collided in a routine training mission. That is what the families had been led to believe.

By presidential order, the whole incident would remain a highly classified secret. The public had been terrified by the attack on Prince Sultan. Like a bash on the head, it had finally hit home how vulnerable they were to an unconventional attack. The public outcry had the potential to bring the presidency down, and the last thing he wanted was to throw fuel to the fire.

So he wouldn't ever tell them how very close it had been. It would remain a huge secret. At least that was his hope.

The lumbering transport approached the hangar, swung into the parking spot, then shut down her engines. Charlie was the first one to climb down the crew ladder. He was wearing dress blues, a row of medals on his chest. Aria followed him down to where he stood blinking at the sun, his short hair bristling back in the wind. He was looking across the tarmac, toward the rear of the aircraft, to where the enormous taildoor was just coming down. He glanced toward Aria as she placed her hand on his arm.

Behind her, Shannon carefully made her way down the ladder. Walking forward, she stood beside her sister. Charlie stared at them both. The resemblance was striking. Same black hair and high cheekbones, and an identical smile. Shannon held on tight to Aria's hand.

Without talking, Charlie moved to the rear of the aircraft. The ramp was now down. A group of honor guard soldiers, dressed in formal blue and gray, moved solemnly inside the enormous aircraft to bring their fallen comrades out.

One by one, they lifted the flag-draped wooden coffins and carried them down the sloping ramp. A row of black hearses was waiting in line. The identical coffins were gently placed inside each limousine, while the families watched in anguish from the side.

Charlie stood near the aircraft until the remains of Colonel Wisner and Captain Bennett were brought down. He stood at attention while the coffins filed by, his face firm as stone, his finger at the tip of his brow in a salute of respect for his friends.

It took only a few minutes to unload the caskets from the transport. Then the motorcade set off for Arlington National Cemetery. A rental car was waiting. Charlie and the two women climbed inside. Charlie slipped the car into gear and followed the line of black limousines.

Four hours later, Charlie was making his way down Route 17, the old road that led from Washington south, rambling its way along the coastline of Virginia, cutting through coastal fishing towns and old farming plantations. As it meandered south, the road crossed no less than three dozen rivers. Tall pines and white birch lined both sides of the highway. Charlie was only going forty-five. He was not in a hurry. He was ready for life to slow down.

Aria was sitting beside him in a light, blue cotton dress. Shannon was restlessly sleeping in the back. The windows were rolled down. An ocean breeze blew a cool wind through the car. The smell of salt and fresh pine seemed to be everywhere—typical for southeastern Virginia.

The memorial service was over and Charlie felt so relieved. For the past forty-eight hours, it had been something to dread. But it had brought him a sense of closure, and a surprising feeling of relief. It had helped him to see that his life would go on.

Aria cocked her head and pushed a strand of black hair from her eyes, then leaned sideways in her seat. "Want to listen to some music?" she asked. Charlie nodded his head. Aria punched at the stereo until she found a classic rock station, then turned up the volume and leaned back once again. A song from the sixties began to play on the air.

Layla—you got me on my knees, Layla—

Charlie glanced over. He was smiling for the first time in days. "Did you know Eric Clapton wrote this song on the back of a grocery sack," he said.

Aria giggled and answered. "Of course. Everyone knows that!"

Shannon woke up and leaned forward, positioning herself between the two bucket seats. "Excuse me," she said in heavily-accented English. "I don't want to bother you, but its getting late and I'm very hungry. Do you think that we could we get something to eat?"

Charlie nodded down the road. "There's a McDonald's up ahead. Would that be okay, or do you want something fancy?"

Shannon stared for a moment as the huge restaurant came into view, its shiny glass and yellow arches gleaming in the sun. Turning to Aria, she lowered her voice. "I've never heard of McDonald's. Is that okay with you? It looks kind of nice. Do you think that we have enough money?"

Aria laughed, then reached out to take her sister by the hand. "Shannon," she said, "you have so much to learn! Welcome to America. This will be fun!"